W9-DAC-199

HuNTed

HuNteD

DISCARD

JERRY B. JENKINS
TIM LaHAYE

with CHRiS FABRY

TYNDALE HOUSE PUBLISHERS, INC.
WHEATON, ILLINOIS

Visit Tyndale's exciting Web site at www.tyndale.com

Discover the latest Left Behind news at www.leftbehind.com

TYNDALE is a registered trademark of Tyndale House Publishers, Inc.

Tyndale's quill logo is a trademark of Tyndale House Publishers, Inc.

Hunted is a special edition compilation of the following Left Behind: The Kids titles:

#35: The Rise of False Messiahs copyright © 2004 by Jerry B. Jenkins and Tim LaHaye. All rights reserved.

#36: Ominous Choices copyright © 2004 by Jerry B. Jenkins and Tim LaHaye. All rights reserved.

#37: Heat Wave copyright © 2004 by Jerry B. Jenkins and Tim LaHaye. All rights reserved.

Cover photograph of side mirror © by Randy Allbritton/Getty Images. All rights reserved.

Cover photograph of woods © by Ron Chapple/Getty Images. All rights reserved.

Authors' photo copyright © 1998 by Reg Francklyn. All rights reserved.

Left Behind is a registered trademark of Tyndale House Publishers, Inc.

Published in association with the literary agency of Alive Communications, Inc., 7680 Goddard Street, Suite 200, Colorado Springs, CO 80920.

Scripture quotations are taken from the *Holy Bible,* New Living Translation, copyright © 1996. Used by permission of Tyndale House Publishers, Inc., Wheaton, Illinois 60189. All rights reserved.

Some Scripture taken from the New King James Version. Copyright © 1979, 1980, 1982 by Thomas Nelson, Inc. Used by permission. All rights reserved.

Designed by Jessie McGrath

Library of Congress Cataloging-in-publication data

Jenkins, Jerry B.
    Hunted / Jerry B. Jenkins, Tim LaHaye, with Chris Fabry.
       p. cm. — (Left behind—the kids ; #35-#37)
    This is a special combined edition of three previously published Left behind : the kids titles.
    Summary: Four teens battle the forces of evil when they are left behind after the Rapture.
    ISBN 1-4143-0272-X (hardcover)
    1. Children's stories, American. [1. End of the world—Fiction. 2. Christian life—Fiction.]
I. LaHaye, Tim F.   II. Fabry, Chris, 1961-   III. Title.
    PZ7.J4138Hu 2005
[Fic]dc22   2004027646

Printed in the United States of America

10   09   08   07   06   05
 9   8   7   6   5   4   3   2   1

JUDD Thompson Jr. said a quick prayer and wondered if it would be his last. He glanced at Tom Gowin, the young believer from South Carolina who lay on the dusty floor, his head turned, a trickle of blood running from his mouth.

Lionel Washington was beside Judd, his hands also cuffed behind him. Lionel was near tears, his head down, sweat pouring from his forehead.

Judd wondered where they had made their mistake. Were they wrong to come to South Carolina? Chang Wong kept up with developments around the world. Surely he knew the danger they faced.

"Keep your head up," Judd whispered to Lionel.

Someone slapped Judd on the back of the head. "Shut up!" Albert yelled, pushing Judd hard. "Get in the next room."

The bounty hunters herded Judd and Lionel into the

living room of the tiny house and shoved them onto a shabby couch by the front door. The man with the long scar on his face, Max, took out a cigarette and lit it. Judd noticed Nicks littering the kitchen table, payment for bringing in two bodies without the mark of Carpathia.

Max threw a leather pouch at Albert. "Put the money in there. We don't want anybody wiping us out while we're gone."

"You know there's nobody out here—," Albert began.

"Just do it," Max said, opening the door.

"Where you going?"

"The truck needs fuel." He glanced at Judd and Lionel. "And make sure the other one's still alive. If he isn't, we'll load them all up and take them to the GC."

The door slammed behind Max, and the truck chugged to a small outbuilding. Judd watched through a side window as Max unlocked a creaky door. Empty metal cans crashed until the man found one with gasoline.

Albert grabbed Nicks from the table and floor and stuffed them into the pouch. He jammed a few bills into his pockets, and Judd gave Lionel a look. Albert smiled as he flitted about the room gathering money, humming an off-key version of a country song.

"We're going to do a little celebratin' tonight! After we turn you in and find that other nest of Judah-ites, we'll have enough money to move out of here and get a place near the city where the real money is."

Judd bit his lip. The pain from being shot by the weird weapon and having his hands cuffed tightly behind him had dulled his senses. It was difficult to breathe, let alone think clearly. His shoulder muscles ached as he shifted on the rickety couch.

"Too bad you and your friend are settling for chicken feed," Lionel said.

"Shut up," Albert said.

"Up in Atlanta, there's probably thousands of people without the mark. We could lead you to them."

The man grinned. "You ain't from Atlanta. I can tell you're from up north somewhere."

"I didn't know it mattered where we're from," Lionel said. "Isn't an unmarked Northerner worth just as much?"

Albert rolled his eyes. "Max says the GC is real interested in you two. They might pay us more than the regular rate."

Lionel glanced at Judd and leaned toward him, then whispered, "You think Tom's still alive? His head hit pretty hard on the floor."

Judd shrugged and the truck started up again, a plume of blue smoke rising from the tailpipe. Max pulled up to the house and ran inside. Albert handed him the bulging pouch of money.

"He kept some of it," Judd said.

Albert backhanded Judd's face. Judd tasted blood in his mouth.

"Judah-ites," Albert sneered. "He's just trying to get us to turn against each other."

"Look in his pockets," Judd said.

Another hard blow, a kick this time, sent Judd reeling. The couch crackled, and if Lionel hadn't been sitting beside him, Judd was sure they would have toppled.

"He took some of the money!" Judd yelled.

Max glared at his partner. "It had better all be here."

"I might have picked up a few Nicks by mistake . . ."

Max frowned at Albert who held out his hand. "I swear it was a mistake." He dug into his pockets, emptying the contents on the table.

Max grabbed the Nicks and shoved them into the pouch. "I'm going to count this. If it's short—"

"Lemme look," Albert said, fishing in his pockets.

Judd saw movement to his right. Someone peered through the crack in the door where Tom was being held. Judd studied the face—a young man, a little older than Judd. Brown hair. *Luke?*

The man made a signal Judd couldn't understand, then mouthed, "Stay there."

Judd nodded and whispered to Lionel. When Judd glanced back, the door was closed.

The veins in Max's neck were sticking out. "Check on the other kid and make sure he's alive."

"Wait," Judd said, trying to stand.

"You shut up," Albert said, kicking Judd in the stomach and sending him back onto the couch. Judd tried to stall the man, but he went straight for the door. He jiggled the handle several times. "How did this get locked?"

Max squinted. "Out of the way!"

With one kick, the door cracked and flew open. Max and Albert disappeared into the room, and both let out a string of curses.

"The window!" Albert yelled. "He got out through the window!"

4

Vicki Byrne closed her eyes and tried to calm herself. The e-mail from Chang Wong in New Babylon was the worst news she could imagine. Bounty hunters in the South were looking for anyone without the mark of Carpathia. Judd and Lionel had walked into a trap.

Mark turned the speakerphone on so everyone could hear Carl Meninger's voice. Carl had worked for the Global Community in Florida and now lived in South Carolina.

"Tom and Luke headed for the fort hours ago," Carl said. "That's where they were supposed to meet Judd and Lionel."

"Have you had any contact with Tom and Luke?" Vicki said.

"We talked by radio several times. They saw Judd and Lionel's plane and even spotted them rowing across the river. They were going to meet them when we lost contact. I thought they had just gone out of range, but maybe they were caught."

"How far from the meeting place are you right now?" Mark said.

"It's a hike. We're a long way up the river on an old plantation."

"Those bounty hunters could be coming to you next," Vicki said.

"We don't see many people up here," Carl said. "We've taken a lot of precautions since our other hideout was discovered."

Carl said he would check back when he heard any

news, and Mark hung up. An eerie silence fell over the group.

Finally, Zeke said, "I think we ought to pray."

The kids prayed for Judd, Lionel, Tom, and Luke. Vicki wiped away tears. A few minutes into the session, she got up and went outside.

Zeke joined her under one of the awnings the group had constructed between cabins. "I know you're upset, but you can't give up hope."

"I have to do something. The GC is making all the moves. It's like we're trapped."

"You know how long it would take you to get to South Carolina from here? The best thing you can do is pray."

"I don't want to pray. I want to do something!" Vicki sobbed.

Zeke nodded, his long hair swishing against his chubby shoulders. "I know exactly how you feel. When the GC picked up my dad, I wanted to go in there with guns blazing and get him out. You know how hard it is to know someone you love's going to die?"

Vicki couldn't speak.

Zeke put a hand on her shoulder. "Dad was ready, and Judd and Lionel are too."

"Don't talk like that! Judd's coming back, and I'm going to help him!"

Vicki ran inside the building. "I'm sorry to interrupt, but I need a vehicle."

Marshall Jameson stood. "Vicki, you can't be serious."

"I have to help them."

Shelly hugged Vicki and they both cried.

Mark ran a hand through his hair. "Vicki, this is insane."

She turned to Zeke. "Isn't there a part of you that wishes you had tried to save your dad? Don't you ever wonder if you might have been able to help him?"

Zeke just stared at her.

Colin Dial stepped forward. "If this program that Commander Fulcire created goes through, there'll be a million eyes watching. If everyone knows they can make money finding people without the mark of Carpathia, we'll be a prime target."

"The program hasn't started up here," Vicki said. "Besides, I'll stick to back roads—"

Becky Dial put a hand on Vicki's shoulder. "I know how upset you are, but Colin's right. You can't go anywhere right now. We have to trust God."

"He helped you by sending that angel Anak," Charlie said. "Maybe God will send an angel to Judd."

Vicki looked from face to face, sensing their concern. Everyone in the room wanted Judd and Lionel to return safely.

"I'm going to my cabin," Vicki said. "Call me the moment you hear anything."

Vicki raced away, wiping tears from her face. She collapsed on her bunk and sobbed, crying out to God.

———————————

Judd caught his breath as the two men in the next room shoved wicker furniture away from the window. Lionel struggled to his feet and moved toward the kitchen.

"What are you doing?" Judd said.

Lionel turned and felt along the tabletop. His eyes lit and he scampered back to the couch. With his hands still cuffed behind him, he held out his pocketknife. "He took this and some clips from me earlier." He sat on the couch, leaning forward, trying to open the small blade.

Max returned and Lionel sat back, hiding the knife in his palm.

"Get these two into the back of the truck," Max said, glaring at Judd and Lionel. "And switch your gun to kill. No more trying to be nice to these kids."

Albert hustled Lionel and Judd into the back of the truck and closed the tailgate. Max had fastened plywood over the broken window, and it was dark inside.

"You try to get away and it'll be the last time," Albert said.

The plastic cuffs were tight around Judd's wrist, and Lionel said he had lost most of the feeling in his hands. Lionel told Judd to scoot close. He pricked Judd's arm once with the blade, and Judd helped guide the knife to the plastic strip.

Lionel pulled the blade back and forth along the plastic. With the sawing motion they hoped to cut a notch into the thick plastic.

"Good thing they didn't have the metal cuffs or there would be no way we'd get them off," Lionel said. "You think the guy you saw was Luke?"

"I've never seen him before, but I can't imagine who else it would be."

Judd held still as Lionel worked. Max and Albert

hadn't returned, and Judd wondered if they had followed Tom into the woods. After a few minutes, Lionel pulled the knife away, and Judd managed to get his little finger to the middle of the cuffs.

"I don't feel any notch at all," Judd said. "It's not working."

"I have another blade with a serrated edge. Let me try that."

Judd helped guide the blade again, but this time the edge cut his arm and he yelped.

"Sorry, man," Lionel said.

Minutes later the bounty hunters returned, and Judd heard the clatter of a weapon in the front seat.

"You know I don't do well at that place," Albert whined.

"It's not like there's a bunch of gators down there," Max said. "Just take these two and have them processed. I'll stay here and wait on the dogs so we can find the other one."

"Max, let me stay."

Max spoke through clenched teeth. "Go. I'll find the other one."

The door closed and the truck started. Lionel kept working on the cuffs as they bounced along the bumpy road.

"You ever think it would end this way?" Lionel said. "Guess you won't get to see Vicki again."

"Concentrate!"

Judd didn't want to think about anything but getting free. Now, as Albert drove along the deeply rutted road,

Judd thought of Vicki. Unless Tom got back to his group and told the story, no one would know about Judd's and Lionel's fate. *Is this God's plan?* Judd thought. *How could this possibly glorify God?*

Years before, Bruce Barnes had said, "Pray as if everything depends on God, but work as if everything depends on you."

Lionel stopped for a moment and worked out a cramp in his hand. "Feel it and see if we're making any progress."

Judd ran a little finger around the plastic, feeling for a notch. Lionel had been working the new blade long enough to get a cramp, but Judd's heart sank when the surface was completely smooth.

2

JUDD leaned forward and tried to relax. He had been straining to help Lionel cut the plastic bands since the beginning of their bumpy ride and now felt despair. He imagined the Global Community facility as a dark place with some kind of courtyard where they executed prisoners. He shook his head and tried to concentrate.

"Give me the knife and let me try your cuffs," Judd said.

Lionel passed the knife to Judd but lost his grip, and it clattered onto the truck bed. Judd stretched to reach it, the cuffs cutting into his wrists. He had tried twisting his hands, but that only made the pain worse. His hands were swelling, which made it difficult to grip the knife.

"I don't think it's going to work," Lionel said.

"What, you're giving up?"

Lionel grunted. "We've been through a lot of stuff, man. Remember when we were trying to save Nada and her parents and those locusts attacked?"

11

"Don't do this, Lionel."

"I gave up a long time ago."

When Judd tried rolling over so he could see Lionel, the truck hit a bump. His body flew up a few inches, and he found himself looking at the back of Lionel's head. "What do you mean?"

"Control," Lionel said. "I gave it up a long time ago because somebody else is running this show. We'd have been dead by now if God hadn't taken care of us. And he'll take care of us now, one way or another."

"So you're ready to take the blade?"

Lionel quivered. "I had a dream the other night in Petra. I saw this sharp blade dripping blood and it was mine."

"Why didn't you tell me? We could have postponed the trip."

Lionel chuckled. "The night before that I dreamed I was riding in the pouch of a kangaroo and we were flying over water."

"A kangaroo?"

"Yeah, I could guide him by reaching up and pulling his ears."

"You're strange," Judd said.

"I'm just saying there was no reason for me to tell you the dream when the other ones I've had were so strange."

Judd settled back again and gripped the knife. "You didn't make a dent in these handcuffs."

"I didn't think I would, but I figured we ought to at least try."

Judd looked around the back of the truck bed. A little

12

light was coming through the tiny windows on the sides of the camper. He spotted some rope and small chains at the front. A cardboard box lay on its side with a few rolls of duct tape inside.

"Maybe if you hold the knife on the plastic and I try to twist my arms we can break it," Lionel said.

The road was smoother now, and Judd no longer heard gravel striking the under-side of the truck. He rolled over again, held out the knife, and let Lionel guide it into position.

Lionel grimaced in pain as he jerked the cuffs, trying to snap the plastic. They worked for several minutes without results before Judd felt the truck speed up. The tires whirred and Judd knew they were on asphalt. Albert's muffled curses came from the front, and Judd wondered whom the man was talking to. Something clattered in the front seat, and the truck swerved wildly to the right. Judd rolled onto Lionel and dropped the knife, hoping he hadn't injured Lionel.

Another sound beside them. More tires on pavement. Was there another vehicle?

A high-pitched sound came from the front, and Judd recognized the high-tech weapon. The burst sent a wave of pain through him as he recalled the intense sting of the weapon. Tires screeched beside them, and gravel flew against the side of the truck. Albert sped up, swerving to his left, then to his right, sending Judd and Lionel rolling. Judd tried to hook his foot on something, but Albert swerved again, throwing the two to the other side of the truck bed.

The second vehicle was closing in on them, bumping them from behind and trying to get around. When Judd heard the shotgun blast, he screamed.

———————————

Vicki lay on her bed, her face buried in a pillow. She cried so hard she didn't hear Shelly walk in. The girl put a hand on Vicki's back and sat on the edge of the bunk.

"Why did I do it?" Vicki moaned.

"Do what?"

"I was the one who suggested Judd take that flight to South Carolina, remember? If he winds up getting . . . if he gets hurt, it's my fault."

"You know that's not true."

"I told Chloe Williams that Judd was in France and she—"

"I know how it happened, but you can't blame yourself. We have to trust God that—"

"Trust God?!" Vicki screamed. "We trusted God for Bruce, and look what happened to him. We trusted God for Ryan, and he still got trapped during the earthquake. We trusted God for Natalie and Zeke's dad and Chaya. There's a long list we've trusted to God, and they're all dead."

Shelly looked at the floor, and Vicki shoved her face back into the pillow. "He and Lionel are going to die and it's because of me."

Vicki sobbed and Shelly seemed content to sit, not saying anything.

After a few minutes, Vicki sat up and Shelly pulled her

close. "You're upset and not thinking straight. You're the one who's said all along that God's in control. He's working his plan, and though we might not understand it—"

"It's too hard! I don't want to be part of his plan anymore. I don't want to hide or worry about how we're going to eat or if the GC is going to come rushing in on us any moment. Why does God expect so much?"

"Shh," Shelly said, patting Vicki on the back. "God's all we have right now. I've seen you stand up under a lot of pressure, and we're not going to let this stop us from believing that he wants what's best for us."

"Oh, Shelly, I'm so scared." Vicki put her head on Shelly's shoulder and cried. "I can't imagine what's happening to Judd and Lionel right now. I don't want to sleep. I'm afraid I'll have an awful dream about the two of them getting their heads chopped off."

"Listen to me. You know God protected us from the GC with that angel. It's obvious he has more for us to do. Do you think he still has more for Judd and Lionel to do?"

Vicki nodded. "I hope so. It's just that I keep hearing that creepy guy's voice who answered Judd's phone."

"I understand. Right now the best thing we can do is pray. And when you're all prayed out, we'll find something to do. I'll stay with you until we hear from them."

"You will?"

"You bet."

Judd flinched when shotgun pellets slammed against the truck bed and left dents in the metal. The truck immediately dipped to the left, and a horrible scraping made Judd want to plug his ears, but he couldn't. The truck slowed as the smell of hot rubber filled the camper. The tire flopped, ka-thumped, and smoked while Albert tried to keep the truck on the road. He finally veered off, came to a bumpy stop, and called Max on the radio.

The other vehicle screeched to a halt somewhere near the truck. Judd and Lionel tried to see out the small window, but a voice called out to them. "Judd, Lionel, stay down!"

"That wasn't Tom," Lionel said as he and Judd quickly dropped to the floor and lay flat.

A click and a hum sounded from the truck cab. The right front door opened, and Albert plopped to the ground.

"He's coming around the right side!" Judd said.

"Shut up, Judah-ite!" Albert screamed. "I should have taken care of you when I had the chance."

The person at the other vehicle yelled at Albert. "Come around with your hands up and nobody gets hurt."

"It's not me who's about to get hurt." Albert laughed. A shadow passed the side window of the truck. Footsteps on the other side, Tom's. Judd wondered how he had gotten out of his handcuffs.

"Put down your weapon, Albert," Tom said.

As soon as Judd heard the weapon fire, he ducked and pulled his knees to his chest. The piercing hum jarred him again. There was no return fire from the shotgun, and Judd wondered what was happening. "Tom, he's got the gun set to kill. Don't take any chances."

Albert screamed again and banged on the truck's plywood covering. Judd turned and whispered, "I was hoping he'd give away his location."

Albert fired his weapon again and someone yelped.

"Ha-ha! I gotcha, you little no-account Judah—"

Albert's voice cut off midsentence, and Judd heard a terrific thump. Had Tom been killed? Why had Albert gone suddenly silent? Judd was sure the man would turn the gun on him and Lionel before taking them to the GC.

The back door opened, and a young man with sandy hair and rippling muscles looked inside. "I'm Luke Gowin. You must be Judd and Lionel."

Judd sat up and sighed. "Is Tom—?"

Tom appeared beside his brother. "Right here. I drew old Albert into the open, and Luke did his linebacker routine."

Albert lay on the ground, holding his stomach and panting. Judd felt a strange mix of anger and pity toward the man. A few months ago Judd would have prayed for him and tried to convince him of the truth about God. Now that Albert had the mark of Carpathia, Judd knew his fate was sealed. He felt sorry the man had no chance for heaven, but he was mad at him for trying to harm believers.

"Please don't hurt me anymore," Albert gasped.

Tom limped to retrieve the weapon and threw it in their car, along with another energy clip from the front. After he handed Luke one of the plastic handcuffs, Luke looped the cuffs through Albert's belt, secured Albert's arm behind him, and lifted him into the back of the truck.

Luke's arms were massive and bronzed by the sun. Judd wondered what the boy had done other than play football to be in such good shape. One snip of Luke's pliers and Judd's hands were free. He rubbed his wrists and raised his hands in the air, trying to get the blood flowing again. Both hands were swollen and had turned a pale blue, but soon they were back to their normal size and color.

"Better get you guys out of here before Max comes," Luke said. He turned to Albert. "We didn't mean to hurt you. And tell your buddy we could have easily killed you today, but that's not our way. We ask you to stop hunting us and leave us alone. If you don't . . . well, God help you."

"I should have set the gun to kill a long time ago," Albert threatened. "Max and I will find you. You're not gettin' away next time."

Luke plastered a piece of duct tape across Albert's mouth and closed the tailgate as Judd and Lionel rushed to the car and jumped in the back.

Luke crawled behind the wheel and told Lionel and Judd what had happened. "Those two guys went after Tom when he and I split up in the woods. I got away, circled back, and hid our car a little farther into the woods. When I saw they had Tom, I knew I had to follow them, but I didn't have a weapon. I raced to one of our supply houses and found the shotgun. When I came back, the truck was gone. I had no idea you guys had been captured too. I went back to the fort and found it empty, so I decided to go looking for those two guys."

"They could have taken me straight to the GC," Tom said.

Luke smiled. "Little brother, it was just a test of your faith in me."

"How did you find their house?" Judd said.

"It took a while. Fortunately I heard the truck when that Max guy took the two dead people to the GC. I back-tracked and had just located the house when he got back."

"How did you get Tom out without anyone hearing?" Judd said.

Luke shrugged. "I managed to get through the window and move some of that furniture without making much noise. Tom looked stone cold on the floor, but I had my snippers with me and we got out of there. We were all set to spring on them, but they put you guys in the truck. We decided to take our chances on the road."

"I can't thank you enough for helping us," Judd said. "Did you know they were bounty hunters?"

"We'd heard some rumors from a few people that something was up, but nothing concrete. The GC was always looking for us, but this changes everything. We're going to have to be even more careful."

Luke made his way through a series of back roads, stopping to listen for vehicles passing. They didn't radio ahead to the safe house for fear someone might be listen-ing. When a car passed in the distance, Luke pulled behind a deserted shack, and they got out to wait for nightfall.

"You think Max and Albert will still try to find us?" Lionel said.

"Bet on it," Luke said. "They're in this for the money. And there will probably be more like them roaming the low country for as many people without the mark as they can find."

Judd sat with his back to the shack, his head in his hands. He had been prepared to die, to give his life, and God had used Luke to spare it again. He patted his pockets, forgetting Max had taken his cell phone.

"We can set you up with the latest once we're back at the hideout," Tom said when he found out what Judd was looking for. "You should see all the technical stuff we've gotten from the Co-op."

Lionel smiled at Judd. "Who did you want to call?"

3

VICKI and Shelly stayed together the rest of the day talking and praying. They made frequent trips to the main cabin to see if anyone had heard from South Carolina. Sad faces at the computer left Vicki feeling sorry she had come.

"You mentioned we should do something," Vicki said as she and Shelly walked to their cabin. "I think I have an idea."

Vicki led Shelly to a vacant shack and walked inside. The door creaked on its hinges, and dust was piled on the rickety furniture. After Vicki explained her idea, Shelly agreed to help. "We should get Marshall's okay first."

Marshall smiled when Vicki told him their plan. "I have some paint and material you could use for curtains."

The two girls got busy fixing up the cottage. They asked Charlie to help them carry the furniture outside to clean it. By nightfall, the inside was spotless and ready for paint, but Vicki and Shelly were exhausted.

Vicki couldn't stop thinking about Judd, but plunging into a project forced her to keep going, and it felt good to be doing something constructive. She skipped dinner, saying she wasn't hungry, washed up, and retreated to her bunk in the cabin. There she continued writing in her journal.

> *I can't think about Judd dying. The thought is too horrible. I keep hearing that man's voice who answered the phone and it makes me sick. From the time Bruce Barnes started teaching the Bible, I've known that things would get worse. But it always seemed like something far off, an evil in New Babylon. Now the evil has spread so much that we'll have to worry about normal citizens, not just the GC. But a life without Judd . . .*

Vicki put down her pen as someone approached her cabin. Out of breath, Darrion raced inside and fell panting next to Vicki with a cell phone. "It's for you."

Vicki studied Darrion's face for any hint if this was good news or bad, but Darrion quickly rose and ran out the door.

"Hello?"

"Vick, it's Judd."

Vicki covered her mouth with a hand. "Judd . . . you're alive. This isn't your last request or anything, is it?"

Judd laughed and his voice sounded tired. "We just made it to Tom and Luke's place in South Carolina. You wouldn't believe what happened."

"Tell me. Are you all right?"

"I was until I got shot," Judd said.

Vicki gasped as Judd told her about the weapon the two men had used. "Carl Meninger's looking at it now, but it shoots some kind of laser or heat ray that can kill you. Fortunately it was on stun when he shot me."

Judd went through their flight from Petra, telling Vicki everything about their pilot, Mr. Whalum, how they had made it to the fort in South Carolina only to be chased by two bounty hunters. When Judd described their escape, Vicki felt like she was living it herself.

"Luke was your angel," Vicki said. She told Judd about God's warning and their trip to western Wisconsin. "How's Lionel?"

"Pretty good. We're both scratched up from running through the woods, but I'm looking forward to a shower or a bath and a long sleep. Tom got the worst of it. They think his leg might be infected, so they gave him medicine."

"Any idea when you'll head this way? You're still planning on coming, right?"

"We have to talk about that," Judd said seriously.

Vicki's heart fell. Could Judd have changed his mind? Maybe he didn't feel the same about her. "Go ahead," she said.

Judd took a breath. "We're meeting tomorrow morning to talk about our strategy. It's going to be a tough call whether to stay put or—"

"Judd, get to the part about coming here, okay?"

Judd sighed. "When you're in a situation like we were in, you do some heavy thinking. I thought we were going to die. And every minute I was running I was trying to get back to you. I know God's in control and we're living for him, but a part of me is living to see you again."

Vicki choked back the tears. "Really?"

"I would have paid Mr. Whalum a million dollars to fly us to Wisconsin. And I'm trying not to let those feelings affect our next move, but it's really hard."

"I'm waiting for you," Vicki said. "Just knowing you're all right will keep me going." She told Judd about Zeke, Marshall Jameson, and the setup in Avery.

"What about the problems you had with Mark?"

"We sort of patched things up before the angel's visit. We haven't really talked since we've been here, but I think he'll be okay as long as I don't do anything stupid."

"You?" Judd chuckled.

Vicki's laughter turned to tears. "Judd, I was so worried about you. I was just writing that I didn't know what I'd do if the GC . . ."

"I know. I feel the same about you. We've come a long way since those first days after the disappearances."

"Do you think it's selfish of us to be so concerned about each other?"

"I don't think it's selfish to really love someone."

Vicki heard someone in the background open a door, and Judd put his hand over the phone. Finally he said, "I need to go. I'll call you tomorrow and we can talk more."

"I can't wait," Vicki said.

There were no showers at the plantation, so Judd settled for a lukewarm tub in one of the upstairs bathrooms.

The plantation house was near a slow-moving river miles from any town. Barbed wire and signs with skulls and crossbones warned people to keep out of the contaminated area, and it had worked. A barrier that seemed to be built by the Global Community blocked the only road to the house. And with the help of Chang Wong in New Babylon, planting false information about the area, Judd hoped to guarantee the GC would stay away.

The house had fallen into disrepair over the past fifty years. Banisters that had once been polished to shine like mirrors were rotting and in some places lay broken in pieces. Judd hadn't seen the whole house, but the kitchen seemed like the most usable room. Carl had helped Tom and Luke tap into an electrical wire some distance away, so no one knew there was anyone living on the property.

The bathroom floor was so rickety that Judd wondered if the water-filled tub might fall through. He gingerly stepped in and lay back. When the water settled, he thought about God's mark on his forehead. That every believer had this mark made it easy to spot friend or foe, and over the past few months he had become accustomed to it. Now, he again saw it as a miracle. Though Nicolae forced people to take his mark, God had placed his identifier on people who willingly chose to be forgiven.

He splashed water on his face and watched it drip into the tub. He wondered how he would have acted at the guillotine. Would he have begged for his life? Would he have taken the mark? No, God wouldn't let that happen. Still, Judd wondered where the courage others had shown came from. Was it something God gave the person at the time he or she faced the blade?

While thunder sounded in the distance, Judd dressed and went to the bedroom he and Lionel shared. Together they watched a storm roll in from the coast. Lightning bolts flashed as God put on a light show. Tom had described the wall of water from the meteor that crashed down into the ocean. For some reason, God had wanted this house to stand.

A few minutes after rain began pelting the roof, the ceiling started dripping in a steady stream. Carl Meninger brought in a bucket. "We still have a few holes to plug, so this is our emergency backup system."

From Vicki's e-mails, Judd knew Carl had worked for the Global Community and had helped the kids while they were living in the schoolhouse. He had escaped the GC after Vicki's final satellite transmission to young people.

"How's Tom doing?" Lionel said.

Carl winced. "His leg's pretty nasty, but we have a lady here who used to be a nurse. He should be fine if he takes care of it."

Carl explained that they had moved from a different hiding place on a small island to this plantation. "What the GC meant for evil, God used for our good. We have lots more room here and it's even safer. Plus, we've learned we have to be more careful about who we trust."

"Not an easy lesson to learn," Lionel said.

Judd slept through the night and went downstairs after the group meeting had started. Tom sat in the center of about twenty people with his leg elevated and bandaged. Luke introduced Judd and Lionel to those who hadn't met them the night before. The oldest people were a couple in their fifties Luke had met on an excursion before leaving the island. The couple had become believers after Luke encouraged them to read Tsion Ben-Judah's Web site.

The youngest members were a little younger than Judd. Luke and Tom had found them on an island not far from Beaufort. Their ancestors were African slaves, and though they were glad to be safe, the kids felt strange living on a plantation.

"You all know the developments and the new danger we're in," Luke began. He pulled out a sheet of paper. "This came from Judd's friend Chang just this morning." Luke handed the message to Carl, who read the text of Chang's warning about the new bounty hunter scheme.

"Over the next few days we're going to figure out our action plan," Luke said when Carl finished.

"What do you mean?" a girl said.

Carl stood. "There are a number of things we can do. We can play it safe and hide, we can concentrate on Internet outreach and plan small trips—like getting Judd and Lionel back north—or we can go on the offensive. Try to beat the GC at their own game."

"We're looking for as many ideas as you can come up with," Luke said. "Everybody will be heard."

Lionel raised a hand. "About Judd and me, how are we going to get from here to Wisconsin?"

"That's a good question," Carl said. "Chang is supposed to send us some more detailed information about the bounty hunters and where they're being used. I'd like to wait until we have that and contact the Co-op before we commit."

Judd nodded. "You've risked your lives for us, and we both appreciate it. We'd be lying if we said we wanted to stay, but we'll wait as long as we need to."

Vicki worked at the cottage the next day with a feeling she couldn't describe. Everything seemed lighter. Her heart felt freer, and she hummed as she painted. She had always hated the chores her mother gave her. "When you live in a small space you have to keep things clean," her mother would say.

"Then let's live in a real house like other people," Vicki would say. These conversations usually became heated arguments that wound up getting Vicki grounded. Now she wished her mother could see her efforts.

Maybe Mom can see me, Vicki thought. *I wonder what she thinks of Judd. And what does Dad think?*

Vicki imagined a conversation between Judd and her parents. She had always thought of Judd's family as high-class, from a different income level with expensive cars, houses, and friends. But the disappearances had leveled the playing field, both for those left behind and those taken. There was no difference now between Vicki's parents and Judd's. All four were in heaven where even the poorest person on earth was rich.

I wonder if Mom and Dad have actually talked with Judd's parents.

Shelly arrived with more paint and asked Vicki why she was smiling.

"I'd never be able to explain it in a hundred years," Vicki said.

Vicki had asked Maggie Carlson to sew curtains, and the woman had them completed later that evening. Conrad helped secure them over the windows, and Maggie fluffed the corners. "Do you think she'll like them?"

"She'll love it," Vicki said, slipping an arm around the older woman.

The next morning at breakfast, Vicki could barely contain her excitement. Almost everyone in the group knew what Vicki and Shelly were up to, but all had kept the secret. Before the morning meeting, Marshall asked Colin and Becky Dial to accompany him outside. Vicki glanced at Shelly and giggled as they followed.

When Colin and Becky arrived at the cottage, Marshall turned. "One of the qualities of believers who are maturing is self-giving love. People see a need or become aware of another person's pain and they decide to help, not because they are going to get points in heaven or pats on the back, but because they know it's something Jesus would have done."

Colin cocked his head and looked around as others joined the small group. "What's this about?"

Marshall smiled. "You two lost your house and everything in it. For men that's a hard thing, but not the end of the world. A house is a roof and a place to sleep. For wives, it's different. Becky, you lost a home and all the ways you tried to turn those four walls into a place of refuge for your family and friends."

Becky nodded and wiped away a tear.

"We know it's been hard on you, so a couple of younger people suggested we try to make the transition a little easier." Marshall motioned for Vicki and Shelly. "Will you do the honors?"

Vicki stepped forward and opened the door. Though the outside of the cottage had remained the same, the inside had been transformed with the paint, curtains, and cleaning the others had done.

When Becky looked inside, her mouth opened in amazement. She glanced at her husband, who simply smiled and nudged her inside.

"It won't replace your old home," Vicki said, "but we hope you like it."

Becky sat on the bed, put her face in her hands, and wept. She reached out a hand to Vicki and squeezed, then did the same to Shelly.

Then everyone but Colin and Becky moved outside.

Charlie furrowed his brow and squinted at the newly washed window. "Doesn't she like it?"

"More than she can say," Vicki said.

4

JUDD and Lionel met with Carl and found he had some of the latest gadgets and phones from the Co-op. "Sometimes they deliver supplies, food, and clothes, and other times they have stuff like this." Carl held up a tiny phone about three inches square.

"How do you punch in the numbers on something that small?" Lionel said.

"You don't. It's all voice activated. And look at this." Carl removed a soft plastic piece from the back of the phone and placed it in his ear. "You talk and listen through this without using your hands. You can look at the display to see who's calling, but you never have to hold anything. Some are so small you can actually fix the transmitters to one of your teeth."

Carl handed Judd and Lionel separate phones and told them to put in the earpieces. "Now watch this. Intercom. Twenty-one. Twenty-two."

Instantly a tone sounded in Judd's ear and Carl's voice came through the tiny speaker. "You can communicate with anyone in the group at a moment's notice from anywhere, as long as they have their earpiece in. With the heightened alert, we're asking everyone to wear these at all times."

"And the intercom works how far?" Lionel said.

"The technology is global, so you could be anywhere in the world and still talk to each other without ever dialing."

"If you can spare some of these, I'd like to take them to Wisconsin with me."

"Just tell me how many you need," Carl said.

The group talked excitedly over meals about their next move. Some took turns at the computer typing out suggestions, while others used pen and paper.

Luke coordinated lookout assignments. One man was a carpenter and had built a small observation tower atop the plantation house accessed through an upstairs room. The land was flat, and anyone could see clearly with the help of high-powered binoculars.

Judd and Lionel took a four-hour shift in the tower the next afternoon, and Judd used the time to call Vicki. He told her about the group and that their trip north was on hold until they heard from Chang Wong. Vicki said she understood, but Judd could hear the disappointment in her voice.

"There's something I haven't told you," Vicki said. "When the angel Anak warned us to leave Colin Dial's house, he also said something that's been bothering me."

"What did he say?"

Judd heard pages flipping. "I want to get this right. Here it is. Just before he disappeared, he stood right next to me and said, 'You will see your friends again before the glorious appearing of the King of kings and Lord of lords. But one you love will see much pain and will not return whole.' What do you think that means?"

"You think he was talking about me?"

"I don't know. I guess somehow the angel knows about us." Vicki paused. "But I don't know if he meant love in the regular way or the special kind of love . . . I have for you."

"Maybe it's some kind of warning. Or that could have been fulfilled when Tom hurt his leg. If the infection gets worse, there's a chance he could lose it."

"Yeah, it could be, but I had the impression he meant somebody in our original group."

After Judd said good-bye, Lionel put the binoculars down. "What's your gut feeling?"

"I honestly don't know if we should try to move now or wait and—"

"Not about that, about Vicki. What's going to happen with you two?"

Judd looked out the tower window. In the distance he saw the river moving peacefully through the countryside. Large trees dotted the unused fields toward the south. He could imagine a hundred people working them, hot and sweaty, harvesting, planting, tilling the soil. He turned to Lionel. "You know me as well as anybody. What do you think?"

Lionel shook his head. "I'd say you're pretty gone on her, and assuming we can get back, I'm going to have to find some fancy clothes to wear to the wedding."

Judd smiled. "If it happens, would you be willing to be my best man?"

Lionel cackled and stomped his feet. "I was hoping you'd ask."

Sam Goldberg put the finishing touches on another edition of his Petra Diaries and read over his words in the computer building. Sam had included excerpts from the latest message of Dr. Tsion Ben-Judah, who had focused that morning on the words of Jesus. Tsion repeated parables and gave an explanation of each story. Dr. Ben-Judah said he would review the Sermon on the Mount tomorrow.

Sam had begun to notice something strange going on in the crowd as Tsion and Micah spoke. Most people at the site were believers, but every day new people came forward to pray and Sam rejoiced as they received God's forgiveness. Still, hundreds and perhaps thousands were undecided. Another smaller group disagreed with Tsion and Micah and said Jesus was not God.

Sam wrote in his Petra Diaries:

> As Tsion or Micah begin to speak, these defiant ones and those who are not sure about Jesus often fall to the ground as if in pain. They struggle and cry out, tear their clothing, and throw dirt in the air. If you have ever read the story of Jacob when he struggled with the angel of

God, this looks exactly like that. They are fighting the very God who has died to save them and calls to them even now.

The Bible talks about this kind of spiritual warfare. I have never seen it so dramatic as here in Petra. The people can't walk away from the teaching. It is right in front of them every day, and they cannot escape the voices of truth speaking so clearly.

If you are reading this and you feel this same wrestling in your soul, do not resist God. He loves you and wants to come into your life and forgive you, change you, and make you a new person. Allow him to do that today and end this fight with the God who loved you enough to die for you.

Sam hit the send button and prayed that someone outside Petra would respond to the words. When he opened his eyes, Naomi Tiberius walked into the room. Naomi had become the main computer person at the site, helping train and coordinate communication with Chang Wong in New Babylon. Naomi was a little older than Sam, but he felt attracted to her. Though she had helped Sam become part of her computer team, she hadn't shown much interest outside their work together.

Sam had decided this would be the day he would talk with her about his feelings. He motioned for her and she smiled. A blip on Sam's screen showed he had a new batch of e-mail, but that could wait.

"Do you need help?" Naomi said as she walked up to him.

Do I ever, Sam thought. He glanced at the floor, took a breath, and looked into her eyes. "I have something to ask you that's pretty important."

Naomi sat and stared at the computer. "The monitor looks fine. Is something wrong with one of your programs?"

"No, this is not about computers. It's about us."

"Us?" Naomi said, raising an eyebrow.

"Naomi, I don't know how to say this . . . I've tried not to let my feelings get in the way of our work together, but—"

Naomi put a hand on Sam's shoulder and smiled. "I have sensed that you felt something more than friendship for me." She glanced away, then turned her chair toward him. "I think you're very sweet and kind, and you work very hard at everything you do. You have a heart for God. You're handsome, easy to talk with—"

"Okay," Sam said, sensing bad news, "just get to the point."

Naomi bit her lip. "I don't have the same feelings for you that you have for me."

"Is it my age?"

"Partly perhaps, but—"

"You just said how great I am, handsome, a heart for God. Why can't you like me?"

"I do like you. You're a great friend, and a friend is to be treasured. But friends are always honest with each other. And I would be lying to say my feelings go beyond friendship."

Sam paused. "Do you think you ever . . . you know . . . would your feelings ever change?"

"Again, I must be honest. I don't believe so." Sam looked away, and she grabbed his chair and turned it. "I'm very flattered that you are attracted to me. I'm honored that you've talked to me in such a straightforward way. But you don't want me to lie, do you?"

Sam held up both hands. "It's okay. I won't mention it again."

"Sam—"

"And you don't have to worry about this affecting my work. I'll keep going as long as you need the help."

"Sam, look at me."

Sam sighed and looked at the floor. "I feel like a fool."

"Don't. You're very brave. You were honest with me and you risked getting hurt. I admire that."

"Yeah. I've got a lot of great qualities, but nothing that interests you."

"Sam—"

"It's okay. I understand what you're saying, and I thank you for trying to let me down easy. Now, I have some work to catch up on."

"Sam, don't be upset."

He clenched his teeth. "I'm not."

Sam clicked on his e-mail box and pulled up several messages. Some were in response to recent editions of the Petra Diaries, and others were from kids in the Young Tribulation Force. As Naomi walked away, Sam put his head on the desk. No matter what she said, he still felt awful inside and knew he wouldn't be able to concentrate. He started to turn the computer off when he noticed a message from someone whose last name was Ben-Eliezar.

This is it, Sam thought. *I've been waiting for so long.*

Vicki was elated about Becky Dial's reaction to the spruced-up cottage. The gesture had helped the woman's depression. Vicki had a chance to talk with her a few days later.

"It's not so much the cottage that helped," Becky said, "but to know you guys went to all that trouble and were thinking about me really means a lot."

Judd had called Vicki the day after, just as he had said, but news of his possible return didn't come until a few days later. Vicki took the call in the meeting room and rushed to her cabin to talk.

"I don't know how to say this," Judd said, "but travel right now doesn't look good."

"Is it the bounty hunters?" Vicki said.

"Yeah, I talked with Chang late last night. The GC response to the bounty hunters is positive. The guy in charge of the Rebel Apprehension Program—"

"Kruno Fulcire," Vicki said.

"Right. He's expanding the program throughout the whole United North American States. Chang says that means bounty hunters will be everywhere. Think of it, Vick—with the GC or Morale Monitors, at least you can spot them by their uniforms. Bounty hunters won't be wearing any identifying clothing. And with the kind of money the GC is offering, you can bet these people will target believers and look for as many as they can find."

"Any word on the two who were after you?"

"Chang got into the database and found out they were questioned. They're scouring the countryside for us, so we're on heightened alert. People are keeping watch all day."

"I know what that's like."

Judd paused. "I can't tell you how disappointed I am."

"Me too. But you're safe, and at least we're on the same continent now."

"Part of me wants to forget what the others are saying and just grab a couple of motorcycles and drive up there."

"Sounds exciting but not very safe."

"We also talked about finding a Co-op driver, but with the bounty hunters on the loose, the Co-op will be affected too."

"What was the meeting like? Is everybody in agreement?"

"There are a couple of people who evidently didn't want to risk taking us in. I think they'll be okay, but we have to be sensitive to everybody's feelings."

"So bottom line, you have no idea when—"

"I know exactly when I'll be there, and that's as soon as I can. The very second I get the chance."

———

Sam found Mr. Stein speaking with a group of older believers in a cave. When he got the man alone, he showed him a copy of the e-mail from Aron Ben-Eliezar.

"This is one of the sons of the rabbi we helped escape Jerusalem?" Mr. Stein said.

"I'm sure of it. I didn't tell him where I was. He must think I'm in Israel because he asks to see me in Tel Aviv. Read what he says."

> Sam,
> I finally received your note. Thank you for writing. I'm glad to know my parents are safe, but I don't believe they are followers of Ben-Judah. I know they aren't foolish enough to buy what Carpathia says, but they wouldn't turn their backs on our faith.
>
> Joel and I would like to talk with you, but not by e-mail or phone. And please, don't tell my parents about contacting me. If you can come late tomorrow night, we will wait for you.
>
> Shalom,
> Aron

Aron gave a location and a specific time at the bottom of the page. Mr. Stein folded the paper and took a deep breath. "Something about this troubles me."

"You think they are loyal to the Global Community?"

Mr. Stein shook his head. "No. I think they are lost lambs who need a shepherd, but I don't know what to do."

"Let me go see them. I'll talk with them and tell them the truth."

Mr. Stein pursed his lips.

"The Co-op has pilots. I could ride with one of them."

"Wait here," Mr. Stein said. He climbed down the steep stairway cut into the rock and disappeared.

Sam leaned against the wall and looked out on hundreds of thousands who had made their home in the ancient city. He looked toward the computer building and sighed. *I guess Naomi was kind with what she said, Lord, but it still hurts.*

A few minutes later Mr. Stein returned, his face tight. "I have spoken with the elders about the matter, and they are praying for direction. Unless they disagree with the plan, I will accompany you and we will find Aron and Joel together."

5

SAM shook hands with Mac McCullum and boarded the plane that had carried more materials to Petra. The Tribulation Force didn't have to worry about feeding the people here, but there were still ongoing computer and building needs.

Mac talked loudly and didn't hide the fact that he thought it was dangerous to send two believers into Israel. "But if the elders have given their approval, they must have a good reason."

"We all submit to their authority," Mr. Stein said. "If they had told us not to go, there would have been no question."

"Who are you looking for?" Mac said.

"They are sons of a rabbi and his wife who are now in Petra," Mr. Stein said.

Mac asked why the parents weren't going to talk with them, and Sam explained Aron's e-mail. "We're asking God to help us reach them and bring them out safely."

"Well, I'll be prayin' for you," Mac drawled. "But if those two have resisted the truth this long, I don't hold out much hope for them. How do you know they haven't taken Carpathia's mark?"

"From Aron's e-mail, it sounds like they hate Carpathia like many of the undecided in Petra," Sam said.

"I hope it's not some kind of trap," Mac said.

Mr. Stein asked Mac why he hadn't stayed in Petra, and Mac smiled. "I'd get too fat eating all that manna. Plus, I'm having more fun than a coon in a cornfield flying all over the place with Albie."

"Who's Albie?" Sam said.

"Another Trib Force pilot. I moved in with him after I left the Strong Building in Chicago. We're staying in Al Basrah now, when we aren't flying, which is pretty much all the time. Albie's an expert at trading on the black market." Sam scrunched his eyebrows and Mac said, "You know, getting things without the GC knowing about it and for as little cost as possible. Albie can find just about anything if you can pay the price. That's where this plane came from."

"Do you have phony identification?" Sam said.

"Nah, after what happened in Greece, I know God's looking out for us flyboys. He's got things in control."

Sam watched the Tel Aviv skyline come into view and dialed the number Judd had given him for the man known only as Sabir. Sabir had agreed to pick up Sam and Mr. Stein at an airfield Mac and Albie used. When they landed, Mr. Stein spotted a small car at the end of the runway and Mac slowed the engines. "Should be fine from here. Check with Chang when you want to head back to Petra."

Sam and Mr. Stein thanked Mac and made their way through a chain-link fence that had been cut with wire cutters. Sabir, a short, Middle Eastern man with graying hair and glasses, welcomed them and as they drove told his story of being a former terrorist. Sam hadn't heard about Judd and Lionel's close call with the GC in Jerusalem, and he was thrilled at Sabir's version of the story. Sabir's wife had flown to Petra, and he handed Sam a note to give to her when Sam returned.

As they drove toward Tel Aviv, Sabir gave tips for avoiding the GC. Both Sam and Mr. Stein had hats on and wore long-sleeved shirts so no one could tell they didn't have the mark of Carpathia.

"Why don't you come back to Petra with us after we are through here?" Mr. Stein said as Sabir stopped the car in an alley. "You can take the message to your wife yourself."

"I would like that very much, but so far God hasn't given me peace about leaving. Just the other day I woke up from a sound sleep and felt urged to get in my car. I started it and sat behind the wheel for a good five minutes asking God where I should go.

"I heard no voices, no signs from the sky, so I started driving. A half hour later I was in front of a darkened storefront. I stopped at the curb to get my bearings and saw movement inside. Three people walked out a door and scurried into the night. Something told me I should follow, and I did, with my lights off.

"When they discovered I was there, they began to run. I got out and said, 'In the name of Jesus, stop!' All three stopped dead in their tracks. They turned and walked toward me, and when I turned on my headlights I saw all three had the mark of the believer."

"What were they doing there?" Sam said.

"Hiding. They had not taken the mark of Carpathia and had just become believers a few days earlier. Some people had discovered their hiding place, and they were afraid the GC was coming the next morning. I got them to a safe place before the sun rose."

Mr. Stein patted Sabir's arm. "God has you where he wants you for now, but if you feel in danger, please let us know."

Sabir gave Sam and Mr. Stein final directions and drove away. The sun had set as the two walked through alleys and narrow walkways. A poster caught Sam's eye, and he stopped to examine it. "See the Miraculous Power of Orcus!" The poster gave the date and time, and Sam realized the performance would be that very night.

"I don't like the looks of that," Mr. Stein said, glancing at his watch. "Come on, we only have a few minutes."

Sam was shocked at the difference between the safety he felt in Petra and the evil he sensed in Tel Aviv. The few people they saw in darkened alleys and walkways moved with heads down, fear etched on their faces.

When they reached the meeting place, a public park, Sam and Mr. Stein waited until the correct time and gingerly moved into the open. A block away a stage had been set up with lasers flashing and music blaring. Sam guessed that Aron Ben-Eliezar had picked this place because of the crowds. It would be easier to blend in with thousands than to meet in a private place.

Mr. Stein motioned toward a small fountain, and they sat on a bench, studying the growing mob swarming toward the stage. In the distance, young people whooped and hollered, chanting Carpathia's name and falling in front of a statue suspended above the crowd.

"Aron should be here by now," Sam whispered.

Something beeped to Sam's right, and he noticed a small mound covered by leaves and grass. Sam shoved the debris away and found a walkie-talkie on the ground.

"Okay, pick up the radio and move to your right," a scratchy voice said.

Sam picked up the walkie-talkie and walked toward the street with Mr. Stein. Hundreds made their way toward the stage, and Sam pulled his hat low and tried not to make eye contact with anyone.

"Stop there," the voice said when they reached the edge of the sidewalk. "Look up."

Sam tilted his head and saw a curtain flutter on the third floor of the building in front of them. "Go to the back entrance and take the stairs. Don't let anyone see you come in."

Sam and Mr. Stein followed the directions. The stairwell had a huge crack in the wall, and plaster was falling onto the steps. When they entered a hallway, a door opened at the other end. Mr. Stein whispered a prayer as they walked toward the open door. Once inside, the door closed and a thin man with a beard stepped forward. He had a bandage on his forehead, but there was no mark of Carpathia on his right hand.

Sam introduced himself and Mr. Stein, and the man stared at them. "I didn't know you were a kid." The man looked at Mr. Stein. "You really know my parents are safe in Petra?"

"Rabbi Ben-Eliezar accompanied us to Masada before going on to Petra," Mr. Stein said. "We have not told them we made contact with you. Are you Aron or Joel?"

"Joel."

"Where is your brother?"

Joel moved to the front window and opened the curtain a few inches. "Don't worry about him. Tell me about my parents."

Mr. Stein told him how he had met the Ben-Eliezars, their concern about their sons, and how they had tried repeatedly to contact them. Joel bit his lip as he listened, his eyes turning to the window.

When Mr. Stein carefully described how they had believed in the message about Jesus, Joel shook his head. "That is the part I can't accept."

"It is true. It is why we have come all this way at such personal risk. We want to tell you the truth about God."

Joel rolled his eyes. "I have no need to believe in God. There is a scientific explanation for all the questions we have."

"Even with everything that's happened?" Sam said. "The disappearances, the earthquake, the—"

"People believe in God because they've been told to. They have an emotional attachment to their faith because it helps them get through. It helps them deal with their pain. I rely on myself and hard work. If a crisis comes, like an earthquake or another natural disaster, I try harder."

"And what if all your efforts are striving after wind?" Mr. Stein said. "What if you come to the end and find you cannot try harder?"

Joel glared at Mr. Stein. "The only comfort we have in life is to know we have done something worthwhile. We've tried to think independently and struggled to improve the world."

"What happens after you die?" Sam said.

"Nothing. It's over. You get one chance to make a difference and that's it."

"With everything going on in the world, and with Nicolae executing people without his mark," Mr. Stein said, "does it not make you consider placing your faith in the true God?"

"I have faith in myself that I can improve the world. Outside of that, I have no use for faith."

The door opened and a man who looked slightly younger than Joel came in, breathless. "It's about to start."

Joel introduced his brother, and Aron shook hands with Mr. Stein and Sam. Sam studied his face and hand and didn't see any sign of Carpathia's mark. Mr. Stein repeated the information about his parents, but Joel stopped him. "I want to see how they begin this. Go in the next room."

The window of the shabby apartment faced the stage.

Joel grabbed binoculars and watched the introduction of guests as Sam and Mr. Stein went into the bedroom with Aron.

Aron paced as Mr. Stein and Sam sat. "My parents are all right?" he said.

Sam nodded. "Why haven't you answered them?"

"Things have been happening. I came to live with my brother here in Tel Aviv shortly after the Global Community went after those people in the desert. We have tried to exist since then, but my brother, he is not well. . . ."

"Are you open to hearing the truth we have discovered?" Mr. Stein said.

"Perhaps," Aron said. He turned and leaned against the wall. "Ever since Joel took the mark, he has regretted the decision."

Mr. Stein stood. "He took the mark of Carpathia?"

"Yes, though he didn't worship the image."

"Listen to me carefully," Mr. Stein said. "Your soul is at stake. Your brother has made a decision he will regret for eternity. Why haven't you taken the mark?"

"I was hungry. You need it to buy anything. But something seemed wrong about it—not just taking an identification number, but actually identifying yourself with Carpathia."

"You were right not to take it. Now let me tell you why."

Mr. Stein began with an overview of how sin began in the perfect world God had created. The evil one tempted humans, and they chose against God's way. "Throughout the Bible, Satan has opposed God. Now, in these last days, Satan is trying to destroy, just like he has always done. Nicolae Carpathia is the ultimate evil and will stop at nothing to thwart God's plan for good."

"What is that plan?" Aron said.

"To save people from their sins. God sent his own Son to die as a sacrifice for you and me. If we put our trust in Jesus, the Messiah, and ask him to forgive us from our sins, God will do that. Those who were taken in the disappearances, like your sister, Meira, were ones who believed the truth about Jesus. But there is still time to choose—"

"Come and see this," Joel yelled from the next room. "Hurry!"

Sam rushed to the front window and squinted. In the distance a huge monitor showed two men wielding swords that were as long as Sam was tall. The fight seemed staged, but the sound of the steel blades striking each other was real. Finally, one of the men ducked and made a move to his left, avoiding the razor-sharp blade by inches, and struck a blow to the other man's right arm. The crowd gasped as the first man staggered, his severed arm dropping to the stage with a sickening thud.

Blood gushed from the wound, and people near the stage fell back, screaming. The injured man's sword fell, and he slipped to his knees, trying to stop the fatal flow of blood. His opponent held up his sword with both hands and the crowd cheered, encouraging him to finish the injured man.

"It's like watching the Roman gladiators," Sam muttered.

Suddenly a curtain parted, and a man stepped forward. He wore normal-looking clothes, and his hair reached his shoulders. Sam noticed his eyes, which seemed to bore into the man with the severed arm. The longhaired man stooped and picked up the limb from the stage.

The crowd hushed. The hero worship for the winner turned to silence as the man placed the severed arm back in place, grasped it with both hands at the point of the injury, and said, "I have been given power by the potentate. Therefore, under the authority of the risen lord, Nicolae Carpathia, I pronounce this wound healed."

The injured man lifted his once-severed arm and raised a bloody fist above his head. "It's back! He healed my arm!"

6

"**DID** they do that with mirrors?" Sam said, his mouth still open at what he had just seen.

"It has to be a trick," Aron said.

Mr. Stein shook his head. "It is real power, but not the power of God. It is the power of the evil one."

Joel raised an eyebrow. "You mean Bible hocus-pocus?"

"Do not be deceived. You're seeing Scripture come to life. Leon Fortunato calls down fire from heaven by the power of Nicolae. This faker may attempt other miracles tonight to mock God."

The man with the healed arm picked up his sword and raised it in triumph with his new arm. People near the stage fell to their knees and worshiped the miracle worker.

"Do not praise me, for I am only one sent by god," Orcus said as he pointed to the statue of Nicolae. "I am simply his servant. Turn your affection to the one who has the power of life and death and who lives to serve you."

"Praise lord Carpathia!" the healed man said.

"Praise him!" the crowd shouted.

Smoke billowed from the image hovering over the crowd, and everyone lay down before it. Muffled praise rose from the people, and some began singing "Hail Carpathia."

When Orcus raised a hand, everyone quieted. "Your praise has been heard, and I assure you, lord Carpathia appreciates your reverence tonight. And to show you how much he loves you—" he swept his hand forward—"let there be light!"

A great flash of white light bathed the audience. Instead of night, it seemed like day. Sam shielded his eyes and studied the lasers backstage. The light wasn't coming from them but from overhead.

Joel rubbed his forehead so hard that the bandage came off. Sam saw the mark of Carpathia beside scratches and blotched skin. "I've tried to get this off with sandpaper, even tried to cut the skin. But maybe Orcus is right. If he can do these things by the power of Nicolae . . ."

"I need to talk to you now," Mr. Stein whispered to Aron.

Sam followed and Mr. Stein closed the door. "Your father and mother did not want to believe what I told them about God. But after I explained what the Bible says and they heard Dr. Ben-Judah, their eyes were opened. They understood God wanted a relationship with them and that the only way to escape the judgment coming upon this world was to receive the gift of Jesus Christ."

Aron sat and ran a hand through his hair. "I've wanted these past three years to be a bad dream. When you wrote, I thought you were mistaken. My parents could never turn their backs on their Jewish faith—"

"They haven't. Jesus came to fulfill everything the Bible predicted."

With that, Mr. Stein walked Aron through the many prophecies foretelling the coming Messiah. These showed clearly that Jesus had uniquely fulfilled each prophecy and was truly the Son of God. Aron focused on Mr. Stein's words and nodded, asking questions and listening carefully. "If what you're saying is true, my brother has no hope."

"You are right. Once a person voluntarily takes the mark, their eternity is sealed."

"Even if he took it to help me?"

Mr. Stein knelt before Aron. "Don't let your brother's choice affect your destiny. You will not be called to account for his decision. Accept the gift God is offering now."

"Look at this!" Joel shouted from the other room.

Sam ran into the other room with the others and looked out the window. The miracle worker had moved into the crowd and held both swords high above his head. The crowd parted as he walked. "Don't imagine that I have come to bring a sword to divide people. No, like Nicolae, I have come to bring peace."

Instantly, the swords turned into doves, which flew

over the crowd. People *ooh*ed and *ahh*ed as the birds circled Orcus. "The enemies of our god want us to war and fight with each other. They are like snakes in our midst." The man clapped, and the birds stopped flapping and fell, quickly turning into long, hissing snakes. The miracle worker caught both snakes and held them high so everyone could see. People moved back, some shrieking and fainting.

"There are snakes among us, but our god has helped us identify them. Anyone without the mark of loyalty to the potentate is an enemy of peace. Look around you now and make sure there are no snakes here."

"Over there!" someone screamed. Spotlights swung wildly and stopped on a woman cowering next to a tree. Suddenly, the miracle worker was next to her, both snakes hissing in his hands.

"How did he get over there so fast?" Sam mumbled.

"Are you an enemy of the most high god?" the miracle worker screamed.

The woman trembled and people around her scattered, forming a thirty-foot human ring. Orcus held the snakes higher and asked again if she was an enemy, waving the snakes violently until they became swords again.

"I am Jewish," the woman said, her voice shaking. "I'm not against peace, but I don't want—"

"Silence! I don't care what religion or creed you follow. If you are not willing to show allegiance to Nicolae Carpathia, you are an enemy. Now, will you take his mark?"

The woman fell to her knees and held out her hands, as if in prayer, begging the man. "I can see you are a great man, but please, I cannot show loyalty to a man who kills my people."

With one motion the miracle worker swung both swords and killed the woman where she knelt. The crowd paused, then broke into wild applause, hooting and whistling approval. The man wiped her blood from the blades and turned. "The Jews and Judah-ites are enemies of world peace. They must be identified and eliminated, and you can help. Report anyone without the mark to the Global Community immediately. It doesn't matter if they are strangers, friends, or even close family members. As long as they are living on earth without the mark, they deserve to be cut off!"

The crowd roared, some dancing around the woman's body and spitting. Sam remembered the two witnesses, Eli and Moishe, and how their bodies were treated. He cringed at the cruelty.

"If you know of someone who does not have the mark and do not report them, you are just as guilty," Orcus continued.

"I've seen enough," Aron said, glancing at Mr. Stein. "What do I need to do?"

"Wait," Joel said. "You're not thinking of following these wackos, are you? Didn't you see what just happened? I thought I was wrong, but this proves you need to take Carpathia's mark now."

Aron ignored him and went into the room with Mr. Stein and Sam. When the door was shut, Mr. Stein said,

"Becoming a believer in Christ is simple. You recognize that you are a sinner before God. Do you acknowledge that?"

Aron nodded. "I know I've done wrong things, but I can't see how God can forgive me. Don't I have to do something to make up for it?"

Mr. Stein grabbed a Bible. "In Romans we read this. 'When we were utterly helpless, Christ came at just the right time and died for us sinners. Now, no one is likely to die for a good person, though someone might be willing to die for a person who is especially good. But God showed his great love for us by sending Christ to die for us while we were still sinners. And since we have been made right in God's sight by the blood of Christ, he will certainly save us from God's judgment. For since we were restored to friendship with God by the death of his Son while we were still his enemies, we will certainly be delivered from eternal punishment by his life. So now we can rejoice in our wonderful new relationship with God—all because of what our Lord Jesus Christ has done for us in making us friends of God.' "

"So God becomes our friend simply because we ask him to forgive us?"

Mr. Stein leaned closer. "You could never do anything to wipe away your own sins. We all deserve the judgment of God. But Christ lived a perfect life and took your punishment. Now, if you ask God's forgiveness, he looks at you not just as a person who is going to heaven, but as a person cleansed by Jesus, perfect."

Aron sat and stared ahead. Sam had gone through this

same process as Judd and Lionel tried to convince him of the truth. For some the decision was immediate. For others, especially those who were Jewish, it was a more difficult process. There were hurdles they had to overcome that others didn't. Aron had no doubt been raised to believe Christianity was different from Judaism, and for a Jew to embrace Jesus meant that you turned your back on your faith. Sam knew that wasn't true, but would Aron see it?

"So God accepts me just the way I am?" Aron said. "That's almost too hard to believe. I mean, it's too easy."

Mr. Stein smiled. "This is the grace of God. He loved you so much, he sent his Son to die for you. Reach out to him now, Aron."

Aron closed his eyes. "Yes. I need to do this now."

The window in the front room opened and Joel shouted something. Sam opened the door a crack and saw Joel leaning out. "Two Judah-ites! Third floor. I'll keep them here."

Sam closed the door and whispered, "Your brother is telling someone we're here."

Aron shot up from his chair and ran to the nearest window. Mr. Stein pleaded with him to pray. "It doesn't matter what happens to us here as long as you are washed in the blood of the lamb. Don't put this off."

"I'll do it as soon as we're safe," Aron said. "Come on."

The three climbed out the window onto a fire escape and made their way down. When they were nearly to the street, two uniformed GC Peacekeepers appeared. Sam tried to turn and run, but another Peacekeeper leaned out the upstairs window. They were trapped.

A Peacekeeper led Sam and Mr. Stein to a car, but they took Aron in a separate vehicle. Mr. Stein tried to shout to him what to pray in order to become a believer, but the Peacekeeper struck Mr. Stein with a nightstick and closed the back door.

Sam was terrified as they drove to the GC station. He had heard stories of people who were given the opportunity to receive the mark of Carpathia or have their heads chopped off. He had watched the concert where Z-Van had killed a Christ follower on stage. Now it was his turn.

"I guess this wasn't God's plan for us," Sam said. "We're going to be killed, and Aron won't be able to become a believer."

"Quiet back there," the Peacekeeper said, rapping on the cage between the front and back seats.

"We must pray for God's help," Mr. Stein whispered. The man leaned close to Sam. In a very soft voice he prayed, "Father, I agree with the psalm David prayed when he was in the wilderness of Judah. 'O God, you are my God; I earnestly search for you. My soul thirsts for you; my whole body longs for you in this parched and weary land where there is no water.'

"Sam and I praise you for your unfailing love, and we will honor you as long as we live. Father, I would lift up my hands to you if they weren't secured behind me, but I praise you now for leading us here and helping us explain the truth to Aron.

"I think how much you have helped me; I sing for joy in the shadow of your protecting wings. I follow close behind you; your strong right hand holds me securely."

Mr. Stein paused and Sam took up the prayer. "Father, help Aron understand the message he's been given and to cry out to you. All those who trust in you will give praise to you, and those who are against you will be silenced."

The Global Community station was in an older section of town, but the building had been renovated and turned into a sparkling GC facility. The outside was made of stone, and a statue of Nicolae Carpathia towered in front. People were lined up, even at this hour, to take the mark. A few yards from the loyalty application center was the ghastly specter of the guillotine, standing like a soldier at attention.

Sam shivered and leaned close to Mr. Stein. "Will they give us a chance to take the mark, or just take us directly to the guillotine?"

Mr. Stein shrugged. "I was hoping we would be able to have some contact with Aron."

The car stopped in front of the building, and the Peacekeeper got out and went inside the station. The other car with Aron pulled in behind them.

"O God, give us the strength for what we are about to endure," Mr. Stein prayed softly.

Sam's heart pounded in his chest. He couldn't take his eyes away from the guillotine. When the Peacekeeper returned and roughly pulled him from the car, Sam knew he had only minutes and perhaps seconds to live.

7

JUDD'S favorite spot in the plantation house was what Luke called the "Yankee Computer Room" because the house had been used as a hospital for Union soldiers during the Civil War. Many had scrawled their names on walls or into the wood trim, and the owners had left the ancient marks. The room had a comfortable chair and a portable computer, and Judd had fallen asleep several times while writing Vicki.

Though the kids had been separated for quite some time, their Web site had kept going strong. With reports coming in from kids around the world, updates on Dr. Ben-Judah's writings, The Cube, files of information, and Sam's Petra Diaries, there was a wealth of information available to anyone.

But Judd also knew the Global Community was monitoring anything coming from suspected Judah-ites. Tsion Ben-Judah's Web site was a popular destination for

GC officials who wanted to see the latest on the "enemy camp." Anything posted on the kids' Web site had to be checked and rechecked to make sure it didn't give out vital information.

Judd loved talking with Vicki, but he also liked writing his thoughts. He had changed a couple of the paragraphs when it seemed they didn't say exactly what he wanted.

Vicki had written about their work on Colin and Becky Dial's cottage. Judd responded:

> I've only known you since the disappearances, but one word I'd use to describe you is giving. You were that way with Ryan Daley, giving him understanding and a big sister to look up to. You've been giving with Charlie. When nobody else wanted to deal with him, you did. I think you're the most giving person I know.

Compliments did not come easy for Judd, but the more he wrote, the easier it was to encourage people. He sent the e-mail and looked through incoming messages. One from Petra caught his attention. He opened it and found it was from Naomi Tiberius. Judd had met Naomi briefly and remembered she was the main computer whiz in Petra.

> Judd,
> I wanted you and the others in the Young Trib Force to know about Sam. He and Mr. Stein have gone to Israel looking for the sons of a rabbi friend. We know

from the pilot that they arrived safely in Tel Aviv. Sam was supposed to check in with us after he made contact with the two sons, but we haven't heard anything.

There is a miracle fair going on in the city, so there are many people who would probably like to see Sam, Mr. Stein, and any other believer harmed. Please ask your friends to pray for him and keep praying until we hear something.

Judd wrote a quick response thanking Naomi for the alert. He checked his unread mail and found an old message from Sam. It explained where Sam was going and that he was trying to make contact with Rabbi Ben-Eliezar's sons. *We are expecting great things and are so glad the elders have approved this trip,* Sam wrote.

Judd couldn't believe he had missed Sam's message and immediately sent an urgent request to everyone he knew. *Put our friends Sam and Mr. Stein at the top of your prayer list,* he wrote. He explained what he knew and included a portion of Sam's e-mail, leaving out the specifics of the trip in case anyone in the GC might read it. *Ask God to give them protection in a very dangerous situation.*

Judd was curious about the reference Naomi had made to the miracle fair. He found a GC Web site that listed the fairs, and to his surprise discovered they were scheduled around the world in the next few weeks. At hundreds of locations people could watch a self-proclaimed healer do miraculous things. One Web site advertised special coverage and included a button that said, "Watch now!"

Judd clicked the button and was instantly taken to a Web site originating from somewhere in Europe. A crowd had gathered around a stage with a lone man standing at the center. A gallon of blood dipped from the sea was placed beside him on a small table. The man poured some blood into a glass and held it up. "Anyone like a drink? It's fresh."

The thick, red liquid repulsed the crowd, so he poured it back into the container. The camera zoomed in. "By the power given me in the name of the most high Nicolae Carpathia, I declare this so-called plague to be a fraud."

When the man poured the liquid into a glass, out came clear water. Judd sat up quickly. The fluid in the big container was still bright red. What was poured into the glass was clear.

"Do I have any volunteers now?" the man said.

Several raised their hands. A young woman took a sip from the glass. She smiled, looked at those around her, and said, "It tastes really good." She drained the rest.

The sun shone brightly on the crowd, and the man asked for a bigger container of blood. Like a spotlight, the rays beat down, and people began crying for relief.

"Would you like some refreshment from the sea?" the man said, pointing to the huge red container.

The crowd shouted no, but a worker grabbed the container with a mechanical arm and raised it over them. People screamed, thinking they would be soaked with blood, but when the miracle man tripped a lever, the bottom of the container opened, spilling fresh, cool water on the people.

"I will do even better than that," the man yelled from the stage. He closed his eyes and motioned toward the sky. The sun quickly darkened, and the camera panned overhead. A cloud formed, then spread out and unleashed a gentle rain.

"Bless the name of Nicolae," the man said. "He sends a cooling rain on those who praise him and follow peace." He sneered. "But on those who remain his enemies, on those who refuse his goodwill and insist on their own way, he calls down fire."

A lightning bolt struck, and the crowd squealed. No one seemed hurt, but everyone got the message. "Do not worry. If you are for Nicolae, who can be against you?"

Sam sat in the cell with Mr. Stein, surprised they had been shoved along a corridor to a processing center instead of to the guillotine. The man at the front had asked their names and Sam and Mr. Stein gave them. There was no sense trying to fool the GC about their identities. Neither of them had Nicolae's mark, which was punishable by death.

"Are you Jewish?" the man said.

Mr. Stein nodded. "Both of us."

The Peacekeeper had smirked and shook his head. "Two more for the transport in the morning."

"What do you mean?" Mr. Stein said. "You're sending us—"

The Peacekeeper had backhanded Mr. Stein so hard

that Sam thought his friend would fall to the ground. Sam tried to steady him with his body.

"Take them away," the man said to a guard.

"It's okay," Sam whispered when Mr. Stein regained his balance. "Let's go."

The guard had led them to a long line of cells, taken off their cuffs, and shoved them into the last room. Mr. Stein wiped blood from his lip. Sam tried to turn on water from a tiny faucet in the corner, but nothing came out. The toilet in the room smelled hideous.

"What did he mean about the transport?" Sam said.

Mr. Stein shrugged.

A man across the hall slid to the front of his cell. "Are you a Jew?"

"Yes," Sam said.

"They're kicking all of us out of here. They said the guillotine was too good for us, so they're shipping us off to camps."

"Do you know how long you can live without food and water?" another man said from a cell farther away.

"No," Sam said innocently.

"You're about to find out," he said. "They want to torture us for not taking Carpathia's mark. We're traitors and enemies of the risen potentate. Others get a quick drop of the blade, but we get weeks, maybe months, of starvation and mistreatment."

"I knew this would happen," Mr. Stein whispered, "but I never dreamed I would see it with my own eyes."

The main door opened, and a guard pushed Aron through. Aron fell face-first on the concrete floor. The

Peacekeeper jerked him up and threw him into an empty cell at the front and locked the door.

Sam counted seventeen others. A few with the mark of Carpathia who had no doubt broken some law, but most of them were Jews who had not taken the mark. He and Mr. Stein were the only believers.

Mr. Stein called to Aron, but the man didn't move. When Mr. Stein shouted louder, several others told him to be quiet.

"He's either knocked out or dead, so shut up!" a man with Carpathia's mark said.

Mr. Stein and Sam sat on a cot and prayed quietly for Aron.

Vicki and the others gathered in the main cabin in Wisconsin and prayed for Sam Goldberg and Mr. Stein. Though most in the group had never met them, they spoke as if they were close friends.

"Please don't let the GC get to them," Charlie prayed in his simple way. "And if they do, get them out of there. You know they were trying to help others come to know you, so please help them. Amen."

Sam watched for any sign of movement from Aron but saw none. He and Mr. Stein continued to pray, then sang a few choruses, even though some inmates seemed angered by their voices.

Mr. Stein walked to the front of the cell. "Gentlemen,

I know not all of you can understand me, but I have been sent here to tell you good news—"

"Why do you think we can't understand you?" a graying old man said. "You're speaking perfect Hebrew."

Mr. Stein turned and winked at Sam. "For those of you without the mark of Carpathia, I say this. On behalf of the true King of kings and Lord of lords, you have a chance to turn from your sin and your rejection of God and begin a relationship with him."

Most of the men turned over on their bunks, but a few seemed to listen. Mr. Stein was careful not to talk too loud and bring in the guards, but he explained plainly how the men could receive Jesus Christ. When he was finished, Sam noticed Aron moving slightly. Sam called for him and Aron stood.

"If you are ready to pray, do it now before it is too late," Mr. Stein said. "O God, I know that I am a sinner and that I deserve to be punished for my sin. But right now I reach out to you in faith and ask you to take away that sin through the blood of your Son, Jesus. I believe he died on the cross in my place, took my punishment, and rose again three days later, a victor over death. I give my life to you now. Lead me in the paths you desire. Save me from my sin. And I pray all this in the name of Jesus, the Messiah. Amen."

Sam kept his eyes shut tightly as Mr. Stein prayed. He prayed for each of the men and that the guards wouldn't break in during Mr. Stein's prayer. When Mr. Stein finished, Sam looked first at Aron, but the man was again on the floor.

Of the seventeen men, three had the mark of the true believer on their foreheads. Mr. Stein pointed to them, and the three were amazed he could tell they had believed. He explained the mark of God and how everyone who prayed received one.

Finally, Aron stood and Sam was overcome with emotion. The man had the mark of the true believer as well.

"We may not know where they are taking us," Mr. Stein said through tears, "but we know our eternal destination. Our home in heaven has been sealed, and one day we will walk there because of the grace and love of our God."

Mr. Stein asked the three their names and encouraged them with words from the Scriptures. Guards arrived to quiet everyone and turn out the lights.

"Better get some sleep, Jews," one of the Peacekeepers snarled. "You'll be leaving before daylight."

The men grumbled, but Sam settled onto his bunk. Mr. Stein got the attention of one of the guards. "This young man is still a teenager. Tell me you won't have compassion on one so young."

"He's old enough to make his own decisions," the man said. "He didn't take the mark, and he's a Jew. He'll ride with the rest of you."

Sam closed his eyes and thought about Petra. He wished he could be there once more to climb the rock formations and say good-bye to the people he loved. He thought of Naomi. Though she didn't feel the same way he felt for her, she had shown him kindness.

Sam wondered if Judd and the others in the Young Tribulation Force would ever find out what had happened to him. *They will,* Sam thought, *when they get to heaven.*

Sam didn't think he could get to sleep. He imagined the ride to some sickening camp where the GC would put them to work until they dropped. He almost preferred the quick ending of the guillotine to what his mind conjured up.

Later Sam fell into a deep sleep and dreamed of writing a final edition of his Petra Diaries and sending it to everyone in the Young Tribulation Force. In the dream, Dr. Tsion Ben-Judah put Sam's writings on the screen above Petra so everyone could read it.

Sam awakened, smiling. The main door opened and a bright light shone in his face. It was time to leave.

SAM stirred, sitting up on his bunk and watching the guard at the door. The men inside breathed heavily in their sleep and a few snored. Mr. Stein slept soundly, and Sam hated to awaken him.

After the light went out, Sam wondered if the guard was simply checking on them. He glanced at Aron's cell and saw the man was sleeping or unconscious. Sam lay down quietly and waited.

The guard moved slowly past the sleeping prisoners, his footsteps quiet. It was 4:00 A.M. If they were going to be taken before sunup, they would probably be roused in the next hour, but this seemed too early.

Sam listened carefully and was convinced the man had gone, so he settled back on his pillow and sighed deeply. Before he closed his eyes he glanced at his cell door. A man stood there staring at him.

Sam resisted the urge to scream, but his eyes widened

and his heart raced furiously. Sam was sure he had never seen this stranger. He wore sandals, a long, flowing robe, had a short beard and piercing eyes. He had no mark, either of the true believer or of Carpathia.

Sam kept his eyes on the man and sat up. "Is it time for us to go?" he whispered.

"Yes." The man's voice was deep, and something about it made Sam want to trust him.

"Are you taking us to the transport?"

The man shook his head.

"Then why are you here?"

"I come in the name of the Lord our God. He is strong and mighty to save. Though the evil one is set on the destruction of the people of God, he will not touch you. There are many praying for you and your friends."

Sam wanted to pinch himself to make sure he wasn't dreaming. He fell out of bed and onto his knees. Tears streaked his cheeks. "I'm not worthy for the Lord to take such an interest in me. Others have died. Why should I be saved?"

Sam felt a hand touch his face, lifting him up. The angel stood next to him, the cell door still closed. "Write these things as an encouragement to those around the world, young one. Tell of the Lord's mighty deeds and give praise to the one who lifts those who are weary of heart."

"You mean my diary—yes, I will." The angel's touch ignited a fire inside Sam, and he couldn't wait to tell Judd and the others. Sam looked at the cell door. They still had to get away from the jail without any guards noticing.

And how would they tell Mac about needing a ride with-out the cell phone?

"Do not let your heart be troubled," the angel said. "Trust in God and the one he has sent to protect you."

Sam nodded weakly. He recalled the story of the apos-tle Peter being set free by an angel while Peter was chained to two sleeping guards. If God could do that, surely he could help Sam and the others escape.

"Awaken your friend and I will get the others," the angel said. "We must leave quickly."

Sam put a hand on Mr. Stein's shoulder and shook him gently. He opened his eyes and gave Sam a startled look. "Have they come for us?"

"Yes," Sam said, "but not the guards. God has sent someone to rescue us." He pointed at the man who had moved to Aron's cell. There was a metal clank on the floor as handcuffs fell from his wrists.

Aron rubbed his wrists and stood. The angel spoke from the hall and without moving so much as a finger, the door swung open and Aron stepped outside.

Sam reached for their cell door, and it unlatched as if someone had flipped a switch in another room. Mr. Stein and Sam moved into the hall as the angel awakened the other believers and motioned to them to get up. Sam and Mr. Stein edged as close to the angel as they could as he approached the main door. In spite of the noise of the six inmates walking out of their cells, the others kept snoring.

The main door opened as noiselessly as the cell doors. Sam walked into a holding area, where a guard sat slumped in a chair and another leaned forward on a desk, his hat covering his face. The angel pointed to a shelf above the sleeping guards, and Sam spotted their cell phone in a plastic bag. The angel nodded, and Sam grabbed it.

Each door opened for them as if it were automatic. When they reached the street, they found a sleek minivan parked in front. Sabir got out, smiling, and welcomed the six. Sam turned to thank the angel, but he had vanished like a vapor.

Sam couldn't hold back his praise. "We thank you, O God, for your protection and your love for us," he said, his arms outstretched toward heaven.

"Come," Mr. Stein said. "We will thank God once we are on our way."

Sabir explained that he had been awakened from a dead sleep and told to come to the GC station. "I got in my little car and a man stood before me, shaking his head. He pointed to this vehicle, and I found the keys in the ignition. If I had brought the small one, we never would have been able to fit all of you in."

"Where are we going?" Mr. Stein said.

"To the airport," Sabir said. "My instructions were very clear. I should accompany you on the flight."

"You're going to see your wife!" Sam said.

"I suppose many prayers will be answered tonight. I said I would stay until God directed me, and now he has."

"Mac needs to know—"

"The angel said everything had been arranged," Sabir said.

As they drove near where the miracle fair had taken place, Aron touched the window and looked out sadly. "What about Joel? Is there no hope?"

"Your brother made a foolish decision," Mr. Stein said. "He closed himself to the truth and took the mark of Carp—"

"But I was just as closed," Aron said. "He took the mark partly for me so I could have food."

Mr. Stein turned. "We spoke with your brother before you came in. He seemed upset we had even come. He countered our message at every point."

"He was angry at himself. He knew what you would say about God."

"He turned us in to the authorities," Sam said. "I know you love your brother, and your parents will be saddened by the choice he made, but we can't go back."

Aron nodded. "I understand, and yet my heart breaks for him."

The man buried his head in his hands, and Sam put an arm around him. "My father also made a foolish choice and died before I could speak with him again. I'm so sorry."

Sabir drove to the airfield and parked in the same spot where Sam and Mr. Stein had been picked up the night before. A plane waited on the runway, and they scurried through the fence and quickly boarded. Mac McCullum gave them the thumbs-up sign and had Mr. Stein secure the door.

"When we get in the air, I want to hear all about this," Mac said.

The GC radioed Mac just after takeoff, but he ignored their call. He motioned Sam forward, and Sam sat in the copilot's chair.

When Sam had told him everything, Mac said, "I've seen a lot of strange things in the past few weeks. Bullets going through helicopters, angels blinding the GC, but when I got the call to come get you guys—"

"Someone called you?" Sam said.

"Figure of speech. I was asleep, waiting to hear about my next flight from Chang Wong or Chloe Williams. All of a sudden I was awake and knew I ought to come here. It was as clear as if you'd sent me a fax or called and given specific directions. I just knew."

Sam looked around the cockpit, and Mac asked what he wanted. "Something to take notes with. I need to start a new installment of my Petra Diaries right away."

The reunion in Petra was more than Sam could have hoped for. The four new believers were welcomed warmly as Tsion Ben-Judah announced their arrival at the morning meeting. Several counselors had been trained by Dr. Ben-Judah himself to take new believers and help them learn the basics of the faith. They surrounded the men after Tsion had finished introducing them and whisked them away.

Micah prayed for Jews who were being arrested around the world. "You know, Lord, that these people are being mistreated and killed simply because they have Jewish ancestors. The Global Community considers them traitors, and they are being paraded across international television, humiliated every day. We ask that you would surround these with your love and mercy, and show them the truth that you want them to turn from their sin and accept Jesus Christ as their Savior."

Micah asked the assembly to gather in small clusters. The wonderful sound of voices uniting in prayer echoed off the red rocks.

Sam and Mr. Stein hadn't had a chance to locate Rabbi Ben-Eliezar and his wife, and Aron was anxious to see them. When the groups finished praying, Tsion Ben-Judah introduced Mr. Stein. "This man's own child turned to Christ and he disowned her. After her death, he became a true believer and stands before us today to tell of the mercies of God."

Mr. Stein stepped forward. Sam was proud that he would have a chance to speak to so many. "For those of you who have not yet believed, I plead with you to consider the truth. Christ died for your sins, and he paid the penalty for your disobedience. Do not run from him any longer, but accept his love right now."

A few people near Sam fell to the ground, wrestling with the truth of God. Sam closed his eyes and prayed they might respond while Mr. Stein spoke.

"I would like to ask Rabbi and Mrs. Ben-Eliezar to come forward," Mr. Stein continued. "Are you here?"

From the back of the crowd came a faint cry from Rabbi Ben-Eliezar. He and his wife walked as quickly as they could through the masses. Like the Red Sea, people parted and allowed them to walk through and up a steep walkway that led to Mr. Stein. As they came, he described meeting them and their struggle to believe in Jesus.

Finally, they reached the rocky cliff, and Mr. Stein draped an arm around the rabbi. "They spoke to us of their sons some time ago. When Micah talked about praying for relatives and friends who do not yet believe, my young friend Sam Goldberg took him seriously. He began praying and trying to contact Aron and Joel."

Mr. Stein turned. "Rabbi, Mrs. Ben-Eliezar, behold your son."

Aron stepped out of the shadows of a cave. The rabbi and his wife were so overcome, Sam thought they were going to topple off the ledge, but they gained their balance and rushed to Aron, hugging him and weeping.

"Their other son was unfortunately caught up in the desire to follow Nicolae Carpathia, but we can rejoice that this one has believed and has returned."

A great roar rose from the crowd as they yelled their praises to God. When the noise died down, Mr. Stein looked at the struggling group near Sam. "What about you? Will you receive the gift of God now?"

9

THE DAYS passed quickly for Judd and Lionel in South Carolina. Sam's escape from the GC was all anyone could talk about for a week. Sam's description of the angel and their return to Petra thrilled the group so much that Judd hooked up a video connection with Sam and had him speak to their group.

As time passed, Judd read sketchy reports of bounty hunters discovering more people without the mark. He sent a message to Chang Wong asking for any information on the identity and location of the bounty hunters in South Carolina.

One afternoon Judd was talking to Luke and Tom about their lives before the disappearances. Luke said he had always dreamed of being a shrimper and having his own boat.

"Is that how you got those muscles?" Judd said.

Luke smiled. "I guess. I've always felt like I've been cut

out for physical stuff, you know, hard work. I like using my hands, where old Tom here—" he patted his brother's back—"uses his brain, what little he has."

Tom socked Luke in the shoulder. "All brawn and no brain makes Luke a dull boy."

Luke picked a long piece of grass and put it between his teeth. "I've been thinking more about why we've been left here. If those verses about us all being part of a body are right—and it's in the Bible so it has to be—all we need to do is figure out what part we are and do what we were made to do."

"Luke just figured out he's an armpit," Tom snickered. "Smells like one, doesn't he?"

Judd laughed and Luke shook his head. "I'm trying to be serious."

Tom rubbed his face with his hands. "I'm sorry. Go ahead, armp—I mean, Luke."

"I never got to go into the army," Luke continued, "or become one of those special-forces people, but I've grown up around these rivers and marshes and know them like the back of my hand. Instead of sitting here, we could be out there stopping the bounty hunters and finding people who might become believers."

"You gonna do this all over the country?" Tom said. "You read what Chang said. Pretty soon the GC will expand the program, and there'll be more bounty hunters than believers."

"The point is, we can do something now if we want."

"Maybe that's how Lionel and I could get north," Judd said. "We could go along with you."

Luke nodded. "The key is finding the bounty hunter network."

"But what are you going to do once you find them?" Tom said. "Kill them?"

Luke spat the grass onto the ground. "No, that wouldn't be right. But we can sure slow them down, don't you think?"

Vicki gathered with the others in the main cabin to watch the latest from the Global Community News Network. A special Web site had been set up to highlight miracles performed around the world. Many miracle workers looked like average citizens wearing regular clothes, while others dressed in weird outfits. One man tried to imitate the sackcloth Eli and Moishe had worn.

Most of the miracle workers were men, but there were a few women as well. All claimed they had come under the authority of the risen lord, Nicolae Carpathia, and all had been given power by him.

"Are these demons dressed like people, or are they real people?" Tanya Spivey asked.

Marshall Jameson pursed his lips. "If they're not demons, they're at least humans under the spell of Carpathia."

"I don't like watching this," Charlie said, backing away from the monitor.

Mark pulled up a spreadsheet of information he had documented since the rise of the miracle workers. "The number on the left is how many miracles have been performed. As you go across, you see what types of things they're doing."

"Those are all the same things Jesus did while he was on earth," Darrion said.

"Exactly," Mark said. "They're counterfeiting Christ's miracles just like they have to fake everything else, like the mark on the forehead."

The blood-to-water miracles seemed most popular. One woman had changed water to blood, then changed it to wine. There had been reattached limbs, healing of skin diseases, three blind people given back their sight, and twenty-three lame people made to walk.

The GCNN anchor announced that viewers were in for a treat today because a man in England had asked a miracle worker to heal his sick daughter who lived in Australia. The miracle worker had asked GCNN to set up a live video feed from the man's home, and the network had agreed.

The miracle worker was dressed all in black and stood before a massive image of Nicolae. Five thousand people crammed into the large amphitheater, and crowds spilled out of the venue into the street. Everyone applauded as the miracle worker appeared onstage, accompanied by the father of the sick daughter.

"We are here not to present a sideshow or even entertain you. We have gathered to celebrate the life-giving power of our lord and king." The man knelt before Nicolae's statue. When he stood, he motioned to someone backstage, and workers wheeled a massive monitor into view. The picture rolled and the audio crackled and buzzed.

Conrad shook his head. "If he can heal all those people, you'd think they'd be able to fix the satellite feed."

The miracle worker stared at the monitor, his jaw set, then turned to the crowd. "What you are about to witness has never been attempted before, and it will prove that Nicolae is god and should be worshiped."

"What's he going to do?" Janie said.

"Whatever it is, it's not going to glorify God," Vicki said.

The picture from the satellite feed stopped rolling, and a reporter on the scene in Australia came into view. The woman's face was tight and her eyes red. She stood in front of a simple, ranch-style house with several vehicles parked in the driveway.

"What is the matter, my friend?" the miracle worker said.

The reporter waited through the time delay and said, "Sir, our crew arrived here only a few minutes ago. I went inside to explain what was happening and found those inside watching our coverage."

"So it appears we are a hit with audiences around the world!" The crowd laughed, and the miracle man held up a hand. "Is the young lady still in the house?"

"Yes, but . . ."

The miracle worker raised his lips in a smile. "Go ahead, tell me."

"She is only about sixteen years old. When we got here, a local doctor was with her. Something must have gone wrong . . ." The reporter's chin quivered. She looked at the ground and pulled the microphone away.

"What's happened to my daughter?" the father shouted. "Have they taken her away?"

"Tell him," the miracle worker said, speaking as if he already knew what had happened.

"She is dead. The doctor came out just before we went on with you and told us. It happened a little while ago."

The crowd gasped and the father fell to his knees. He was in such grief that he could only whimper and moan. Finally, he looked up at the miracle worker. "I know you are sent from god, and whatever you ask lord Carpathia, he can do. Please, help my little girl."

The miracle worker closed his eyes and seemed to drink in the man's words. He looked at the audience and shouted, "I tell you the truth. I have not found anyone in the whole of the Global Community with such great faith. In the midst of such distressing news, he looks to the only one who can help."

The miracle man looked at the monitor and told the crew in Australia to pick up their camera and take it inside. When they hesitated, he shouted at them, and the picture wobbled as they hauled the equipment inside.

The living room was filled with people crying and grieving the girl's death. A man with a black satchel and a stethoscope around his neck talked with the woman.

"That is my wife," the father said.

The woman shook a white handkerchief at the camera and moved back. The doctor put out a hand to stop the camera and the reporter, but the miracle man spoke in soothing tones. "Doctor, tell us about the girl's condition."

"This is highly irregular," the doctor said, "I must ask you to leave at once. This family is in the midst of a terrible loss—"

"I know of their loss, and I am here to tell you that you will see victory instead of defeat. Doctor, are you sure the girl no longer lives?"

The doctor suddenly saw himself on television and looked startled. "Yes, of course I am sure. She has no pulse, and she is not breathing. She went into cardiac arrest and died twenty minutes ago."

"What would you say if I could tell you that the mother and father will see this girl alive again?"

"Impossible," the doctor said. "Even if her heart and lungs could begin again, there has been so much damage to the brain that she could no longer—"

"That is enough," the miracle man said. "Take the camera into the girl's room."

"But as I said—"

"Now!" the miracle man shouted.

The camera moved rapidly, family pictures flashing by as the camera raced to the end of a darkened hallway. A door opened and the operator adjusted for the low light.

"Remove the covering," the miracle man said.

The reporter put down her microphone and gently peeled back the white sheet over the body. A thin, dark-haired girl lay on the bed, her face pale and peaceful. The father wept loudly onstage, and the miracle man did nothing to stop him. Suddenly the mother ran into the room, screaming and yelling for everyone to get out.

"Silence!" the miracle man said.

The woman fell back against the bedroom wall. The camera zoomed in on the girl's face. Vicki watched as the miracle man turned and asked the father the girl's name.

"Talitha," the father said.

The miracle man held up both hands and the crowd grew quiet. Kneeling in prayer, the father tried to control his weeping but couldn't. Muffled sobs came from the mother.

Vicki shuddered, guessing what would happen next. The old liar, the one God said from the beginning was a murderer and a thief, had enlisted this new breed of false prophets, Nicolae's messiahs.

The miracle man leaned close to his microphone and whispered, "Talitha, wake up."

The words sent a chill down Vicki's spine. He said it again, this time louder, as if the corpse couldn't hear. "Talitha, wake up!"

The screen swayed as the cameraman took a step closer. The girl's eyes fluttered once, then again. A shriek came from the other side of the bedroom. The white sheet covering the girl's body rose slowly as she took a breath.

Thousands gasped in the massive crowd. The father tried to stand but fell forward toward the monitor, crying tears of joy. Vicki and the others in the cabin groaned.

"Talitha, arise!" the miracle man ordered.

The girl's eyes opened fully and she sat up. In the amphitheater, the crowd went wild—some screaming, others yelling shouts of praise to Nicolae. The image of Nicolae began quaking at the noise and belched fire and smoke from its mouth. At the home in Australia, the young girl stood and her mother embraced her.

The reporter's microphone shook as she stepped in front of the camera. "If I hadn't seen it with my own eyes, I'm not sure I would have believed it. This girl, who had no pulse, no signs of life for nearly half an hour, is now walking toward her family. She is alive!"

At this, the crowd raised such a shout that Mark muted the computer speakers. People ran toward the stage, struggling to reach out and touch the miracle man. Cameras switched from the frenzied faces in the crowd, to the weeping father, to the belching image of Nicolae red with fire, to the scene of family members mobbing the young girl in Australia, to the miracle man, smiling, lifting his hands toward the statue, and mouthing the words to "Hail Carpathia."

Vicki and the group sat, stunned at the evil they had witnessed.

Janie broke the silence. "I don't understand. I thought only God could raise the dead."

"The power of evil is real now more than ever," Marshall said. "Tsion has talked about this many times. Satan is being allowed to deceive, kill, and destroy like never before. I don't understand it either, except to say that Satan can only do the things God allows."

Vicki watched the video feed a little longer, then headed back to her cabin with a heavy heart. The last thing she saw was the girl who had been dead kneeling before a statue of Nicolae.

JUDD helped the others put together what Luke called
Bounty Hunter Defense kits or BHDs. He noticed some
sour looks from the group, and Judd commented later to
Lionel about the lack of organization in the South
Carolina hideout. At their next meeting, Judd brought up
his observations, and the others stiffened.

"Everybody follows Luke and Tom," Judd said.
"There's no give-and-take."

"Somebody has to be in charge," Carl Meninger said.
"If we voted on everything, we'd never have tried to help
you."

Judd nodded. "I think there have to be leaders, no
question. But if others just follow, they start feeling left
out."

A teenage girl named Shawnda raised a hand. "We
came up with our own ideas at the last hideout, and that's
when we let somebody in who ratted us out to the GC."

"I can understand being cautious," Judd said. "The

goal isn't to make sure everybody has a vote so we rule by majority, but you might be missing out on gifts people have by not including them."

Lionel lifted a hand. "One of the advantages to having this many believers together is the wisdom of numbers. Proverbs says, 'So don't go to war without wise guidance; victory depends on having many counselors.' If we're not working together, we're going to pull apart."

"I wish Tom were here," Luke said, "but he's on watch right now. Let's hear what everybody has to say."

People looked at each other nervously. Finally, Shawnda cleared her throat to speak but was interrupted by two short beeps from the intercom. "We've got movement in the marsh," Tom said. "Somebody's headed this way."

Luke looked at Judd. "Want to take a vote on what we should do?"

Chang Wong tried to keep his mind on the tasks at hand but found it difficult. His father was dead, and Chang couldn't shake the thought of the guillotine plunging onto his father's neck. He had dreamed of the man screaming Chang's name just before the beheading. Chang spent the next day erasing any mention of his father's death from GC records. He did not want his boss, Aurelio Figueroa, or anyone else in New Babylon knowing his dad had turned against Nicolae Carpathia at the end.

Chang knew he would see his father again in heaven, and that fact kept him going. But he felt a heaviness, a weight on his shoulders each day he came to work and followed orders.

Chang's sister, Ming Toy, was still in China with their mother, and Chang encouraged Ming to stay there and not risk traveling to the underground hideout in San Diego. Things in China were terrible, but any movement of believers anywhere was extremely dangerous.

Chang spent most of his time outside of work talking and planning with the adult Trib Force, but he had a special interest in the Young Trib Force as well. High on his priority list was helping Judd and Lionel move north to Wisconsin, but with daily reports about new bounty hunters scattered across the South, Chang felt sick. He could see no way Judd and Lionel could leave soon.

Though Chang felt lonely without believers to talk with face-to-face, he prayed almost constantly as he worked at his desk in the palace. The most evil being in the universe was in the same building, but Chang could pour out his heart to God and know that God heard every word, every request, and every praise. Once, Chang had seen Nicolae walking in the courtyard with several GC officials. Chang was praying for the safe evacuation of several Tribulation Force members, and Nicolae had looked directly at him.

Can he read my thoughts? Chang decided to test him. You are evil in the flesh, the total opposite of the loving God I serve.

Nicolae looked away and joined another conversation, and Chang was convinced the man couldn't know his thoughts. Only the true God had that kind of power.

As Chang continued his work, accessing data for his boss, he stumbled onto some information from the United North American States. He had been searching for details about the location of bounty hunters. The document before him contained a grid of the southern states with dots. Chang clicked on the dots, and a picture of each bounty hunter popped up with details about where each person lived, their previous occupation, how old they were, if they were married, and other data.

Chang copied the file and decided to wait until he was back in his apartment to send it to Judd. "God, you know what they need to make it back to their friends. I pray this will help them in some way, and if it be your will, help them reach their friends."

Chang opened his eyes and was startled to see a GC Peacekeeper standing beside his desk. "Chang Wong?"

"Yes?"

"You're to come with me immediately."

"Is something wrong?"

"No questions. We're going to Director Akbar's office."

Judd was amazed at the way the group flew into action and worked together to make the house look like no one lived there. They had obviously practiced this procedure.

Luke pulled out rickety chairs and a broken table from a pantry. Others raced to the kitchen, gathered dishes and silverware, and hid them upstairs. Carl Meninger took care of the computer equipment and brought the radio with him to the hidden cellar. Within a few minutes the house was transformed into a run-down building.

"We've got two bogeys, both headed toward the house via the main road," Tom said over the radio. "They don't look familiar."

"Take your positions," Luke said.

Everyone ran in different directions, and Judd stared at Luke. "What do you want Lionel and me to do?"

He pointed toward the cellar door, then stopped and cocked his head. "Wait a minute. If these are bounty hunters and they don't turn back at the signs, this might be a good chance to try out our idea. Take one of the BHDs and crawl into the tall grass beside the house. Make sure they don't see you."

Judd and Lionel raced to the supply room, grabbed a kit, hurried out the back, and crawled into the grass. When they were far enough to get a good look at the marsh, they stopped and opened the kit.

"What if it's the guys who caught us, Max and Albert?" Lionel said.

"They'll wish they hadn't come looking for us," Judd said.

A few minutes passed before Tom whispered that a male and female had passed him and were at the warning signs.

"They're coming through the fence. Everybody get ready," Tom whispered.

Judd took out a weird contraption Carl had put together: a curved telescope that allowed the viewer to see around corners or above something taller. Judd fit the pieces together and raised the scope to the top of the grass.

"See anything?" Lionel said.

"Yeah, two coming this way. They're looking at the signs."

"Maybe that'll stop them."

Judd paused, zooming in. "No, they're headed our way."

"All right, looks like we're having company," Luke said into the earpiece. "Tom, follow those guys at a close distance. Judd and Lionel are to the east of the house waiting. We're testing the BHDs."

"You're gonna jump them?" Tom whispered. "What'll you do after that? They'll know somebody's in the house and we'll have to leave."

A long pause. "You're right, little brother. Judd and Lionel, you two keep down out there."

"Got it," Judd said.

Judd and Lionel were far enough away from the house that the two intruders would have to step on them to find them. Judd felt itchy with all the bugs in the weeds, but as the strangers approached, he couldn't move.

"A hundred yards," Luke said. "I'm in the observation tower. Everybody hold your position, except you, Tom, and give me a report if they're coming into the cellar."

Judd put the scope away and waited. Wind blew the grass above his head. What if the two came around the house and found them? Then what? He took a breath and waited.

Chang had been questioned by his boss, Aurelio Figueroa, before, but he had never been in Director Akbar's office. The director's secretary glanced up when he walked in and motioned to a conference room. Chang sank into a leather chair as the Peacekeeper pulled up a questionnaire on a computer screen. Chang saw his picture with the vital statistics such as his age, height, weight, nationality, how long he had been employed by the Global Community, etc.

Has someone found out about my father?

When the Peacekeeper finished taking information, he excused himself, walked out of the room, and closed the door.

Chang realized how isolated he was. If the GC discovered he was the mole, they would have him executed on the spot and the rest of the Trib Force wouldn't know of his death. It might even put the others in danger, since Chang's computer at home carried the contact information for just about everyone.

Chang tried to calm himself. This was exactly what the GC wanted, to upset him enough that he'd appear nervous and say things he didn't want to say. Chang told himself that David Hassid had covered his tracks well and that no one but Chang could access the information in his computer.

By the time Suhail Akbar and the Peacekeeper walked into the room, Chang had stopped sweating.

"I hope we're not keeping you from anything important," Akbar said with a smile.

"What you deem important, Director, is of the greatest importance to me," Chang replied.

Akbar sat. He was in his early forties, from Pakistan, and gave Chang the impression he meant business. He looked over the screen and checked the stats as the Peacekeeper looked on. Chang wondered why two were needed for this meeting, but he quickly put the thought out of his mind.

"I suppose you're wondering why we've called you here," Akbar said, crossing his legs and raising an eyebrow.

"Yes, sir."

"You know we've been searching for an informant inside the palace. A mole."

"Yes, I've been questioned about that already."

"I know, and you passed. But we're putting all employees through another interview. We know the mole is still here."

"How, sir?"

Akbar clicked on the computer, and a copy of Buck Williams's *The Truth* appeared onscreen. "This, for one. Have you read it?"

"I thought this material was forbidden."

"Good man. It is. But we have to keep tabs on the enemy." He pointed to a section of the first page. "There's information here that no one could possibly know unless he were here in the palace or had a friend inside."

"He tells the truth?"

Akbar frowned. "He gives an accurate account of things that happen here, conversations, activities."

Chang's stomach tightened. If Akbar hooked him up to a lie detector right now and asked if he had ever had contact with Buck Williams, he was sure he would fail. "And you're talking to me because . . . ?"

Akbar smiled and leaned forward. "How well do you know your boss, Mr. Figueroa? How well do you know your fellow employees, like the one who sits in the next cubicle—" he snapped his fingers at the Peacekeeper— "what is her name?"

"Rasha, sir."

"Have you noticed anything unusual about any of these people and how they act?"

Chang's muscles loosened. He could talk all day about his fellow workers. And he would give Akbar as much information as he wanted.

———————————

Judd lay as still and as low as possible in the grass. Mosquitoes buzzed around his head, and he wanted to swat at them but couldn't.

"I thought they said nobody ever comes to this place," Lionel whispered.

"I guess there's always a first."

The two strangers tromped up the gravel walkway that led to the house. Soon they were on the porch. Judd strained to see their faces, but they were too far away.

"Full alert everyone," Luke said. "They're going inside."

11

JUDD raised his head and stared at the two on the front porch. One leaned down and looked in the windows, putting his hand to the glass and peering inside. The female knocked and yelled, "Anybody home?" Satisfied, she opened the door.

"No mark of the believer, no uniform, and unarmed," Judd whispered into the intercom. "What should we do, Luke?"

"Everybody hold your positions," Luke said. "Maybe they'll take some food and leave."

Judd heard movement to his left and saw Tom snaking toward the house through the tall grass. He found Judd and Lionel and lay down beside them. "We've never had anybody just walk onto the property like that," Tom said when he caught his breath.

Judd described the two.

Tom nodded. "They could be bounty hunters and we'd never know it until they pulled guns out of their back pockets."

"Shouldn't we jump them before they find someone?" Judd said.

Tom spoke into the intercom. "Luke, we think it might be better to surprise these two rather than the other way around. What do you think?"

"They're in the kitchen," Luke said. "If you can get the jump on them, go ahead."

Tom stood. "Lionel, you stick with me. Judd, go around to the back door and wait for my signal. Let's go."

Chang fully answered Director Akbar's questions about his coworkers. He said Aurelio Figueroa was the most loyal employee he had known. The more Chang spoke, the more frustrated Akbar became.

"So you haven't seen anyone in the department who might be funneling information to Buck Williams?"

Only when I look in the mirror, Chang thought. "I know it would make sense for the person to be fluent in computers and technology, sir, but I can't say there's anyone who fits the profile of a Judah-ite near me."

"That's all," Akbar said, waving a hand and clicking on the computer for the next person to interrogate.

Chang went back to his desk, counting the minutes until he could go home and send the information he had gleaned about the bounty hunters to Judd and Lionel.

Judd moved quietly to the back door and waited for Tom's signal. The man and woman rummaged inside. The kids had cleaned out the refrigerator and stored supplies behind a false wall near the pantry, so there wasn't much food left.

"Okay, Judd, now," Tom whispered in Judd's earpiece.

Judd flew inside the door as Lionel and Tom burst into the kitchen. Tom pointed the advanced weapon at the man and woman. They held up their hands and dropped the food, two rancid apples and some moldy bread.

"Hands behind your head, on the floor!" Tom yelled.

Luke ran in and patted them down. "No weapons."

Judd had them hold out their right hands and saw they had no mark of Carpathia. He helped them up and pulled out two chairs.

The man had a week's worth of beard. He was thin, with dark hair and blue eyes. His forehead was a dark red, sunburned from exposure. The woman also had dark hair and a pretty face. She looked ghostly thin, and her lips were parched.

"You two look like you could use something to eat," Luke said. He motioned to Tom who brought fresh bread and cheese from the pantry and put it on the table.

The two devoured the food in seconds, then drank fresh water. Luke sat beside them and asked where they had come from.

"Savannah," the man said. "We were trying to get to a relative's house in Charleston, but we ran into trouble."

"Bounty hunters?" Tom said.

"I guess," the man said. "They were looking for anyone without the mark. We hid in a shack on the beach, then traveled at night."

"Why didn't you stop when you saw our warning signs?" Luke said.

The woman leaned forward. "We were so hungry and tired, we didn't care. We figured if there was radiation, at least we'd die trying to find food. What is this place?"

"Not so fast," Tom said. "How do we know you're not working with the bounty hunters or the GC?"

The man shook his head. "I don't know that we can convince you, other than the fact we haven't taken Carpathia's mark."

"Why didn't you?" Lionel said.

"Why didn't *you*?" the man said.

Luke slammed a rickety chair to the floor and it cracked. "We're not the ones asking for food. Now stop jerking us around."

The man held up both hands. "Okay, we've gotten off on the wrong foot." He wiped his hands on his shirt. "I'm Lee McCarty. This is my sister, Brooke."

"And you want us to believe you walked from Savannah with nothing but the clothes on your back and wound up here?" Luke said.

"You don't have to believe anything, but it's the truth. We had enough provisions to make it to Charleston—at least that's what we thought."

"We had to leave our stuff when those guys chased us," Brooke said. "That was a couple of days ago."

Lee pushed back from the table and stood. "Thanks for the food. We're sorry we bothered you."

"We can't let them go back out there," Lionel said, turning to Tom and Luke.

"Sit down," Tom said. "You're the first people we've seen since we found this place, so we're a little skittish. Tell us something about yourselves."

Lee sat and Brooke picked up their story. "Our parents were divorced when we were in high school."

"Names?" Luke said.

"Linda and John."

"Where did you go to school?"

"Milton High in Florida."

Tom wrote down the information as Luke asked who her favorite teacher was and the name of the principal. Brooke answered quickly, and Judd felt sorry for her.

"Look, it's obvious you don't trust us and don't want us here," Lee said. "We'll head north to Charleston tonight—"

"And draw every bounty hunter in the county to us?" Luke said.

"I'd like to hear more about your story," Lionel said. "Keep going."

Brooke nodded. "After the divorce I went to live with Mom and Lee went with Dad. Dad got some kind of religion after the divorce so Mom tried to get Lee back, but that's when the disappearances happened. We all freaked. A lot of our high school was just gone. Dad disappeared, and Mom started drinking. She got killed in the earthquake."

Judd shook his head as Luke drilled Brooke with another question. "What have you been doing since then?"

"We went to live with an uncle and then some friends," Lee said. "We've pretty much just tried to exist."

"I'll ask again. Why didn't you take Carpathia's mark? It would have been a lot easier for you."

Brooke hung her head. Lee glanced at her and sighed. "Dad kept a diary of sorts on his computer. He tried to get me to go with him to church and Bible studies, but I didn't want any part of it. Brooke and I read the journal or whatever he was keeping. He'd been writing out prayers for us, asking God to save our souls and show us the truth."

Brooke looked up. "He said the Lord was coming back for his own and that Satan was going to take control of the earth. My dad wrote that the Antichrist would one day make everyone take a mark and that he hoped his kids would never have to go through that."

"I guess your dad's worst fears came true," Luke said.

"If you've known all that, why didn't you believe like your dad?" Tom said.

"How do you know we haven't?" Brooke said.

"We know," Luke said.

Lee sighed. "I guess if we have to take the mark, we will. We've been avoiding it this whole time—"

"Even though you know they'll kill you if you don't take it?" Luke said.

"We felt like we'd be betraying our dad to take the mark, and we'd betray Mom if we believed what Dad was saying."

"So you're caught in the middle, just like when your mom and dad split up," Lionel said.

"Yeah," Brooke said.

Lionel stayed with Lee and Brooke while Judd and the others went into the next room. Carl Meninger joined them and said he had listened to their conversation through the intercom and had looked up the information Lee and Brooke had given.

"It all checks out," Carl said. "The high school, the teacher she mentioned. Her mom was arrested for drunk driving twice, and there's a Linda McCarty listed among the dead after the earthquake."

Luke scratched his head. "How did they just happen to stumble onto us out here?"

"Maybe it was God leading them," Tom said. "Anyway, all we have to do is explain the truth, and they'll be part of the group."

"You think it'll be that easy?" Luke said.

"There's something else I haven't told you," Carl said, handing Luke a piece of paper. "Chang Wong just sent this. It's a list of the names and locations of every bounty hunter working for the Global Community. With this, Judd and Lionel have a better shot at going north."

Luke nodded. "Okay, but first we explain our beliefs to these two."

"Let Lionel try," Judd said. "I think they kind of connected with him."

"Good. Judd, take him aside and explain. We'll see how they respond. Tom, watch the perimeter from the tower. We're not taking any chances."

Lionel pulled the regular chairs from the storage area and sat at the table next to Lee and Brooke. Brooke asked how Lionel had gotten to the South Carolina hideout and he smiled. "It's a long story."

"We've got time," Lee said.

"Well, I can tell you what happened right after the disappearances." Lionel began there and described what happened to his family. He told them how he had met Judd, Vicki, Ryan, and Pastor Bruce Barnes. "Bruce showed us a video of the former pastor of the church talking about how believers in Christ would one day be taken away or raptured. That's what happened to my family."

"And our dad," Brooke said.

"Right." Lionel explained what the Bible said about God's forgiveness and that a person couldn't work their way to heaven. "God already loves you enough to die for you, and he did that when Christ died on the cross."

Lee nodded. "I get it. If we ask God to forgive us, he will, not because of anything we've done, but because he sacrificed himself."

"Right. It's a good thing you didn't take the mark of Carpathia because that would keep you from becoming a believer."

"Why is that?" Brooke said.

Lionel explained that taking the mark and worshiping Carpathia meant you had chosen once and for all against God. When that decision was made, there was no changing your mind.

As Lionel explained more, he got the feeling that they

had already been exposed to the message. They both said it was new to them, except for what their father had written, but they seemed to understand things quickly and didn't ask as many questions as others who had become believers. It almost felt too easy when they asked Lionel if he would pray with them.

"Sure," Lionel said. He closed his eyes and began. Lee and Brooke prayed out loud with him. At one point, Brooke choked up and had to whisper the words. When Lionel finished, he looked at them and they both smiled.

"I feel a lot better, don't you?" Brooke said to her brother.

"Yeah. I'd never have believed just saying a prayer could change things so much. Mom was wrong and Dad was right."

Lionel shook hands with Lee and hugged Brooke. He was about to take them into the next room to tell the others when he noticed something that made his heart drop.

"You guys wait here," Lionel said. "I want to bring Judd and the others in so you can tell them the good news."

"Great!" Brooke said.

Lionel closed the kitchen door behind him and found Judd, Tom, and Luke in the next room talking to Carl.

"How'd it go in there?" Tom said.

Lionel took a breath. "They listened, then prayed. Everything was fine until I looked at their foreheads. They don't have the mark of the believer."

12

JUDD moved toward the room where Lee and Brooke sat, but Lionel stopped him. "We have to figure out what we're going to say."

"Maybe they didn't understand," Judd suggested. "They might be mixed up."

"They understood," Lionel said. "The way they acted after they prayed seemed calculated."

"But if it's a trap," Judd said, "wouldn't they know about the mark of the believer?"

"Maybe they think that's a hoax and we don't have any mark," Tom said.

"I'll bet you anything they have some kind of transmitter," Lionel said.

"We should take care of them now," Luke whispered.

"What do you mean?" Judd said.

"What I said."

"We can't kill these people. I don't care if they aren't

who they say they are. We can't take the chance that they're two innocent—"

"All right. Then we tie them up until we figure out what to do," Luke said.

"We have to go back in soon or they're going to get suspicious," Lionel said.

"Play it like they're part of our family now," Judd said. "We'll keep the others hidden."

"I've got an idea how we can stall whoever they're working with," Lionel said. "Follow my lead."

As the four walked into the room, Lionel beamed and gestured with a hand. "I want you guys to meet our newest members. They're true believers now."

Judd, Luke, and Tom shook hands with Lee. Brooke hugged Judd and said, "I'm so glad we found this place. I can feel the Lord working in my heart already."

"Are there other believers here?" Lee said.

"No, we're the only ones," Luke said quickly.

"But there's something we need to tell you," Lionel said. "A group of believers is supposed to show up in the next couple of days. We've been in contact with them."

"How many?" Lee said.

"A dozen, maybe more. We'll be in touch tonight."

"How do you guys contact each other?" Brooke said.

Judd was sure the two were searching for information, and he was glad Lionel had thought of his plan. The others could get away while the GC or whomever Lee and Brooke were working with got ready to pounce.

"We have a cell phone," Lionel said. "We try to limit our calls to make sure the GC doesn't track us."

"That's smart," Brooke said. "I hate the way the GC operate."

"Me too," Lee said.

"I'll show you around the place," Lionel said. "Let me take you outside first."

Judd, Tom, and Luke quickly met with the others in the cellar while Lionel kept Lee and Brooke occupied. Carl got in touch with Chang Wong in New Babylon with his hastily constructed communications center and asked if there were any GC programs using agents without the mark.

I'm not aware of any, Chang wrote, *but I wouldn't put it past that Kruno Fulcire guy. Let me check it out.*

When Carl asked Chang for a place to escape, Chang suggested talking with Chloe Williams. "She has a better idea of the safe houses and Co-op facilities in your area."

"Vicki can help us," Judd said. "She talked with Chloe a few days ago."

Lionel took Lee and Brooke outside, telling them the history of the property and making up the rest. He could tell they wanted to go inside and explore, but he knew that would lead to more questions and possibly discovering the other believers. "It's time for our teaching," Lionel said, leading them back to the kitchen.

"But we're already believers," Brooke said. "We need to listen to more stuff?"

"Yeah, when you receive God's forgiveness, he puts a hunger in your heart to know more about him. Do you feel that?"

Lee cocked his head. "As a matter of fact, I do have a lot of questions."

Lionel gave them more water and called for Judd. "We're going to have our teaching now. You want to tell the others?"

"Yeah, I'll go get them," Judd said.

Lionel thought of people in one of three camps: believers in God, followers of Carpathia who had no chance of responding to the truth, or people with neither the mark of God nor Carpathia who could still respond. A thought flashed in his mind as he handed Bibles to Lee and Brooke. *If they don't have Carpathia's mark, maybe the truth will get to them. Even if they are Global Community or helping bounty hunters, if God's Word reaches their hearts, they could become believers!*

The thought excited Lionel, and he couldn't wait to go through the material he had chosen. He had them turn to the Gospel of John.

"Why don't you read?" Lionel said.

" 'In the beginning the Word already existed,' " Lee read. " 'He was with God, and he was God. He was in the beginning with God. He created everything there is. Nothing exists that he didn't make. Life itself was in him, and this life gives light to everyone.' "

"Any idea who John is talking about?" Lionel said.

"I don't even know who John is, let alone who this 'he' is who was with God," Brooke said.

"He's talking about Jesus," Lionel said. "The Trinity is made up of God the Father, God the Son, and God the Holy Spirit."

114

"Why are there three of them?" Brooke said.

Lionel paused and said a brief prayer for them, asking God to take away their blindness.

Judd retreated to a corner of the cellar and called the Wisconsin group. Mark answered and asked how things were going.

"I don't mean to be short, but we've got a situation here and Vicki can help."

Mark handed the phone to Vicki, and Judd quickly explained what had happened. Vicki gave him Chloe's number without question.

"You guys have to get out of there now," Vicki said. "The GC could raid you any minute."

"We feel safe, but we need a destination. I'm thinking, if we head north, Lionel and I might as well keep going until we get to Wisconsin."

"I like that idea." Vicki asked Judd to keep her updated on their plans. "We'll be praying like crazy."

Judd spoke with George Sebastian at the San Diego underground, who passed the phone to Chloe Williams. She seemed upset at first that Judd had called, but when Judd explained their problem, she understood.

Over the past few months, a series of safe houses, homes, and underground shelters had been developed across the country. It was not as sophisticated as Chloe would have liked, but Judd was thrilled they had options.

Judd took information about the groups and ran

upstairs. The meeting with Lee and Brooke continued, and by the look on Lionel's face, things weren't going well. Brooke noticed Judd's cell phone and asked if he had heard anything from the other believers.

"I did talk to someone, but we won't know until later tonight when they'll be arriving and how many," Judd said.

The mood was tense throughout the day as the four tried to keep Lee and Brooke occupied. Tom suggested they sleep in an upstairs room he and Luke had cleared out. When they were settled, Judd and the others retreated to the cellar.

Carl Meninger had a video display of the upstairs room onscreen as Lee and Brooke sat on separate beds facing each other. "I wouldn't normally do this, but since we think these two might be—"

"Shh, listen," Luke said, pointing to the screen. Brooke scratched her forehead.

"Don't do that," Lee said. "You'll rub it off."

"I can't help it—it itches!"

"You'll be able to take it off soon, but if these people think we have the mark of Carpathia, we're both dead."

"Can you believe that performance during the prayer?" Brooke said, taking off her shoe and pulling a tiny object out.

Lionel moved toward the screen. "What's she doing?"

Carl shook his head. "She's calling her boss. That's a phone."

Brooke rattled off a series of numbers. Carl turned up the volume, but they couldn't hear much through the tiny speakers. He put on headphones and relayed what Brooke said.

"She's definitely talking to her boss," Carl said. "She just asked them to hold off on the raid until they get more information about the group coming to the house." Carl pressed the headphone close to his ear and nodded. "Okay, I recognize the protocol they're using. These two are definitely working for the GC."

Judd shivered, thinking how easily the two could have duped them. Carl unplugged the headphones when Brooke moved to the other side of the room.

"They bit on everything we said." Brooke laughed. "The whole thing about our parents, our dad getting religion." She paused. "No, they're pretty primitive as far as technology. We haven't seen any computers at all, so there's no way for them to check our Florida information. I wish they could—it would throw them even further off the track. . . . Yeah, we'll let you know later when the next group is coming in and from which direction. . . . No, sit tight. I think we'll have some good news for Commander Fulcire once this thing is over."

"That's it then," Luke said. "Somehow they've covered up the mark of Carpathia and are leading the GC to us."

"And it makes sense that they couldn't understand what I was saying about God," Lionel said. "They couldn't even pretend to believe."

"But how did they find us?" Tom said.

Judd gave Luke and Tom the information about the safe houses, and Judd and Lionel went upstairs to prepare dinner. When it was time, the six of them gathered around the table, and Judd said a brief prayer. Judd didn't feel right praying for people who didn't exist, so he simply asked God to bless the food and protect their friends. Brooke and Lee said an enthusiastic, "Amen."

Everyone went outside after the meal, giving the kids in the cellar enough time to move their things to an outside shed. They would wear the clothes on their backs and take as much computer equipment and tools as possible in backpacks. Moving on foot wasn't going to be easy, but Carl had found someone who could give them a ride to the next safe house.

"God sure was good to lead us here," Lee said. "I can't believe we're actually going to get to see our dad again."

"I look forward to seeing my family again too," Lionel said. "Almost as much as I want to see old Nicolae finally fall."

"How's that supposed to happen?" Brooke said cheerily, though Judd detected an edge to the question.

"The Bible says Nicolae is going to fight God with his armies but that he'll be captured, along with his false prophet. They'll both be thrown into a lake of fire, and the army will be wiped out."

"Wow," Brooke said. "Nicolae seems so powerful. You think that can actually happen?"

"I *know* it will," Lionel said. "I've read the end of the book."

At the selected time, the cell phone rang and Tom answered. He walked a few paces into the front yard and spoke softly. Judd knew the call was from the cellar, and Brooke and Lee strained to hear what Tom said. As Tom walked back to the group, Judd noticed Brooke touch her shoe.

"There's twenty of them," Tom said when he returned. "They're at a safe house south of us."

"Twenty?" Lee said.

"We've got room," Tom said, "but they can't get here until late tomorrow night. Some kind of car problem."

"That'll give us more time to fix up the place," Brooke said.

"Good thinking," Luke said, motioning for Brooke and Lee to follow. "Let me take you guys down to the river. You know, God's love is like a mighty river. There's a ton of verses that talk about that. . . ."

Judd, Lionel, and Tom quickly ran to the house and helped the others with the last of their things. There were tearful good-byes to Tom. Carl gave him a big hug and said they would wait for him at the Barnwell, Georgia, safe house.

"Hopefully we'll meet tomorrow night after we get things settled with these two," Tom said.

"I've left a few surprises for the GC downstairs," Carl said. "Don't go poking around down there. And you'll be without any kind of computer connection."

"It's okay," Tom said. "We'll catch up tomorrow night."

After dark that night, Judd sat up with Lee and Brooke, talking about the ways God had changed his life. Judd didn't hold back explaining exactly what God had done, thinking it might have some effect, even on people with Carpathia's mark.

Tom came in a few minutes before midnight and gave Judd a nod. The others had escaped without being noticed. Judd couldn't wait until it was his turn to leave, but he knew they had to come up with a good plan to keep Lee and Brooke occupied.

One more night and we'll be on the move north, Judd thought.

EARLY the next morning Judd took the call from Carl Meninger letting them know the group was safe in a hideout at Barnwell, Georgia. Carl and the others had walked miles through the low country until they had reached a major roadway running north and south. There, they hooked up with a fearless Co-op member who had risked his life and his truck to help the kids escape.

"I've e-mailed Chang from here, and he says the GC have called in the big guns for tonight's raid," Carl said. "There's a group north of Charleston who want to help transport you. The pickup will be at the same place as ours, but they'll take you to a different location to be safe."

Judd noticed Lee and Brooke listening near the door. "Okay, then we'll expect you guys late tonight. Can't wait

121

to roll out the red carpet. We're fixing up some rooms so you'll feel welcome."

"I couldn't help overhearing," Brooke said when Judd hung up. "The new members are definitely coming?"

"Yeah, and I talked with Luke about setting up watch for them. They'll be coming from the south, so we'll need some lookouts to welcome them and make sure we don't get any unfriendlies."

"What do you mean?"

"Global Community."

"You don't think they know about this place, do you?"

Judd took a breath. "The GC know a lot about everything. They could be following our people, or bounty hunters could be out there. We need people on all points of the perimeter." Judd handed Brooke a radio. "We'll use these to communicate."

"Lee and I will be honored to help."

Throughout the day, Luke and Tom coordinated the meeting place with believers in Walterboro, South Carolina. The two mapped out their trail as Judd, Lionel, Lee, and Brooke worked on upstairs rooms.

"Some of these are clean," Lee said. "Were there people staying here before?"

"We haven't been here long," Lionel said. "From what I've heard, a lot of people have moved through here in the past couple of years."

Judd broke away from the others and went to the cellar to call Vicki. He remembered Carl's reminder and noticed wires running along the foundation and several weird contraptions under the staircase.

Vicki was glad to hear from Judd and said she felt good about their escape plan. "We've been praying for you guys nonstop."

Judd told her that he would try to e-mail or call as soon as they arrived at their location, but not to worry. "Lionel and I have been kicking around an idea for after we get out of here."

"What's that?"

"It's clear that coming up there is going to be risky right now if we try to fly in or even drive. The GC is cracking down on anybody without the mark."

"Then you need to stay there until it's safe," Vicki said.

"Not necessarily. We've mapped out a list of safe houses nearby that Chloe Williams gave us. We'll need more as we go north, but what if we get enough supplies together and hoof it to Wisconsin?"

"You're not serious."

"Totally. There's no way the GC can patrol the forests, what's left of them, and if we can make it to different safe houses every few days for rations and maybe grab some rides with Co-op members, it could happen. I don't know how long it would take, but at least we'd be moving in your direction."

"Judd, you know how much I want you back here, but this sounds . . ." Vicki giggled.

"What?" Judd said.

"I was just thinking about a story I read about a guy . . ." Vicki paused. "No, I don't want to say it."

"Come on, tell me."

"Well, he wanted to show his girlfriend how much he loved her, so he started out in California and walked all the way to his girlfriend's house in Pennsylvania and proposed to her."

Judd smiled. "Sounds pretty devoted."

"I wasn't saying that to make you . . . you know, to plant some kind of idea or anything . . . oh no, I've really done it this time."

Judd chuckled. "That story obviously didn't happen during the Tribulation."

"Right, that just popped into my head. I'm sorry."

There were footsteps above so Judd lowered his voice. "Listen, there are a lot of miles between us right now, but I'm going to make it back. When I do, we're going to be a great team again."

"Be careful, Judd."

Vicki hung up with Judd and wished she could do something to help him. Her days at the Wisconsin hideout were good, with plenty of work and new opportunities for reaching out through the Internet. The kids' Web site had been listed as forbidden by the Global Community, but that only made people want to read it more. It was like the list of "banned books" Vicki remembered at her local library. The controversy made more people want to read them, though she didn't understand how you could check out a "banned" book.

The Global Community had developed a program that infected The Cube, the kids' high-tech presentation of the gospel, but Jim Dekker, who had created the program, quickly discovered how to defeat the virus. With the rise of the miracle workers around the world, many undecided wrote with questions, and Vicki found many believers who were confused. They couldn't understand how these false messiahs could do the same types of miracles that first-century Christians had witnessed.

Vicki spent most of her time answering e-mails, helping with the mundane cleanup and cooking, or fixing up run-down cabins. Charlie was a big help moving heavy things and finding new lumber. Phoenix spent most of his waking hours following Charlie around and never let the young man out of his sight.

Other than Judd, the person who weighed most heavily on her mind was Cheryl Tifanne. Cheryl had become a believer shortly after being rescued from a GC holding facility in Iowa, and the girl was pregnant. She wasn't due for another few months, but Vicki wondered if the girl would be strong enough to deliver the baby.

Cheryl had asked Josey and Tom Fogarty to be the parents of the child after he or she was born, but Cheryl was having second thoughts. As the baby began to move in Cheryl's womb, it became more real and Cheryl wondered if she had made a mistake promising the child to someone else.

"If I hadn't become a believer, I would have probably had an abortion," Cheryl said. "Now I can see that every life is precious, even though the baby's father abandoned me."

"You'll probably stay right here with the Fogartys," Vicki said. "You'll help raise the child."

"But it's going to be hard just handing the baby over," Cheryl said.

"From what I know about pregnancies, your emotions are going to go all over the place. It's important to keep asking one question: what's best for the baby? If you keep that in front at all times, you won't be swayed by how you feel. You'll do the best for the child."

Cheryl nodded. "It's not going to be easy, though. I can't imagine holding the little thing in my arms and then giving it away."

Vicki put an arm around the girl. "God will show you what to do when the time's right. And he'll give you the strength to do something good."

Cheryl caught her breath. "Did you feel that? He kicked! Right here. Feel."

Vicki put a hand on Cheryl's stomach and felt something pressing against her. A bump appeared on Cheryl's skin and Vicki giggled.

"I think that's an elbow. Can you believe it, Vicki? A brand-new life coming into the world and at a time like this." Cheryl trembled as the baby moved again. "I'm scared for the little thing. How are we ever going to take care of it?"

Vicki didn't answer. She knew there were no guarantees for any of them. The GC could find out about their camp and wipe it out in a few minutes if they wanted. But for some reason God had left them here, scared and outnumbered, for a reason.

Judd tried to stay calm throughout the day as he and Lionel led another study of Scripture. Lee and Brooke tried to act interested, but Judd could tell the Bible annoyed them. Judd scooted close and asked Brooke to read a few verses. As she staggered through the words, Judd looked closely at her forehead. Whoever had covered their marks had done a good job. All of Brooke's scratching had left a crease in the makeup, and Judd thought he saw air bubbles under the rubber-like covering.

Tom and Luke gathered the radios and a few BHDs, put them in backpacks, and hid them in the woods to the north of the house. When the six gathered for dinner, Tom gave Judd a discreet thumbs-up.

"Why don't you lead us in a prayer tonight, Brooke?" Luke said.

"Oh, I-I-I couldn't, really."

"Nonsense. I know you're new and all, but you've got to get over being nervous about praying in public. Give it a shot."

"Yeah, go ahead," Lee said with a smile.

"Okay." She folded her hands and closed her eyes.

Judd felt a twinge of guilt listening to the girl stammer. He wanted to punch Luke for suggesting it. All they needed was for her to slip and pray something to lord Carpathia and the whole Global Community would come down on them. When Brooke finished with, "I pray to Jesus, amen," Judd heaved a sigh of relief.

Two hours later, Luke handed Brooke and Lee a radio

127

and asked them to follow. He placed Tom at a spot near the river, then left Lionel a few hundred yards to the south in a marshy area.

"We'll leave you two together by the fence there," Luke said. "You'll have the best view if anybody comes up the road."

"Let's hope it's your friends, the believers," Lee said.

"Exactly," Luke said. "Judd and I will walk west toward that field. That'll give us a better view of the air in case the GC decides to join us."

"Got it," Lee said.

Judd and Luke jogged west through the tall grass. A faint orange glow shimmered on the horizon as the last of the sun played through the trees.

"How far do the radios reach?" Judd whispered when they hit the tree line and headed north.

"Two, maybe three miles. Far enough that when we get out of range, there won't be anything those two can do about it."

Judd hustled after Luke. They had left Tom near the river because of his bad leg. He was closest to the meeting point.

Judd stopped when he heard a creaking sound. "Is that a helicopter?"

Luke shook his head. "It's just cicadas. Come on."

Tom checked in on the radio and the others answered. Luke had been careful to place everyone out of sight of Lee and Brooke.

"Nothing here," Lee said into the radio.

"Check," Luke said. He turned to Judd. "I'll bet a

hundred Nicks they've called their GC comrades. You could see the gleam in their eyes when we dropped them off. They're out for blood."

"It's sad, really," Judd whispered.

"What do you mean?"

"You know the GC had to brainwash them. Who knows what would have happened if Nicolae's goons hadn't gotten to them."

Judd's mind played back the scene in Israel where he had injured a Morale Monitor. Judd had never heard whether the boy had lived or died, but he knew they were in a war. Nicolae Carpathia would stop at nothing to wipe out his enemies, and Judd was in that group.

"All right, we're in place," Luke said when they had run to the back of the property. "Everybody check in."

"Everything's quiet over here," Tom said.

"Same here," Lionel said.

Luke stared at the radio, waiting for Brooke or Lee. Finally, Brooke's voice cut through the static. "Nothing over here. Luke, where did you and Judd go? We lost sight of you."

"See that little copse of trees on the knoll? We're about a hundred yards farther to the west."

"Wave to us."

"Something's not right," Judd whispered.

Luke nodded and keyed the microphone. "I don't want to give our position away. What's wrong?"

"It's just that we can't see any of you, and we don't want to get separated. You know, in case the GC come," Brooke said.

"I should have thought of this," Luke muttered. He keyed the mike again. "Okay, how about I come back to you and Lee goes with Judd?"

"Are you crazy?" Judd whispered.

"That's good," Brooke said. "I'll head toward you now."

"What are you doing?" Judd said. "You can't switch places—"

"You head toward the meeting place, and I'll stall these two," Luke said to Judd.

"How?"

"I don't know, I'll think of—"

"Hold your positions, guys," Lionel said over the radio. "I see movement. Brooke, Lee, do you see something moving this way from the road?"

"No, there's nothing . . . wait. Yes. Now I see it."

Two clicks sounded on the radio, the secret signal for everyone to run. Luke took off into the brush and Judd followed, his heart racing. The soft light of the sunset had given way to a creeping darkness, and Judd found himself at Luke's heels, dodging trees and crashing through the underbrush. Had Lionel's report about movement been true or a ruse to keep Luke away from Lee and Brooke? Had the GC moved in to arrest the small band of the Young Tribulation Force?

Judd gasped for breath as they plunged deeper into the woods. He hoped they would find Lionel and Tom at their meeting place.

14

JUDD ran as fast as he could through the thick brush. They passed a swampy area, and Judd made sure he followed Luke's exact steps. He hoped Lionel would catch up with Tom, who knew the area well.

Brooke's voice cut through the songs of crickets and grasshoppers. "We think that's a deer moving on the road. Luke, are you on your way?"

Luke stopped and tried to still his breathing. Judd bent double, his hands on his knees.

"I'll just come over there and you meet me," Brooke said.

"Negative," Luke said. "I thought I saw headlights coming this way. It could be our people."

The radio was silent for a few moments, and then Brooke's excited voice came again. "Okay, tell us if you see anything else."

"Maintain radio silence until I give the word," Luke said, then clicked the radio twice.

Luke started running again at an even pace. Judd was beginning to think their plan would work. When they reached the clearing, Judd helped Luke pull out the hidden backpacks, and they both put one on. Luke knelt, his eyes darting back and forth at the scene. The moonlight cast an eerie glow through the trees.

"Where are they?" Judd whispered.

Luke put a finger to his lips. "Somebody's coming."

Tom crashed through the brush and fell into the clearing. He held his injured leg and gasped for breath. "Didn't think I was going to make it."

"Where's Lionel?" Judd said.

"Didn't see him. I thought he'd catch up with me before I got here."

Tom reached for a backpack, but Luke waved him off. "You don't need the extra weight on that leg. I'll carry it."

"You don't think he's back there waiting, do you?" Judd said.

Luke stood, concentrating on the sounds around them. "I hear something."

The three squatted and Luke grabbed a large stick. Luke's muscles tensed as he got a firm grip. Footsteps sloshed through water behind them, and then Lionel ran in from the west and plopped down in the middle of the group. "I went too far," he gasped. "Tried to find Tom . . . then got turned around . . . sorry."

"It's okay," Luke whispered, pulling out a compass.

"Did you really see something on the road?" Judd said.

Lionel pulled his backpack on, shifted its weight

forward, and shook his head. "Thought you guys could use some help. Brooke was about to come your way."

Luke pointed northeast. "Tom sticks with me and you two bring up the rear. We're headed two miles in that direction, then—"

Tom held up a hand and glanced into the brush.

"What is it?" Luke said.

"I don't know, I thought I—"

The brush crashed around them as Lee and Brooke hurtled into the clearing. Judd's first thought was to run, but when he saw Brooke reach into her boot, he knew he had to stop her. He lunged, but Brooke stepped back, avoiding him, and Lee's sharp kick to Judd's stomach crushed air from his lungs.

Before Brooke could push the button on the phone, Luke threw the extra backpack and knocked the phone into the brush.

Brooke fell back. "You Judah-ites are dead!"

"So you're not real believers after all," Tom said. "What a surprise."

"All four of you on the ground. Now!" Lee yelled.

"You're forgetting something, GC boy," Luke drawled. "There's four of us and two of you." He grabbed Lee by a wrist, turned his arm behind him, and the man went down hard. Brooke screamed, and Judd clamped a hand over her mouth.

"Hand me some duct tape, Tom," Luke said.

Luke taped their mouths, hands, and feet. Lionel found the phone and gave it to Luke, who dropped it on a rock and smashed it with one stomp.

"How many are coming for us?" Luke said, ripping the tape from Lee's mouth. "And no yelling."

"I'm not telling you anything."

Luke knelt beside Lee. "I know a big snake pit not far from here. You two should feel right at home."

Brooke's eyes widened, and she shook her head violently.

"I don't know how many exactly," Lee said. "Enough to flank the road and capture as many Judah-ites as you said were coming."

Luke glanced at Tom. "That changes things. Get on the phone to our people and tell them to hold their position. We'll head to the—" Luke stopped, then pulled Tom to the side, whispering something in his ear. Tom nodded and walked several yards away and held the phone to his ear.

"You're not going to get away," Lee said. "If we don't get you, the bounty hunters will."

"Maybe you're right," Luke said. "Maybe we'll get caught. But when your Global Community crumbles, remember we told you what would happen. You're on the losing side."

Truck brakes squealed in the distance. Lee started to call out, but Luke slapped the tape back on his mouth.

Judd looked back as they headed east toward the river. Lee and Brooke lay squirming on the ground like earthworms. Judd had caught his breath from Lee's kick, but his heart pounded like a jackhammer. The GC were at the house and would be searching for them.

After they had run a hundred yards east, Luke pointed

left and they switched directions. A few minutes later, he
held up a hand. "I'm hoping they think we're headed for
the river and that we're trying to meet our group downstream. They shouldn't find Lee and Brooke for a while,
so it should give us some time. You guys ready?"

Everyone nodded and followed Luke. A series of
explosions erupted, and Judd wondered if the GC was
destroying the house or if the blasts were Carl Meninger's
work. The four slogged through a marsh and onto dry
ground. With Global Community troops nearby and
bounty hunters ahead of them, Judd smiled. He was
finally going home.

Vicki stayed up the entire night with Shelly, Janie,
Darrion, and Tanya. The five prayed for Judd and the
others, asking God to protect them and the rest of the
southern Young Tribulation Force. Vicki was amazed at
how quickly the time passed as they prayed, read passages
out loud, and talked. Cheryl tried to join them but
couldn't stay awake.

Marshall Jameson had given Vicki an old road atlas he
had found, and Vicki turned to the South Carolina page.
She held the map as they prayed, wondering if Judd and
Lionel were on any of the small roads she saw.

The angel's words came back to her. Was it possible
that something would happen to Judd on the way? Vicki
prayed silently, not wanting the others to know her fears.

At 5:30 A.M., after hours of prayer, the phone rang
and Vicki beat the others to it. "Hello?" she said.

"It's Judd. We made it."

Vicki fell to her knees, tears welling in her eyes. The others crowded around and tried to listen, hugging each other and thanking God.

"We made it to Walterboro about fifteen minutes ago," Judd said. "You won't believe where we're holed up. It's an old Baptist church the GC thinks is condemned. There's a basement with an underground hideout."

Vicki ran a finger over the wrinkled map in her hand and found Walterboro. She flipped back to the main page and tried to judge the distance between Wisconsin and South Carolina. It was such a long way. When she could speak, Vicki said, "How's Lionel?"

"Good. We're both tired and scratched up. I'll write and tell you all about it."

Vicki hung up and thanked everyone for staying up with her, then went to her bunk. She thanked God again for keeping Judd and Lionel safe and fell asleep asking him to bring them back soon.

Over the next few days, Judd and Lionel planned their trip north, contacting Chloe Williams about the different safe houses along the way. Judd found out that Carl Meninger had indeed set explosives inside the plantation house to destroy materials left behind.

"They weren't meant to hurt anybody, but I'm not going to cry if GC soldiers lost their lives."

Judd furrowed his brow. "We're not here to kill people. The GC will label us terrorists if we start—"

"Look," Luke said, "we're in a battle. You don't think there are casualties in war? They're chopping off the heads of believers every day."

"But why stoop to their level?" Judd said.

Luke stared at Judd. "If we'd have taken care of those two back at the house, we'd probably still be there."

"Right. Kill all the GC we can," Judd said, throwing his arms in the air.

One of the Walterboro believers came in to quiet them, but they still argued.

"Tom and I are going out tonight on a little mission," Luke said. "We could use the help."

Lionel shook his head. "If you're going to do something violent, we can't support you. We'll pray for you and ask God to protect you, but we don't see this as the answer."

"Fine," Luke said. "Just remember who rescued your nervous hides."

Judd checked with Chang Wong, who said there were three reported injuries at the plantation house but no troops killed. Chang said he felt more and more isolated in New Babylon and longed to escape.

For the next three nights, Luke and Tom slipped into the darkness with supplies and blackened faces. News came over GCNN of fires deliberately set in South Carolina. All were said to be the homes of bounty hunters.

"Maybe they'll get the message and stop what they're doing," Luke said.

But a week later, Luke and Tom failed to return from a night mission. Everyone assumed they had gone to

Barnwell to join their other friends, but no one was sure. Judd and Lionel made final preparations to leave, though they didn't want to until they found out about Luke and Tom.

The next afternoon, the Global Community made a startling announcement. The Walterboro group surrounded the television in their dark underground as Commander Kruno Fulcire held a press conference.

"I will allow questions, but before that I have an important message and directive for all citizens of the Global Community," Fulcire said. "We have conducted a pilot program, a test for the entire world. I'm pleased to say that our bounty hunters have had great success in ferreting out our enemies. There have been hundreds of people in the southern region of the UNAS delivered to GC headquarters.

"We want to thank those who have participated, some at great personal cost and peril. I have communication from the highest levels who say they appreciate your efforts."

Fulcire looked at his notes. "However, with recent terrorist actions taken against GC forces and especially targeting bounty hunters, we have an alternate plan we hope will be instituted not only in the southern region, but in all the United North American States, and eventually, throughout the entire Global Community."

Fulcire held up a shaded map of the southern region. "I have authority from the very top to issue this proclamation. If you are listening to my voice and you are in this shaded area and still have not complied with taking the loyalty mark to our risen lord, you have forty-eight hours to receive that mark.

"After the forty-eight-hour period, we will observe a zero tolerance policy and institute a vigilante law. This means any loyal citizen with a valid mark may kill an unmarked resident on sight. There is no longer any excuse to have neglected your duty. You must come forward at once.

"Citizens who exercise their rights and eliminate lawbreakers will be rewarded. Simply bring the body to the nearest GC facility for processing."

Judd couldn't believe what he was hearing. They had escaped the GC and bounty hunters, and now ordinary citizens would be their enemies. People in the room clucked their tongues and tsk tsked.

"Sir, what happens if a citizen mistakenly kills a person with a valid mark?" a reporter said after Fulcire finished his remarks.

"The murder of a loyal Carpathianite is punishable by death," Fulcire said. "Anyone, no matter what the intentions, must be sure the person they accuse of being an enemy does not have the mark here or here." He pointed to his forehead and right hand. "I suggest caution, but if you know someone is a Judah-ite or simply doesn't have the sense to take the mark, your action will be rewarded."

"Is there a preferable way to execute enemies of the Global Community?" a female reporter said.

Fulcire smiled. "A dead traitor is a dead traitor. The weapon is up to the loyal citizen. Personally I would like to see these people suffer, but that is up to the vigilante."

The crowd of reporters laughed, and Lionel turned to Judd. "What does this do to our plans about heading north?"

"If we're ever going to leave, now is the time," Judd said.

15

JUDD and Lionel crammed supplies into backpacks, and one of the Walterboro group gave them a solar cell phone. They had mapped out a series of safe houses and campsites through South Carolina, North Carolina, Virginia, Kentucky, Indiana, Illinois, and finally Wisconsin. Judd checked with Chloe Williams to find Co-op flights or trucks headed in that direction, but Chloe confirmed Chang Wong's fears. Some Co-op drivers had been caught, while others had cut down their routes and had trouble just getting supplies to needy groups.

Judd had not only mapped out their travels but also tried to estimate the time for each leg of the trip. On some days, if someone gave them a ride, they could travel as much as fifty miles. Other days, when they were hiking through mountains, they could go five or ten miles at most. They planned to hike through the night and hide during the day, either at a safe house or somewhere in the woods.

The Walterboro group gathered round them after dark, put their hands on Judd and Lionel, and prayed for their safety. Though they hadn't stayed long, Judd felt like they were part of his family. They had risked their lives, and Judd was emotional as the believers huddled around them.

One of the members had agreed to drive them from Walterboro to Barnwell, where the members of Luke and Tom's group stayed. The man had disabled the car's brake lights and they set out after midnight, driving by moonlight. When they saw headlights of an oncoming car, they pulled over and hid until it passed.

Carl Meninger met them in the wee hours of the morning and showed Judd and Lionel where they would sleep, but both agreed to stay up the rest of the night and sleep during the day. Carl took them to the makeshift computer room, and Judd and Lionel spent a few hours writing e-mails and finding out more about the Global Community's latest actions.

Judd became so engrossed that he didn't notice Carl walk into the room, tears in his eyes. "What's wrong?" Judd said.

"We just saw a report about the bounty hunters," Carl said. "Tom and Luke are dead."

The news hit Judd like a punch in the stomach. He staggered from the computer to the TV in the next room.

"More now on the deaths of two young men thought to be the arsonists terrorizing South Carolina," the reporter said. The picture switched to grainy video shot the night before and three bounty hunters standing by two bodies.

"This is them, all right," one man said. "We caught them with gasoline they used to start the fires last night."

The camera moved closer, showing the faces of Judd's friends. The two brothers who had saved Judd's life lay lifeless on a wooden pallet. Someone had tried to rub the shoe polish from their faces, but the Global Community spokesman said their identities weren't important. "What is important," the man said, "is that a message is sent to our enemies. As you can see, neither of these two had the mark of loyalty, so the bounty hunters will receive their reward, as will any citizen who finds and exposes anyone not bearing lord Carpathia's mark."

Judd went back to the computer and sat, numb from the news. After a brief memorial service for Luke and Tom, Judd wrote Vicki: *I can't help thinking they wasted their lives trying to stop the bounty hunters. They could have done so much more for the cause. I don't want that to happen to us.*

Over the next few weeks, Vicki waited for Judd's calls each morning and kept track of his progress with the atlas and a pen. Judd would give his location, and Vicki drew lines from South Carolina, through North Carolina, and into Virginia. Vicki had a celebration when Judd crossed into a new state.

Judd and Lionel were taking great care in their travels, but Vicki couldn't help but worry when they'd report seeing a GC squad car or even a normal citizen. Their job, as Judd told it, was to walk or ride as far as they could each night, taking as few chances as possible. If they had the choice to go ten miles over a mountain with no chance of seeing anyone, or going five through a more populated stretch, they went over the mountain.

"The thing that scares us most is dogs," Judd said one morning. "The ones that have survived all the plagues seem meaner, and they bark their heads off at anybody on foot."

The next day, Vicki didn't get a call from Judd until late in the afternoon. She worried throughout the day until the phone rang.

"We found a cave just before sunup," Judd said from a Kentucky cave, "but since this place is so remote, we decided to find the safe house. It was set back on a hill overlooking a little town, but when we got there, several GC officers surrounded the place."

"Those poor people," Vicki said.

"The GC stormed it and came out with nothing."

"You think the people were tipped off?"

"I hope so. Anyway, we won't be able to get the ride we thought we would."

"I don't like how long this is taking," Vicki said.

"We're being safe," Judd said.

Vicki tried to keep her mind on other things, like working on the kids' Web site. The best activity she found was cleaning and fixing up run-down cabins. The physical work helped keep her mind busy. She, Charlie, and the others completed the cleaning or construction of a new cabin about every two weeks.

Every few days, Marshall Jameson would get a call for Zeke from some secret believer who had heard about what the man could do to people's appearances. Zeke had set up shop in one of the renovated cabins and thrived on helping people. With the coming of Carpathia's mark, there was only so much Zeke could do, but everyone who visited him went away happy.

In her weak moments, Vicki counted the cost of not flying to meet Judd in France. They would be together now if she had, but she wouldn't be available to Cheryl.

Cheryl had reached the halfway point of her pregnancy but didn't seem to gain much weight. She tried to eat healthy but felt sick to her stomach most of the time. She slept late each morning and could remain up only a few hours before going back to bed. Marshall, who had some medical training, admitted they needed to find someone to help with the baby's delivery.

Mark searched the Web for any information. Josey and Tom Fogarty were so concerned that Tom offered to drive to find a doctor, but they couldn't locate one. Vicki sat with Cheryl and tried to calm her. Several times the girl was afraid she had lost the baby, and then it started to move again and Cheryl sighed with relief.

"Zeke can do just about everything else— you think he could help?" Cheryl said.

Vicki smiled. "You're lucky you have so many people who care about you. We're going to find some help." But deep inside, Vicki wondered if they would or if the job would be Marshall's.

After the event with the Global Community in Kentucky, Judd and Lionel covered even less ground each day and camped about every other night. They both grew dirty, unable to take showers for days at a time, and let their beards grow. Lionel said Judd looked like a mountain man, while Judd said Lionel looked like a fuzzy cartoon character.

"Which one?" Lionel said.

Judd just laughed and waved a hand. They had become closer since hearing of the deaths of Luke and Tom. Judd felt more comfortable talking with Lionel about Vicki, and Lionel shared some of his fears about the final years of the Great Tribulation.

"We're playing for keeps now," Lionel said. "It's like everybody in the world is hunting us, and all we're trying to do is survive."

"Everybody in the world needs what we have," Judd said, "but if they've taken Carpathia's mark, they won't be able to believe."

Judd had never traveled through this part of the country, except by interstate, and he was surprised at how beautiful the land was. Even with the earthquake and the fires that had consumed grass and trees, he could still see the beauty of God's creation.

When they reached the Ohio River and prepared to cross, they decided against using bridges for fear they'd be spotted, so they found a small boat and pushed across. The river was swifter than Judd anticipated, and they drifted a mile downstream.

Three days of hard traveling through rugged terrain left them on the outskirts of Salem, Indiana. They found the safe house in the wee hours of the morning and called from nearby. A groggy-voiced man answered and hurried to open the door of an old farm equipment store.

The man, Eustice Honaker, pulled them inside and put a finger to his lips. He led them through the building to a secret compartment under the stairs. The room was belowground, only about five feet high, and housed nearly a dozen people sleeping on cots.

Eustice pulled Judd and Lionel to the corner and whispered, trying not to awaken anyone, "There was a boat stolen a few nights ago along the river."

"That was us," Judd said.

Eustice pushed a tattered baseball cap back and scratched a bald spot. "The GC has scoured the country-side for you two. Somebody spotted you from a bridge, I guess."

"We didn't see anybody in the woods while we traveled," Lionel said.

"They're out there, and they've enlisted everybody in this half of the state to find you. I thought you'd been caught."

What was supposed to be an overnight stay turned into weeks as Eustice and the others convinced Judd and Lionel that to leave would be suicide for both them and the local group. If Judd had felt isolated before, he now felt so cooped up he could scream. There was no Internet connection, so he got his news about other believers from Vicki and those he talked with via phone. Vicki read him huge chunks of Buck Williams's *The Truth*, and Judd relayed the words to his new friends.

Since there was no sunlight inside the hideout, Judd snuck out before sunup and put the phone in some weeds where he knew it would recharge, then retrieved it late the next night. The only news about local happenings came from a local radio station.

After moving several hundred miles and feeling the freedom of being their own bosses, Judd and Lionel felt like their future was in someone else's hands. Several times the group had given the okay for them to leave, only to have the Global Community strike up another round of raids. The weeks turned to a month, then two. Finally, five months since leaving Israel, Judd and Lionel began the final leg of their journey.

Eustice and the others gathered around and prayed, as so many of the groups had done. They also prayed for the Wisconsin believers and Cheryl's baby in particular.

As Judd slipped into the muggy Indiana night, he knew he was closer than ever to reconnecting with his friends.

"You ready for this?" Lionel said.

Judd nodded. "I've never been so ready."

Vicki raced to the main cabin for Marshall Jameson. Cheryl Tifanne had been complaining of pain in her stomach for hours, and everyone hoped it would go away. She still had several weeks to go before giving birth, but Vicki could tell from the girl's sweating and increased pain that something terrible was happening.

Marshall had tracked down a midwife who was a believer and through a coded e-mail had discovered she lived about two hours away. Marshall sent a message, grabbed his coat, and headed for his vehicle. Mark followed him out the door.

Vicki glanced at the clock. If it took Marshall two hours to get there and two hours to get back, it would be 4:00 A.M. before he returned.

When Cheryl screamed, Vicki rushed inside the cabin.

Shelly held the girl's hand, placing a cold cloth on her forehead. "She's not getting any better, and her stomach's getting tighter."

"Just hang on, Cheryl," Vicki said. "Help is on the way."

Judd took the lead and headed up a rocky slope in the moonlight. "How does it feel?" he said to Lionel.

"Nothing against those people, but I was about to go crazy."

They had been walking two hours, Judd making sure they were headed north. A cool breeze blew out of the west. "I don't care if we spend the rest of the trip outside. The fresh air is like a taste of heaven."

Just after midnight they came to a ridge that Judd thought must have been created by the wrath of the Lamb earthquake. On the left of the hill was a swiftly moving stream, and to the right was a rock face that heaved up.

"Your call," Judd said. "You want to go around?"

"Nah, let's go over the top. I'm ready for some adventure."

The climb up the slope wasn't difficult. There were some loose stones, but the grade was about as steep as a ski slope Judd had climbed as a kid. But when they reached the top, Judd's mouth gaped. The other side was a sheer drop.

"You sure you don't want to go around?" Judd said.

Lionel looked at his watch. "We'll save time this way. Come on."

Lionel led the way. Judd was glad there were only a few clouds out or they wouldn't have been able to see the footholds. About halfway down, Lionel held up a hand and told Judd to wait. "Let me get closer to the bottom before you climb down."

Judd sat back against a boulder, and a cascade of tiny rocks skittered down the hill. Lionel shielded his face with a hand and scowled.

"Sorry," Judd said in a loud whisper.

The passing clouds looked like a train, spreading out across the black sky. Judd wondered if Vicki was still up. He thought about calling her but decided against it.

Lionel moved slowly, so Judd got another foothold and stepped onto the boulder so he could relax. As he put his weight on the huge rock, he felt something move. Another cascade of tiny rocks plunged down the incline, and then the boulder itself tipped forward.

"Hey, look out!" Judd yelled, jumping from the rock and sliding down a jagged slope.

The boulder moved like a turtle, slow and easy as it tilted. Then, as the ground shifted and the earth beneath it gave way, the rock gained momentum and crashed down the hillside.

Judd grabbed a bush growing straight out of the hill and hung on. He glanced down, seeing Lionel frantically trying to move out of the way. Judd screamed as the rock bounced left, heading straight for Lionel.

16

JUDD Thompson Jr. let go of the bush and scampered to his left, trying to escape certain death. Tiny rocks fell as he searched for footing, his feet pumping like a cartoon character's. Lionel was down there, but all Judd could think about was getting out of the way.

Judd lunged for a flat rock and hung on with both hands. He glanced back as the rock reared in the air like a stony stallion and hovered, blocking the clouds and sky. Just as he thought he would be squashed, the rock tipped to the right and began a free fall toward the bottom. Smaller rocks and dust covered Judd's face.

The ground shuddered with each turn of the rock. Judd pulled himself to a sitting position while the boulder crashed to the bottom.

As the dust settled and Judd caught his breath, he looked for Lionel. He had had plenty of time to get out of the way, and Judd wondered if he had jumped into the bushes by the stream.

"Guess we should have gone around, huh?" Judd called out.

No response.

"That rock was as big as a house. Good thing we got out of the way."

Still no response.

"Hey, Lionel, where are you?"

Crickets chirped and frogs croaked. Hearing the trickle of water gave Judd an eerie feeling. Everything was peaceful, as if nothing had happened.

"Come on, man, this isn't funny. You think I tried to knock that rock down?"

Judd surveyed the damage. The crashing rock had left several craters in its wake, which would make it even more difficult to get down. Any moment he expected Lionel to jump out from behind a bush and scold him.

Judd carefully took a few steps left to a small ridge. As he slowly climbed down, something hissed near his foot. He jumped and slid a few feet. When he heard the hiss again, he leaped to the ground, a good fifteen-foot drop.

His knees ached after the fall, but he was glad to be away from the snake. "Lionel?"

Judd listened closely. Rocks skittered down the hill and came to rest near him. Either Lionel was hiding in the bushes or . . .

"Lionel, I just heard a snake."

Something moved and moaned softly. Judd called Lionel's name again, but only crickets and frogs responded. Something swooped over him, a fluttering of wings and a caw. Judd ducked, then saw the outline of a

crow against the night sky. When the bird lighted in a
nearby tree, Judd moved toward the boulder. What he
saw when he rounded the corner took his breath away.

Vicki Byrne held Cheryl Tifanne's hand and prayed with
all her might. Vicki feared the baby was in trouble, but
the greater fear was that Cheryl was about to deliver it
without the help of the midwife.

Sweat poured from Cheryl's forehead, the girl turning
her head from side to side and moaning. When the cabin
door opened and Vicki turned, Cheryl dug her fingernails
into Vicki's arm.

"Don't leave me," Cheryl said through clenched teeth.

"Don't worry."

Shelly came in with Josey Fogarty. Josey carried a box
and placed it on the nightstand. "There's some pain
medication in here—"

"Good," Vicki said, grabbing a bottle.

"Wait," Josey said. "If she's in labor, she shouldn't
take anything."

"I need something for the pain!" Cheryl screamed.

Josey pulled Vicki's arm and whispered, "This medicine will go right to the baby. It could endanger the
child."

"But don't they give women medicine for pain before
they have their babies?" Vicki said. "That's what
happened with my mom."

"They can give them all kinds of things, but the
patients are on monitors, checking heartbeats and oxygen

levels. We don't have any equipment, and the medicine is the wrong kind."

"Vicki!" Cheryl shouted.

"I'm right here," Vicki said, then turned back to Josey. "We have to give her something."

"Not until we know for sure what's happening," Josey said.

Shelly reached in her pocket, and plastic rattled. She pulled out a half-eaten roll of candy. "We could give her this."

"That won't do anything," Vicki said.

"But if she thinks it's medicine, maybe it'll calm her down."

Josey nodded. "It's worth a try."

"Give me one," Vicki said.

Cheryl's hands shook as she sat up and grabbed a glass of water. She popped the piece of candy in her mouth without looking at it and downed the glass, water dripping from the corners of her mouth and onto her bedsheets. Cheryl closed her eyes and lay back, trying to catch her breath.

"Try to relax," Josey said. "You and the baby are going to be fine."

"Is the doctor coming?" Cheryl said.

"She's a midwife—it's like a doctor, without the hospital," Vicki said.

"How long before she comes?" Cheryl gasped.

"Won't be long," Vicki said as she glanced at Shelly and Josey.

Vicki had been in the room during part of her

mother's labor with her little sister, Jeanni. It had been a long process, and Vicki hadn't seen the worst of it, certainly not the kind of pain Cheryl was going through.

"Call Marshall and ask him if there's anything else we can do for her," Vicki whispered to Shelly. "The minute he makes contact with that midwife, have him call us."

Vicki took Cheryl's temperature and it was normal. "Stay still. Help will be here soon."

Judd moved around the rock, horrified. Lionel lay motionless on the ground. The left side of his body appeared to be pinned under the boulder.

Judd stared at the scene, unable to move. Was Lionel breathing? Had the rock crushed the life from him? Judd finally knelt and placed a hand on Lionel's neck. *A pulse.*

Lionel's head lolled to the side, and he opened his eyes. "It hurts."

"What does?"

"My arm."

Judd let his eyes adjust to the dim light. He had thought Lionel's whole body was under the rock, but only his left arm was pinned. "I'll have you out of here in a few minutes, just hang on."

"I'm not going anywhere," Lionel mumbled.

Judd looked around for something to wedge under the rock and came back with the biggest stick he could find. He shoved it as far under the rock as he could and pushed, but the wood cracked. He had a sinking feeling there was no way the rock would move.

"Hold on. I'm going to try something else," Judd said.

Lionel said something and Judd leaned close. "What?"

"Backpack . . . can you get it off?"

Judd pulled one side of Lionel's backpack off, then loosened the strap on the other side and pulled it free. He placed it under Lionel's head, and the boy sighed and nodded.

Judd found a sharp rock near the stream and began digging a few feet from Lionel's trapped arm. He hoped to dig a hole big enough to pull Lionel free, but a few scrapes against the earth and his heart sank. Lionel was pinned under a rock weighing thousands of pounds. Without some kind of jack or mechanical device, he was stuck.

Judd ran a hand through his hair and took the cell phone from his backpack. He dialed the safe house in Salem, but there was no answer. There was no one to call, no one he could think of to help. He would enlist the prayer support of others in the Young Tribulation Force, of course, but where else could he turn? He and Lionel were on their own.

Judd walked toward the stream again, racking his brain. If only they had gone around the hill. If only he hadn't sat on the boulder.

"God, you sent that angel, Anak, to Vicki and the others. It would only take one finger for him to lift this rock and help Lionel. Please, I need your help. I need to get Lionel out of there, and there's simply no way."

Judd walked back to his friend and sat. "How're you feeling?"

Lionel's eyes fluttered. "I tried to get out of the way, but I tripped. I'm lucky the rock didn't roll one more time or I'd be flat as a manhole cover." He took a breath and blew it out. "There's no way to get me out, is there?"

"There's a way. I just haven't found it yet." Judd rummaged through his backpack and pulled out a flashlight. Though the area surrounding him was bathed in moonlight, under the rock it was dark. Judd switched the flashlight on and pointed it toward Lionel's trapped arm. Blood streaked Lionel's shirt and pooled in the dirt.

If I don't get him out of here, he could bleed to death.

Vicki looked for any improvement in Cheryl's condition but found none. The girl thrashed and squirmed, holding her stomach. When the phone rang, Vicki thought it was Marshall with the midwife. She quickly answered but heard Judd's voice.

"We've got a situation here," Judd said with emotion. "There's been an accident."

"What happened? Are you all right?"

"I'm fine. A little scratched up, but fine." After he explained what had happened to Lionel, Vicki covered the phone and relayed the message to the others.

"Tell everybody to pray," Judd said. "I need wisdom about what to do."

"He should put a tourniquet on that arm to stop the bleeding," Josey said, taking the phone. "You have to make this decision carefully, Judd, but if you think there's no chance to save that arm—"

159

Judd interrupted and Vicki strained to hear but couldn't. Finally, Josey said, "If the bleeding doesn't stop, you have to stop it. A tourniquet will do that. At least he won't bleed to death."

The two talked a few minutes, and Josey handed the phone back to Vicki. "Judd, can you get back to the last safe house and get help?"

"It's an option, but not a very good one."

Vicki explained what was going on with Cheryl, and Judd said he would pray for her. Judd promised he would call and give them an update by morning.

When she hung up, Vicki felt low. Cheryl's condition seemed worse, and Lionel was in grave danger. She asked Conrad to carefully word a prayer alert and send it over the kids' Web site.

Shelly put a hand on Vicki's shoulder. "God's going to help us. I'm sure of it."

Vicki nodded. "I just wish he would hurry."

Judd pointed the flashlight under the rock. The boulder completely covered Lionel's hand and forearm, but there was a small crevice that left Lionel's elbow uncovered. His arm was swollen, and blood pulsed from the wound.

"How do you feel?" Judd said.

Lionel blinked. "My head feels kind of light, like I'm going to be sick."

Judd examined the arm and concluded that Lionel's hand and forearm were crushed. Whether they would ever heal once he got out of there—if he got out of there—Judd didn't know. But from what Josey said, his first priority was to stop the bleeding.

"I'm going to put a tourniquet around your arm before I leave," Judd said.

"Leave? Where are you going?"

"For help. There's no way I can move this thing. Maybe I can get back to the people in Salem."

"Even if they come, how are they going to move it?"

"That place was an old farm equipment store. They're bound to have something. A couple of inches and you're out of there."

"Then what?" Lionel said.

Judd patted Lionel's shoulder. "We'll figure that out." He took off his belt and carefully strapped it around Lionel's arm above the elbow. He pulled it tight, and Lionel winced as Judd made a mark on the belt for the new hole. "Where's your knife?"

"Left front pants pocket. Sorry, but I can't reach it at the moment."

Judd smiled. That Lionel still had a sense of humor was a good sign. Judd found the knife and spent several minutes jabbing a hole in the belt. "This isn't going to feel good, but it's necessary."

"Whatever," Lionel said.

Judd took a breath, then pulled the belt as tight as he could around Lionel's arm. Lionel's scream echoed through the woods, and Judd nearly let go, but he knew this was Lionel's best chance of getting out alive.

Lionel wiped his forehead with his right hand. "Sorry I yelled like that."

"Don't be," Judd said, putting the knife in Lionel's right pocket. He pulled out the cell phone and dialed the safe house in Salem again. No answer. Judd handed the phone to Lionel. "Keep this and call Vicki if you need someone to talk to."

"But you might need it."

Judd shook his head and opened Lionel's backpack. He sorted the food and made sure Lionel could get to it, then gave Lionel all but one bottle of water. "I'll be back before sunup. Sundown tonight at the latest. Can you hang in there that long?"

"Only one way to find out," Lionel said. "Don't take any chances back there."

Judd nodded and checked Lionel's arm to make sure the bleeding had stopped.

"There'll be a lot of people praying for you. Concentrate on staying alive."

"That's been my full-time job since the disappearances."

Judd grabbed his flashlight from the backpack, headed into the night, and took a final look back. Lionel waved and tried to smile.

17

VICKI held Cheryl's hand and looked out the window. How could they have been so wrong about the due date? Was the baby in danger? Maybe it had already died.

Vicki shook her head. She couldn't think that way. They had to assume it was alive and work as hard as they could.

Cheryl squeezed Vicki's arm. Her breathing was short and her hands shook. "Something's wrong, isn't it?" Cheryl panted. "Am I going to lose the baby?"

Vicki patted her shoulder. "This just took us by surprise. You're a little early, but Marshall will get help. As soon as he gets back we'll all feel a lot better."

Cheryl put her head on the pillow and grimaced. Her breathing came rapidly, along with short moans of pain.

"Where does it hurt?" Vicki said.

Cheryl grabbed low on her stomach. "There's a lot of pressure. It feels like my stomach's going to explode."

The girl leaned forward, and Vicki noticed wetness on Cheryl's pants. Cheryl gasped.

Josey rushed to them. "Don't be scared. That was just your water breaking."

"What water?"

"A sac of fluid protects the baby. If it breaks, it usually means the baby is moving further down. We're going to see that little one tonight."

When Josey moved in to help Cheryl, Vicki stepped out of the way. Vicki wasn't ready for this. The baby couldn't be born tonight, could it? In the last few months Vicki had read lots on the Internet about giving birth. She had walked Cheryl through a class on how to breathe during labor, but now, all her reading and coaching seemed worthless. She felt helpless, without a clue about what would happen next.

She whispered the only prayer she could think of. "God, help us."

Judd went as fast as he could toward the stream, pointing his flashlight at the bank and making sure of his footing. It would take extra time going around the hill this way, but he wouldn't risk climbing up and sending more rocks onto Lionel.

Judd talked as he walked, trying to keep himself moving. His words became prayers as he asked God for wisdom. He prayed for Cheryl, the baby, and that Vicki would be able to help. He asked God to bring Marshall and the midwife back quickly and to spare the life of this child.

But Judd's thoughts kept coming back to Lionel. Had he checked the bleeding well enough? If the tourniquet wasn't tight, Lionel could die. Judd cringed as he imagined getting back to the rock and finding Lionel's body.

Judd stepped onto a rock jutting out over the stream. "God, I've got to trust you to take care of Lionel. You have to show yourself mighty in this, because I'm too weak to do anything else."

Judd moved through the darkened woods as quickly as he could. Someone at the safe house had to help.

Lionel wanted to scream for Judd to turn around. He didn't want to be left alone, but he knew it was his only chance. Every breath sent pain pulsing and throbbing through his arm.

Lying on his back in the rocks and dirt was the most uncomfortable position he could think of. *This is where I'll spend the next few hours, so I'd better get used to it.*

Lionel mustered the strength to pull the backpack closer with his right hand. Judd had emptied the contents on the ground so it would be easier to grab the cell phone, his flashlight, or something to eat. He bunched the backpack up and put his head back, out of breath. Pain shot through his arm and shoulder.

Lionel felt something move on his neck, and he smacked it. Whether it was a spider or some other insect he didn't know. The warmth of his skin probably attracted it, he thought. *And if I attract spiders, what else will I find out here?*

The stream caught his attention, and he tried to concentrate on it instead of the pain. His mom had bought a noise reducer for his room when he was young, so growing up he had gone to sleep to electronic crickets, a heartbeat, or a babbling brook. The only problem with the water sound was that it made his younger brother, Ronnie, want to go to the bathroom. His mom would kiss them good night, turn on the device, and leave. As soon as she was out the door, so was Ronnie, hopping sideways to the bathroom.

The thought made Lionel laugh, which also made his arm hurt. He listened to the water running over the smooth rocks and tried to imagine what it looked like in the moonlight. Such a peaceful sound. He could go to sleep so easily listening to that.

No! He couldn't go to sleep. If he went to sleep, he might never wake up. He put a finger on his arm just below the belt Judd had tightened. There was blood, he was sure of it. No way was he going to sleep.

Lionel grabbed a peanut-butter sandwich with his free hand and unwrapped it. Supplies at the Salem safe house had dwindled, but the people had given them enough food for two days. Lionel didn't know how long it had been since he had eaten a cheeseburger or any meat. Without the mark of the beast, those hiding had to settle for any food they could scrounge up or what the Commodity Co-op could provide. That usually meant something out of a can and stale bread. Lionel pretended the sandwich was a juicy burger from his favorite restaurant.

How long had it been since he had eaten at a restaurant, walked through a mall, shopped for clothes, or listened to music on the radio? How long since he had done anything *normal?* The disappearances of his family had been a little more than four years ago, but it seemed like a lifetime.

Four years. Lionel was now seventeen. He should have been looking for his first car, stashing cash to buy some old beater he could call his own.

He winced as another wave of pain hit. Lionel thought of his father. Charles had been a heavy-equipment operator. If he were here, he'd have this rock off in no time. But he wasn't, and Lionel wouldn't see him again until . . .

Lionel reached for his sandwich but dropped it. He started to blow away the dust and tiny rocks stuck to the jelly, but he wasn't hungry anymore. He put the sandwich back on the wrapper and pushed it aside.

Lionel closed his eyes and imagined his father sitting in a crane, lifting the huge rock. His dad could always fix things, and Lionel couldn't remember him ever failing at mechanical work. The only thing that threw him was dealing with Lionel's older sister, Clarice. She knew how to push his buttons and get him flustered. A two-ton rock would have been a piece of cake, but an argument with Clarice, that was something else.

The pain returned, and Lionel reached for a bottle of water. Judd had forgotten to loosen the top, so Lionel struggled to unscrew it. He tried holding it under his arm, but the bottle slipped. Finally, he put the cap in his mouth and cracked the seal, sending a dribble of water down his neck. Lionel took a drink and screwed the cap back on.

Something moved in the bushes by the stream, and Lionel instinctively tried to sit up, sending a new wave of pain through his left arm. He cried out, then lay back and turned toward the bushes. "Judd?"

No answer.

"Hey, no fair trying to scare me!"

Crickets and frogs and the stream. *Is it my imagination?* He found the flashlight and flicked it on. Just before the flurry and scurry of feet, Lionel saw two eyes.

Vicki tried to calm Cheryl as she prepared to deliver the baby. Shelly helped Cheryl get into a clean nightshirt while Josey put new sheets on the bed. Tom Fogarty, the former cop, offered to help. Josey thanked him, and Vicki noticed Charlie pacing outside the door of the cabin.

When Cheryl was settled, Conrad pulled Vicki outside and showed her a printout of responses to the prayer alert. "We've had more than a hundred notes so far, and it's only been on the Web site a few minutes."

"We're going to need the support," Vicki said.

"How close is she?"

"Josey thinks it could be soon. I hope Marshall hurries."

"Mark's with him. He'll call as soon as they find the midwife."

168

When Cheryl screamed again, Vicki rushed to the door. Charlie grabbed her arm. "If there's anything I can do, let me know."

Vicki nodded and ran into the cabin.

Lionel couldn't breathe for a few seconds as the animal disappeared into the bushes. He couldn't tell what or how large it was. *Great,* he thought, *now I'm being stalked.*

Lionel picked up the ant-covered sandwich. *Did the food attract the animal? Maybe it was my blood.*

Throughout their trip from South Carolina, Judd and Lionel had seen animals. Moving mostly at night, the two had run across opossums and skunks, but they had also seen several coyotes and what looked like wolves.

Lionel waved the flashlight, trying to catch the eyes again. A shrill sound split the night. *The cell phone!* Lionel reached for it but knocked it away. He strained, popping something in his left arm. He screamed in pain, then grabbed the phone. When he caught his breath, he pushed the receive button. "Hello?"

"Judd? It's Chang."

Lionel told Chang where Judd was and what had happened.

"I'm surprised you're still able to talk," Chang said. "Have you taken anything for the pain?"

"We didn't bring any medicine."

Chang asked for his location and punched in the coordinates on his computer. "I have to be careful about how much I try to do these days. They're still after that pesky mole in the palace." He clicked the keyboard and sighed. "The closest group of believers is where you've just come from. But . . ."

"What is it?"

A few more clicks. "Oh no."

"Tell me what you see."

"Do you have any way to get in touch with Judd?"

"No. I have the phone with me."

"The Global Community is conducting a midnight raid on that group. Judd could be walking into a trap."

Lionel's heart beat wildly. "We have to pray he sees them before he gets there."

Chang prayed and said he would check in later. The phone call had sapped Lionel's strength, and he wondered what had popped in his arm. He reached for the belt Judd had tightened and felt blood, but it seemed thicker. He put his head on the backpack, closed his eyes, and thought about the people in Salem. He and Judd had stayed with them longer than anyone else on their trip north, and though tempers had flared at times because of the close quarters, Lionel had a deep respect and love for the people.

Lionel imagined the GC storming the place, finding the hideout, and hauling the people out one by one. The GC loved torching things during their raids to destroy evidence and instill fear in believers. With the vigilante law in effect, his friends would be unable to escape.

A sickening thought raced through Lionel's mind. Had he and Judd been the reason the group was discovered? Had someone seen them stealing away earlier and called the Global Community? The idea turned Lionel's stomach.

Something moved to Lionel's right, and he grabbed the flashlight. A flash of red. Two eyes darted through the bushes and were gone.

Then something hissed to his right. Judd had said something about a snake when he was coming down the hill. Maybe it was his mind playing tricks. Maybe the whole thing—

Hiss . . .

Lionel slowly turned his head and came face-to-face with a coiled snake, only a few inches from his face.

18

LIONEL froze in horror. He had never liked snakes. When he was a kid, he couldn't bring himself to touch a page with a snake's picture on it. He'd had nightmares of hundreds of snakes writhing in his front yard. Those dreams sent him to his mom and dad's room quicker than the noise reducer sent Ronnie to the bathroom.

Lionel was close enough to see the snake's tongue slither in and out of its mouth. He looked at its eyes and thought of the nature show he had seen that said you could tell if a snake was poisonous by the shape of its head. The snake didn't rattle, but the markings were strange. Perhaps it was a copperhead.

The thing is probably looking for food, Lionel told himself. *He'll realize I'm too big and go away.*

The snake inched closer, angling toward the rock and Lionel's trapped arm.

"Nice snake," Lionel whispered, then rolled his eyes. *I'm talking to the thing like it's a puppy.*

The snake's head pulled back a few inches, and Lionel was sure it would strike. He closed his eyes and fumbled for the flashlight or phone, anything to throw.

Movement in the bush startled him, and a small animal jumped out and danced around the snake, pawing and nipping. *A fox!* The snake retreated, trying to find safety under the huge rock, but the fox hopped forward, blocking its way and dodging the snake's strikes.

Lionel wanted to cheer the fox on, but he was afraid it would scare the animal. Instead, he lay still and watched the action, silently praying.

The fox chased its enemy to the hillside and out of sight, but Lionel wondered if the snake was really gone. He had always heard that snakes don't attack people unless you enter their territory, but he'd never believed it.

He closed his eyes and took a breath. Though he hadn't moved, the excitement of the encounter had raised his heart rate. His skin glistened with sweat, and the cool air of the early morning gave him a chill.

The fox returned, sniffing at the air by the rock and licking its paws. The animal was thin and wiry, and Lionel could see its hipbones sticking out. The fox didn't pay attention to Lionel, as if this heroic act were a normal part of its day.

"Hey, boy, thanks for the help," Lionel whispered.

The fox looked up. Lionel expected it to bolt, but it just stared at him. Lionel picked up the sandwich, and the fox darted backward toward the hill, then slowly sniffed at the air.

"I have something for you, if you want it. It's not

much, but it's all I have. You want it?" Lionel held out the
sandwich, hoping the fox would approach.

Instead, it sat, studying the food and the teenager. It
put its front paws on the ground and stretched.

Suddenly, Lionel felt a wave of pain and nausea.
Whether it was the adrenaline rush of the encounter with
the snake or too much blood loss he couldn't tell, but he
felt tired and cold. He draped the backpack over him just
before he lost consciousness.

Vicki talked with Marshall by phone, the man giving
instructions for what they should do. Mark was driving to
the midwife's house, and they were still a few miles away.
"Make Cheryl as comfortable as possible," Marshall said.
"We'll call as soon as we find her."

"Her water broke, and she's feeling a lot of pressure,"
Vicki said.

Marshall paused. "So she's further along than we
thought. Okay, Wanda doesn't use a phone, but she
might be by her computer. Write her."

Vicki found the address for the midwife and quickly
wrote a message, asking if there was anything more they
could do for Cheryl. As she waited, Vicki noticed reports
about miracle workers from around the world. These
were the new breed of Nicolae's messiahs, changing water
to wine, healing the sick, and doing various magic tricks
to confuse the world.

A return message from Wanda came a few minutes
later.

Your friend is going to want to push, but don't let her. The passage the baby has to come through has to dilate—or open up enough for the baby's head to come through. There's a chance she could be ready, but from what you've said I doubt it. I can tell you how to check, but I'd rather be there. Get a watch and figure out how many minutes between contractions. Your friends in the car should be close to me. If they have a phone, I'll call you from the road.

Wanda

Vicki borrowed Conrad's watch and hurried back to Cheryl. When a contraction came, her stomach tightened, she closed her eyes and grabbed whatever was near. The first contraction lasted about forty-five seconds. Vicki pressed the stopwatch button and counted.

One minute.

Josey put another pillow behind Cheryl and encouraged her to relax until the next contraction.

Two minutes.

Vicki watched the timer count up, praying more time would pass before the pain began again.

Three minutes.

Shelly took Vicki's arm in hers. "Are you ready to become Aunt Vicki?"

Vicki forced a smile. "Aunt Vicki is fine. I'm just not ready for Dr. Vicki."

"Ow, ow, ow!" Cheryl screamed. "Here it comes again!"

Vicki glanced at the watch. Three minutes, twenty-eight seconds.

Lionel opened his eyes slowly. It was still dark, but he had no idea how long he had been asleep. Five minutes? An hour? A slight wind blew from the east and he shivered.

The fox was close, sniffing at the sandwich in Lionel's hand. Lionel remained still and watched the animal inch forward like a hungry pup. It licked at the peanut butter and backed away, then moved forward again and took a bite. When it came back for more, Lionel let go, and the fox pulled the sandwich near the rock and devoured it.

"Hope you enjoy that," Lionel whispered. "You deserve it."

Lionel felt strangely comforted by the animal and wondered if God had sent it. Could an angel appear as a fox? He shook his head. The loss of blood was even affecting his theology.

Lionel tried to think of a verse that applied to his situation. There was something in the Psalms about God being a refuge in times of trouble. In other places it described God as a rock, but Lionel didn't want to think about that. He reached for his left arm again and noticed the blood was almost dry. The tourniquet had worked.

He sipped some water and watched the fox lick its lips. The sandwich was gone, and there was nothing to keep the animal near. Still, it stayed, and Lionel was grateful.

As soon as Judd had gotten past the hill and the stream, he quickened his pace and ran toward Salem over the path they had followed. Normally, he and Lionel watched the compass and headed northwest, making sure they stayed in the woods or other places with few people. The jog back seemed unfamiliar, but Judd knew he was going in the right direction. When he finally reached the edge of town, he got his bearings and headed for the hideout.

Judd prayed for Lionel as he ran. What had begun as the last leg of their journey had turned into a nightmare. In the past few months two of his friends had died at the hands of the Global Community. Chang Wong, his contact in New Babylon, constantly lived under the pressure of being watched inside Nicolae Carpathia's palace. The farther Judd ran, the angrier he became at Carpathia, GC Peacekeepers, Morale Monitors, bounty hunters, and Satan himself.

Judd stopped by a tree a hundred yards from the hideout and caught his breath. He realized he was angry, not just at the evil around him but also at God for allowing it. The whole thing was somehow part of God's plan, but Judd didn't understand it.

A sudden flash in the distance caught his attention. Judd studied the landscape in the moonlight and figured it was the reflection of headlights on a window. He moved into the open pasture, angling toward a barn and running close to the ground.

A single beam of light swept over the field. Judd hit the ground immediately and rolled, trying to find a low point. The beam swept over him just as he spun into a dip in the field.

Judd wondered who would be out at this time of night. He waited a few minutes, listening for voices, but only heard cars in the distance. When enough time had gone by, he peeked toward the light but saw nothing. He rose and darted toward the barn. Suddenly, a radio crackled and Judd's heart sank. He reached the barn and put his back flat against the outside wall. He was in shadows and felt safer, but he had to get a look at the safe house.

He crept through shadows inside the barn. Though it still smelled of hay and animals, it was empty, save for an old hay baler and some rusted plows. He climbed into the loft, the soft moonlight shining through the weathered boards.

Judd pressed his face close to a hole and spotted the farm machine shop where he and Lionel had stayed. Several men stood at the side of the building. An orange glow appeared, and Judd realized a few people were smoking.

No one at the hideout smokes, Judd thought, *and they wouldn't be outside anyway.*

Judd had a bad feeling the safe house wasn't so safe. He looked out another opening in the barn and spied an old tractor parked a few yards away. Judd wanted to find help for Lionel, but he had to make sure his friends at the safe house were okay.

Within a few minutes after finishing the sandwich, the fox left. Lionel felt more alone than ever. He nearly cried when the little red animal turned and headed into the woods.

"Okay, Lord," Lionel prayed aloud, "you were good enough to send me someone to keep me company and chase that snake away. Now I need somebody strong enough to lift this rock."

The crickets and frogs lulled Lionel back to sleep.

Judd crawled the final few yards to the abandoned tractor and hid behind its massive wheel. He counted five men by the door to the safe house. They kept quiet, looking out at the field.

Finally, a man in a GC uniform approached, and the men stood at attention. "Commander Fulcire wants you to know you'll be rewarded for your actions tonight," the Peacekeeper said. "Because of your alertness, we were able to detain a number of unmarked citizens tonight."

The group applauded, then whooped again when they heard they would divide the bounty for each of the citizens equally.

"Though the prisoners wouldn't give information before they were . . . uh, taken care of," the Peacekeeper said, "we believe the first report to be true. There are two more heading north, and if you'd like to be part of that search party, follow me."

After the group went inside the former safe house, Judd caught his breath. Someone had seen Lionel and him leaving the safe house. Judd had to throw these men off the track and get help to Lionel before they found him. But how?

Judd duckwalked to the GC cruiser, reached through the open window, and grabbed the microphone to the radio. "All GC Peacekeepers, repeat, all GC Peacekeepers," Judd said in an official tone, "we have an alert of two unmarked citizens now crossing Highway 56, just east of town. These may be the two spotted earlier. Out."

Judd threw the microphone into the car and hustled back to his hiding place. The men poured from the building followed by the Peacekeeper who tugged at the microphone on his shoulder.

"Verify that last transmission," the Peacekeeper said.

The radio remained silent, but already the men had jumped in their cars and were racing toward the highway. Judd didn't know how long he had before they figured out his call was a hoax, but he knew he had to look for help somewhere else. He glanced at the sky. Only a few more hours before daylight.

Vicki counted the minutes between contractions. A few came within two minutes of each other, while others came five minutes or more apart. Cheryl grew weaker with each round of contractions, sometimes writhing and shouting in pain. Josey did what she could to keep the girl calm but gave Vicki a worried look. Cheryl was panting, taking in short gasps of air between screams. Josey whispered that Cheryl could pass out from lack of oxygen if she didn't breathe slower.

On the next contraction, Cheryl let out a piercing scream. "I can't take it anymore! I want to push. I have to!"

"Call Marshall," Josey said, holding Cheryl down.

Shelly stood at the foot of the bed. "Guys, look at this!"

Vicki rushed to Shelly's side and gasped. She could see the top of the baby's head in the birth canal.

19

VICKI felt a mix of awe and fear. Her mouth dropped open at the sight of the baby's head, but she nearly fainted when she realized they would have to deliver it alone.

"Calm down," Josey said to Cheryl.

"I can't calm down! I'm about to have a baby!"

"Call Marshall again," Vicki said to Shelly as she moved closer to the bed. The top of the baby's head was hairy.

"Can I push?" Cheryl said.

"Wait," Vicki said. "Wanda told us not to let you—"

Cheryl screamed.

"They've got Wanda," Shelly said, holding the phone.

"Let me talk to her," Josey said.

Vicki was glad someone else was taking charge. She didn't want to be the one caring for the baby. What if she dropped it? She had heard stories of women giving birth in cabs, police cars, and even grocery stores, but she never thought she would see one born in a secret hideout.

"Yes," Josey said, "we can see the top. Okay. Uh-huh. All right."

Vicki stepped aside as Josey examined Cheryl. Vicki put a hand on the girl's shoulder. The last contraction had passed, and another was coming quickly.

"All right, she's ready to push," Josey said.

"I can?" Cheryl said with relief.

"Wanda says to wait until the next one comes, then take a deep breath and push through the contraction."

"I don't know what that means," Cheryl said.

"I'll help you, honey, just relax until—"

"Here it comes!"

Vicki moved to the foot of the bed. When the contraction began, Cheryl took a breath, held it, and closed her eyes. Her face turned red, and Josey told her to take another breath, but the girl kept pushing. Vicki looked down and saw the baby's head move an inch forward.

This is really happening, Vicki thought.

"Shelly, get some of those sterile cloths," Josey said.

"I don't know what to do," Vicki said.

"Just help me encourage Cheryl," Josey said. "You're doing fine."

Vicki found herself breathing and pushing along with Cheryl, her heart beating like a drum. "You're doing great, Cheryl! Good girl! It won't be long now."

The contraction wound down and Cheryl sat back, panting like a dog. Josey wiped her forehead and held the phone to her ear as Wanda gave instructions.

184

Cheryl's eyes widened, and she clutched the bedsheet. "Here comes another one!"

With each gasp of air and each push, the baby's head moved farther forward. Suddenly, Vicki saw the face of the child.

"The head's out!" Josey cried into the phone.

Vicki studied the child. "Its face is blue. Maybe that's normal, but—"

"Here," Josey said, shoving the phone into Vicki's ear.

"Tell me what you see," Wanda said.

Vicki could hardly contain her emotion. She had known Cheryl for several months and had talked with her about the baby, but in all that time of feeling it move, it had all seemed so far away. Now, staring at the child's face, Vicki wiped away tears of joy.

"The little face is pointing up, toward the ceiling," Vicki said, "and its color is kind of blue-green, like the color of your veins, and it's got the cutest—"

"Okay, listen carefully. I want you to put your fingers near the baby's neck. Don't let Cheryl push. Just feel the baby's neck and tell me if there's anything there. Hurry."

Vicki used both hands and felt around the baby's neck. "Yeah, there's something here."

"What's it feel like?"

"I don't know. It's kind of like a big, fat worm. Kind of squishy."

"That's what I was afraid of."

"What?"

"Vicki, we don't have much time. That thing around the baby's neck is the umbilical cord. We have to move it fast."

185

"How?"

"We need to reduce the pressure by easing the cord over the baby's head."

"I don't think I can—"

"You have to," Wanda pleaded. "It may already be too late, but you have to try."

"Okay, but how?"

"Grab the cord with your fingers."

"I'm trying, but I don't want to hurt—"

"Hurry, Vicki! See if you can pull the cord toward you. Does it move?"

"It's slippery."

"What's going on?" Cheryl said. "Is the baby okay?"

"Lie back and rest," Josey said.

"Can you pull it?" Wanda said.

"Yeah, it came forward a few inches, but that's all—"

"Good. That might be enough. Now I want you to take the cord and lift it over the baby's head. Just pull it over right now."

Vicki strained as she grasped the cord. "It's really tight. I'm afraid it's going to—"

"It won't break. Just pull it over. Did you do it?"

"No, it's stuck."

"You have to push it to the other side right now. I don't care how you do it—"

"—this is so scary!"

"—just do it!"

"Please, God," Vicki prayed, "please, God, please, God, please, God!"

Vicki took a step to her left and used both hands.

With the cord tight against the top of the baby's head, she managed to ease it over and down toward its left shoulder. The child kept its eyes closed and didn't move.

"I need to push again!" Cheryl said.

"Is the cord over the head?" Wanda said.

"Yeah, I got it."

"Then tell her to push."

"Go ahead and push," Vicki said.

While Cheryl bore down again, Wanda spoke into Vicki's ear. "Get ready for the little thing to come out pretty quickly. It'll be sort of slick and a little bloody, but you'll be okay. Have someone there get a pair of sharp scissors or a knife and some shoestrings."

"Shoestrings?"

"Don't ask questions. Just do it."

"Take another deep breath," Josey said to Cheryl.

Vicki asked Shelly to get the scissors and more cloths as one of the baby's shoulders came out. Vicki kicked off her shoes and quickly removed the laces as she watched the baby's progress. "How will we know if the baby's okay?"

"Let's just get it out of there first," Wanda said.

Vicki took two of the cloths and held them in front of her. She felt like her dad, who played catcher for their church's softball team. With another push from Cheryl, the baby came sliding out, hands wiggling toward the ceiling. Vicki held the child gingerly, overwhelmed at the sight.

"It's a boy!" Josey said.

"Really?" Cheryl said, sitting up to have her first look at the child. "It's really a boy?"

"Don't hold the baby too low," Wanda said to Vicki. "Hold him about the same height as the bed where the mother is. That way we'll keep the blood flow even."

"Okay," Vicki said. "Now what?"

"Wipe the baby off, and don't hold him like a piece of china. Hold him like you know what you're doing."

Shelly brought scissors while Josey tied Vicki's shoelaces tightly at two spots on the cord.

"Why isn't he crying?" Vicki said.

"Cut the cord," Wanda said.

It took Vicki two tries to cut the umbilical cord. Blood splattered the floor.

"Is something wrong?" Cheryl said.

Josey kept the phone to Vicki's ear as Vicki cleaned the boy off. "Wanda, he's still blue—he's not crying."

"You need to clear the airway," Wanda said. "It could be mucus."

"What do I do?"

"Open his mouth a little and swab it out. Just put your finger in there."

Vicki put her finger near the boy's mouth. The child looked like a doll with his tiny lips and perfect fingers. His nose was flat, but Vicki knew that would change. She cleaned some clear liquid from the child's mouth and held him up with both hands. "Please, God!"

"Now stroke his back with your hand," Wanda said. "Not too hard, but hard enough to get his little lungs going."

Cheryl leaned over and nearly fell out of bed. "Is he going to be okay? Tell me he's going to be all right."

Vicki glanced at Josey. Tears welled in the woman's eyes.

"It's not working," Vicki said, rubbing the baby's back.

"Okay, tip the baby's head back a little to open his airway. His chin should point to the ceiling. Now I want you to do this gently. Vicki, do you understand?"

"Yes, gently." Vicki held the baby in the crook of her left arm and tipped his head back. The child's mouth opened slightly.

"I want you to put your mouth over the baby's nose and mouth and gently blow. Just once, and don't do it hard, very gently."

"Please, God." Vicki placed her lips over the baby's nose and mouth and gave a puff of air. The child's throat gurgled, and Vicki felt his chest move slightly. He arched his back, squinted, and opened his mouth wide.

"What's happening?" Cheryl said.

Before Vicki could answer, a tiny, bubbling cry echoed through the cabin. Vicki shook with emotion. It was the most wonderful sound she had ever heard.

"Oh, thank you, thank you, thank you."

"I heard that," Wanda whooped on the phone. "My watch says 2:23. That'll be the official time of birth, Dr. Vicki."

"Thank you so much for what you did," Vicki sobbed.

"It wasn't me, young lady," Wanda said. "You did everything I asked and more. Congratulations."

"What now?"

"We'll want to keep the baby warm. Unwrap him and put him on the mother's chest, skin to skin. Then cover

189

them with blankets and cloths. The baby may want to nurse, that's good. Also, find something for the baby's head, like a little cap. Most of the heat is lost through the head."

Vicki handed the baby to Cheryl, and the girl snuggled him as Shelly covered them. Wanda gave instructions, and Josey and Shelly cleaned the room.

Vicki answered a knock at the door. Conrad stood with tears in his eyes. "We were listening out here and praying for you. I can't believe what you did."

"Thanks," Vicki whispered.

Charlie stepped forward. Phoenix was just behind him, wagging his tail and whining. "I found some pictures of little babies on the Internet and every one had a little cap on."

Charlie handed Vicki the tops of some floppy, white socks he had cut with scissors and decorated with markers. There were crude stars, moons, and some pictures Vicki couldn't identify.

"Those are the wise men coming to the baby Jesus," Charlie said. "I thought that would be good to put on his first hat."

"It's perfect," Vicki said.

She closed the door and pulled the covers back. The baby slept as she placed the floppy hat on his head and leaned down to kiss the child. "You're lucky you have a lot of people who were praying for you, little guy."

"He's lucky he had you taking care of him," Cheryl said, glowing with joy.

"I'll bet you're glad that's over," Vicki said.

"I'm so thirsty and hungry too."

Josey brought some fruit, water, and bread, and Cheryl ate with her eyes closed. Every few moments she pulled the covers back and looked into the face of her son. "I can't imagine what God must have gone through, giving up Jesus on the cross."

The door opened and Josey led her husband, Tom, into the room. The man smiled at Vicki, then quietly crept to Cheryl's bedside. "I heard it got pretty rough in here."

Cheryl smiled. "Nothing we couldn't handle." She pulled the bundle out from under the covers, and the baby's hat flopped in front of his face. Josey tried to stop her, but Cheryl shifted in the bed, then handed the boy to Tom.

Tom Fogarty was speechless. Josey looked over his shoulder and smiled, pulling the hat out of the boy's face. The child's eyelids scrunched tightly together, and Vicki noticed little white spots, like pimples, on his small, flat nose.

"Mr. Fogarty, I want you to meet your son, Ryan Victor."

"My son?"

"And let Mom hold him when you're finished," Cheryl said.

Vicki hugged Cheryl and wept. She couldn't wait to call Judd and tell him the good news.

JUDD'S mind raced as he prowled through the neighborhood, running away from the safe house. The believers who had helped him and Lionel were either dead or on the run—he knew that from the Peacekeepers' conversation.

"God, I don't know what to do," Judd prayed. "Give me some kind of sign."

He stayed away from streetlights while he walked, wondering when someone would discover him. He was a marked man without the tattoo of Carpathia and instant cash for any citizen who caught him.

Judd walked more than a mile until he came to a main road leading to town. He and Lionel had avoided such places the past few months, but now he knew he had to take the risk.

He spotted a blue sign with an *H* in the middle. Medical help. No matter what he did for Lionel, it would be worthless to simply get him out from under the rock without treating his arm. A plan slowly formed in Judd's mind as he ran toward the hospital.

Lionel awoke to a chirping noise. At first he thought it was some kind of bird, maybe a vulture. Then he realized it was the cell phone and smiled.

The night had turned colder, and in his sleep Lionel had tucked his right arm under him for warmth and had drawn his legs up toward his body. A soft breeze blew through trees, and Lionel smelled rain. *Great, that's all I need. The stream will rise and I'll drown.*

Lionel grabbed the phone on the third ring and answered.

"Lionel? It's Vicki."

Vicki's voice cheered him, and Lionel explained that Judd had left the phone and had gone for help.

"How are you?" Vicki said. "Judd told me a little about what happened."

"There's not much to tell. I've got this big rock on my arm, and I can't move. I've had a couple of animal visitors in the night, but that's about all. How's Cheryl?"

"She's doing well. She had the baby." Vicki described what had happened with Ryan Victor.

Lionel was astonished. "Hey, if you can deliver a baby and save his life, you could probably help me out. You want to come down here?"

"You don't know how much I'd give to do that. Are you in a lot of pain?"

"Only when I move." Lionel smiled, then thought about Chang's news of the safe house raid. He decided not to worry Vicki. "I'm really cold, but as soon as Judd gets back I'll be fine."

Vicki paused. "What if Judd doesn't come back?"

"He wouldn't leave me here."

"I know, and I don't want to think about this, but what if he runs into trouble? There's enough GC and vigilantes to catch all of us."

"Is this your way of cheering me up? I don't think Florence Nightingale would have done it this way."

Vicki chuckled, then grew serious. "I'm saying this for your own good. You have to think about what to do in the worst case."

"You don't understand. There's nothing I can do. God's going to have to swoop down and roll this stone away, preferably not on the rest of me."

"Maybe there's somebody else in the area you could call."

"Yeah, I'll just try the Yellow Pages. Come on, Vicki. I'm stuck. The only other thing I could do is get my pocketknife out and . . ."

"What?"

"Nothing. I was just trying to be funny."

"I had Conrad put out a message on the Web site—"

"No. I don't want to alert the GC."

"We didn't give your location. We just put out an SOS so people could pray."

The phone began to break up. "Looks like the phone is running low. It'll recharge once the sun comes out. I'll call you the minute I hear anything from Judd. Okay?"

"All right. But call me at first light."

Lionel hung up and put his head back on the ground. He reached for his arm and found the blood crusted and dry. That was the good news. The bad news was that everything was swollen. Lionel knew he risked infection, but he had no medicine and no way to treat the wound.

The conversation with Vicki had given him an idea, as far-fetched as it seemed. He could use his pocketknife—

No, things would have to get a lot worse for him to consider that.

Lionel set his jaw and closed his eyes. Judd was coming back. He would find a way to get the rock off, treat his wound, and they would keep going. He might lose the use of that arm, but he'd rather be alive than dead.

Judd would come back. That was the plan, and Lionel chose to believe it. Judd had to come back.

The hospital was a series of buildings that had survived the wrath of the Lamb earthquake. It was nearly 4 A.M. when Judd reached the darkened parking lot. He noticed a section for staff and saw a row of expensive autos. These were no doubt doctors' vehicles, and at the end, taking up two parking spaces, was a sleek-looking Humvee. The thing had to cost more Nicks than all the nurses were paid in a year.

Judd looked for a security camera but didn't see one. He spotted a night watchman at the front of the emergency room and carefully tiptoed to the back of the first building. He had no plan, other than to somehow get help for Lionel. The sight of the Humvee made him think the vehicle might have a jack that would lift the rock, but how would he get medicine?

Judd peeked in a window in the back and saw a nurse in scrubs at a small desk. The blinds were pulled at the next few windows. Then Judd came upon a patient room with two beds. Only one was occupied.

The door opened and a man who looked to be in his late thirties entered. He pulled the chart at the end of the bed, looked it over, then examined the male patient. "I'd say you were pretty lucky tonight," the doctor said, shining a light in the man's eyes. "Those Judah-ites can be pretty ornery."

"Yeah, and to think there was a nest of them right in our own town," the patient said.

"I think this knock on your head's nothing to worry about, but we're going to keep you a few more hours. I'm headed out, but Dr. Parker will be here in a few minutes. He'll take care of you."

Judd ducked as the doctor left the room. If the shift was changing, doctors and nurses would be going home. Judd made a quick decision and headed for the parking lot.

Vicki heard the van and snapped awake. Wanda was inside the cabin examining Cheryl and the baby before Vicki wiped the sleep from her eyes. Wanda was older, with graying hair and a sagging face. There were bags under her eyes, and wrinkles everywhere, but there was something fresh about her—she seemed to light up the room as she did her work. Cheryl pointed at Vicki and Wanda turned, the mark of the true believer on the woman's forehead.

"So this is the young lady with the future in medicine," Wanda said, smiling and hugging Vicki. She kissed Vicki's cheek and took a step back. "You're a pretty little thing. You're sure you didn't go to medical school?"

Vicki giggled. "I actually didn't even make it out of high school."

"Well, you did excellent work with Cheryl and Ryan. Both look like they'll be fine. He came a little early and doesn't weigh much, but if he eats right, he should fill out in no time. He's also a little jaundiced."

Vicki furrowed her brow. "What's that?"

"It's common. You can tell by the skin. See, it's yellow. Best thing to do is put Ryan in the sunlight and let him sleep. You don't want him to get burnt, but the sun's rays start . . . well, all you need to know is that he needs to be in the sun a couple of hours a day."

Vicki yawned and Wanda told her to get some sleep. "I'll still be here when you wake up."

"Good," Vicki said. "I have a lot of questions, and I'd love to hear your story. We don't get many visitors, except for the ones who come to see Zeke."

Wanda smiled. "Get some rest."

Judd found a small piece of pipe on the ground and slid under the Humvee, watching from the shadows as a few workers exited the hospital. He was careful not to touch the car and set off an alarm. He waited nearly thirty minutes, watching cars arrive and people in uniforms rush inside. Just as he was about to give up, the Humvee chirped and the engine started.

Judging from the shoes and the way the person walked toward the vehicle, Judd guessed it was a man. Maybe a doctor. When the man came around the back of the vehicle, Judd scooted out and caught up to him as the door opened. The man wore a white jacket and had a stethoscope draped around his neck.

"Hey," Judd said as he sprang from the shadows.

The man threw his hands in the air. "My wallet's in my back pocket. I've only got about fifty Nicks but you can have—"

"Put your hands down. I don't want your money. Get in."

The man turned slowly. "Look, buddy, don't shoot. If you're looking for drugs—"

"Don't turn around. Just get inside. I don't want to hurt you."

After the man got inside, Judd opened the back door quickly and slid in. "We're driving out of here and to the back of the hospital, not past the guard, got it?"

"Yeah, but I hope you don't want me to go inside. You can't get in that way."

Judd knew Lionel needed medicine, but there was no way he could enter through the front. Judd's eyes landed on the rearview mirror. The man stared at Judd, the mark of Carpathia clear on his forehead. It was the same doctor he had seen through the window.

"Tell me what you want. Maybe I can help."

"A friend of mine's hurt. His arm is trapped under a rock."

"Where?"

"I can't tell you his location—"

"No, where on the arm?"

"Just below the elbow. The rock's huge. I put a tourniquet on him to stop the bleeding."

"How long has he been there?"

Judd looked at his watch. "A few hours."

"And he was conscious when you left him?"

"Yeah, he was talking, and I told him I'd be back before sunup."

The man put the vehicle in gear and backed out.

"Hey, where are you going?" Judd said.

"Duck your head so the guard doesn't see you. The windows are tinted, but if you pass a lighted area people can still see inside. I have some medical supplies at my house. We'll go there and then to your friend."

Judd shoved the pipe into the back of the seat. "Okay, but remember I have this."

The doctor drove by the guard, and Judd relaxed a little. He was tired, hungry, and thirsty.

"Looks like you have a few scratches yourself," the doctor said. "Anybody look at those?"

"I'm okay."

"Patrick Rose," the doctor said, reaching back.

Judd hesitated, then shook the man's hand. "I'm Judd."

The doctor glanced back, and Judd pulled away.

"Look, I can tell you're not a hoodlum. I don't think you're going to rob me, and I believe your story about your friend, so relax. I'm going to help you."

"What are you going to do?"

"We'll get some meds, then find him."

"Does this car have a jack?"

"I'm sure it does, but I've never seen it. The dealer sends someone out if I blow a tire, but I've only had this a few months. You can look for the jack while I get my black bag."

"I'll be going with you into the house."

"Suit yourself."

"Are you married?" Judd said.

The doctor raised his left hand. He wore no ring. "Not anymore. I lost my wife a few years ago."

They drove through a residential area and came to a house with an unattached garage. Dr. Rose stopped the car and held up his hands. Judd told him to put his hands down and stepped in behind him.

Traces of light shone on the horizon as the man put a key in the front door and opened it. Judd followed, looking at the gourmet kitchen with pots and pans hanging from the ceiling. Counters glistened when Dr. Rose hit the light switch. The refrigerator looked big enough to hold food for an army.

Judd was distracted and didn't hear the soft padding of feet down the hall. Dr. Rose turned, smiling. "I want you to meet Princess."

Something growled in the hallway, and a huge dog stepped into the light.

21

JUDD took a step back and stared at the dog. It was a Great Dane mix and looked like a horse. The dog snarled, the hair on its back standing up straight. Judd had confronted dogs before, but he had never faced an animal this big.

"If I were you, I'd take your hands out slowly and stay very still," Dr. Rose said. "Princess doesn't like unannounced company. In fact, she doesn't like company at all."

"I have a gun," Judd said shakily.

"No, you have a pipe. I saw it in the car. Now drop it or I'm going to order Princess to—"

At the sound of her name, Princess perked up her ears and Judd interrupted the man. "No! Don't say it." The pipe clanged on the polished, wooden floor.

The dog sniffed the pipe and nudged it with her nose. Judd remained still, glancing at the back door.

"Sit down," Dr. Rose said. "Slowly. I'll get you something to eat. You up for eggs? I make a mean omelette."

"I don't have time. I have to get back to my friend."

Dr. Rose opened the refrigerator and pulled out some food. In a few moments he had the burners going and was whipping eggs in a metal bowl.

"I noticed you don't have the mark," Dr. Rose said. Judd sat silently watching Princess. "That could mean you've had no contact with civilization for a while, or it could mean you're an enemy of the Global Community. A Judah-ite, perhaps."

"I'll never take Carpathia's mark."

Dr. Rose mixed ingredients and poured eggs into a hot skillet. The smell of food cooking seemed like heaven, but Judd was prepared to jump and run.

"You'll eventually die, you know. They'll catch you and lop off your head."

"Carpathia's mark means a worse death than they could ever put me through."

Dr. Rose pushed the omelette onto a plate and put it in front of Judd. He noticed Princess had turned her attention to the eggs, thick drops of saliva running from both jowls. Dr. Rose fixed another omelette, cut off a large chunk, and tossed it to Princess. She caught it and swallowed it with one gulp.

"It keeps her coat nice and shiny," Dr. Rose said.

Judd felt guilty about eating, but the food looked so good and he was so hungry that he dived in. Nothing had ever tasted better.

The man opened the refrigerator and pulled out a carafe of orange juice. Because of Judd's life in the underground, he hadn't tasted juice for a long time. The sweet drink stung his stomach as he drained the glass.

"So, are you a Judah-ite?"

"What difference does it make? If I don't have the mark you can take me to the GC and get your reward."

Dr. Rose glanced around the kitchen. "Does it look like I need money?"

"You're not going to turn me in?"

Dr. Rose took a mouthful of food and sat back. "I became a doctor so I could help people. And I've never been impressed with Nicolae, though he did bring sanity when the world fell apart. Coming back from the dead was nothing short of a medical miracle, but I can see through the act."

"You don't think Nicolae is god?"

"Maybe he is. Maybe he isn't. At the end of the day, it doesn't do much for my patients. Which brings us to your friend."

Judd glanced out the window as the sun rose through the clouds.

Lionel shielded his face from the light rain with his hand. He had finally gotten more comfortable when the soft pattering of drops struck his face. He pulled the backpack over his face as the rain came harder.

Lionel's watch was on his left wrist, beneath the rock. He had the urge several times in the night to check the time, and he had even tried to look at it before remembering he couldn't.

Lionel glanced behind him and saw the cell phone in a puddle of water. He grabbed it, tried to dry it off, and stuck it in the backpack. He wanted to call Vicki, but that would have to wait.

Lionel thought again about the fox and the snake. Had that been a dream? It had seemed so real, but he knew his mind could play tricks.

"God," Lionel prayed, "I know Judd would have come back if he could, so he's either trying to get to me, or the GC have him. I trust you to help him. You are our strength."

Lionel thought about his prayer. God was his *strength*. It would take God's power to move the stone. *Unless* . . .

Maybe the reason God hadn't sent an angel or brought Judd back was because God wanted Lionel to act. Did God want to show his strength through Lionel's weakness?

Lionel reached in his pocket and pulled out the knife. It was the one his father had given him as a birthday present when he was thirteen. The bounty hunters in South Carolina almost took it away, but he managed to get it back. Lionel opened the main blade and ran his finger along the edge. Was it sharp enough?

"God, I need you to make it clear whether I should wait for Judd or do something else."

Judd couldn't understand why Dr. Rose was acting like a friend. Could Judd trust anyone with the mark of

Carpathia? The man's eternal destiny was sealed, so there was no sense explaining the truth of God and the Bible. And yet, the man didn't seem concerned that Judd was an enemy of the Global Community.

Judd explained Lionel's injury, and with each bit of information Dr. Rose became more concerned. Judd told him about the tourniquet and what his arm looked like.

"He needs attention right now," Dr. Rose said, "but I don't think trying to lift that rock is going to do much. You may have saved his life with the tourniquet, but if he's exposed for too long, things could get bad."

"He could lose the arm?"

"He's already lost it. The question is whether the rest of him will survive."

Judd felt sick. Lionel's injury was Judd's fault. If only he hadn't sat on that boulder.

"I'll get my stuff and you can show me the way," Dr. Rose said.

"Why are you helping me? You're just endangering yourself, and for what?"

"I figure, if you've made it this far, and if you're willing to risk your life for your friend, you deserve a chance. The GC may catch you. That's none of my business. My job is to help anybody I find who's hurt."

Judd stared into the man's eyes. *What other choice do I have?*

"I'll get my stuff and meet you in the car."

Judd stood from the table and froze as Princess growled.

"Princess, sit," Dr. Rose said.

The dog sat.

"Princess, friend."

The dog cocked his head, and Dr. Rose said the word *friend* again. To Judd's surprise, Princess stood on her hind legs, put her front paws on Judd's shoulders, and licked his face.

A few minutes later, Judd and the doctor were in the Humvee, heading for the woods. Judd asked to use the man's phone and dialed Lionel. It rang but there was no answer.

Dr. Rose turned on the radio to a GC report of a midnight raid on Judah-ites. He quickly switched it off.

"Before we got to your house, you mentioned you had a wife," Judd said, breaking the silence. "What happened to her?"

"She disappeared. She was carrying our first child."

"Were you with her at the time?"

Dr. Rose shook his head. "I was at the hospital. The whole place was crazy that night. Women with babies disappearing from their wombs. Patients freaking out because their roommates had vanished. Nurses were gone. The security guard's clothes were in a pile outside the emergency room.

"We started getting accident victims after that. Car accidents, that kind of thing. I called the house in the morning, but there was no answer. I figured my wife had gone to see her family, but they didn't answer either. I got home about three the next afternoon. Her car was in the garage, but she wasn't at the house. I finally found her nightgown in the bed upstairs. She was gone."

"What do you think happened?"

Dr. Rose shook his head. "I've heard all the theories, but it doesn't matter. They're not coming back."

"I know where they are."

Dr. Rose rolled his eyes. "Are you sure you want to risk preaching to me? I might turn you in."

Judd pointed the way past the safe house.

After a few moments the doctor turned. "All right, tell me. Where do you think they are?"

"First, I'll guess about your wife. She was religious, right?"

"Not until the last few months."

"Something happened that changed her, and she wanted you to change too."

Dr. Rose shrugged. "I guess you could put it that way."

"And the same thing happened to her family."

"Her mom and dad were already religious wackos. Teri just bought into it a little late. How did you know?"

"It fits," Judd said. "It's because they believed the same thing about Jesus that they were taken."

"Right. And if you know all this, why are you still here?"

"My family was taken just like your wife and unborn baby."

"I'm sorry."

"I'd heard about God all my life. I never really took it seriously. Now I'm trying to tell as many as I can about the truth."

"What truth?"

"That God loved you enough to die for you. That he made a way to come to him through his Son, Jesus."

"Yeah, Teri listened to a Jesus station on the radio," Dr. Rose said, furrowing his brow. "So what happens to us? Will we ever see them again?"

Judd pursed his lips. "Those who accept the gift God offers will see those who disappeared again. That's one of God's promises."

Dr. Rose slammed on his brakes and slid to the right. Judd wore a seat belt, but he still went flying forward.

"That's what frosts me about you people. You're so sure about everything, and it's all in the future. Someday you'll do this, and someday God's going to make everything better. At least Carpathia does stuff for us right now."

"Carpathia is the enemy of God. Those who follow him and take his mark—"

"What? They don't have a chance at your little after-death party?" He shifted and pulled back onto the road.

Judd recognized the street and some of the buildings. They were close to the turnoff where they would find Lionel. Judd didn't want to anger the doctor, but he didn't feel right about keeping quiet. "I'm telling you straight what I believe. I don't want you to get mad and turn me into the GC—"

"If I wanted to do that, believe me, your head would already be rolling on the ground." He paused. "What's your Bible say about me?"

Judd took a breath. "Taking the mark of Nicolae and worshiping his image means you've made your choice."

Dr. Rose gritted his teeth, but before he could speak, his beeper went off. He studied the number as he drove. "This could be a problem."

He pulled the Humvee to the roadside and dialed a number. "This is Dr. Rose. . . . Yes . . . okay, but listen, I'm on an emergency. . . . No, I understand. I'll be right there." He threw the car into gear and made a U-turn, cutting off an oncoming car.

"What's going on?"

"Emergency at the hospital. Some rebels ambushed a high-ranking GC official. They need me to patch him up."

"Can't somebody else do it?"

"Head of the hospital picked me and wouldn't take no for an answer."

"What about Lionel?"

"So that's his name, huh? Lionel will have to hold out until we can get to him." Dr. Rose scowled. "Of course, if we don't get to him in time, God'll just take him to heaven, right?"

22

LIONEL pulled the phone from his backpack and dialed Vicki. He needed to talk through his options with someone he loved. The phone was still wet, and Lionel couldn't see the readout on the phone's face.

"Must need more of a charge," Lionel said, placing the phone on the ground. A cloud moved and the sun peeked through, but the phone was still in the shadow of the rock.

Lionel put his head back. His whole body ached. He had read the verse about Christians being members of a body, and that if one member hurt, the others did too. Lionel felt that verse with his back, neck, and ankle that he had hurt trying to get out of the rock's way. His right hand was scraped and crusted with blood. His hair felt like it was full of ants, though Lionel couldn't tell if bugs were really crawling on him or not.

Lionel pushed the phone as far away as he could, but he couldn't reach the sunshine. *Soon,* Lionel thought, *the sun will move this way and I'll call Vicki.*

Lionel had to think clearly. If Judd didn't return, what would he do? How long could he survive on the food and water left? And how long could he last if the sun beat down on him all day? He looked around for the second sandwich and unwrapped it.

Lionel remembered how his mom cut the edges from his sandwiches when he was little. Now, with his stomach growling, he devoured the crust. He made a quick inventory of his food and found one more sandwich, packages of crackers and potato chips, and a few cookies. He had four small bottles of water. That was enough to keep him going through the day. Judd would be back by evening unless . . .

Lionel watched a cotton-candy cloud float through the sky. He closed his eyes and looked again, studying the shape. It looked like a face, with two eyes and a nose. Suddenly, Lionel saw Nicolae Carpathia's face, the old devil himself looking down. Nicolae looked like he was laughing.

Lionel closed his eyes. More than ever, he knew he was in a battle. From the moment Lionel had prayed to accept Jesus as Lord and Savior, he had stepped into a war, not of flesh and blood, but an unseen battle of good versus evil. Lionel had sensed it early. Satan and his followers must have loved it that Lionel lied to his parents about his faith, but after the disappearances, Lionel knew he had to respond to the truth of the Bible. That decision hurtled him into a daily struggle against the forces of evil.

But Lionel knew no matter how fierce the battle, he

was on the winning side. The evil one would try to get him
to fight with his own friends, whisper things to get him to
doubt, but Lionel had to follow God and listen to him.

Lionel opened his eyes. The cloud was gone and he
was glad. He looked around but saw no sign of the fox or
snake. The rippling stream was soothing, but he also realized he had to go to the bathroom.

A rumbling stirred the peaceful scene. An engine
revved. Was he imagining this or was it real?

Judd remained silent on the trip back to the hospital. He
thought about asking the doctor to let him out, but
someone would spot him in broad daylight. Judd said a
quick prayer and ducked as Dr. Rose pulled into the parking lot. The man turned off the engine and took the keys
from the ignition. "I don't suppose it'd be smart of you to
go inside with me."

"Unless you want to get me killed."

Dr. Rose sighed. "Look, I'm sorry about your friend.
I'll try to make this quick. Will you stay here?"

Judd nodded.

Dr. Rose handed him the keys. "Use these if you need
to put the windows down. Don't take the car. I'll report
you if you do, and the GC will be on you." He got out
and hurried toward the hospital.

Judd sat quietly in the backseat, watching the emergency entrance and counting the number of GC cruisers.
All Dr. Rose had to do was tell one Peacekeeper and Judd
was toast. He didn't like trusting anyone who wasn't a

believer, but there was something about this man that made Judd think he wouldn't turn him in.

Judd wished he could call Vicki. He had promised to get in touch, but Lionel needed the phone more. Judd opened the glove compartment, pulled out the owner's manual, and found a diagram that led him to a storage compartment in the back. He studied the jack, wondering if it would move the giant rock.

Judd put the jack in the backseat and waited. *Am I doing the right thing staying here?*

Vicki awoke around 9 A.M. and asked if anyone had called. Shelly shook her head. Vicki tried dialing Lionel but got a weird ring.

The baby, Ryan Victor, was sleeping when Vicki peeked in on him. Wanda had examined him and trimmed his cord. Cheryl was sleeping, so Vicki held the baby. Wanda paced the room, and Vicki asked if something was wrong.

"The baby's fine," Wanda whispered. "Really healthy, even though he's a little early. He's nursing and getting enough to eat. I'm concerned about the mother. The birth took a lot out of her. If she were in a hospital they'd have given her an IV with lots of fluid. She can't stay awake long enough to eat or drink anything."

"What could that be?"

"Might be that she's just tired. I'm hoping that's all it is and that we'll get her through this." She put a hand on Vicki's shoulder. "You need to motivate her."

"I don't understand."

Wanda sat and patted the bench for Vicki to join her. The baby stuck out his tongue and made a sucking sound, then turned and went back to sleep.

"Cheryl has given the baby to the Fogartys, right?" Wanda said.

Vicki nodded.

"I've seen it happen before. If the mom is weak and something goes wrong, she can lose her will to keep going. For the baby's sake, you've got to help that girl take care of herself. Even if the Fogartys raise him, he's going to need his mother's milk. You can get formula on the black market, but it's pretty difficult to find."

Wanda took the baby from Vicki and explained more about what Vicki should do, and Vicki took notes. Finally, she asked how Wanda had become a believer.

"I was a nurse for a number of years. Then I trained couples about the birthing process. You know, breathing techniques, that stuff. I even went with couples to the hospital and stayed with them when the baby came."

"What made you want to do that?"

"My father was a doctor. He used to talk about the miracle of birth, how every one of them was a gift from God. Delivering babies interested me, but I didn't think God had anything to do with it.

"One night I was helping a couple who had gone through a difficult pregnancy. The mother had been on bed rest for weeks, and the labor was going way into the night. The doctor finally decided they had to do a C-section."

"That's where they operate on the mom?"

"Right. I was there when they took her to surgery. The doctor did a perfect procedure. All the monitors said both the mother and baby were fine. The doctor made the last cut, put both hands around the baby, and lifted her out. I saw the little one's face. The doctor looked at the mother and said, 'You have a beautiful baby girl.' Then the doctor's hands flew into the air, and the baby's umbilical cord dropped to the floor. That child had simply disappeared before our eyes."

"It must have been awful."

Wanda nodded. "The mother started screaming, asking what they had done with the baby. One of the nurses fainted.

"That's when I started thinking more about God and what my father had said. I read my Bible, but it didn't make much sense. I found some answers on the Internet and prayed a prayer they listed. I kept working at the hospital until the wrath of the Lamb earthquake, and then I moved up here to get away from the GC. God brought several pregnant moms to me, and I got sort of a reputation. I'm glad to still be part of bringing little ones into the world, but I have to tell you I don't know what kind of world it's going to be."

"It would be a lot worse for us if you weren't in it."

Wanda cradled the baby and hummed an old hymn. "I used to think my parents were crazy for believing all that stuff about Jesus coming back. I just wish it hadn't taken all that's happened to convince me."

Lionel raised his head as far has he could, shielding his eyes from the sun with his hand. He pushed the bottles of water and food under the rock to keep them cool.

The engine revved again. Could it be Judd? Maybe he's forgotten the way.

Lionel listened as the rumbling stopped, and then he heard voices. Perhaps Judd had made it to the safe house and had gotten help before the GC raid.

Someone whistled and a dog barked. Then another. Lionel's heart sank. He was trapped and the GC was closing in.

Judd rested in the backseat of the Humvee. When it got too hot, he cracked the windows a few inches to let in some fresh air. Throughout the morning, Judd listened to conversations of people passing. Some talked about the expensive vehicles, upset that doctors made so much money. Most discussed their work or things at home.

". . . and it was all over the news about the Judah-ites they caught last night," one woman said.

"I didn't hear about it until this morning," another answered, "but I'm not surprised. There were a lot of them around before the GC started the mark of loyalty, and then they just disappeared. . . ."

Every few minutes, Judd glanced at the hospital to make sure the GC weren't coming for him. He had scouted his escape route if someone came. Judd could jump out and run through a residential section or barrel away in the doctor's Humvee, but that would mean maneuvering out of the parking lot, which Judd didn't think he could do quickly.

He looked at his watch and tapped his foot. Dr. Rose was taking too long.

Lionel lay perfectly still, listening for any movement. He guessed the vehicle rumbling in the distance had stopped because of the trees a few hundred yards away. He hoped the rain had washed away their tracks, but the dogs worried him. Whoever was out there was looking for him or some other rebel.

Rebel. Lionel liked the word. He was a rebel, trying to free the captives. He was a child of the king, on a mission not just to save his own life but also to save others. But how long would he be a rebel?

"God, keep me safe right here," he prayed silently.

Judd was startled at the knock on the window. He had dozed off on the plush seats, and the car felt like it was one hundred degrees.

Dr. Rose opened the front door and hopped in, handing Judd a Styrofoam box. "Here's some lunch from the cafeteria. No guarantees."

Judd glanced at his watch. It was ten minutes after noon! "What took so long?"

"The GC had an accident. From what I can tell, it wasn't caused by rebels, but that's who they're blaming."

"How much longer you gonna be?"

Dr. Rose shook his head. "One of the guys still has internal bleeding. They want me to stay until everybody's stabilized."

Judd slammed the box of food on the seat. "And how long will that take?"

"I told you I don't know. Now you can get mad or work with me. I found out from one of the guys that there's a detail of GC with dogs looking for rebels north of town."

"That's where Lionel is."

"That's what I thought." Dr. Rose scratched his head. "You know, it might be best if they find him. They could bring him back here and let me—"

"You know the first thing they'll do to him," Judd said. "They'll take him to the guillotine. They won't waste a hospital bed for someone they're going to kill."

Dr. Rose got out of the car. "Eat something. I'll be back as soon as I can."

23

LIONEL couldn't see movement above him, but he could hear the searchers getting closer. Radios squawked. A female laughed.

Small rocks skittered down the embankment, and Lionel closed his eyes. The men were right above him on top of the hill. His only chance now was to lay still and keep out of sight. The rock on his arm had trapped him, but it was also hiding him.

"Tell me again what we're supposed to be looking for," a man said with a drawl.

"You know they caught a bunch of Judah-ites under the old feed store," another man said.

"Yep."

"Well, before they took them to the guillotine one of the younger ones told the GC about a couple of guys heading north last night."

"So we're looking for two?"

"Yeah. One black, one white."

So the GC hasn't caught Judd, Lionel thought. *But where could he be?*

Several others joined the two at the top of the hill. A man with a nasally voice took control. From what he heard, Lionel guessed there were a few Peacekeepers and Morale Monitors along with volunteers.

"The dogs haven't picked up anything, but I'm not willing to give up," Nasal Voice said. "From the information we have, the two on the loose were Judah-ites, maybe high up in the so-called Tribulation Force. As you know, there's an extra bounty for those."

Lionel wondered who in the Salem group had talked. He felt sorry for the people who had faced the blade and couldn't blame them for giving information.

"My guess is, we're a little off their trail," Nasal Voice continued.

"Which way, sir?"

Lionel's heart pounded. If the group came down the hill, they would spot him. If they came to the stream they would see him too.

"Our best bet is to get back to the vehicles and push a little farther east where there aren't as many trees. We'll have helicopter support later in the afternoon."

"Maybe a few of us should follow that stream," a man said. "We could spread out—"

"I'll give the orders," Nasal Voice barked, "and we'll stick together and head east. I don't think the Judah-ites would have the guts to try to go through land like this. It's too hard."

Someone threw a rock that landed in the stream behind Lionel. It splashed with a loud *ka-thunk*. The group moved away, and Lionel sighed. They had missed him this time, but a helicopter would surely spot him. He picked up the phone and dialed Vicki's number.

Judd watched the doctor go into the hospital, then opened the Styrofoam box. He found some cold French fries and an even colder grilled cheese sandwich. He shoved a few fries into his mouth, took a bite of the sandwich, and thought of Lionel. If he had remained conscious and hadn't lost too much blood, there was still a chance he was alive. But if the doctor was forced to stay at the hospital, Judd was out of ideas.

He pushed the food away, put his head on the seat in front of him, and prayed.

Vicki was trying to get Cheryl to eat lunch when Shelly brought the phone. "Lionel wants to talk."

Vicki took the phone and walked to the other side of the room. Lionel sounded a little better than before, but something about his voice scared her. He explained what had happened since they last talked. The bleeding had stopped and Lionel felt stronger, but the prospect of the GC being in the woods along with the execution of his friends back at the hideout had terrified him.

"I wanted to talk to you before I go ahead with what I'm about to do," Lionel said.

"I don't understand," Vicki said.

"There's a verse somewhere in the New Testament. It's Jesus talking about it being better for a man to poke out his eyes than for his whole body to go to hell."

"Lionel, stop."

"I can't remember what Jesus was teaching there, but I figure it's better for me to be able to live without my arm than to stay here and die or get caught by the GC."

"Lionel—"

"Please, just listen. I know you care a lot about me. So I have to ask your help."

"I'd do anything for you, but—"

"It's my arm. I've got a pocketknife here, and I think it's sharp enough—"

"Stop it!"

"Vicki, I know it's hard to think about, but this might be my only chance. I have no idea where Judd is—I don't think the GC caught him, but I can't be sure. There's a chopper coming this afternoon, so if I don't get out, they're sure to see me, and you know what they'll do. I have no feeling in my left arm, and I think the bones were crushed."

Vicki felt woozy. Lionel was talking about something so horrible she could hardly listen. But this could be his only chance to live. She tried to put aside the sick feeling in her stomach. "All right. What do you need to know?"

"Is there anyone there who knows about medical stuff? I'm going to need help."

Vicki told him about Wanda. "Her specialty is babies. I'm not sure she could—"

"Put her on."

Vicki quickly explained the situation to Wanda. The woman took a breath and held a hand over the phone. "Even if he does this cleanly, he's going to have to get some medical treatment."

"There's not much chance of that," Vicki said.

"If someone doesn't clean the wound, he could get an infection and die. Plus, he needs—"

"If he doesn't get out, he's going to be dead anyway," Vicki said.

Wanda spoke with Lionel, asking him if he could see any blood or feel any broken bones. Vicki walked out of the cabin and called everyone together. It was time to pray.

Lionel talked with a woman he had never met, asking questions he never thought he would ask, about to do something he never dreamed of doing. In order to save his life, he was going to have to amputate his own arm.

He had heard of mountain climbers doing this, and he had even heard an old radio broadcast once about a man whose leg had been trapped by a falling tree. *It has been done before,* he told himself.

"There's no way you're going to cut through the bone with a pocketknife," Wanda said. "How is your arm positioned?"

"It's turned up, with the elbow pointing toward the ground."

"That's good. Now you're going to have to find a way around the bone. Can you reach your elbow with your right hand?"

Lionel reached under the rock as far as he could. "Just barely."

"Is the arm numb? Pinch yourself, or put the knife blade up to the skin below the tourniquet and see if you can feel anything."

Lionel preferred pinching himself. He used his fingernails but only felt slight pressure.

"All right," Wanda said. "I knew a hunter once who had to do this to his leg."

"What happened to him?"

"He wasn't being chased by the GC like you, but he lived. Last I heard he had taken up fishing." Wanda paused. "Lionel, how far are you from medical help?"

"I don't know. Probably a couple of hours from the town. But finding anybody who would take me in will be the problem."

"We'll pray. Now, if you're ready, I can try and walk you through this."

The clouds were gone, and the sun beat down on Lionel's face. The stream swelled with the night's rain and pushed the edges of its banks. A black bird flew overhead, and Lionel heard the familiar caw of the crow.

In order to perform the procedure, Lionel knew he would have to talk with Wanda, put the phone down, pick up the knife, and continue. "I've always wanted to be a doctor, so here goes."

Vicki couldn't bear hearing Wanda's instructions to Lionel, so she and the others gathered in the main cabin. Phoenix seemed to sense something was wrong, and he whined at the door. Before leaving to join Wanda, Marshall Jameson suggested they pray short, sentence prayers.

"Dear God," Charlie prayed, "I want to ask you to show Lionel exactly what he needs to do to get out from under that rock."

"And, Lord," Darrion continued, "help Wanda know what to say. Give her wisdom."

"Father," Mark said, "you know how much Lionel means to us. I pray you would give him your strength, through your Holy Spirit."

There was a pause, and Vicki heard a few sniffles around the room.

"I can't imagine what Lionel's going through right now," Shelly prayed, "but you are the Great Physician. You answered our prayers for Cheryl and baby Ryan, and now we pray you would help Lionel."

"Nothing happens without you knowing about it," Janie said. "It's hard to even think about, but we put our trust in you, and we give Lionel and his life to you."

Conrad slipped into the room and knelt with the others. When he caught his breath, he prayed, "Father, I know Lionel's started the operation. Guide his hand, and help Wanda and Marshall as they talk to him. Don't let him pass out, Lord, and keep the GC away."

Vicki felt overcome with emotion. She tried to

remember the first time she had seen Lionel. She had heard about him from Lionel's older sister. Clarice had shared a seat on the school bus with Vicki, and Vicki had seen her family's picture, but the day after the disappearances was the first time she had actually met Lionel. She saw him first near New Hope Village Church, Lionel on his bike and Vicki on foot. Lionel had the same features as his sister, a cute face and round nose, but Vicki could tell the boy had been crying that day. They were both scared. Their family members had vanished.

As she thought of the emotion of that day, Vicki brushed a tear from her face and cleared her throat. "Father, I know that as much as we love and care for Lionel, you love him even more. You gave your only Son to die for him. So we ask you to comfort us with that love, and help us not be afraid."

"Give us the chance to help Lionel when he comes back to us," Zeke said.

"Yes, Lord."

"Amen."

Vicki put her head in her hands. Never had she heard the kids pray so strongly or more sincerely. Words came straight from the heart as they pleaded with God to spare Lionel. After a few minutes, the kids didn't pause between prayers, picking up from the last word and continuing in one long petition for Lionel's life. At one point, Josey Fogarty asked the kids to break into groups of two. The room came alive with voices, some shaking with emotion.

As the voices grew louder, the door opened. Vicki looked up and saw Wanda with the phone in her hand.

Marshall walked in beside her. Neither smiled or gave a
hint of what had happened.

Finally, with his chin trembling, Marshall said, "It's
over."

Throughout the afternoon, Judd felt like he was going
crazy. He watched for any sign of Dr. Rose, but he didn't
return. Several times Judd reached for the door handle to
leave or studied the keys, wondering if it was time to
make a getaway, but something told him to wait.

Finally, as evening approached, a figure rushed
through the emergency room exit and headed for the
Humvee. Dr. Rose hopped in, and Judd threw him the
keys. The man squealed his tires on the way out, waving
and smiling at the scowling security guard.

"Did you hear anything from the GC about Lionel?"
Judd said.

"I heard one Peacekeeper say there's a chopper out
there, but I don't know if they found anything."

Judd sighed and rolled his window down a little
to let fresh air in. "Thanks for not sending them to get
me."

"Thank me when you find your friend."

For a second, Judd had the sinking feeling that the
doctor was leading him into a trap. He dismissed the
thought, knowing there was nothing he could do but try
and get to Lionel as quickly as he could.

Judd gave the man directions and ducked when they
saw someone on the street. A GC cruiser flashed his

lights, and Dr. Rose cursed. "Get down in the back and don't say anything."

Judd held his breath as the doctor rolled down his window. He spoke angrily to the patrolman. "I just patched up three of your friends at the hospital—the least you can do is let me go home and get some sleep."

The man went back to his car, then returned, apologizing to the doctor and telling him to have a nice evening.

Dr. Rose pulled away and found the route Judd and Lionel had taken into the woods. Skirting trees and sometimes going over the small ones, the doctor was able to navigate the way in half the time it would have taken them to walk.

As the sun set, they came to an area near the woods with tire tracks. Judd found food wrappers in the dirt and assumed the GC had been there. He grabbed the tire jack and led the doctor to the stream. The two followed it until they came to the hill from the night before. It was the first time Judd had seen it in daylight, and the height of the incline took his breath away. He climbed over some smaller rocks and spotted the boulder that had fallen on Lionel.

"Would you mind waiting here?" Judd said.

"Go ahead."

Judd walked slowly, hoping his friend would still be alive. "Lionel?" he called out.

No answer.

"I brought some help," Judd continued. "You don't

have to worry about that helicopter or any of those Peace-keepers looking for you."

Judd reached the huge rock that held his friend, took a breath, and peeked around the corner. What he saw made him drop the jack and fall to his knees.

24

JUDD stared in disbelief. Lionel was gone—at least his
body was gone. Judd turned away as Dr. Rose raced
forward and knelt by the empty water bottles and blood.

"These are the kind of people you're following," Judd
said with disgust. "They chopped off his arm so they
could drag him away and cut off his head."

Dr. Rose scanned the area. "I don't think the GC did
this."

"How can you defend them?"

"I'm not defending. Look at the ground. The only
footprints here are yours and your friend's."

"Then how—?"

"Either somebody got here before us, or—"

"Or what?"

"Or he did this himself."

"That's impossible. Nobody would be able to . . ."
Judd stopped when he remembered Lionel's pocketknife.
The thought of Lionel cutting off his own arm to escape

sickened him. He looked around for the backpack and the phone, but they were gone.

Dr. Rose followed some footprints and a trail of blood to the edge of the stream. "He's still losing a lot of blood. See the trail? Looks like he walked over to the stream to clean the wound."

"Is that bad?"

"Cleaning it's the right thing, but this water could cause an infection. We need to find him—fast."

Judd waded into the stream and searched for any foot-prints on the other side. "If there were dogs out here, he could have waded in to throw them off his trail."

A sound broke over the trickling of water, and Judd recognized the *thwock-thwock-thwock* of a helicopter. He instinctively ducked, but Dr. Rose pointed east. "They're over there."

Dr. Rose stumbled out of the stream and climbed up the other side of the bank. Judd followed, jumping out of the way of a small water snake. As the chopper moved farther away, the sound grew faint.

The light was fading, and Judd figured they had only a few more minutes of daylight. With their eyes glued to the ground, the two moved by the stream, looking for any sign of Lionel.

Nothing.

Judd was about to turn around and go the other way, but something in the woods caught his eye. "Lionel?" Judd whispered.

It was the most wonderful and terrible sight Judd had ever seen. The young man who had been with him since the start of the Young Tribulation Force—Lionel Washington, the strong, resourceful, solid, and steady member—stumbled out from behind a rock, his right arm held up in a wave, his shirt covered with blood. Judd's belt was still tightly wrapped around what was left of Lionel's left arm.

Judd rushed to his friend and grabbed him as Lionel collapsed.

"I didn't think you were coming back."

"Sorry it took me so long," Judd said through tears. "It's okay. We're here. This is Dr. Rose."

Dr. Rose examined Lionel's arm. "What did you do this with?"

"My pocketknife. A woman on the phone helped me. After I got away from the rock, I think I passed out. I don't know for how long."

"Is he going to be okay?" Judd whispered.

Dr. Rose ignored Judd's question, pulled out a light, and flashed it in Lionel's eyes. He asked Lionel a series of quick questions, then helped Judd carry him back across the stream. "We have to get to the car."

Lionel's head lolled back as they carried him. "You don't have the mark, Doctor. Why not?"

Dr. Rose looked at Judd. "He's not seeing clearly. That concerns me."

Judd winked at Lionel and whispered, "I'll explain in the car."

Lionel floated in and out of consciousness as Judd and Dr. Rose helped move him toward the car. His thoughts swirled in a sea of dull pain. What day was it? Why had this man with the mark of Carpathia come with Judd? Lionel reached to scratch his left hand, then realized it wasn't there.

As they walked along the wooded area he saw the fox. The animal licked its paws, turned its head, and was gone.

When they reached the car, Judd spread a blanket on the backseat and helped Lionel get settled. Dr. Rose handed him three pills. "These will ease the pain."

Lionel put the pills on his tongue and washed them down with a gulp of water. He put his head on the seat and closed his eyes.

Judd wrapped Lionel's injured arm with a piece of fabric torn from a blanket, and Dr. Rose told him how to apply it. Judd pulled the pack off Lionel's back and looked inside. The bloody pocketknife lay at the bottom. Judd clenched his teeth and decided to leave it alone. Instead, he took the phone, also spattered with blood, and called Vicki.

"Lionel?" Vicki answered. "Is that you?"

"No, it's me, Vick. We've got him now."

"Oh, thank you, God!" Vicki said. Her voice muffled as she told the others Judd was calling. "Are you all right?"

"After seeing Lionel, I'll never complain again. I hear somebody with you helped him."

Vicki told Judd what had happened in Wisconsin, and

Judd couldn't believe how God had answered their prayers. Judd explained that he had found a doctor who was going to help Lionel.

"A believer?" Vicki said.

"No. I can't explain right now."

"Judd, how do you know he's not going to take you to the GC and turn you over to them?"

"I don't know that for sure. I'm taking this one decision at a time."

"We'll be praying. Just let us know what happens."

Judd hung up and stashed the phone in his pocket.

Dr. Rose looked in the rearview mirror. "Who was that?" He put up a hand before Judd could answer. "Don't tell me. I don't want to know."

"Some friends of ours we're trying to get back to. It's been a long time."

"I'm not going to be able to take him to the hospital," Dr. Rose said. "First thing they do these days is check for the mark of Carpathia. I'll need to stop there and get some supplies though. Then we can head to my place."

Judd spent a few tense moments in the parking lot, wondering whether the doctor would bring the GC back with him, but the man returned alone, just like he said.

It was dark when they arrived at his house, and they quickly carried Lionel inside. Princess met them at the door and followed them downstairs where they placed Lionel on a pool table. Judd couldn't bear watching the doctor sew Lionel's wound, so he went to the kitchen and flipped on the television to catch up with the latest from the Global Community.

The world was still in awe of the miracle workers. These false messiahs performed miraculous deeds for the sick, diseased, maimed, and disabled. One program featured a collection of video clips from around the world. After a miracle had been performed, the video made sure viewers knew this was all done by Nicolae's power.

Judd switched channels and found live coverage of yet another Z-Van concert. This time Z-Van had taken his crew into a remote country in Africa. As a camera panned the audience, Judd was surprised to see people with no mark on their foreheads. An announcer explained that because of technical difficulties with materials, many in this region had not been able to take Carpathia's mark.

Though people in the audience could not understand the man's words, Z-Van screamed his lyrics, pranced, danced, and flew over the stage. When he soared into the air with his demonic message, the crowd seemed mesmerized. A huge hologram of Nicolae appeared and spoke a message in the local language. Judd was about to turn the coverage off when a camera jerked wildly away from Z-Van and tilted. The producer quickly cut to another camera that focused on people in the crowd. Instead of enjoying Z-Van's show, they seemed upset, pointing at the sky and shrieking.

Finally, the screen showed a wide shot of the scene. Z-Van stood cowering on the stage. Musicians ran for their lives. A man stood several yards from the microphones, but it was clear everyone in the crowd heard him.

"My name is Christopher," the man said, "and I come to you on behalf of the true and living God."

Princess darted into the kitchen, the hair on her back standing on end.

Christopher explained the gospel and told people they should ask God's forgiveness for their sin. "That forgiveness is offered through God's only Son, Jesus Christ."

Another angel, Nahum, appeared next to Christopher and warned of the coming fall of Babylon. He urged people not to take the mark of Carpathia, that it would mean death to their souls. "Anyone who accepts the mark of the beast and worships his image seals their fate for all eternity."

"Accept the mercy of God now," Christopher said.

It was clear to Judd that people working behind the scenes were frantically trying to get the program off the air. Z-Van paced the stage like a caged lion, sneering at the angels who didn't seem to notice him. As Christopher led a prayer, people near the stage prayed and received the mark of the true believer. Judd closed his eyes and gave thanks that God was still working.

"What are you watching?" Dr. Rose said.

Judd stood, frightened by the voice. "Just a concert." He turned the TV off. *What do I talk with this man about now?*

Dr. Rose grabbed a beer from the refrigerator, popped the top, and leaned against the kitchen counter. "Your friend is pretty shaken. I cleaned and dressed the wound. It's not going to look as nice as if I'd done it at the hospital, but he'll live."

"Thanks. I-I know you took a risk helping us."

"That's what a doctor's supposed to do, right?"

"Not a loyal doctor for the Global Community. Your first duty is to help Nicolae rid the world of people like me."

Dr. Rose frowned. "Yeah, maybe I just added to the human pollution."

"Where should I go with him? We can't stay here."

"No, you can't." The man rubbed his eyes, and Judd remembered how long they had both been awake. "Your friend needs to be in the hospital for a few days, but since we can't arrange that, I'd suggest you get on that phone and find someplace for both of you. Without the proper attention, the arm could get infected. He could still die if you're not careful."

Dr. Rose walked to the stairway leading to his bedroom and turned. He took a long drink and stared at Judd. "You really think you know where my wife and baby are?"

Judd nodded.

Dr. Rose pointed to the mark on his forehead. "And because of this I'm not going?"

Judd pursed his lips and nodded again.

"I don't get it. I've tried to help people. You'd think God would take that into account."

"It's not about doing good things."

Before Judd could explain more, the doctor moved into the shadows. "I guess I had my chance." His voice cracked as he spoke again. "Do me a favor, would you?"

"If I can."

"Assuming you make it to where my wife and baby are, would you tell her I love her?"

The man's voice trailed off, and he whispered something Judd couldn't hear. It was clear he was in despair, and Judd wanted to say something to make him feel better, but what? What could he say to someone facing eternal separation from God and the people he loved?

Dr. Rose picked up the phone and dialed a number. "Judy, it's Pat. I'm taking a couple of days off. I really need to be away. Don't try my beeper or phone." He put the phone down, climbed the stairs, and Princess followed, whimpering. The door closed.

Judd grew tired. He found a pillow in the living room and carried it to the stairs leading to the basement.

The gunshot startled him. It came from Dr. Rose's bedroom. He dropped the pillow and took the stairs three at a time. Judd stopped at Dr. Rose's door and shook his head. He didn't look inside. He knew what he would find.

25

LIONEL awoke with a headache and for the hundredth time reached for his forehead with the left hand that was no longer there. Several times during the day he reached to scratch his arm or pull it across his body, but he grabbed nothing but air.

He opened his eyes and tried to get used to the low light in their new hiding place. After moving Dr. Rose's body, Judd had used the man's computer to communicate with Chloe Steele. Chloe had found a safe house for them across the Ohio border where one of the members was a family doctor. The trip had been traumatic for Lionel. He had lost more blood, and some of the stitches had come out as Judd took back roads and cut across fields with the Humvee. But they had rendezvoused successfully with the new group, and the doctor had put Lionel on strict bed rest.

The safe house was dug into the earth at a historical

site that had been all but forgotten by the Global Community. Most historical sites had been changed to somehow include Nicolae Carpathia and the Global Community. This one had been declared a disaster after the wrath of the Lamb earthquake, but the people there had fixed it up and used it to treat sick and desperate believers. The addition of the Humvee was welcomed, and Judd and Lionel felt good that the vehicle would be used for something positive.

Because of the way the safe house was situated, not many people came and went for fear of GC raids. And with what had happened in Indiana, the last thing Judd and Lionel wanted to do was be responsible for tipping the GC off.

Vicki had protested the decision, saying they could drive from Wisconsin and pick up Lionel and Judd, but even she had finally admitted that wasn't practical. Driving near any populated area, no matter what time of day, was dangerous for anyone without Carpathia's mark. Lionel felt bad they were still separated, and as the days wore on and his health improved, he longed to go north, not just to see Vicki, Mark, and the others, but also to find Zeke and see if the man could fit him with some kind of device for his missing arm.

Lionel not only regained his strength but also learned to function with only one hand. Eating wasn't a problem since Lionel could use one hand with most of the food. The doctor and everyone else in the new safe house had been amazed at what Lionel had done.

Their routine was much the same as other safe houses

they had visited. During the day, people tried to sleep and stay quiet. At night, people used outdated computer connections to plan their next supply shipments with the Tribulation Force Co-op.

"When do you think we'll head north?" Lionel asked Judd a few weeks after they had arrived.

"I want you at 100 percent," Judd said. "It won't surprise me if this last leg of the trip is the hardest."

Vicki and the others in Wisconsin had rejoiced when they heard Lionel and Judd were safe, but Vicki despaired when she heard it would take a few weeks before Lionel could travel.

Cheryl had recovered from the birth of baby Ryan more quickly than Wanda expected. The woman had stayed an extra few days, helping Cheryl get used to feeding the baby and training the Fogartys on raising a child without doctor's visits.

Charlie had come up with the most surprising find of their stay. Months earlier, Marshall Jameson had discovered a GC warehouse on a routine Web search. From what Marshall could tell, the metal buildings held weapons and ammunition for GC forces in the Midwest. In a daring, nighttime raid, Charlie had accompanied Mark, Conrad, and the newest member of the team, Ty Spivey, to the facility, in spite of protests from Shelly, Tanya, and Vicki.

Instead of guns and bullet clips, they found medicine and food. Mark had deactivated the main alarm so the three strolled through the compound, taking much-needed pain relievers, cough medicine, and bandages.

Charlie had broken away from the other two and had found a tiny section of the building with baby formula, disposable diapers, and even shampoo. They brought all the supplies they could carry and made it back to the hideout before sunup.

Later, Tom Fogarty found information that the supplies had been confiscated by the GC and were supposed to be destroyed. *The GC wants everyone depending on them for everything,* Fogarty wrote the Trib Force. *Maybe some GC general or higher-up decided to put that stuff away in case it was ever needed. Maybe the guy was killed. I don't know, but I do know where the stuff in those buildings can get the best use.*

A week later a convoy of fearless Co-op drivers showed up with five semitrailers. One of the semis became buried in a sandy area near the buildings. Another reached a Trib Force storage center in Iowa and provided food and medicine for hundreds of families. But the three other trucks had been chased and apprehended by the GC. The drivers were beaten and questioned before being executed.

"No more of these missions until we know it's safe," Marshall Jameson said.

Vicki was even more depressed after the drivers' deaths. She had hoped to convince the others that Judd and Lionel needed to be in Wisconsin instead of Ohio. But with each day, a new report of GC activity seemed to block their return.

Vicki took comfort in the new life of Ryan Victor. The Fogartys were overjoyed with caring for the baby. The diapers Charlie had found were huge on the child, but Shelly rigged up a way to make them work. Everyone took turns holding him and helping Cheryl with anything she needed. It was almost like the boy had an unlimited set of brothers and sisters.

Vicki tried to stay current on the events around the world and especially news from Petra. Tsion Ben-Judah's letters continued to encourage people to stay strong as they passed the four-year mark of the Tribulation.

Sam Goldberg wrote more Petra Diaries, which made Vicki feel like she was in the ancient city. Sam's descriptions of Tsion Ben-Judah's messages, along with the testimonies of Micah and others, made her want to travel there. Sam described the battle going on for the soul of his new friend, and the kids prayed the boy would decide for God soon.

Sam Goldberg had tried everything to reach his new friend, Lev Taubman. Lev had moved with his family from Chicago to Jerusalem just before the disappearances, and they had spent the months before the escape to Petra hiding from the Global Community in secret passageways underneath the Holy City. Lev's father, mother, and older sister shared a small hut in Petra, and Sam had spent a lot of time talking with them.

They watched reports of miracles performed by

devoted Carpathia followers, and Lev seemed moved by the dead raised to life and the people healed.

"You know what Dr. Ben-Judah says about them," Sam said.

"How could I not hear?" Lev said. "Fakers. Deceivers. They are not using the power of God, but the power of the evil one. Am I right?"

"Yes, but do you understand Tsion's message? These miracle workers were sent to draw you away from the true God to worship a false one."

Each day, as Tsion or Chaim followed the main teaching with an evangelistic message, Sam prayed for Lev and his family and the others who still had not believed in Christ. Each day he searched the foreheads of Lev's family for the mark of the believer, and each day Sam was disappointed.

Nothing could stop Sam from singing, praying, and celebrating with the people who had been turned around by the preaching and teaching. But Sam's heart ached when he thought of Lev and his family, who were so close to the truth.

Sam had found another new friend in Chang Wong, the teenager in New Babylon Judd talked so much about. Chang had written Sam about one of his Petra Diaries, and the two had struck up a friendship. Sam asked Chang his opinion about unbelievers in Petra.

Chang wrote:

> *Let me remind you that these people are just like you and me before the disappearances. There was a cloud over*

our understanding. You know this from Tsion's message. We are in a war for people's souls.

Paul writes, "For we are not fighting against people made of flesh and blood, but against the evil rulers and authorities of the unseen world, against those mighty powers of darkness who rule this world, and against wicked spirits in the heavenly realms." There is something holding back your friend, and I will pray that God will break through before it's too late.

My sister told me what happened to her in China recently. Three angels visited a group of unbelievers and preached the Good News to them. Some twenty-five of them received the mark of the believer before they were executed. God is at work. He is still calling people to follow him, so do not give up.

A few weeks later, Sam invited Lev to listen to Dr. Ben-Judah's teaching. That day, Tsion was to speak of the fruit of the Spirit from Galatians.

"I'll go with you if you'll go with me later," Lev said.

"Where?"

"Into the Negev. I hear a miracle worker is visiting us."

Sam frowned. "I have heard the rumors too."

"You don't believe he'll come?"

Sam shook his head. "I'm sure he will. Nicolae will try anything to get people to believe the lie that he is god—"

"I knew you would close your mind to this. My father said there was no sense inviting you."

"You and your family are in grave danger, and you don't understand it."

"My father read about the miracle workers in Mr. Williams's *The Truth.*"

"And Mr. Williams made it clear every time he mentioned them that they are fakes. You can't trust them."

"My family will go, and we will at least hear them out. My father thinks they may give us a reprieve about the mark—"

"You're still considering taking Carpathia's mark? After all you've seen and heard here?"

Now it was Lev shaking his head. "You're so closed minded. You probably wouldn't even come to the debate they're talking about."

"What debate?"

"The one between your Dr. Ben-Judah and Leon Fortunato. Don't look at me that way. It's from a reliable person. They said it would be televised so the whole world could hear."

"I would welcome such a debate," Sam said. "Maybe you will finally see the truth."

"I still don't know who or what to believe, but getting out of this place for a couple of hours and walking into the desert to see a show, that interests me."

Sam thought of all he had seen God do while coming to Petra. People had been protected from bullets, missiles, and an army sent against them. What more did Lev need? Sam's lip trembled, and he looked away.

Lev grabbed his shoulder and turned him around. "Why are you crying?"

Sam stared. "I beg you not to go. You must convince

your family not to follow the false messiahs. It could mean death to you."

Lev smiled. "I appreciate how much you care. I'll talk to my family."

Sam wandered back to camp, walking a different way than normal and praying, asking God to show him something new to speak to Lev. He spotted a man in his early thirties sitting by a campfire. Sam recognized him as a pilot friend of the American Rayford Steele. Sam walked closer, and the man motioned for him to sit.

"You look troubled, my young friend. My name is Abdullah."

Though he didn't know this man, Sam poured out Lev's story easily.

Abdullah listened and leaned forward when Sam finished. "I am not an outgoing person. Some would call me shy. But what you talk about has troubled me too. I have been pleading with those who are undecided, asking them not to go out. I've told them the only safety they can be assured of is here in Petra, and the only safety for their souls is in accepting the forgiveness of Jesus Christ."

"But what if they don't listen?" Sam said. "What if they go out anyway?"

Abdullah took a stick and traced it in the ashes surrounding the campfire. "There is only one way I know to make this piece of wood catch fire." He stuck it in the yellow blaze until the stick burned, then pulled it out. Flames licked at the wood and ran to the end. "The fire of God is ignited through the prayers of his people. I don't mean that God only acts on what we ask, but I have never

seen a person come to God without prayer somehow
being a part of it." Abdullah threw the stick into the
flames. "How much have you prayed for your friend?"

"Every day."

"Good. Double that. Triple it. Pray every hour. I will
add him to my list as well. Ask others to join you. Get on
that e-mail thing the young people have—"

"The Young Trib Force?"

"Yes. Ask everyone to pray with lots of hardness."

"But what if nothing happens? What if we pray and
Lev still goes out there?"

Abdullah stood. "When you are at war, you do not
know how it will end. However, in this one, we know
God wins, so we have the advantage. But we do not know
what will happen in these battles for people's lives. Keep
praying and asking God to work—pray that the eyes of
Lev's heart will be opened. Pray that God will receive
glory from Lev's life. And that he will finally understand
the truth."

Abdullah's eyes twinkled in the firelight. "The results
are not up to you. You can't make people believe. You
must simply be faithful. If God brings someone to you,
pray for them. Speak to them. Love them."

Sam watched the stick burn. "Why don't we pray right
now?"

Abdullah smiled, clapped Sam's neck with a hand,
and shook him gently. "Now you're talking with my
language."

26

AS LIONEL improved over the next few weeks, Judd spent more time at the computer, reading *The Truth*, Sam's Petra Diaries, and anything else about the outside world. Judd was glad Lionel was making progress, but each time Judd saw him, he felt somehow betrayed, like Lionel had hurt himself to keep Judd away from Vicki. Of course, Judd knew this wasn't true, but something was going on inside him, a bitterness he knew had to be worked out.

Before the disappearances, Judd had felt this way about his parents. They were trying to hold him back, keep him from doing things, making his life hard.

Now Judd had a new perspective. His parents had tried to give him freedom and let him make his own decisions. At the time, Judd figured they had no clue about his bad decisions, including turning his back on the church and God. But now Judd wondered if they *had* known. Had they sensed the battle inside him?

Thinking of his parents reminded Judd of the good times. When he was young, there was the excitement of summer, baseball, campouts, and vacation trips. Fall meant school, football, raking leaves, and preparing for the holidays. Winter was Christmas, snowball fights, skiing, and hockey. And spring meant baseball, heading outside, and planning for summer. The seasons had led from one to another in perfect sequence. It was part of the rhythm of life Judd took for granted.

But since the disappearances, those seasons had been interrupted. He used to be concerned about the weather and was bummed if it rained. Now he and the others stayed inside, scared to go out for fear of the Global Community. They did things at night, and Judd began to appreciate nocturnal animals and studied their living habits.

As the temperature turned colder, then plummeted severely, he resigned himself to staying in Ohio with their new friends. There was no way he and Lionel could set out on foot, and taking a vehicle was too dangerous. His trip north was on hold.

During this "underground season" as Judd called it, he looked forward to two things: writing or talking with Vicki and communicating with anyone else outside their group. Judd loved sending e-mails to Sam in Petra. He wrote Rayford Steele in San Diego and Chang Wong in New Babylon.

He also enjoyed writing Zeke in Wisconsin and hearing another perspective of things going on there. Zeke e-mailed texts of devotional messages by Marshall Jameson, and Judd was impressed by the tough issues he tackled. Marshall addressed becoming discouraged while being cooped up, fear of the Global Community, anger at God for making them go through the horrors of the Tribulation, and more. The one Judd was most interested in was a weeklong message Marshall had given on marriage. Several days were devoted to how husbands and wives were supposed to treat each other, but Marshall had begun by talking about whether it was good or bad to be focused on romantic relationships during such a terrible time.

The words challenged Judd to think more about Vicki, and they exchanged several e-mails about the material. What would a romance between Judd and Vicki do to their main purpose of spreading God's truth? Would it in any way take away from that goal, or would they be more effective together?

As Judd thought about the questions, an e-mail from Chang Wong in New Babylon arrived. *I wanted you to hear this for yourself,* Chang wrote. *I ran across it and think it shows the kind of evil we're up against.*

Judd opened the audio file and recognized the voices of Nicolae Carpathia and Leon Fortunato.

"If your wizards can do all these tricks, Leon, why can they not turn a whole sea back into salt water?"

"Excellency, that is a lot to ask. You must admit that they have done wonders for the Global Community."

"They have not done as much good as the Judah-ites have done bad, and that is the only scorecard that counts!"

"Your Worship, not to be contrary, but you are aware

that Carpathian disciples all over the world have raised the dead, are you not?"

"I raised *myself* from the dead, Leon. These little tricks, bringing smelly corpses from graves just to amaze people and thrill the relatives, do not really compete with the Judah-ites', do they?"

"Turning wooden sticks into snakes? Impressive. Turning water to blood and then back again, then the water to wine? I thought you would particularly enjoy that one."

"I want converts, man! I want changed minds! When is your television debate with Ben-Judah?"

"Next week."

"And you are prepared?"

"Never more so, Highness."

"This man is clever, Leon."

"More than you, Risen One?"

"Well, of course not. But you must carry the ball. You must carry the day! And while you are at it, be sure to suggest to the cowardly sheep in Petra that an afternoon of miracles is planned, almost in their backyard, for later that same day."

"Sir, I had hoped we could test the area first."

"Test the area? Test the *area*?"

"Forgive me, Excellency, but where you have directed me to have a disciple stage that spectacle is so close to where we lost ground troops and weapons and where we have been unsuccessful in every attempt to interrupt their flying missions, not to mention where, my goodness, we dropped two bombs and a—"

"All right, I *know* what has gone on there, Leon! Who does not?! Test it if you must, but I want it convenient to those people. I want them filing out of that Siq and gathering for *our* event for a change. And when they see what my creature can do, we will start seeing wholesale moves from one camp to the other. You know who I want for that show, do you not?"

"Your best? I mean, one of your—"

"No less. Our goal should be to leave Petra a ghost town!"

"Oh, sir, I—"

"When did you become such a pessimist, Leon? We call you the Most High Reverend Father of Carpathianism, and I have offered myself as a living god, risen from the dead, with powers from on high. Yours is merely a sales job, Leon. Remind the people what their potentate has to offer, and watch them line up. And we have a special, you know."

"A special, sir?"

"Yes! We are running a special! This week only, anyone from Petra will be allowed to take the mark of loyalty with no punishment for having missed the deadline, now long since past. Think of the influence they can have on others just like them."

"The fear factor has worked fairly well, Potentate."

"Well, it *is* sort of a no-more-Mr.-Nice-Guy campaign, one would have to admit. But the time is past for worrying about my image. By now if people do not know who I am and what I am capable of, it is too late for them. But some blow to the other side, some victory over the curse of the bloody seas—that can only help. And I want you to do well against Ben-Judah, Leon. You are learned and devout, and you ask for worship of a living, breathing god who is here and who is not silent. It takes no faith to believe in the deity of one you can see on television every day. I should be the easy, convenient, logical choice."

"Of course, Majesty, and I shall portray you that way."

The conversation sent a chill down Judd's spine. Who was this creature Carpathia mentioned, and what would he do? Was there no end to Carpathia's evil? Judd prayed for Sam Goldberg and his friend who was not yet a believer. He asked God to help convince more people to turn to the true and living God.

There was excitement in Petra as Sam met with Abdullah to pray for Lev and his family. Sam found Abdullah singing near his tent, getting ready for the meeting that would beam Tsion's face via satellite to debate Leon Fortunato. Abdullah was hopeful that this would change many minds, but he was also excited about a flight he was making for the International Commodity Co-op.

"I think this trade we are about to make," Abdullah said, "is so big, only God could pull it off."

Sam smiled and the two began praying. Over the past few weeks, prayer had become more to Sam than simply telling God what he wanted. Sam was being drawn into something deeper, a reliance and trust in God that he couldn't explain. When Sam brought Lev, his family, and his other concerns to God, Sam felt God not only heard his requests but also took them like a weight from his shoulders. While Sam met with Lev later, he noticed he didn't feel as heavyhearted. He could simply talk naturally with his friend and show an interest in him.

The afternoon of the debate, Sam walked to Lev's home but couldn't find him. He asked a woman nearby where the Taubman family was, and she pointed and shook her head. "I don't know why the rabbi puts up with such people."

Sam climbed down to an area leading out of the city and spotted a gathering of thousands. Tsion Ben-Judah and Chaim Rosenzweig were trying to quiet them. None of the people had the mark of the believer.

Sam noticed Lev's father and sister, who moved toward the front. "As soon as this debate is over, we're leaving here for a few hours to hear another speaker," Mr. Taubman said. "He will be right close by, and many believe he is the Christ. Jesus come back to earth to perform miracles and explain the future!"

Chaim stepped forward. "Please! You must not do this! Do you not know you are being deceived? You know of this only through the evil ruler of this world and his False Prophet. Stay here in safety. Put your trust in the Lord!"

Another man yelled something Sam couldn't hear. Then Tsion and Chaim continued pleading with the people. Chaim went so far as to say that these people were being used by the evil one to create chaos in the camp.

Lev's father raised a fist and pushed forward. "You

take too much upon you. Why do you put yourselves above the congregation?"

Sam rushed into the crowd, keeping his eyes on Lev, who was with his mother in the middle of the throng. As he hurried forward, Tsion spoke. "The Lord knows who are his and who is holy. For what cause do you and all those gathered here speak against the Lord? And why would you murmur against Chaim?"

The shouting continued, and Sam reached Lev and caught his arm. "You have to come with me. You and your whole family."

"I can't leave now," Lev said. "Listen, my father is speaking."

"We will not stand with you," Lev's father said. "Is it a small thing that you have taken us from our motherland, our homes where we had plenty, and brought us to this rocky place where all we have to eat is bread and water, and you set yourself up as a prince over us?"

Sam couldn't believe what he was hearing. It was just like the children of Israel in the Old Testament, crying out to Moses in the wilderness. Sam sensed something terrible was about to happen, but he couldn't leave his friend. He pleaded with Lev and Mrs. Taubman. "Come with me to the rocky place where you can see better."

Lev and his mother hesitated, then followed.

Sam glanced at Tsion Ben-Judah. The words of Lev's father and the others seemed to wound the man so much that he cried out to God. "Lord, forgive them, for they know not what they do. I have neither set myself over them nor demanded anything from them except respect for you."

Sam pulled Lev and his mother onto a ledge just as Tsion looked over the crowd and said, "God is telling Chaim and me to separate ourselves from you to save ourselves from his wrath."

People shouted at Tsion and Chaim. Many fell on their faces and cried out. Some stood and shook their fists. Sam couldn't hear their words, but he had a sick feeling.

Lev yelled for his father. The man glanced at the boy, shook his head, and glared. His sister screamed angrily at Tsion. Lev took a step toward his father, but Sam stopped him.

Tsion quieted the crowd and spoke gravely. "Unless you agree with these, it would do well for you to depart from the presence of these wicked men, lest you be consumed in all their sins. From this point on, let it be known that the Lord has sent me to do all these works; I do not do them in my own interest. If these men do what is in their minds to do and God visits a plague of death on them, then all shall understand that these men have provoked the Lord."

When Tsion finished, the rocks trembled. Lev and his mother fell back, and Sam grabbed them as a great hole opened under hundreds of people. The angry men and women were swallowed immediately, falling into a deep cavern. Lev's father and sister screamed and plunged down, their arms waving as they fell. The wails echoed from the enormous hole, and just as suddenly as the earth had opened, it closed, and the people inside disappeared.

Thousands scattered, screaming as they ran. Lev shook with fear and his mother yelled, "Get out, before we're killed too!"

Before Sam could stop them, the two had crawled over another ledge and ran for their home. Tsion and Chaim prayed together at the front.

Sam looked back again and watched Lev keep his mother from falling. "Please, God, I pray you won't let their hearts be hardened by this. Lev and Mrs. Taubman still have a chance to believe your truth. Help Tsion as he debates Leon Fortunato. May something he says stir their hearts. And help me to reach out before it is too late."

27

SAM climbed over the ledge as thousands scattered from the area. The image of people plunging to their deaths stuck with him. He heard Lev's mother weeping when he approached their small home, so he sat outside the door and prayed for them.

A half hour later, the door opened and Lev stepped outside and sat next to Sam. The two were silent for some time.

Then Lev looked at Sam with tears in his eyes. "Why would God do that to my father and sister?"

"I'm so sorry for your loss," Sam said, his chin quivering.

"I was just thinking about the miracle workers," Lev said. "If my father's and sister's bodies were here, we could take them to the miracle workers and they could be raised. I've seen that happen on the reports."

Sam shook his head. "Those people cannot offer you

or anyone else real life. They are fakes. They want you to worship Nicolae."

"I don't care. I want my father back."

Sam closed his eyes and thought of his own father. "I know what it's like to lose a dad. It's painful, but your father's choice doesn't have to be yours. Do not harden your heart toward the one who loves you."

"How can God love me if he takes away my father?"

"Your father spoke out against God's leaders. God is cutting out those who don't believe. You must follow him before it is too late."

Lev shook his head. "I have to help my mother. She is all I have now."

"Please, listen to the debate. Tsion will explain things."

"I'll try to listen," Lev said.

After Lev had gone back inside, Sam lingered a few moments, praying for him. He ran to find Mr. Stein but was stopped short by the voice of Tsion Ben-Judah. Sam climbed back over a ridge and saw Tsion in front of a crowd. A camera stood before him.

"I would ask that all pray during the broadcast that the Lord give me his wisdom and his words. And as for you who still plan to venture away from this safe place, let me plead with you one more time not to do it, not to make yourself vulnerable to the evil one. Let the Global Community and their Antichrist and his False Prophet make ridiculous claims about fake miracle workers. Do not fall into their trap.

"Messiah himself warned his disciples of this very

thing. He told them, 'Many false prophets shall rise, and shall deceive many. And because iniquity shall abound, the love of many shall wax cold. But he who endures to the end, he shall be saved. And this gospel of the kingdom shall be preached in all the world for a witness unto all nations.' "

Sam glanced at the huge screen above the stage. Was Tsion being carried over GCNN live?

" 'If any man says to you, "Lo, here is Christ," believe it not,' " Tsion continued. " 'For there shall arise false Christs and false prophets, and they shall show great signs and wonders—so much so that if it were possible, they would deceive even you. If they say to you, "Behold, he is in the desert," do not go. "Behold, he is in the secret chambers," believe it not.' "

Judd and the others in the Ohio hideout huddled together to stay warm and kept the television sound low. One of the leaders led in prayer that God would give Tsion success and boldness.

Something was wrong at the Global Community News Network. Tsion was already on the air and warning people not to follow the false Christs. A woman from New Babylon appeared on-screen and asked Dr. Ben-Judah to stand by to speak with the Most High Reverend Father Fortunato.

"Thank you, ma'am, but rather than stand by, as you flip your switches and do whatever it is you have to do to make this work, let me begin by saying that I do not recognize Mr. Fortunato as most high anything, let alone reverend or father."

The screen split and Leon Fortunato appeared in one of his colorful outfits. A few people in the hideout snickered, and Judd closed his eyes. He would give anything to be back with his friends in Wisconsin, listening to their comments about Leon's clothes.

"Greetings, Dr. Ben-Judah, my esteemed opponent. I heard some of that and may I say I regret that you have characteristically chosen to begin what has been intended as a cordial debate with a vicious character attack. I shall not lower myself to this and wish only to pass along my welcome and best wishes."

Tsion didn't say anything, and Judd wondered if he could hear. Finally, the rabbi said, "Is it my turn, then? Shall I open by stating the case for Jesus as the Christ, the Messiah, the Son of the living—"

The woman broke into the conversation and tried to avoid the conflict. After a few moments of banter, Leon Fortunato began. Judd thought the man looked more composed, even gentle, as he started his remarks. "My premise is simple. I proclaim Nicolae Carpathia, risen from the dead, as the one true god, worthy of worship, and the savior of mankind. He is the one who surfaced at the time of the greatest calamity in the history of the world and has pulled together the global community in peace and harmony and love. You claim Jesus of Nazareth as both the Son of God and one with God, which makes no sense and cannot be proven. This leaves you and your followers worshiping a man who was no doubt very spiritual, very bright, perhaps enlightened, but who is now dead. If he were alive and as all-powerful as you say, I challenge him to strike me dead where I sit."

"I don't believe this," Lionel whispered. "I wish God would strike him right now."

But nothing happened. Leon smiled, cocked his head, and said, "Hail Carpathia, our lord and risen king."

Tsion Ben-Judah jumped into the debate. "I trust you will spare us the rest of the hymn written by and about the egomaniac who murders those who disagree with him. I raise up Jesus the Christ, the Messiah, fully God and fully man, born of a virgin, the perfect lamb who was worthy to be slain for the sins of the whole world. If he is but a man, his sacrificial death was only human and we who believe in him would be lost.

"But Scripture proves him to be all that he claimed to be. His birth was foretold hundreds, yea, thousands of years before it was fulfilled in every minute detail. He himself fulfills at least 109 separate and distinct prophecies that prove he is the Messiah."

Judd's heart welled up, and tears stung his eyes. Tsion's message was as rapid-fire as a machine gun, and Judd was thrilled that people around the world could hear it.

"The uniqueness and genius of Christianity," Tsion continued, "is that the Virgin Birth allowed for the only begotten Son of God to identify with human beings without surrendering his godly, holy nature. Thus he could die for the sins of the whole world. His Father's resurrecting him from the dead three days later proves that God was satisfied with his sacrifice for our sins.

"Not only that, but I have discovered, in my exhaustive study of the Scriptures, more than 170 prophecies by Jesus himself in the four Gospels alone. Many have already been literally fulfilled, guaranteeing that those that relate to still future events will also be literally fulfilled. Only God himself could write history in advance—incredible evidence of the deity of Jesus Christ and the supernatural nature of God."

Leon stared into the camera. Judd wondered if Nicolae himself was watching this spectacle, and if so, how red Carpathia's face must be.

"But we *know* our king and potentate arose from the dead," Fortunato said, "because we saw it with our own eyes. If there is one anywhere on this earth who saw Jesus resurrected, let him speak now or forever hold his peace. Where is he? Where is this Son of God, this man of miracles, this king, this Savior of mankind? If your Jesus is who you say he is, why are you hiding in the desert and living on bread and water?

"The god of this world lives in a palace and provides good gifts to all those who worship him."

"Mr. Fortunato," Tsion calmly said, "would you tell the viewers how many people have died by the guillotine because of your loving god? Would you admit that Global Community troops and equipment were swallowed by the earth near Petra, and that two bombs and a deadly missile struck here, yet no one has been injured and no structure jeopardized? Will you not also admit that Global Community Security and Intelligence Peacekeeping forces have spent millions of Nicks on attacking all traffic in and out of this place, and not one plane, flier, or volunteer has been scratched?"

Leon ignored Tsion's questions and praised Carpathia for his worldwide rebuilding effort. "Those who die by the blade choose this for themselves. Nicolae is not willing that any should perish but that all should be loyal and committed to him."

"But, sir, the population has been cut to half what it once was, the seas are dead from the curse of blood— prophesied in the Bible and sent by God. Yet the believers—his children, at least the ones who have survived the murderous persecution of the man you would enthrone as god—are provided water and food from heaven, not just here, but in many areas around the world."

Leon praised Nicolae as a man of peace and accused Ben-Judah followers of being the problem. At one point he criticized Tsion as one of the "disloyal Jews."

"Mr. Fortunato, I wear the title as a badge of honor. I am humbled beyond measure to be one of God's chosen people. Indeed, the entire Bible is testament to his plan for us for the ages, and it is being played out for the whole world to see even as we speak."

Fortunato smiled. "But are you not the ones who killed Jesus?"

"On the contrary," Tsion said. "Jesus himself was a Jew, as you well know. And the fact is that the actual killing of Christ was at the hands of Gentiles. He stood before a Gentile judge, and Gentile soldiers put him on the cross.

"Oh, there was an offense against him on the part of

Israel that the nation and her people must bear. In the Old Testament book of Zechariah, chapter 12, verse 10 prophesies that God will 'pour upon the house of David, and upon the inhabitants of Jerusalem, the spirit of grace and of supplications; and they shall look unto me whom they have pierced, and they shall mourn for him.'

"Israel must confess a specific national sin against the Messiah before we will be blessed. In Hosea 5:15, God says he will 'go and return to my place, till they acknowledge their offense, and seek my face; in their affliction they will seek me earnestly.'

"The offense? Rejecting the messiahship of Jesus. We repent of that by pleading for his return. He will come yet again and set up his earthly kingdom, and not only I but also the Word of God itself predicts the doom of the evil ruler of this world when that kingdom is established."

"Well," Leon said, "thank you for that fascinating history lesson. But I rejoice that *my* lord and king is alive and well, and I see him and speak with him every day. Thank you for being a quick and worthy opponent."

Judd shook his head. "Fortunato never answered any of Tsion's arguments."

"What did you expect?" Lionel said.

Sam was mesmerized by the interaction between Tsion and Fortunato. Hundreds of thousands of supporters gathered, many with heads bowed in prayer.

Leon looked into the camera and tilted his head, as if he were talking to the crowd. "I would like to greet the many citizens of the Global Community who reside with you temporarily," he said, "and invite them to enjoy the benefits and privileges of the outside world. I trust many will join one of our prophets and teachers and workers of miracles when he ministers in your area less than an hour from now. He will—"

Tsion interrupted, "The Scriptures tell us that many deceivers are entered into the world, who confess not that Jesus Christ is come in the flesh. Such a one is a deceiver and an antichrist."

"If you'll allow me to finish, sir—"

"Whoever abides not in the doctrine of Christ, has not God. He who abides in the doctrine of Christ, he has both the Father and the Son. If any come to you and bring not this doctrine, do not receive him into your house, neither bid him Godspeed, for he who bids Godspeed partakes of his evil deeds."

"All right then, you've worked in all your tiresome Bible verses. I shall be content to merely thank you and—"

"For as long as you have me on international television, Mr. Fortunato, I feel obligated to preach the gospel of Christ and to speak forth the words of Scripture. The Bible says the Word shall not return void, and so I would like to quote—"

The screen went blank as the Global Community finally cut Tsion off. A cheer rose from the crowd for Tsion, and Sam noticed Lev Taubman a few feet behind him.

"How long have you been here?" Sam said.

"I saw most of it."

Lev looked tired or scared. Sam couldn't tell which. Suddenly, a group of people shaking their fists at Tsion moved toward the Siq to go outside Petra. Others screamed warnings, but the people wouldn't listen.

"Are you leaving with them?" Sam said to Lev.

Before Lev could respond, Tsion cried out over the noise, " 'Be sober, be vigilant; because your adversary the devil walks about like a roaring lion, seeking whom he may devour.' "

Sam watched the people walk toward the desert. He had heard the GC had constructed a stage almost two miles from the entrance to Petra.

Lev turned. "The Global Community is offering forgiveness for not taking the mark, even though the deadline is long passed. It's tempting."

"And what do you think?"

Lev ran a hand through his hair. "I need to stay with my mother."

Sam took the boy by his shoulders. "Lev, I have been praying for you nonstop. God wants you to come to him. He wants you to choose life."

"I am thankful that you care, and after what happened to my father and sister, believe me, I have more questions, but—"

"Let me help you answer them. What is keeping you from believing in Jesus as your Messiah?"

Lev shook his head. "I don't know. I'm confused. What Dr. Ben-Judah said makes sense. . . ." He licked his lips. "Let's go up to the high place. I have a pair of strong binoculars. If this is a trick by the GC, I will do as you say."

"Don't put the decision off," Sam said, but Lev was gone, running toward his house for the binoculars.

28

SAM climbed with Lev up to the high place and looked out over the desert. The concert stage had been set up quickly, and people moved in a long line toward it. As an airplane landed on the runway nearby, a helicopter flew out to meet it.

"One of the reasons it makes no sense to go out there is the protection we have here," Sam said, handing the binoculars to Lev. "The helicopter pilot is my friend Abdullah Smith. He says the GC tries to shoot our planes and helicopters down, but it is no use. God is protecting us."

Several hundred people walked through the hot sand toward the venue. Lev clicked the binoculars to increase the power and punched Sam in the shoulder. "Looks like your friends in the chopper are going to the show as well."

Sam grabbed the glasses and looked closely. Sure enough, Abdullah's chopper flew toward the stage. Sam watched the reaction of armed Peacekeepers as the chopper set down a hundred feet from the stage, whipping up a sandy cloud. There was a brief standoff, with the chopper starting up again, and then the GC left the craft alone.

While the crowd made its way to the stage, Sam continued explaining the Scriptures about Jesus. It was the same message Lev had heard from Chaim and Tsion for many weeks, but Sam thought that perhaps this time the words would sink in and the boy's heart would soften.

When the people were in place, someone onstage captured their attention. Sam and Lev couldn't see the stage, but they could tell from the crowd reaction that the people were impressed.

Suddenly the crowd looked up, shading their eyes from the sun. A white cloud appeared over the gathering and blocked the hot rays.

"What do you make of that?" Lev said.

Sam kept his eyes on the people. The cloud disappeared, and moments later a spring of water gushed from the middle of the group, and people drank from it.

Lev took the binoculars. "They're passing around a basket of food."

Sam shook his head. "I see what's happening. Whoever is up there is trying to prove he can do God's miracles. Lev, you need to pray—"

"A hundred people just fell to the ground! It looks like they're dead!"

Sam took the binoculars and viewed the chaos. People shrieked, some turned and ran, and then everyone froze.

"Look there," Lev said, pointing to a small cloud of

dust rolling like a tumbleweed toward the gathering. "What could that be?"

Sam glanced at the cloud and shook his head, focusing on the group again. "I don't know, but the people look deathly afraid of it."

Suddenly the spring turned to blood. People backed away, then fled toward Petra. Many screamed and staggered in the sand, trying desperately to retreat.

"The dust cloud just changed direction," Lev said. "It's headed for all those people. Could that be some kind of animal?"

The chopper started, and a cloud of dust kicked up and covered the area. Sam strained to see through the binoculars. When the sand cleared, Lev let out a shriek. Bodies dotted the path back to Petra. The stage was gone. There were no Peacekeepers or vehicles or anything that had been there only moments ago.

Sam, his hands shaking, gave the binoculars to Lev, but the boy was on his knees, tears streaming from his face. "That could have been me out there. If I had gone, I would be dead right now."

Sam knelt beside him. "Take this last chance to turn to God and away from the enemy of your soul. Nicolae and his followers would like you to curse the true God and take Nicolae's mark, but God—"

"I'm ready," Lev interrupted. "And not just because I'm afraid. I do believe what you've said about Jesus. I opened the Scriptures and read the passages Tsion has given. I don't know why I haven't seen it before, but I'm ready to pray."

Sam put a hand on the boy's shoulder and prayed. Lev repeated Sam's words softly. "Heavenly Father, thank you for sending your Son, Jesus, to pay the penalty for my sin. I believe that he died in my place, and right now I ask you to forgive me of my sin. I'm sorry I've rejected you and the gift you've offered, but now I reach out and take it by faith. And because Jesus rose from the dead, I know you have prepared the way for me to spend eternity with you. Thank you for saving me from death today, for saving my soul, and I ask you to come into my life and lead me and show me your path for the rest of my days. In Jesus' name. Amen."

When Lev looked up, Sam saw the mark of the believer on his forehead. Lev wiped tears from his eyes and stood. "Let's go talk with my mother."

Vicki couldn't wait until midnight each night. That was the time she and Judd agreed to communicate with each other. They limited themselves to three times a week talking by phone, and the other nights they used the computer.

In one e-mail, Judd described his thoughts about Lionel. *I feel awful that I resent him. I know there's no part of him that wanted that to happen, and he's been through so much pain during the healing process. Yesterday I awoke out of a dead sleep and heard him gasping for breath. I thought he was dying, Vick, but when I got to him, he was crying. He said his arm really hurt, and he was just sad about the things he'd never be able to do again.*

All that must make it even harder for you, Vicki wrote.

Yeah. Deep down I know that what happened is not anybody's fault. But when I think of not being able to be there with you, all those ugly feelings come back.

Vicki had slept on it and had brought up the subject the next night on the phone. "I've been thinking more about you and Lionel." She paused. Over time she and Judd had been able to share some deep things without holding back.

"God protected you and Lionel from the GC," Vicki continued. "Even though the others in that group were killed, he spared you two for a reason. I don't know why we've had to be apart so long, and my heart aches just as much as yours about the separation, but one of the good things for me has been that I know we don't have to be together in order to show love to each other. I'd hate to think of this happening, but if we never saw each other again before the return of Jesus, that would be okay. If God wants us together, I know we will be. If he just wants us to be friends and help each other along the next few years, then that's okay too."

"Totally surrendered," Judd muttered.

"What?"

"I was just thinking about being surrendered to God. Letting him control things and resting in his love for us takes a lot of the pressure off. I can't imagine not seeing you, but you're right. If God wants us to stay apart, I can handle it. But I don't think he wants that, do you?"

"I hope not," Vicki said quickly, then laughed.

"When you look at things that way, with God in

control, there's no way I can blame Lionel for us not being together."

"Tell Lionel Zeke is working on a gadget he thinks Lionel will be able to use. I hope we'll be able to see him soon too."

Vicki and Judd always ended their conversations and e-mails with prayer. Sometimes one would pray, sometimes both. Most of their talks lasted hours, and several times the sun had come up before they finished.

The Wisconsin group had a routine of eating the morning meal together, then having a time of teaching and prayer. It was Vicki's turn to give a brief devotional one morning, and she happened to see the latest Petra Diary from Sam. She brought a printed copy to the meeting and gave everyone the good news that the boy they had prayed for, Lev Taubman, and his mother had become believers.

"Let me read the latest entry that proves we don't wrestle against flesh and blood, but against a spiritual enemy. Sam writes, 'Lev and I saw something incredible happen in the desert, but it wasn't until I spoke with my friend Abdullah that I found out what really happened. Abdullah was in the desert when people from Petra ventured out to see the miracle worker.

" 'Abdullah said the man looked like a younger version of Leon Fortunato, and the man said he was not from this world and that he had been given power by the risen lord, Nicolae Carpathia.

" 'The first miracle the guy did was bring in a cloud that blocked the sun. Then the guy made the cloud disappear, not move or fall apart, but vanish. Next he turned the microphone and stand into a giant snake. Everybody recoiled, but just as fast as he turned it into a snake, it was a microphone and stand again.

" 'Then from the middle of the crowd came a spring of water gushing straight into the air. People drank from it. The man asked if people were hungry and produced a basket of real bread, warm and chewy. Everyone in the crowd took some, but the basket never emptied.

" 'Do you see the mockery of this? Miracles God performed in the Bible were produced by this faker to gain people's trust. And they fell for it big-time. The man, or being, whatever he was, said he was a disciple of Carpathia. And while his behavior had been nice up to that point, he then said that Carpathia's patience had run out and that he would administer Carpathia's mark. He simply pointed at people, and they had the mark of Nicolae.

" 'This is where the story really gets ugly. The man killed more than a hundred at one time. People went crazy. Then the man raised the dead people back to life. It went on like that, the man convincing people their friends were really dead. Then a little cloud of dust appeared on the horizon.

" 'I have to tell you, Lev and I saw this cloud moving straight for the stage and audience, but we didn't know what it was. Abdullah said the man onstage told the people the cloud contained snakes, vipers with a deadly venom. That's when the spring of water turned to blood and the man called the people fools and said Nicolae wanted them dead. He told them to run but warned that the vipers would kill them before they reached Petra.

" 'And that is what happened. The cloud caught up to the people, and there was a line of bodies in the sand. Abdullah was sitting in the helicopter with two of his friends when the evil man appeared before them. The wonder-worker didn't open his mouth, but they heard him say, "I know who you are. I know you by name. Your god is weak and your faith a sham, and your time is limited. You shall surely die." ' "

Vicki glanced at the group and saw looks of disbelief. Shelly and Janie shook from the horrific story.

Charlie looked up with glassy eyes. "Didn't any of them survive?"

"All of the people on foot died. Abdullah and the others in the chopper were okay because they were believers. Sam wrote that when the dust settled, everything on the desert—the stage, the vehicles, the Peacekeepers—was gone."

"It was all an illusion?" Tanya said.

Vicki folded the paper. "I don't know what it was. Tsion told Abdullah and some others that the man was probably a demonic apparition."

"A what?" Charlie said.

"A demon in human form. Tsion referred to Revelation 12 that says that when Satan was cast out of heaven the other bad angels were cast out with him. John 10:10 says Satan wants only to steal and to kill and to destroy. So it all fits.

"Take heart in this," Vicki concluded. "I'll read you the last part of Sam's letter.

" 'Dr. Ben-Judah told his friends that God is doing his "winnowing work." This means he is cleaning the earth of his enemies, wiping them out, and allowing those who still haven't chosen for God to face the consequences. Dr. Ben-Judah concluded with a verse from Romans. "O the depth of the riches both of the wisdom and knowledge of God! How unsearchable are his judgments, and his ways past finding out! For who hath known the mind of the Lord? Or who hath been his counselor? . . . For of him, and through him, and to him, are all things—to whom be glory for ever." '

"Sam finishes with this. 'We need to be careful about the deception of the evil one, but the good news is that there are still more people to reach. May God give each of us new opportunities, even today, to come in contact with the undecided and convince them that God loves them.' "

Sam met with Lev and his mother early the next morning in Petra. The two admitted they had never read much of the Bible. As they munched their morning manna, Sam helped them understand an overview of the Scriptures.

A buzz spread through the million-member camp that everyone should gather after breakfast. Sam took a break from teaching, and the three went to the meeting place. Mrs. Taubman's heart was heavy about losing her daughter and husband, and Sam could tell Lev was struggling too. He tried to comfort them as much as he could before Chaim Rosenzweig, known as Micah, spoke.

"Tsion believes the Lord has told him that no more indecision reigns in the camp. You may confirm that by looking about you. Is there anyone in this place without the mark of the believer? Anyone anywhere? We will not pressure or condemn you. This is just for our information."

Sam looked around at the people near him. Everyone he saw had the mark of the believer.

After a few minutes, Tsion Ben-Judah stepped forward. "The prophet Isaiah predicted that 'it shall come to pass in that day that the remnant of Israel, and such as have escaped of the house of Jacob, will never again depend on him who defeated them, but will depend on the Lord, the Holy One of Israel, in truth.

" 'The remnant will return, the remnant of Jacob, to the Mighty God. For though your people, O Israel, be as the sand of the sea, a remnant of them will return. . . .' And of the evil ruler of this world who has tormented you, Isaiah says further, 'It shall come to pass in that day that his burden will be taken away from your shoulder, and his yoke from your neck, and the yoke will be destroyed.' Praise the God of Abraham, Isaac, and Jacob.

"The prophet Zechariah quoted our Lord God himself, speaking of the land of Israel, that 'two-thirds of it shall be cut off and die, but one-third shall be left in it. I will bring the one-third through the fire, will refine them as silver is refined, and test them as gold is tested. They will call on My name and I will answer them. I will say, "This is My people." And each one will say, "The Lord is my God." '

"My dear friends, you remnant of Israel, this is in accord with the clear teaching of Ezekiel, chapter 37, where our barren nation is seen in the last days to be a valley of dry bones, referred to by the Lord himself as 'the whole house of Israel. They indeed say, "Our bones are dry, our hope is lost, and we ourselves are cut off!" '

"But then, dear ones, God said to Ezekiel, 'Therefore prophesy and say to them, "Thus says the Lord God: 'Behold, O My people, I will open your graves and cause you to come up from your graves, and bring you into the land of Israel. . . . I will put My Spirit in you, and you shall live, and I will place you in your own land. Then you shall know that I, the Lord, have spoken it and performed it.' "' "

Sam looked at Lev and his mother. Sam was grateful he had been part of God's rescue plan for them both.

29

JUDD sat in the early morning darkness, staring at an old map of the United States of America. It had been months since he and Lionel had arrived at the Ohio safe house, and things had changed drastically. An all-out blitz on believers from the Global Community had left few safe places between this location and Wisconsin. Commander Kruno Fulcire appeared daily, rewarding loyal citizens for finding hidden believers.

Judd had even recognized two who were beheaded shortly after they appeared on live broadcasts. Fulcire seethed at those who avoided taking Carpathia's mark. Citizens hunted down the unmarked for cash to help keep themselves alive. Many were hungry, and it became more and more difficult to move supplies.

The food situation for the Ohio safe house had become bleak. They didn't have manna from heaven or quail that flew in for dinner every day like Petra. With an influx of new people, the once huge hiding place got smaller. Judd no longer ruled the computer, and it became difficult to keep his appointments with Vicki.

The doctor who had helped Lionel at the safe house moved with a few others to another location Judd had helped build. The work had been done only at night, and though there were several scares, the GC hadn't discovered their secret operation.

Lionel had been depressed that he couldn't help with the digging and physical work, but he had kept in contact with other Trib Force locations and with Chloe Steele. She had tried to get supplies from the Co-op to their location, but it was difficult with all the GC activity. Lionel had catalogued their supply list and put everyone on a ration system.

Despite the negatives, Judd knew God was still working. Another plague had hit the earth, turning rivers into rushing floods of blood. Judd had traveled past a nearby river every night on his way to the construction area, and the gurgling blood and horrible smell was sickening. One night he had stood in the moonlight, looking at a river so dark it seemed like a bottomless pit. He had found it difficult to sleep, having nightmares about blood washing over him, and that was the last time he walked close to the river.

The bloody water caused people to focus less on hunting down people without Carpathia's mark and more on staying alive, which had been good for believers. People were still coming to the truth and giving their lives to God through the kids' Web site, which Judd had all but

abandoned with the construction project. Lionel kept
Judd up-to-date with new contacts and anything he
learned.

Reports from around the world came in about sightings of angels preaching in remote areas. Lionel nearly
attacked Judd early one morning as he came in, muddy
and sweating from a night of work.

"You've got to see this," Lionel said, pulling Judd
toward the computer.

Judd stared at the message from Chang.

> I just heard a story from our Co-op group in Argen-
> tina. Rayford Steele is one of the pilots. Rayford and some
> others found themselves in a group of locals moving
> through the countryside. They finally found someone who
> spoke English and asked where everyone was going.
>
> The people said they had been invited by three men
> who came to their door and told them to meet together to
> hear good news. They told them not to be afraid, even
> though none of these people had the mark of Carpathia.
> Pretty soon, the GC showed up, about a hundred
> troops.

Judd felt goose bumps as he read. He wiped a finger
clean, pressed the computer's down arrow, and read the
rest of the message.

> The GC told them they couldn't meet together and
> that they had twenty-four hours to take the mark of
> Carpathia or face death. But the people didn't pay atten-

tion. Then, as the man on the bullhorn shouted his final warning, someone called for silence.

"One of the angels," Judd said under his breath as he scrolled down.

It was the angel Christopher. He introduced his coworkers, Nahum and Caleb, and then ordered the GC troops to leave the area or face death by God's hand. They did leave, and after that the angels repeated the message we have heard about all around the world.

Judd secretly wished he would be visited by some kind of angel that could pick him up and drop him in Wisconsin. He had seen angelic visitors on television and had heard about them from Vicki and others, but he had never seen or spoken with one in person.

Now, as he sat looking at the map and estimating the number of miles between him and Vicki, he ran his finger along the waterways. Many of them had changed since the great earthquake, but he wondered if he had some kind of boat that would float in the blood. . . .

Judd put his head on the map and closed his eyes. There was word of a Global Community stronghold being built south of the bombed-out city of Chicago. If that was true, Judd knew it would take a miracle to get to Wisconsin.

Judd thought of the verses he had looked up about patience and perseverance. The Bible spoke in various ways about hanging in during the tough times, and Judd had written every reference down and had committed several to memory.

His favorite was from Romans, and Judd softly mouthed the words. " 'We can rejoice, too, when we run into problems and trials, for we know that they are good for us—they help us learn to endure. And endurance develops strength of character in us, and character strengthens our confident expectation of salvation. And this expectation will not disappoint us.' "

I don't want any more character, God, Judd thought. *I just want to get back to Vicki.*

Vicki and the others in Wisconsin made the most of every opportunity given to them to tell people about God. Their main contact with the outside world was through the Internet, and everyone rejoiced when a new person came to Christ. Janie had made red hearts out of some old fabric she had found. Each time they received word of a person receiving the mark of the believer, she put a heart on the wall above the computer. "Another heart snatched from that evil Nicolae," she said.

Jim Dekker, the computer whiz who had worked for the Global Community before coming to live with the kids, had developed another version of The Cube, the high-tech presentation of the gospel. Though hackers loyal to the GC had tried to corrupt the files, Jim had defeated their attempts.

The Fogartys, Tom and Josey, had taken to baby Ryan as soon as he had been born. A few months after his birth, the baby went on formula Charlie and the others had found. Unlike the situation in Ohio, Vicki's group had plenty to eat and a supply that would last months and perhaps years.

As the baby grew, Vicki noticed a sadness in Cheryl. When the Fogartys were with the baby in the main cabin, she avoided them. Cheryl skipped many of their devotion times, saying she needed more sleep or wasn't feeling well. Every time Vicki tried to talk with her about it, Cheryl changed the subject. By the time Ryan started to crawl, Cheryl had moved into a run-down shack by herself farthest away from the others. At each milestone in the baby's life—his first tooth, his first haircut, his first word, which was *dada*—Cheryl withdrew more and more.

Though Cheryl's attitude concerned Vicki, there was still much to be excited about. Tanya and Ty Spivey, along with the other believers who had broken away from the cult in the cave, grew in their faith almost as quickly as Ryan gained weight. They were at every meeting, every prayer vigil, and were some of the first to read Tsion Ben-Judah's Web site and Sam Goldberg's Petra Diaries.

Vicki had become resigned to Judd's absence. She knew how dangerous it was to travel, and though there were nights when she wanted to jump into Marshall Jameson's van and barrel south, she knew it was best to wait.

Her love for Judd grew, even as their talks via computer and phone became less frequent. Both Judd and Vicki had been asked to cut down their time, so Vicki wrote her thoughts and prayers and typed them when others weren't around.

The older women had been a big help to Vicki, especially Josey Fogarty, who counseled her and gave advice when Vicki felt alone. Vicki would hold baby Ryan as he slept, listening to Josey. The woman had spent years waiting on her husband to become a believer, so she had developed a lot of patience.

The most surprising person to help her was Zeke. She figured he wouldn't understand, but Zeke had listened and even gave Vicki a verse to memorize from James. On top of the page, Zeke had scrawled a note. *When you get down and don't think you can go on, look at this. It's almost like God put this in his Word especially for you, though it's helped me a lot since my dad died. Remember, God has a plan, and he's going to do something special with you and Judd.*

The verses came from the first chapter of James. Vicki memorized them, and God brought the words to mind at crucial times. "Dear brothers and sisters, whenever trouble comes your way, let it be an opportunity for joy. For when your faith is tested, your endurance has a chance to grow. So let it grow, for when your endurance is fully developed, you will be strong in character and ready for anything."

"What are you preparing me for?" Vicki prayed. "I'm not sure I want whatever it is. But, God, I trust you. Everything in me trusts you. Please provide some way for us to get back together."

A few days before Ryan's eight-month birthday, which Vicki and the others celebrated with gusto, a vehicle pulled into camp. Zeke had helped many believers take on new identities with false papers and even false marks, but as the GC stepped up their efforts to kill anyone without the mark, Zeke's work tailed off. There was almost no one who needed uniforms to tailor or disguises to invent.

When Marshall Jameson opened the door, Vicki gasped. It was Chad Harris, a friend from Iowa who had taken Vicki and the others in after they had escaped a GC facility. Chad had helped Vicki get through the death of her friend Pete.

Chad shook hands with everyone and smiled at Vicki. "Zeke told me you were here, but I didn't believe I'd ever see you again."

Vicki smiled. "What are you doing here?"

Zeke put a hand on Chad's shoulder. "Take all the time you need. Vicki will show you to my office."

Vicki introduced Chad to the others, and baby Ryan crawled up to him and held out his hands. Chad grinned and picked the boy up. "I remember when you were just a little bump in your mother's tummy."

Finally, Vicki took Chad into the computer room to talk. "The girl who helped us get to your house—"

"Kelly Bradshaw?"

"Yeah, how is she?"

Chad shook his head. "The GC just about cleaned out all of us. They went house to house, looking for anyone without the mark. The ones they didn't find were ratted out by neighbors who'd seen us scrambling around in the night, trying to get food and supplies to each other. Kelly was caught about a month ago trying to get some water and bread to a woman on the other side of town." Chad looked away and wiped at his eyes.

"I'm so sorry. How did you survive?"

"Remember the woods behind my house where we went that night?"

Vicki nodded. Chad had been kind enough to make a picnic and share it with her one night. Their talk had helped her.

"A few of us escaped with all the food we could carry and started living there," Chad said. "We didn't think the GC would bother us, but some teenagers started exploring. You know what they'd do if they ever found us. I heard about Zeke and thought he might be able to give us some uniforms and chase them away."

"But how did you get here?" Vicki said. "A friend of mine has been trying for months to join us from Ohio, but they say it's too dangerous."

"Probably wasn't the smartest thing I've ever done. Took me a couple of nights and a few brushes with the GC, but I made it."

"But there had to be something more than just . . ." Vicki stopped. She remembered that Chad had expressed some feelings for her during their final moments in Iowa.

"The truth is, I really wanted to see you again," Chad said. "I don't know if you've thought of me at all since you were in Iowa, but I haven't stopped thinking about you. I've written a hundred e-mails, then trashed them." Chad scooted his chair closer and leaned forward. "I see a strength in you and a love for others I'm drawn to. I know we weren't together that long and I don't know you that well, but I'd like to get to know you better."

Vicki blushed. "I don't know what to say."

"If you don't feel anything for me, I'll understand. I'll get back in my car, and you'll never hear from me again—"

Vicki put a hand on his arm. "I'm flattered, really. You were so kind to me when I was struggling."

"But there's someone else. The one in Ohio?"

"Yeah."

"He's a lucky guy. I appreciate you being honest with me." Chad stood and walked to the door.

"You didn't really come for Zeke's help?"

Chad turned. "All my friends are gone, Vicki. I'm the only one left."

Vicki stood. "Stay with us. You'll be safe."

Chad nodded and walked through the door. He was the last person Zeke helped with a Global Community uniform. The next night, Chad left without telling Vicki where he was going or what he was going to do.

Two days later a report came over GCNN of the arrest of a man posing as a Peacekeeper.

"The unidentified and unmarked man was apprehended in southeastern Indiana after a high-speed chase," the news anchor said over grainy video shot at night.

Shelly pointed at the screen. "That's Chad!"

"It is not known what type of terrorist plans the man had," the anchor continued, "but he was quickly processed and taken to the nearest loyalty enforcement facility."

Vicki looked at Zeke. "Did he tell you what he was going to do?"

Zeke took a breath. "He made me promise not to tell, but I guess it's okay now. He wanted to know where Judd was staying."

"Judd?"

"Chad said he was going to get him and bring him back here if it was the last thing he ever did."

Vicki put her face in her hands. "He was doing that for me."

"I tried to talk him into staying and waiting for things to cool down a bit, but he wouldn't listen."

The GC report continued, showing others who had been apprehended. Vicki wrote Judd and told him the bad news. They both promised each other they would wait until they were sure God wanted Judd to make the dangerous trip.

30

THE COLD season had ended, and spring had come for Judd and the others hidden in Ohio. Judd flipped through a computer calendar and noticed the anniversary of the disappearances was only a day away. Even though it had been five years since his family had vanished, Judd felt the same ache as the first moment he walked into his house and realized they were gone and never coming back.

Five years of terror and beheadings and natural disasters. Five years of uncertainty, not knowing what was coming next.

Judd got out his notebook and looked at the things he had prayed about in the past few months. At the top of the list was:

Get to Wisconsin. That prayer hadn't been answered, but Judd hoped it would be soon.

Shelly and Conrad. There had been some misunderstanding in Wisconsin, and the two had gone from being best friends to enemies. Judd continued to ask God to give them a spirit of peace in the midst of turmoil.

Carpathia's failure. Though Judd knew those who had taken Carpathia's mark were doomed, he continued to pray for the failure of the Global Community and that the few undecided would turn to the true God. With hundreds of thousands dying because of the lack of drinkable water, that prayer was being answered every day. It seemed even those who followed Nicolae now realized they had been fooled by a cruel dictator who cared about no one but himself. As much as Carpathia, Leon Fortunato, and other GC authorities said it, the world wasn't getting better. Machines, computers, and people were wearing down. Services such as trash pickup and street cleaning were cut off. Roads fell into disrepair, and cities filled with crime.

Chang Wong. Judd continued to pray for his friend. He didn't know how Chang could stay in New Babylon, but he was still there, feeding information to the Tribulation Force and doing everything he could from the palace. Chang reported that the place had become a ghost town. Citizens no longer came to admire the sparkling buildings because the world was a mess. Half the population alive at the time of the Rapture had now died. Carpathia often called for the execution of leaders around the world who he thought weren't loyal enough, and Judd prayed that Chang would remain safe.

The undecided. Judd kept praying for new people to be reached by God's supernatural means. Every day he heard

stories of angels preaching the Good News and the
144,000 Jewish evangelists spreading throughout the
globe, preaching and teaching, apparently protected by
angels. But Satan's evil forces were still at work. The
deceivers were going strong, trying to convince everyone
that they did their miracles by Nicolae's power. Judd wept
at scenes of unmarked people in a remote Philippine
village being lured with the promise of water. Though the
Global Community News Network didn't show it, Judd
knew the same thing that happened near Petra had probably happened to these unfortunate people.

Tsion Ben-Judah. Judd prayed for strength for the
leader of a growing mass of people dedicated to following God no matter what the cost. Tsion continually
taught that God was evening the score with the evil ruler.
*It is not as if the God of gods could not defeat any foe he
chooses,* Dr. Ben-Judah wrote, *but the stench of the other side
evangelizing for evil has offended him and kindled his wrath.
Yet the wrath of God remains balanced by his great mercy and
love. There has been not one report of death or injury to any of
the 144,000 evangelists God has raised up to spread the truth
about his Son.*

Rayford Steele. The leader of the Tribulation Force
wrote Judd that he had also felt the presence of angels
protecting him and his flyers as they moved about the
world. God had protected these freedom flyers from
harm in the Middle East, and he had done so over other
areas as well when the GC tried to intercept them and
force them to land. Judd asked God to continue guarding
these brave pilots.

Buck and Chloe Williams. Judd prayed for Buck's writing in *The Truth*, which was still read by millions throughout the world. Chloe had massive duties with the Co-op, as well as being a mother to little Kenny.

Jacques Madeleine. Judd never forgot the kindness of his friends in France. Though the GC had discovered the anti-Carpathia action at the man's chalet, the group had been able to hide until the GC moved on. From the last report, many had become believers through the ministry.

Westin Jakes. Z-Van's former pilot had been put to work for the Tribulation Force and flew missions around the world. Westin had written many e-mails detailing the harrowing experiences over major cities, but each time God had delivered them from certain death.

Lionel. The transition for Lionel had been difficult. He felt the "phantom pain" of his missing arm, and many days he couldn't sleep because of his experience under the rock. Lionel had been tight-lipped about this, not even sharing with Judd about that night. Judd didn't press him for information but continued to pray with him and find things for Lionel to do.

There were other names on Judd's list like Mac McCullum, Leah Rose, Hannah Palemoon, and Naomi Tiberius, people Judd knew from the Tribulation Force and his travels to Petra. Judd thought often of Nada's parents and asked God to comfort them with the loss of their son and daughter. Judd prayed for Mark, Conrad, and the others in Wisconsin regularly, especially when Vicki brought up a situation. He remembered all the people who had given Lionel and him shelter while traveling north, and he asked God to protect them until the Glorious Appearing.

Finally, Judd prayed for Vicki. He asked God to draw her close and make her an even stronger believer than she already was. Judd thanked God for Vicki's friendship, her support, and for the life she had brought to him, even separated by the miles. "If I didn't have friends like Vicki and Lionel and Mark . . . I don't know if I'd have the will to keep on going."

One evening after a meeting with their Ohio group, Judd opened an e-mail from Sam Goldberg alerting Judd to the fact that the seas of the world had turned from blood to salt water again.

Tsion said this morning that he has been given no special knowledge about this by God, but he wonders if something worse is coming soon.

Judd turned on GCNN and found Carpathia taking credit for lifting the plague. "My people created a formula that has healed the waters." Nicolae beamed. "The plant and animal life of the oceans will surge back to life before long. And now that the oceans are clear again, all our beautiful lake and river waterways will soon be restored as well."

As usual, Carpathia was wrong. The plague of blood lifted from the seas, but as a few more weeks went by it was clear that God had chosen to let the lakes and rivers remain blood-filled. Judd wondered if Tsion was right. Was something worse headed for the earth? Judd opened his Bible to the book of Revelation and studied the text and Tsion's writings side by side.

Vicki looked for any ray of hope for Judd and Lionel to come north over the next few months but found none. There hadn't been another visitor for Zeke since Chad Harris, so the only movement about the country by believers was done by the commodity Co-op, and even that was kept to a minimum. Reports of drivers being stopped, pulled onto the street, and immediately shot were common.

The United North American States had become one of the unhealthiest places on earth to live, and Vicki wished she had taken Judd up on his offer to move to France. Or, she thought, they could have hidden out in Petra. There they were sure to have food, water, and safety.

But Vicki tried not to think of what could have been. Dealing with reality was a full-time job. Baby Ryan had become toddler Ryan, and while the boy's laughter and play habits brought joy to everyone in the camp (especially Charlie and Zeke who made him wooden blocks and toys), more tension had arisen between the Fogartys and Ryan's mother. Cheryl had become moody, staying in her cabin for days at a time and lashing out at anyone who tried to help her.

Vicki grew frustrated, running out of ideas. Josey and Tom Fogarty became fearful that Cheryl might do something careless with the boy when she had him in her cabin. While Ryan was with her, she seemed to become more cheery, but when he returned to the Fogartys, a cloud came over her.

Vicki prayed nonstop for Cheryl, but the Fogartys

called a meeting with Vicki and a few others and asked that Cheryl not be able to see the boy alone. "We're too scared she might take off with him," Josey said. "We love Cheryl, and she's given us the greatest gift we could ever receive, but she's just not stable."

"I've noticed the same thing," Mark said. "She's telling Ryan mean things about Josey and Tom."

"What's she saying?" Vicki said.

Mark sighed. "I was walking by her cabin while she was out at the swing Charlie rigged between the trees. She told Ryan over and over that she was his real mother, that the Fogartys were only taking care of him, and that she was going to take him away as soon as she found a place to go."

Vicki shook her head. "I agree that's terrible, but if you don't let her see him anymore, she could get worse."

"We're going to have to take that chance," Tom said.

Cheryl flew into a rage when Vicki tried to talk with her about the situation. Marshall, Tom, and Zeke came inside when the girl began throwing things. They tried praying with her, but finally Marshall gave her something to make her sleep.

The next few weeks were some of the most difficult Vicki had ever lived through. There were shrieks and cries at night, and Cheryl would show up at the Fogartys' door, asking to see Ryan. It reminded her of the time at the schoolhouse when the locusts had stung Janie and Melinda.

Finally, Marshall and the others decided they would either have to find a new place for Cheryl or move the

Fogartys and Ryan. Everyone felt sad for Cheryl but agreed something had to be done.

Vicki tried one last time to talk with her and explain the situation. Cheryl had been so sweet and had learned so much about the Bible, but now she didn't show up at their regular meetings and seemed hostile when they talked about Scripture.

Cheryl sat in a dark corner of the room, her hair hanging in front of her face while Vicki spoke. "Is there something going on you want to talk about?"

"Yeah, they've taken my baby away."

"But you wanted the Fogartys to have Ryan. Remember?"

Cheryl ran a hand through her hair. "I've changed my mind."

Vicki scooted closer and put a hand on the girl's arm. Cheryl recoiled and pulled both feet into her chair.

"Cheryl, we're really concerned about you. The way you're acting . . . this is not you. I know the kind and gentle person you are, and what you've become lately is somebody different. Please talk to me."

Cheryl set her jaw and didn't look at Vicki. "Get out. And don't come back until you bring my baby."

Vicki wept as she left. Marshall and the others looked for a safe place for Cheryl.

Sam rushed to the communications center when he heard news about something strange in Petra. He found Naomi Tiberius with Abdullah Smith and several of the leaders, including Dr. Tsion Ben-Judah and Chaim Rosenzweig.

Sam had heard from Chang Wong in New Babylon that something was up with Carpathia. Chang had overheard a conversation between Nicolae and his staff lamenting the fact that people in Petra had clean water to drink while the rest of the world suffered. Chang was worried that the GC might try something drastic to tap into the same spring that nourished Petra.

Sam stood in the back of the communications center, close enough to hear the conversation. A missile was fifteen minutes away, and by Abdullah's calculations was headed for a spot where the Global Community had been drilling for water.

Sam went outside to an area overlooking the desert. Sure enough, the GC workers had pulled back. Sam wiped his forehead and looked at the sun. Was it just him or had it gotten hotter? It was almost ten in the morning, but the heat felt like the hottest part of the afternoon.

The leaders and Abdullah walked onto a ledge and looked at the work site. A few minutes later a bright speck moved toward Petra. The missile struck the desert and raised a huge cloud of sand and soil. The explosion roared like thunder, and the ground shook. But no water or blood geyser spouted from the missile that must have cost millions of Nicks. Sam shook his head at the foolishness of the Global Community and wiped his brow again.

Chang's first inkling that something was wrong came as he secretly listened to a conversation coming from Carpathia's office. He had become more and more bold with his listening habits, wearing headphones at his desk so he could follow news of the missile.

Carpathia was upset that their weapon hadn't produced anything more than a crater.

A knock on the door and Krystall, Nicolae's secretary, entered. "Begging your pardon, sir, but we are getting strange reports."

"What kind of reports?"

"Some kind of a heat wave. The lines are jammed. People are—"

Suddenly, shouts came from Chang's office mates. He closed his computer program and took off the headphones. He noticed Rasha by the window with another man named Lars. They were pointing to the street, obviously upset.

Chang heard an explosion, then another, as people crowded around him.

"Get back!" Chang's boss, Aurelio Figueroa, shouted as he burst into the room waving his arms. "Get away from the windows!"

It was too late for Rasha and Lars. The window in front of them gave way, sending shards of glass flying about the room. Both were struck by the broken glass and crumpled to the floor as others screamed. Hot, steamy air blew into the room. A woman tried to help her fallen friends, but her hair curled, then burst into flames from the heat.

"What *is* this?" someone shrieked. "What's happening?"

Chang had the same question. Was this something

Nicolae had planned, or was it God's work? And would believers be affected like those with Carpathia's mark?

Judd awoke to a phone call from an excited Chang Wong. Judd felt groggy and missed the first few words from his friend. Something about heat and people dying.

"Slow down," Judd said, wiping his eyes. "What's going on?"

"The fourth Bowl Judgment from God," Chang said. "I'll explain in a moment, but you must be prepared."

"You mean we're in danger?" Judd said, suddenly awake.

"I don't think so. I think believers will be spared, while this will be a nightmare for unbelievers. But this may be our chance to move much-needed supplies to you and your friends."

Judd's heart raced. He was excited about the prospect of food and supplies for the Ohio group. But the thing that excited him most was that if they could move supplies more easily, *he* might be able to move, and that meant he might get to Wisconsin. *Back to Vicki.*

31

JUDD Thompson Jr. pressed the phone to his ear and walked to a private place in the Ohio hideout. Chang had called from New Babylon to tell Judd about something weird, what he called the "fourth Bowl Judgment." Chang seemed excited about what this might mean for believers.

"Has Dr. Ben-Judah said anything about this?" Judd said.

"I haven't heard anything, but you know he'll come out with something soon."

Judd flipped on the television as he talked, but the only local station was off the air. "Back up and tell me exactly what happened."

Chang took a breath. "I had been listening to Carpathia when his secretary said there were strange reports about a heat wave. Then I heard shouts near my office. Everyone ran to the front window, and my boss

313

warned them to get back. That's when the glass exploded and Rasha . . ." Chang stopped for a moment.

"Who's Rasha?"

"She worked near me. We had several conversations about Judah-ites and all the miraculous things going on. She was a Carpathia follower, but she was really scared that something bad was going to happen to her. I wanted to tell her the truth so many times, but there was no way. She had Carpathia's mark."

"What happened to her?"

"She was at the window when it shattered. Shards of glass flew everywhere. Rasha and another man were cut and fell to the floor as the hot air blew into the room. People went crazy, screaming and running over each other. One woman tried to help Rasha, but her hair burst into flames."

"If that was going on inside, I can't imagine what happened outside."

"It was awful," Chang said. "A woman was walking her dog below us. She let go of the animal and tried to get inside a car, but she burned her hands on the door handles. The dog ran in a circle, trying to find some shade or relief from the heat, but it finally turned into a dog torch."

Judd shuddered. "And the same thing happened to people?"

"They fell out of their cars. Tires exploded. I saw wind-shields melt. My boss ordered everyone into the basement."

"Could you feel the heat?"

"It was a bit warmer, but I wasn't burned. I pretended it was hurting though."

314

"What happened to Rasha and the other guy?"

"They turned into human fire. It was awful. The others ran for the elevator, but I said I would catch the next one. I wanted to run to my quarters and alert the Tribulation Force and you."

As soon as he was off the phone, Judd logged on to Tsion Ben-Judah's Web site. Judd couldn't imagine what the last five years would have been like without the spiritual direction of this man. His Web site alone had helped millions come to know God, and the 144,000 evangelists God had raised up had reached more. Judd noticed a new posting from Tsion and downloaded the file so Lionel and the others could read it. Tsion wrote:

> My dear friends in Christ, I want you to know that we have reached another terrible milestone. For those of you in the former USA and other places where the sun is yet to rise, the deadly fourth Bowl Judgment has struck, as prophesied in the Bible, and every time zone in the world will be affected.
>
> Here in Petra, by ten in the morning, people out in the sun without the seal of God were burned alive. This may seem an unparalleled opportunity to plead once again for the souls of men and women, because millions will lose loved ones. But the Scriptures also indicate that this may come so late in the hearts of the undecided that they will have already been hardened.

Burned alive. Judd couldn't imagine such horror. He had seen scary movies where people had been burned, and the images had stuck in his mind.

Tsion included the Scripture that mentioned the judgment:

> *Revelation 16:8-9 says, "Then the fourth angel poured out his bowl on the sun, and power was given to him to scorch men with fire. And men were scorched with great heat, and they blasphemed the name of God who has power over these plagues; and they did not repent and give Him glory."*

Tsion's message continued, explaining as much as he could, but the man admitted he did not know how long the heat would last. Judd read the brief message again. He had so many questions. Was Chang right about being able to move around during daylight? If cars had exploded in New Babylon, would the Humvee they had hidden near the hideout also explode, or would God somehow spare believers' vehicles?

Judd wished he could talk with Tsion himself, but he knew that wasn't possible. He recalled a conversation with Rayford Steele, who gave his secure phone number and offered to help in making decisions. Judd glanced at his watch. Before he called Vicki with the news, he had to talk with Captain Steele.

Vicki Byrne hadn't slept well the past few nights. Cheryl's moods swung like playground equipment, but the truth was, the situation with the Fogartys had eased a little. Cheryl had said she didn't need to see Ryan much anymore, and Marshall and Zeke were trying to find her another place to live.

But Vicki had to admit that Cheryl wasn't the only reason she was losing sleep. Members of the Young Tribulation Force had grown frustrated. Some wanted to take more chances to find people without the mark of Carpathia. Mark had talked about leaving the group and traveling, but Zeke had convinced him to stay.

The newest members of the group, Ty and Tanya Spivey, along with the others who had broken away from Tanya's father's group, had thought the camp in Wisconsin was the next best thing to heaven when they arrived. Now they felt disappointed at the conflict.

"I know we're all human," Tanya had said to Vicki when they were alone one morning, "but the stuff with Cheryl and the fighting between Conrad and Shelly upset me."

"I'm just as disappointed as you," Vicki said, "but when we become believers we're not promised that everything's going to be easy. In a lot of ways, things got worse when I became a believer."

"That doesn't seem fair. If God loves us, wouldn't he help us solve our problems?"

Vicki couldn't think of a Bible passage that addressed the subject, and she had to admit she felt the same way. She wanted God to fix things. The world's troubles had united the kids for a time, but each day brought new struggles.

Something moved outside the cabin, and Vicki sat up. The moon shone through the curtains, casting an eerie glow. She strained to hear, but all was quiet.

Vicki closed her eyes and prayed for her friends, especially Judd. If God would bring him back, she could put up with any problem.

———————————————

Judd dialed the number to the hideout in San Diego and took a deep breath.

"Steele," Rayford answered.

"I hope I'm not bothering you, Captain. This is Judd Thompson."

"Not a problem. What's up?"

Judd explained what Chang Wong had told him, and Rayford said he had just gotten off the phone with Dr. Ben-Judah. "I wanted to ask him if those with the seal of God would be immune to the heat."

"My question exactly," Judd said. "What did Tsion say?"

"He said they feel some extra warmth there in Petra and some people are a little tired, but like Chang, they're not feeling the effects like unbelievers."

"Then it's true. I could go out tomorrow morning without the GC knowing about it."

"It's likely. I told Tsion this could mean a lot to the Trib Force. As long as we hide before GC officers come out, we're okay."

"Which means you can move supplies around the country."

"Exactly. And with the way the groups are begging for food, this comes at a great time."

"I'm trying to get to the Wisconsin hideout. Do you think it would be safe to drive there tomorrow?"

"You're talking about Avery, right?"

"Yes."

"And what's your location now?"

Judd told him.

"I don't know if I'd chance it unless you have some place to ditch for the night. Wait and see what happens tomorrow. I'll be talking with our people about flights to various groups. Maybe you could tag along."

"Great. But will planes be able to fly in the heat?"

"I hope so. You have to understand we have no idea how long this will last. It could be a few hours, a few days, or weeks. Tsion cautioned that God has never been predictable with these plagues. We know the order they come in, and we used to think that when one ended the next one began. Now we know they can overlap. Tsion just doesn't want to see us caught in the open when the thing ends."

"Me either. But you know the Global Community has to look at something like this as another nail in their coffin."

"The world's in bad shape. People are scrounging for food and the bare necessities. There's no law except survival. Everybody who's smart goes out with a gun."

"Sort of like the Old West."

"Right, except the good guys are the evangelists. Yesterday I got a report about two who preached to a small town in Germany. There were still a few holdouts to Carpathia's mark, and these evangelists found them, but before they could finish speaking, a group of armed men broke into the meeting. They took all the valuables and Nicks the people had and then separated the men from the women."

"I don't like the sound of this."

"Neither did I, until I heard what happened next. It was clear this gang of thieves was up to no good. But as they were leading the women outside, an angel appeared at the door, and with a couple of words the robbers all fell dead."

"What happened to the others?"

"All of them believed the message and received the mark of God."

Judd shook his head. "I'd almost given up about any undecided. It seems like everybody's chosen Carpathia or God."

"This is the greatest rescue mission the earth has ever known. On the video reports about the wrath of the Lamb earthquake, people dug through collapsed buildings for days, even weeks, looking for just one survivor. In one hospital, they found a baby alive fifteen days after the earthquake. I like to think our mission is the same. We have to keep digging, keep praying, keep hoping that we'll find someone who's ready to hear the message."

"I hadn't thought about it that way," Judd said.

"People have lost faith in the GC and its leaders. If there's anyone out there without Carpathia's mark, and we can get to them, I have to believe they'll choose the light instead of darkness. They're going to be suffering as the sun rises every day."

Judd paused. "But hasn't Dr. Ben-Judah said God is actually showing mercy with these judgments?"

"I asked him about that, and he still thinks the fact that more plagues are coming means God still wants people to repent. Most won't and will curse God, but Tsion supports our efforts to find the remaining undecided."

"Then I want to be part of it. And I'll bet there's a bunch of people in Wisconsin who would too and some here in Ohio."

"Let's see what the morning brings," Rayford said. "In the meantime, call Vicki and tell her the good news."

"You know about us?"

"Chloe told me. My guess is you two will be back together within a couple of days."

Judd couldn't help but smile as he hung up. He had tried to stay reserved with Captain Steele, but he was sure some of his excitement had come through on the phone. He quickly dialed Vicki's number.

Vicki awoke with a start. She couldn't tell how long she had been sleeping. Was it an hour? two? The moon had moved little in the window, so she guessed she hadn't been asleep long.

Something outside had startled her. Or had it been a dream? It sounded like Marshall's van, but who could be taking it this time of night?

For the first time in a long while, Vicki worried about the Global Community. What if they had discovered the remote camp? She wrapped a blanket around her shoulders, grabbed a flashlight, and tiptoed outside.

The ground was wet with dew, and the crisp temperature raised goose bumps on her arms. She headed for the main cabin where the others usually gathered and saw footprints heading toward Josey and Tom Fogarty's cabin. When she pointed the flashlight at their front door, she noticed it was open a few inches.

Someone stirred inside, and a light came on.

"Mrs. Fogarty?" Vicki whispered.

A shriek pierced the night.

Vicki rushed toward the cabin as Tom Fogarty swung the door open. "Where is he?"

"Where's who?" Vicki said.

Josey bounded to the door behind him. "He's gone! Ryan's gone!"

32

VICKI rushed inside the cabin and saw Ryan's empty bed. On Ryan's second birthday, Zeke had given the boy a toddler bed in the shape of a car. The child's blanket was gone and a stuffed bear lay on the floor.

Tom Fogarty had run out the door as soon as Vicki arrived. Josey shook while she ran around the room, looking under the bed, checking in the closet. "Sometimes he'll play hide-and-seek and I won't find him until he laughs, but he's never run off at night. Ryan started sleeping at night, you know."

Vicki took Josey's arm and gently pulled her onto the bed. "Tell me what happened."

"We just woke up and he was gone! It's so chilly outside, and the little thing didn't have shoes on."

"I saw footprints outside, but they didn't look like a child's."

Tom Fogarty ran inside breathing hard, his face pale. Marshall followed him in.

"Did you find him?" Josey said.

"We checked Cheryl's cabin," Tom said. "She's not there."

"Look in the other cabins," Josey said. "Check the meeting place or—"

Marshall held up a hand. "Ma'am, the van's gone. I usually keep the keys hidden, but somehow she must have found them."

"You think Cheryl . . . ?" Josey's voice trailed off, and her eyes fluttered. Suddenly she locked eyes with Tom. "Then we have to go after him. We have another car—"

"Hang on," Marshall said. "We're going after her and Ryan. Zeke and Mark have gone for the car. She's gotten a head start, but hopefully she hasn't gone far."

While Tom tried to calm Josey, Vicki followed Marshall outside. "Let me go with you. When we catch up to her I can—"

"We've already decided you need to go," Marshall said. "Get dressed and meet us at the car."

When Judd didn't get an answer in Wisconsin, he e-mailed Vicki and told her the latest news. Then he checked on the latest from the Global Community.

At first, the GC posted all the grisly pictures. Traffic cameras set up near busy intersections showed melting car tires and people jumping from their vehicles. The people just as quickly tried to get back inside, but the door handles were so hot they couldn't touch them. Frantic, drivers rushed for shade or nearby buildings. Shots from these cameras didn't last long because the cameras themselves went blank after a few seconds.

Reporters standing on rooftops showed the slow-moving arc of the sun as it came over the horizon. When the rays reached houses, they began smoking and smoldering. As the sun rose higher, homes caught fire.

Reporters ran for their lives inside buildings, which eventually collapsed from the heat. Judd found one camera shot from a famous university. The view was shielded by trees and looked out on a fountain in the middle of the campus. As the sun beat down, water bubbled. Soon it was boiling and steam rose.

On a gentle slope nearby, a student lay in the shade holding a book, his head propped up on a backpack. He sat up when the water boiled. Suddenly, as trees caught fire and smoke rose, the boy grabbed his backpack and stood.

"Get out of there," Judd whispered to himself.

The boy ran but made the mistake of rushing toward the sunlight. Like a vampire caught in daylight, the boy turned, shielded his face from the hot rays, and fell. First his backpack, then the boy's clothes caught on fire. Finally, he became part of the burning landscape, with trees, bushes, and even the grass igniting.

Judd clicked to one of his favorite sites, which showed famous beaches. The only cameras operating were those where the sun hadn't yet risen, but reports stated the blood was boiling in rivers around the globe.

Everywhere the sun reached, people, animals, plant life, buildings, cars, bridges, and homes were affected.

The world had become the wick of a candle that was quickly burning up, and Judd wondered how many could survive another year before the Glorious Appearing of Jesus Christ.

Judd wrote his friend Sam Goldberg and asked for a report from Petra. He wanted to know exactly what to expect when the sun came up over Ohio.

Vicki rushed to her cabin and dressed, then met Tom, Marshall, and Mark. It took a few minutes for them to back the small four-wheel-drive vehicle from its hiding place. As different people had traveled to the hideout to see Zeke or join the group, one problem Marshall and the others had to deal with was the extra vehicles left in the woods nearby. The group decided to keep the van handy and hide the others. A few cars had been driven into the Mississippi River.

Vicki and Mark climbed in the back, Marshall driving and Tom Fogarty beside him. Vicki thought Tom was perfect for the trip since he had been a former police officer, but she wondered how he had convinced Josey to stay behind.

"Cheryl's obviously been planning this for some time," Tom said. "Vicki, you've talked the most with her. Has she ever said anything about leaving?"

Vicki shook her head. "These past few weeks we haven't talked about much at all. She's been so grouchy that I've had to leave her alone."

The car bounced along the rutted dirt road. When

they reached a paved road, Tom got out and inspected the area. "Go left," he said.

Mark reached for the phone and dialed the hideout. He turned on the speakerphone and asked Conrad to search the computer for anything Cheryl might have written.

"Be right back to you," Conrad said.

"I can't imagine what that little guy's going through right now," Tom said. "Hopefully he'll sleep through this whole thing until we catch them."

Conrad called a few moments later. "I found a deleted message from Wanda, the midwife who helped deliver Cheryl's baby."

"What's it say?" Mark said.

"She was actually writing to Mrs. Fogarty."

"What?" Tom said. "Josey hasn't had any contact with her in months."

"Let me read you the letter," Conrad said.

> "Dear Josey,
>
> "I'm sorry to hear things have gone so badly with little Ryan. Babies can be a handful, especially if he has an illness like you described. If there's anything I can do from this end to help, please let me know. Otherwise, your plan to send Cheryl here with him sounds good. I'd be glad to keep them with me until they can make other arrangements. Be advised that I'm in a different location. I'll include a map on this e-mail, and you can let me know what you want to do. There's plenty of room to park the van, so don't worry about that, but be careful of the GC as you hit town.

"No matter what happens, know that I'll be praying for you and your husband and Ryan through this difficult time. Remember, we serve a great God who can indeed work miracles."

Vicki ran a hand through her hair. "Cheryl wrote to Wanda pretending to be your wife and lied about Ryan being sick!"

Tom shifted in his seat and pursed his lips. "Conrad, are there any other deleted messages there?"

"I'm checking." *Click. Click.* "Okay, found two. The first one looks like . . . yeah, this is the one where she describes Ryan as having an illness and that she wants permission for Cheryl to take Ryan to Wanda's house."

Marshall rolled to a stop at a major road and turned off the headlights. "I'm assuming Wanda is in the same general area where we found her last time?"

"Yeah, I'll give directions in a minute," Conrad said. "Just head toward her old place."

"What's the next message say?" Tom said.

Click. "Oh, boy . . . here we go."

"Dear Wanda,

"Thanks for your kindness and prayers. The situation with Ryan has gotten even worse since I last wrote. Would it be possible, if we can work it out with Marshall and the others, to have Cheryl come alone with Ryan and stay at your place? We would send her in the van.

"I agree with you that God can work miracles. I would like nothing better than to have Ryan back, but all

*the crying and sleepless nights have Tom and me at the
end of our rope. Cheryl has been so good to help us. I
don't know what we'd have done without her. We're all
praying that God will heal Ryan on the way to your place.
You pray with us and we'll look for a good report once
Cheryl is there."*

"She signs the letter, 'Yours in Christ, Josey.' "

Tom slammed his fist so hard on the glove compartment that Vicki thought he had broken his hand.
Marshall drove as fast as he dared, using the moonlight to
navigate. Conrad read the directions to Wanda's house,
and Mark took notes.

"Vicki, you have a new message here from Judd,"
Conrad said. "And it looks like I've missed a couple of his
calls."

Vicki smiled. "I'll read it when I get back."

"Hang on. Zeke has something to say to you guys,"
Conrad said.

"How's my wife doing?" Tom said.

"As well as can be expected," Zeke said. "She tore out
of the cabin when you left. Took three of us to get her
back to her room and settled down. Shelly and Darrion
are with her, and I've got Charlie standing watch to make
sure nobody bothers her."

"What did you want, Zeke?" Marshall said.

"Well, you know I'm not into bad feelings and that
kinda stuff, but I gotta tell you I'm worried about you
guys and little Ryan."

"We're going to catch her, believe me," Tom said.

"I know, but there are GC in that area. I just looked at their list of arrests in the past two weeks, and they've made a bunch of surprise raids. Cheryl could be leading you guys right to the enemy."

"Thanks for the heads up," Mark said, "but I don't think we're going to stop until we find Ryan."

Judd heard a blip and noticed Sam was sending a video message from Petra. Judd turned on the small camera above the screen and saw his friend. Sam wanted to know how Lionel was doing.

"He's adjusted pretty well, but he still has some pain," Judd said. "If we can ever get to Wisconsin, there's a guy who's been working on some kind of contraption he thinks Lionel will be able to use."

"I suppose you've heard what's going on here if you've written at this hour," Sam said.

"Tell me about it," Judd said.

Sam was inside the communications building, but he had someone open the door behind him and Judd could see rock formations in the background. Sam wiped sweat from his forehead. "It's crazy. Some of us noticed it was getting a little warmer, but we had no idea there was a plague until about ten this morning. We heard screams and rushed to see what it was.

"There were some stragglers just outside the camp, undecideds who didn't see the miracle worker. They were literally burned alive where they stood. That's when the reports began coming in from all over the world. We heard from China that everything is dried up, burned, or melted. No one is on the street, except for believers. Some GC apparently tried to use fireproof suits and boots and helmets, but they didn't get very far. One of our sources says believers found piles of burning material on the street."

"So it's kind of like the locusts—the believers can move around without fear they're going to be burned. But one thing still bugs me."

"What's that?"

"If all these buildings are falling in and cars are exploding because of the heat, how do the believers get around? If they walk, they won't get very far. But if they try to use a car or a plane, won't they burn?"

"I don't know how God's doing it, but it seems like the vehicles believers use are immune to the heat. Just like the clothes we wear and our shoes. The same with the hideouts of believers and the supplies."

"Amazing."

"Dr. Ben-Judah just called for prayer that God would give wisdom to the Tribulation Force about how to use this opportunity."

"Great. But you don't feel anything more than just being a little bit warm?"

"Wait a few hours. You'll feel what it's like soon enough."

Judd closed his eyes and smiled. For the first time in months, things would be reversed. Now the GC would hide during the day and be out at night, and the Young Trib Force would move around during the day and sleep at night.

33

VICKI suggested they call Wanda and warn her about Cheryl, but Marshall reminded her that Wanda didn't use a phone. Marshall asked Conrad to send an urgent e-mail to Wanda detailing what they knew.

As they bounced over back roads, Vicki thought about all they had been through in the past few years. The disappearance of her family would have been enough change, but with the earthquake, the plagues, and Nicolae Carpathia hunting down and killing believers, Vicki had little time to think about the past. Survival was a full-time job, and reaching out to those who didn't know God was her main mission.

Still, hardly a day went by that she didn't think of her family, her friends who had died, and the way things could have been. Vicki's nineteenth birthday had come and gone without anyone remembering. Not even Judd. She didn't blame anyone, but she still ached for things to return to normal. Before the disappearances, she had dreamed of going away to school. She thought a college degree might help her get a good job, and who knew, maybe she would find some rich guy and settle down in a Chicago suburb in a real house instead of a trailer. But her parents didn't have the money to send her, and Vicki wasn't scholarship material, at least back then.

Vicki wasn't proud of the way she had lived before the disappearances. She had made bad choices in friends and in the way she lived. She had put partying above every-thing, and she knew she had to tell Judd about some of those things. Maybe he had skeletons too.

Before the vanishings, Vicki hadn't thought of her life in the long term. If something sounded fun, she did it. If she thought something would make her happy, she'd try it. If someone suggested a tattoo or a piercing, she only thought of what people would say the next day at school.

The vanishings and Vicki's new belief in God had changed all that. Suddenly, the truth about Jesus and what he had done for her, the reality that God wanted her to dedicate her life to him, and the fact that there were only seven years until the return of Jesus made her want to change. God himself transformed the hopes and dreams of a normal teenager.

Vicki could never have dreamed what God would do in those first few years. She recalled a quote that summed up her feelings: "The world has not yet seen what God can do with one person who is totally committed to him." As Vicki became more aware of God, his power and love and how much he wanted to help Vicki, she had grown more confident. In spite of her weaknesses, God was using Vicki.

She mulled these things over as they drove into the night, knowing the others at the hideout would be praying. She wondered about Judd's e-mail and felt sad she hadn't asked Conrad to read it to her. It couldn't be anything embarrassing because Judd and Vicki had agreed they wouldn't use e-mails to talk about things that were too personal. When they were on the phone, they discussed their feelings, but in e-mails they stuck to the latest news and happenings. If one or the other did want to say something personal they wrote *private* in the subject line.

Mark handed Vicki a stick of gum, and she thanked him. Vicki couldn't remember the last time she had had a mint or gum. Mark had kept a stash of candy from their trip to the GC warehouse and doled it out at appropriate times. Mark loved giving Ryan candy, and he had become one of the child's favorites.

Vicki stuffed the gum in her mouth and thought of her parents. Her dad had chewed this type of gum on Sunday mornings. She remembered him walking into her bedroom with a fresh minty smell on his breath, asking, pleading with her to come with them to church.

"Sun will be coming up in another hour or so," Marshall said, breaking the silence in the car.

"How much farther to Wanda's place?" Vicki said.

Tom studied Mark's notes. "Wanda didn't give mileage, but from where her place used to be, we have to be close."

"What's our plan?" Mark said.

Tom turned. "We find my boy and—" He squinted out the back window. Something flickered in his eyes.

"What is it?" Vicki said, turning.

"We've got company," Tom said.

Lights flashed in the distance, and a GC squad car approached.

"You think they've seen us?" Vicki said.

"Everybody, hang on," Marshall said. "We're pulling into this field, but I won't be able to use my brakes."

When the squad car came over a hill and reached a dip in the road, Marshall took his foot off the accelerator and turned the wheel sharply, sending them into a field. Mark gripped Vicki's shoulder and pulled her down as the car plunged over an embankment.

After the car came to a stop a few yards into the field, Marshall turned off the engine. "Everybody all right?"

Everyone said they were, then watched breathlessly as the GC squad car approached. Vicki closed her eyes and breathed a brief prayer as the squad car sped past and continued east. When it turned a corner, Marshall started the car and pulled back onto the road.

"Wonder where that guy was going in such a hurry," Mark said.

"Call Conrad and ask if he's heard from Wanda," Marshall said. "I don't like seeing the GC on the prowl."

Tom shook his head a few minutes later. "No return message yet."

Mark groaned and put a hand to his forehead. "Why would Cheryl do this? She knows she's putting us in danger."

"Sounds like she's had kind of a meltdown," Marshall said. "Having the baby, then placing it in the Fogartys' house did her in. She's not thinking rationally."

"Does that mean she's not a believer anymore?" Mark said.

No one spoke.

Finally, Vicki broke the silence. "God hasn't abandoned her. Cheryl's turned her back on what she knows is true and good. I think she'll come around—"

"When the GC catch her and chop her head off?" Tom said. His face was red. "And what about my son? What happens when they give him one of those Nicolae tattoos? What's God going to do with that?"

The thought of little Ryan getting the mark of Carpathia frightened Vicki. Judd had told her about Chang Wong and how he had been drugged and given the mark against his will. Surely God wouldn't hold a little one like Ryan responsible for getting the mark. But the GC would make an example of him, parading him in front of the cameras, pleased that they had taken him from the clutches of the evil Judah-ites.

"We're going to get to her before they do anything to him," Vicki said. "Trust me."

"I hope you're right," Tom said.

"And what do we do with Cheryl after we catch her?" Mark said. "She's a threat to the whole group."

"We just have to keep praying for her," Vicki said. "That's all we can do."

Tom settled in his seat. "As far as I'm concerned, I don't want that girl within a hundred miles of my family."

The group drove toward glimmers of flashing lights ahead. Finally, they slowed near a decaying gas station on the outskirts of a town. Two sets of lights flickered against a building in the distance, but Vicki couldn't see the GC car.

"From these directions," Tom said, "it looks like we can turn left here and take the back road to Wanda's."

Marshall stroked his stubbly beard and glanced in the rearview mirror. "I don't know about you guys, but I'd like to see what those GC caught."

"Same here," Mark said.

Vicki nodded.

Tom pointed at the gas station and suggested they pull behind it. Quietly they all got out, but Tom told Mark and Vicki to wait.

Mark rolled his eyes and got back in the car. "I hate it when older people treat you like a kid."

"They're both stressed about Ryan. It's nothing personal."

"Yeah, well, I still liked it better when we called our own shots. The most exciting thing we've done since coming to Avery is go to that warehouse, and we had to sneak around to do that."

Vicki noticed a lightening in the clouds peeking over the horizon. "We have to get to Wanda's quickly if we want to beat the daylight."

Mark tapped his fingers against the armrest, and Vicki strained to see around the back of the gas station. Another GC squad car approached, then passed the station and turned down a street a few blocks away.

Minutes passed and their friends didn't return. "Maybe they found something," Mark said.

The phone rang and Vicki answered. It was Conrad. "Hold on for this one, Vicki. You're not going to believe it. Zeke and I have been watching reports along the East Coast, and some weird stuff is going on. People are getting burned up. GC and anybody with the mark of Carpathia is at risk."

"What do you mean, burned up?"

"Hang on—we're getting onto Dr. Ben-Judah's Web site. Okay, here it is." He paused, reading through the material. "Does the fourth Bowl Judgment ring a bell?"

Vicki thought a moment. "Wait, isn't that the one where the angel is given power to burn people with fire?"

"Bingo. And it looks like it's happened everywhere the sun's shining. Do you realize what this means?"

"A lot of people are going to die."

"Yeah, but if believers aren't affected, which is what I assume from what I've read of Dr. Ben-Judah's letter, we'll be able to move around during the day."

"What's Conrad want?" Mark said.

"Conrad, thanks. I'll get back to you."

Vicki explained what Conrad had told her and looked toward the horizon. For so long, the sun had caused fear among believers. Now they might not have to be scared of daylight.

"It's been twenty minutes," Mark said. "I think we ought to see what's going on."

"Let's wait another five minutes—"

"Fine, you can stay where you are, but I'm going."

Vicki got out with Mark, switching the phone to vibrate. They stayed away from the street, walking in the same direction as Marshall and Tom, and cut through a hedge. A dog barked in the distance as they skirted a fence and crept through an open area. A few houses were scattered about—some abandoned, others well kept.

The squad-car lights became brighter, but there was still no sign of Marshall or Tom.

A two-story apartment building loomed before them. They walked to the right, stepping gingerly past old barbecues and gardening tools stacked at the end of the building. They stayed low, creeping onto the scene like two cats searching for prey. Mark dropped to his knees, and Vicki followed as they crawled to the top of a knoll and spotted the squad cars near a van.

A child cried out, and Vicki recognized Ryan. The officers had Cheryl against the front of the van, her hands cuffed behind her. A little farther up the street two officers laughed and pointed at something on the ground. Vicki crawled five feet to her left and gasped. Marshall and Tom lay facedown in the street, their hands behind them.

34

VICKI focused on Ryan, who was still inside the van and being cared for by a female officer. The child cried for his mama and struggled with the officer.

"It's okay," Cheryl yelled, tears streaming down her face. "We're going to be okay."

One of the officers near Tom and Marshall keyed his radio. "Two males, one female, and one child. All unmarked."

Vicki wondered if Tom or Marshall had IDs on them. If the GC found out Tom was a former GC officer, they'd take him in for questioning.

Vicki's heart wrenched every time Ryan cried out. She wanted to rush in and grab him but couldn't.

"They must have jumped Tom and Marshall," Mark whispered. "What do you want to do?"

Vicki glanced at the sky. It would still be a few minutes before the sun rose. "Let me pull the car around. I'll get their attention and see if they take the bait."

"What'll you do if they follow?"

"I'll try to lead them into the light. You see what you can do for Tom and the others."

"Maybe I should take the car—"

"No. You'll be better at helping them. Let me go." Vicki scooted backward quietly and ran to the car. The keys were still in the ignition, and Vicki started it and pulled onto the road. She had the sick feeling that perhaps the plague of burning fire wouldn't hit Wisconsin like it had the rest of the world. Could it be over? If so, Vicki and the others were in deep trouble.

Vicki pulled slowly onto the main road and looked at the surrounding hills. The town lay in a valley, so until the sun was higher, there would be patches of shade throughout the area. She stopped in the middle of the road and focused on trees on the ridge. A thin trail of smoke rose like a white snake. Was it some kind of illusion? or dust? The longer she looked, the more convinced she became that it was smoke.

Vicki rolled her window down, peering up at the eerie sight. A spark, then a flash of fire broke out at the tops of trees. As sunlight spread farther, more leaves and branches were caught in the blaze.

A voice brought Vicki back to reality. "You want to step out of the car, miss?"

A man in uniform stood a few feet in front and to the left of Vicki's car. She hadn't heard him approach, and her heart raced wildly when he took a step closer. "Keep your hands where I can see them and get out—"

Vicki punched the accelerator and threw herself flat

on the seat. A gun fired and glass shattered, but she kept her foot down, one hand on the steering wheel. She peeked over the dashboard in time to see she was headed for the curb and swerved as another shot smashed the back windshield, the bullet crashing into the car radio.

As Vicki reached the street where the van was stopped, two GC officers pointed their guns and fired, the other rushing to his car. Vicki ducked again and floored it, hoping none of them would shoot her tires.

She made it past the first few houses and looked up. Before her stretched a wide-open road that led toward the hillside.

Mark waited until he heard the first shot. The GC radio went crazy when the officer reported another unmarked citizen nearby. Mark counted four officers firing as Vicki passed. The female officer carried Ryan away from the van and placed him on the ground near Tom and Marshall.

As the other officers roared away in two of the squad cars, the female officer walked back to Cheryl, and Mark saw his chance. He raced down a slight embankment, careful to keep the van between him and the officer. Cheryl screamed for Ryan.

He reached the back of the van and knelt as the officer pushed Cheryl toward Tom and Marshall. Mark breathed a quick prayer. He wasn't sure what to do, but something told him to get Ryan first.

He duckwalked to the squad car, which was still running, and reached through the open window. He tried to throw the car into gear, but it wouldn't go. He glanced back and noticed Marshall had seen him.

"There's something crawling on my legs!" Marshall yelled at the officer. "Come over here and get it off!"

Mark quietly opened the door, got in, pushed the brake pedal, and put the car in drive. The car moved slowly forward as he scampered away.

As soon as Mark was hidden from view, Marshall shouted, "Hey, looks like your car's going on a trip!"

The officer cursed, and Mark heard footsteps approaching. When the woman passed, he sprinted toward his friends. Mark raced with lightning speed toward Ryan and with one swoop gathered the boy up and darted away.

"Marky!" Ryan said as they ran. The boy giggled, and Mark tried to quiet him. Finally, he put a hand over Ryan's mouth. Mark rushed behind a garage and peered out long enough to see that the female officer had stopped the car. Mark held Ryan tight while he rushed for the abandoned gas station.

Vicki gunned the engine and flew toward the hills. She couldn't see the sun yet, but she could see its effect. A trail of smoke rose from the top of the ridge. If she could reach the curve above her, which looked no more than two miles away, she had a chance.

She flicked on her lights and kept an eye on the rear-view mirror. Racing out of the small town were two squad cars, lights flashing.

Vicki sped up and hit a curve at full speed, her tires dropping off the edge of the pavement, then hopping back on. The squad cars gained ground, so she mashed her foot to the floor and flew down the sloping road and toward the hill. She had to slow to make the next curve, and the car bogged down and the engine revved.

A squad car pulled in directly behind her and another raced beside her. She glanced to her left quickly enough to see there was only one officer in the car. Sirens blared, and someone on a bullhorn ordered her to pull over. Vicki kept her hands glued to the steering wheel and looked to her right. The hill still blocked the sunlight.

"Pull over now!" an officer shouted.

Mark gasped for air and held Ryan tightly against his chest. The boy had giggled as Mark ran from the scene, as if they were playing a game. "Candy," Ryan said.

Mark handed him a soft piece of candy and patted the child's back as they reached the gas station. He expected to see the squad car speed toward them at any moment.

"Marky!" Ryan said, looking around.

"Yeah, Marky's here. Now we need to be really quiet."

Ryan put his hand out. "Blankie! Uh . . . uh! Blankie!"

"We're going to get your blanket, but we need to be quiet, okay?"

Ryan wrinkled his nose. "Blankie . . ."

Mark wished he could have helped Tom and Marshall, but there wasn't time. And if Conrad was right about the heat plague, he wouldn't have to stay hidden long before the GC officers realized the wrath of God.

The gas station was padlocked. Even the restrooms around the back were sealed shut. If anyone came out of their houses or happened to drive by, he and Ryan would be seen.

"Hey," someone whispered.

Mark looked around. On a hillside were a few houses. On the other side was a vacant lot with weeds and bushes.

"Over here," a man said.

Mark focused on what looked like a manhole cover that was slightly open. A hand waved Mark forward. Could it be a GC trick? If so, why would the GC be hiding underground?

Mark looked at the street. No squad car. He hugged Ryan tightly and made a run for the hole. The cover swung open, and a man with a scraggly beard reached out for the boy.

Ryan grabbed Mark's neck and whined. "Scared! Scared!"

"It's okay, buddy. I'm with you."

Vicki heard the ping of bullets off the back of her car and swerved to her right. The car shook, and she smelled something like rubber burning. A glance in the side mirror showed smoke rising from the car. The GC had shot one of her tires.

As she slowed, Vicki noticed sunshine creeping around

346

the mountain. She floored the accelerator and pulled forward as far as she could. When she stopped, the front half of her car was in sunshine, the back in shadows.

"Get out and lay facedown on the pavement!" a GC officer barked.

Vicki opened the door, her hands in front of her. When she closed the door, one of the officers cursed and yelled for her to get down. Immediately Vicki felt a rise in temperature, not unbearable, but definitely hotter.

She lay down, her face near the pavement. The tar bubbled slightly. As a girl, she had ridden her bike on hot asphalt, and this reminded her of the sticky tar on her shoes and tires at the end of the day.

"I'm unarmed," Vicki said. "There's no reason to shoot."

"Shut up!" an officer shouted.

A man with a dark mustache keyed his radio, calling their partner who had been left behind. "We have the runner. Everything okay back there?"

A female officer spoke, her voice shaky. "The girl and two men are still here, but I've lost the kid."

"What do you mean, you lost him?"

"My squad car must have slipped into gear while I put him down. When I got back he was gone."

"I'm heading back there," Officer Mustache said to the other two.

"All three of you'd better leave," Vicki said.

Officer Mustache turned, his hand on his pistol. "I thought we told you to be quiet."

Vicki pushed herself to a sitting position on the hot pavement and noticed that where her shadow fell, the pavement remained cool. "Has the GC contacted you about what's going on with the sun?"

The three looked at each other but didn't respond. Vicki pulled her knees to her chest. Trees on the other side of the road sizzled and popped. "You hear that? When the sun reaches you and your cars, what's happened all over the world is going to happen to you."

"What's she talking about?" a younger officer said.

"You see how this road is bubbling? Look at the smoke behind me on the hillside. There's something going on here, and you guys had better pay attention."

"Cuff her and bring her back to town," Officer Mustache said.

The younger officer moved toward Vicki, pulling handcuffs from his belt. As he got closer, he stared at the bubbling asphalt. "Sir, this tar over here is—"

But Officer Mustache was already in his car, backing away and speeding down the hill.

The younger officer glanced at the trees. Every minute the sunshine inched closer.

"Go ahead and cuff her and get her in the car," the older officer said.

"What if she's right about the sun? You know we had that report from the East Coast before we left the station."

"Just cuff her and we'll get out of here."

The younger officer walked toward Vicki, his face contorted. He took a step into the sunshine and lifted his boot. Hot, gooey tar stuck to it.

"Stand up and move over here," the officer said.

Vicki remained seated. The officer threw the handcuffs to her and told her to put them on.

"You'll have to come over here and get me," Vicki said.

"Go get her," the older officer shouted.

The younger man pursed his lips, hesitated, then walked into the light. At first he didn't seem to have a problem, other than the sticky road. But when Vicki handed the cuffs to him, he screamed and dropped them.

Frightened, the man turned to his partner, holding his hand in front of him. "She made those handcuffs hotter than fire. It left a mark on my hand!"

"This is the fourth Bowl Judgment," Vicki said. "The Bible says if you're following the evil ruler of this world, you're going to be scorched with fire."

The other officer marched toward Vicki rolling his eyes. He was wearing a short-sleeved shirt, and when he reached to retrieve the handcuffs, a blister raised on his forearm. The man cursed and moved into the shadows, rubbing his arm and sneering. "I hate your God and his plagues! No wonder Nicolae wants you and the rest of your kind dead."

The officer reached for his gun and pulled it from its holster. By now the sun had moved forward, and the officers had to step back. Vicki scrambled to the other side of her car as the man fired.

"Come on," the younger officer said. "Let's get out of here before it's too late."

The officers hurried to the car and backed away, tires squealing.

Vicki breathed a sigh of relief. It would be a long day for the GC in Wisconsin.

349

35

MARK crawled into the darkened hole and down rickety stairs. The man inside looked like a castaway from a deserted island. His clothes were dirty and tattered, his beard long enough to touch his chest, and his skin pale.

"You're takin' a big risk out there in daylight without the mark," the man said. "Is this your little brother?"

Mark studied the man's forehead, but there was no mark of the believer or of Nicolae. "No, this is Ryan. The GC stopped his mom just up the street."

"I knew you wasn't GC," the man said. "Come with me."

Ryan clung to Mark's neck as they walked through the room, ducked their heads, and went into another. Mark's eyes adjusted to the dim light, provided by some sort of lamp system around the room.

"Feels like it's gettin' hot out there," the man said. "I've seen the reports."

"What reports?" Mark said.

The man ran a hand over a computer and wiped dust from the screen. "I have to clean everything about once a day." He flicked the computer on and called up images he had saved. Fires engulfed buildings along the East Coast. Scenes of horror Mark could never have imagined flashed, and Mark turned so Ryan couldn't see.

"I expect the same thing's gonna happen here, you think?"

"I'm pretty sure it is."

"Then we need to get your friends off the street, or they'll get burned up."

"There's only one way to make sure we don't get burned," Mark said. "What's your name?"

"Clemson Stoddard," he said, reaching a hand out. "I've been down here since the start of the big war. I was scared of the nuclear stuff at first, but then I kind of liked being out of sight. You're one of the first visitors I've had in ages."

"What is this place?" Mark said.

"There used to be an oil-change place behind the garage. They leveled it after the disappearances, but since I owned the land, I just sealed it up without anybody knowing. Lamps are kerosene. I tapped onto an electric line for my computer and the freezer. Got enough food down here to feed you and your friends for quite a while."

"Why haven't you taken Carpathia's mark?"

Clemson scowled. "He's creepy, don't you think? All that coming back from the dead business. Killin' people

for not puttin' one of his tattoos on. I'm gonna ride this
one out—that's what I'm going to do."

"Have you seen anything about Dr. Ben-Judah on the
Web?"

"Yeah, I've read some of his stuff. I don't mind tellin'
ya I'm not into religion. I try to live a good life and help
people, but I don't go in much for church and all that
Jesus stuff, if you know what I mean."

Vicki watched the squad car race down the hill and take
the turns way too fast. She thought the car would flip, but
the driver slowed enough around curves to keep it on the
road. Up ahead, the sun cast a golden glow. The car sped
up to a frightening speed, but before it could reach the
shade of some trees ahead, it spun out. From Vicki's
perch she saw little puffs of smoke come from each tire.

The squad car came to rest in the middle of the road,
blocking both lanes. To her horror, a large truck pulling a
huge tank bore down on them from the other direction.
The truck tried to stop, but its tires were melting before
her eyes, the wheels sliding on the road like melting
chocolate donuts.

The two officers jumped from their vehicle a second
before the truck collided with the car. An explosion
rocked the valley, sending a ball of flame into the air, and
the officers fell. One finally stood, thrusting a fist toward
the sky before his body was consumed in flames.

Vicki fell to her knees in horror. She covered her face
as the smoke and smell of the fire reached her. "God,

help me get back to Ryan and Cheryl and the others and let them be all right."

———————————

Mark knew Clemson was in serious trouble. He had avoided the Global Community and stayed out of sight from others in the town, but he had no protection from the plagues. Mark discovered the man had been stung by one of the locusts, which had entered through an air vent, but he had obviously avoided the deadly horsemen and hadn't been affected by the wrath of the Lamb earthquake.

"Look, I need to tell you some important stuff, things that will save your life, but I have to check on my friends. Would you mind keeping my little buddy here until I get back?"

"Not a problem," Clemson said. He pulled out a pack of gum and held it up.

"He's too young for that. He just swallows it."

"Right. Well, let me think what else I have here. . . ."

"Do you sing?" Mark said.

Clemson furrowed his brow. "What kind of question is that?"

"He likes 'Twinkle, Twinkle, Little Star' and 'Hush, Little Baby.' "

"Twinkle!" Ryan said.

Clemson laughed, the corners of his eyes wrinkling with delight. "I can give you my country version of that, if you don't mind. Maybe even a little 'You Are My Sunshine'?"

"Sunshine!" Ryan said.

Ryan went to Clemson with his arms outstretched. He seemed fascinated with the man's long beard and pulled at it. "You know how long it's been since I laughed out loud, little guy?"

"Thanks for doing this," Mark said, "but I have to warn you. Don't go outside. Don't even go near the opening. The sun's going to be really hot, and it'll no doubt burn you."

"We'll be all right."

When Mark opened the trapdoor, sunlight flooded into the hidden room. He smelled smoke and heard dry weeds crackling. The last thing he heard before he closed the trapdoor was the warbly sound of Clemson's voice softly singing "Twinkle, Twinkle, Little Star."

Vicki jogged down the hillside as the sun came over the mountain. She expected everything to burst into flames around her, but it didn't. A small stream flowing past the road bubbled and hissed as steam rose, but trees only a few yards away seemed unaffected. Plastic mailboxes melted and pooled on the ground, basketball backboards wilted like dead flowers, and electric lines strung overhead snapped. Vicki had to be careful that she didn't go near any of the downed wires or get hit by falling debris.

Rushing toward town, she noticed another eerie sound overhead. She finally spotted an airplane flying just over the tops of some trees. With its wings on fire, the small plane looked like it was trying to land.

Suddenly, the engine's whine stopped, a wing broke off, and the aircraft plunged. It disappeared in some trees, and another explosion rocked the hillside.

Vicki wiped sweat from her forehead and kept running.

Mark made it to the street where Tom, Marshall, and Cheryl sat and gasped when the female officer pointed her gun at them. Buildings behind the woman blocked the sunshine, but from the sweat stains on the woman's shirt, Mark knew she was feeling the heat. A GC squad car squealed to a stop near the group, and a mustached officer jumped out, yelling at the woman. Mark wasn't close enough to hear, but he figured the man knew they had only a few minutes to get away. *But where's Vicki?*

The woman keyed her radio and called for the other officers, but they didn't answer.

Suddenly, a huge explosion rocked the valley, and a plume of smoke and fire rose into the sky from the east. Mark was close enough now to hear some of the conversation. It sounded like Marshall Jameson and Tom Fogarty were urging the GC officers to find shelter in one of the nearby buildings.

A buzzing from overhead distracted the group, and Mark saw a small plane with its wings on fire trying desperately to land. It disappeared behind the buildings, and seconds later they heard the explosion.

"This must be another judgment from God!" Marshall said. "You need to get out of here—"

"You want us to leave so you can get away," Officer Mustache said. "All of you get up and into the car now."

Something on the hillside distracted Mark. An empty car burst into flames, sending a shower of sparks into the air. Mark panicked. He knew his friends were protected from the plague, but what if they were in a car with unbelievers?

Before he could do anything, the two officers had all three of his friends in the back of the squad car. A house on the hillside crackled, and the roof began to smoke.

Mark moved to his left, toward the main road. When the car was a few yards away, he ran into the road and waved wildly. The squad car was in sunlight, and Mark was afraid it might explode.

Officer Mustache honked his horn and swerved, trying to avoid hitting Mark, but Mark moved right in the car's path. The man slammed on his brakes and stopped a few inches away. Sweat poured from the man's face.

The female officer gasped for air, threw the door open, and drew her gun. "On the ground!" she screamed, her gun pointed at Mark's chest. Suddenly, she dropped the weapon and danced on the pavement like a child running from the tide at the beach. Her ponytail bounced behind her while she ran away from the car in circles. Finally, her hair sprouted flames, and she glowed like a human blowtorch.

Officer Mustache exited the car and immediately put a hand over his head. Sparks flew from his mustache, and he fell and rolled.

Mark turned away, unable to watch. The officers'

screams faded quickly as their bodies were consumed. Mark opened the back doors, and his friends scooted out.

Vicki came upon the squad car and her four friends and couldn't help crying. The two GC officers lay at the side of the road in ash heaps. Vicki wiped away her tears and found the keys to the handcuffs near the female's body. Vicki released Cheryl, Tom, and Marshall before turning to Mark. "Where's Ryan?"

"Come on. I'll show you."

They walked in silence through the town. A few streets over they heard screaming as more fires broke out. Vicki felt like she was walking through the fiery furnace, like the three Old Testament believers Shadrach, Meshach, and Abednego. But this was no furnace—it was the real world burning at the hand of an angry God. Vicki couldn't help but think of hell. She knew there were some who believed it wasn't a real place, but the more she looked around, the more she was convinced that the Bible was true and that hell had to exist.

Mark led them to Clemson's hideout and opened the trapdoor. Vicki heard singing inside and smiled when she realized Ryan was picking up the words to "You Are My Sunshine."

Vicki caught Cheryl's arm and told the others to go inside. Cheryl pulled away and said she needed to see Ryan.

"We need to talk first," Vicki said.

Cheryl nodded and turned as Vicki closed the

entrance. They walked to the middle of the empty lot, and Cheryl folded her arms. "I know what you're going to say, and I deserve whatever it is you guys have decided to do."

"We haven't decided to *do* anything yet. I want to hear it from you—why did you lie to Wanda and take Ryan?"

Cheryl sat in the dirt and buried her head in her hands. "I was so jealous of what Josey had with Ryan. I had done all the work and had gone through all the pain, and she was getting the reward. That little boy was part of me. I felt him growing inside me. Being that close to him was just torture."

"We never should have let you stay that close to him," Vicki said. "If I had it to do over again, I'd have gone with you to another location."

"Where?" Cheryl said. "I don't want to be anywhere but with Ryan."

Vicki kept quiet as Cheryl cried. She had hoped Cheryl would say she was sorry for taking Ryan, but she seemed to be making excuse after excuse.

"Being cooped up at that camp didn't help. There's nothing to do, and every time I saw Ryan I thought about us being together, just him and me. That's how it should have been."

"How did you plan it?"

"The van? I watched Marshall and figured out where he kept his keys. It took a while, but I finally got them. All that time I planned where I would go. At first, I was going to just drive and ask God to show me a place. Then I got scared and decided to write Wanda."

"We found your e-mails to her."

Cheryl smacked her forehead. "I thought I'd deleted those."

"Cheryl, you made a promise to Josey and Tom. You know you can't give Ryan the kind of home—"

"I'm his mother! There's only a little more than a year before Jesus comes back, and I can do as much for him as anybody."

"I think you've ruined that now. How can we trust you when you kidnap—"

"My own son?"

"When you get so moody and won't talk and then endanger all of us by kidnapping a member of the group?"

Vicki watched Cheryl stare at the fires raging on the hillside. She didn't know what to say and silently prayed, "God, please show Cheryl where's she's been wrong. Help her to see the truth about what she's done and admit her mistakes. And give us wisdom with what to do with her. Amen."

36

JUDD Thompson Jr. and Lionel Washington walked out of their Ohio hideout in daylight for the first time since they had arrived. It was difficult convincing others that it was safe to venture out. When everyone read Dr. Ben-Judah's latest message and heard what was going on around the world, they finally let Judd and Lionel go.

Judd uncovered the Humvee, and the two headed away from the hiding place. They were in a remote area, so it took them a few minutes to reach a town, but when they did, Judd wished they hadn't come.

They crossed a river that bubbled like someone was boiling macaroni. The Humvee was engulfed in white-hot steam, then quickly passed through to the other side. They sped by a brick school, smoke billowing through open windows. Playground equipment lay bent and twisted, melting from the intense heat that neither Lionel nor Judd could feel. To them, it seemed like a hot summer day in Chicago, not the inferno that unbelievers felt.

The sky was cloudless so the sun beat down. The normally light blue heavens reflected an orange-yellow from fires on the ground. Homes and businesses smoked and smoldered, threatening fire at any moment.

Judd saw no airplanes or choppers above them. He wondered what a large airport would look like with fires breaking out on grounded planes. *What an awful smell boiling blood must be in the rivers,* he thought.

In a residential section of town, Lionel pointed out finely manicured lawns that had turned from deep green to brown as the grass went up in flames.

They neared a convenience store and slowed when the roof began to curl under the oppressive heat. Huge windows in front burst, spreading glass all the way to the street. Judd backed up a safe distance as hoses to gas pumps melted. A few minutes later the whole thing exploded.

"How is anybody surviving this?" Lionel said.

Judd shook his head. "I guess they have to get underground. But a lot of people in basements are going to have their houses fall on them."

Judd saw a fire department's door open, and an engine rushed out. Firefighters in full gear bounced inside as the truck rolled onto the street. But as soon as the engine hit the street, GC flags on the truck burst into flames. Firefighters flailed their arms and struggled against their seat belts. The red truck slowed, its massive tires melting and spreading onto the pavement. First the driver, then the rest abandoned ship, running toward the firehouse. Before they reached the driveway, they burst into flames. One firefighter ran to the back, managed to turn the water on, and pointed the hose toward his coworkers. Boiling water scalded his friends. They screamed and fell before catching on fire.

Lionel trembled. "It's not even the hot part of the day, and people are dying. Any idea how long this will last?"

"We don't know. Let's get back to the hideout and figure out when to head north."

Mark had learned a long time ago that a person didn't become a believer in God simply because of information, so he had to resist the urge to spell everything out for Clemson. Instead, he asked Clemson about his family, where he had grown up, and his church background.

"I've never been too big on church. My parents went, but I didn't want anything to do with it. I've always felt the Lord knows a person without them having to get dressed up in fancy clothes and making a big show."

"Did you lose anybody in the disappearances?"

"Yeah, lots of people wound up missing. I lived with my mother back then, taking care of her. She was usually up and cookin' breakfast each morning, listenin' to the radio preachers and singin' gospel songs. But that day it was just as quiet as a graveyard. I went out to the pump house to get some apple butter for my toast, and I checked on her, thinkin' somethin' might have happened. Well, you know what I found. Her bed was empty."

"What do you think happened?"

Clemson stroked his beard and picked up a picture of an older woman with shoulder-length hair. "To this day, I don't know what to think. I guess it could have been some kind of sign from God, but I don't know." He paused. "What do you think?"

Mark ran a hand through his hair. He didn't want to preach, but he didn't want to hold back either. "My friends and I have found out that God really exists and that he cares for each of us. In fact, he cared so much that he predicted everything that's happening right now."

"Even this heat wave?"

Mark nodded. "He predicted there would be a ruler that would arise who would lead people away from the truth—"

"Carpathia. I think he's the Antichrist."

"You're right. And the Bible predicted the worldwide earthquake, the stinging locusts—"

"I hated them things. . . ."

"—and even that people would reject his truth, in spite of all the miraculous signs."

"I don't reject anything God does. I believe we all ought to live by the Golden Rule and love others. I've prayed to God before."

"What did you say?"

Clemson shrugged. "I asked him for food and to help me find a safe place to stay, that kind of thing."

"Did he answer?"

Clemson wiped his forehead with a handkerchief. "Sure did. There's lots of people who've been carted off by the GC from around here or who have turned in people without the mark for the reward. I've been protected."

Mark drew closer and got down on one knee. "Clemson, it's not enough just to believe that God exists. The Bible says that the demons believe that. Even Carpathia believes in God."

"I don't think God cares about an old boy like me. He's got plenty to think about without worrying about my troubles."

"So God's not big enough to care for you? To help you find food and shelter?"

"I don't know. . . ."

"The reason we came here was to find that little boy in the next room. But I think God had a bonus in mind." Mark squinted. "Have you been asking God for anything lately?"

"Such as?"

"A sign? Maybe some help? Praying that if God's real, he'd show you and send somebody?"

The man turned white. "How did you know that?"

"I didn't. It was a guess. But since we've found you, I figured God had prepared the way."

Clemson walked to the other side of the room and sat on a rickety stool. "It gets kind of lonesome. I had a dog that stayed with me, but he died about a year ago. He used to stay right beside me like he was scared of what was going on outside." His smile faded. "Bein' all alone gets you to thinking, and I guess over the past few months I've been wonderin' whether or not God was up there and if he cared about all the people dyin'. You think he does?"

"I think the reason that all this bad stuff has happened is that God cares more than any of us can imagine. He wants people to come to know him, to ask forgiveness for their sins, even though he knows that most people will spit in his face."

"Well, if you're so religious why are you still here?"

"One of the reasons he's left us here is so we could reach out to people and help them come to know Jesus personally." Mark told his story briefly, how he had become a true believer in Jesus after the disappearances and had joined the Young Tribulation Force. "I thought I knew God before all this happened, and I thought a lot of other people were just playing church. Some were. But most of my friends who asked me to go to church with them had something I didn't have."

"And what was that?"

"They knew they were forgiven by God because of what Jesus did on the cross. You see, he died so that you could live forever with God and so that you could have a relationship with him right now."

Vicki, Marshall, and Cheryl walked quietly into the room, and Clemson looked up. "And it happened the same way with you people?"

"My parents were these religious nutcases," Vicki said. "They wanted me to go to church with them and read my Bible. I thought Christians were just people who didn't want to have any fun. Now I know the truth, that you can have *real* life, something that lasts, if you give your life to God."

Clemson stared at the floor. "From what I can gather, you people came searching for that little boy because one of you ran off with him. How did that happen?"

No one spoke for a long time. Finally, Cheryl folded her arms and her chin quivered. "Just because we believe in God doesn't mean we'll always make the right decisions." She looked at Vicki and frowned. "I made a big mistake. I can see that now. And there's nothing I can do to make up for it. But I know God is in the business of forgiving people."

Mark looked at Clemson squarely. "Would you like to ask God to forgive you and ask him to come into your life?"

Clemson rubbed his neck with a hand. "I don't know. This has all come on kind of sudden-like. I need some time."

"I understand. But we have to head back, and you need to know that if you go outside during the day without God's protection, you'll die. It's as simple as that."

"I can't make this decision just because I want to live longer."

"Right," Mark said. "But there's no guarantee you'll be alive tomorrow. Half the people in the world have already died. Most of those who were stung by locusts cursed God. But you've been given a second chance. All of us have, and we want to urge you to take it right now."

Tom Fogarty came into the room with Ryan. The child

was humming a crude version of "Jesus Loves Me," and Clemson smiled. "I swear it'd be worth it just to have that kid around. There hasn't been much to smile about the past few years."

Mark held out his hands, and Ryan came to him. "Jesus once called a small child over to him and put the kid right in front of the people he was talking to." Mark stood Ryan in front of Clemson, then clicked on the kids' Web site and found the verse he was looking for. "Jesus said, 'I assure you, unless you turn from your sins and become as little children, you will never get into the Kingdom of Heaven. Therefore, anyone who becomes as humble as this little child is the greatest in the Kingdom of Heaven.' "

"What's that mean, exactly?" Clemson said.

"A little kid depends on others. Ryan can't do much on his own. But he trusts us to take care of him, feed him, and help him. God wants you to put that kind of trust in him."

"I said I didn't want to go to church because it was a show," Clemson said. "The truth is, most of those people in church knew what kind of things I did. Bad things. And I bet if you knew, you wouldn't be so quick to help me."

"Every one of us in this room has sinned," Mark said. He glanced at Cheryl and noticed she had covered her face with her hands. "Because we're sinners, a holy God can't allow us into his presence. That's why he sent his only Son, Jesus, to die for us on the cross. It was his sacrifice in our place that guarantees our forgiveness if we'll ask for it."

"I've always believed in Jesus, that he was God, you know, but I've never really done anything about it."

"Do it now." Mark showed Clemson more verses from the Bible that spoke of God's love. The one that seemed to click with the man came from Romans:

> Therefore, since we have been made right in God's sight by faith, we have peace with God because of what Jesus Christ our Lord has done for us. Because of our faith, Christ has brought us into this place of highest privilege where we now stand, and we confidently and joyfully look forward to sharing God's glory.

"So you're saying I can be right with God and not have to worry about any of this Carpathia stuff?"

"Becoming a believer doesn't mean all your problems go away, but as the Bible says, if God is for you, who can be against you?"

"How do I do this faith thing? Do I have to jump through some hoops or memorize a bunch of stuff?"

"There's another verse in Romans you'll appreciate." Mark called it up on the computer. "Romans 10:13 says, 'Anyone who calls on the name of the Lord will be saved.' "

"Then I want to do some callin' right now," Clemson said.

Mark knelt on the dusty floor with the man. The others gathered around and put a hand on Clemson's shoulder as he prayed along with Mark.

"Dear Jesus—"

"Jesus!" Ryan said.

Everyone laughed, and Mark and Clemson continued. "I come to you now and call on your name in faith. I believe you died in my place on the cross so I could be forgiven. I'm sorry for rejecting you so long, and I ask you now to come into my life and save me. Jesus, I'm sorry for the bad things I've done, and I come to you like a little child, believing that what you've said is true. Take control of me and teach me your ways. You said anybody who calls on your name would be saved, and I believe it. I call on you now, in Jesus' name. Amen."

Clemson stood and gawked at the others. "What's that funny-looking thing on your foreheads?"

37

VICKI was encouraged by the change in Cheryl. Something had happened to the girl as she listened to Mark talk with Clemson. But in a heated meeting with Tom and Marshall, the group agreed Cheryl shouldn't return with them.

Clemson gathered a few of his things and followed the others outside. As the sun rose higher, roofs of buildings curled and fires broke out around them. Vicki saw no animals, no living people, just the rising heat vapor from the charred pavement.

Miraculously, they found the van in perfect condition and began loading Clemson's things inside. Tom had held Ryan the entire time, not even letting the boy get near Cheryl. When they were almost finished loading, Cheryl approached Vicki and asked what the group had decided.

"I don't think going back with us is a good idea,"

Vicki said. "We'll head to Wanda's and see if you can stay there."

"What if I don't want to stay with her?"

Vicki put an arm around Cheryl. "This isn't easy for any of us. Make the most of this time away, and down the road—"

"What happens if I can't get back down the road? Wanda could turn out to be—"

Tom passed, holding Ryan with one hand and holding the phone to his ear with the other. Ryan smiled and waved at Cheryl. She turned to Vicki. "I'll do anything to see my little boy again."

"Then use this time. Let God work on you."

Cheryl nodded and everyone got in the van.

The drive to Wanda's took thirty minutes. Vicki thought their whole ordeal was worth the look on Wanda's face when she saw Ryan. She couldn't believe how big and healthy he looked.

When Vicki had Wanda alone, she explained the situation with Cheryl, and Wanda gave a worried look. "There are people who depend on me. I'm always happy to help, but if this girl keeps me from doing—"

"I have a good feeling about her," Vicki interrupted. "I think she's turned a corner, but she needs help."

"I can keep her busy, but it's going to be up to her to want to change."

They talked until the afternoon, and Vicki and the others decided to return to the cabins the next morning. As evening approached, the sun lowered, and Vicki had never seen such a sunset. Smoke from the rising fires mixed with the fading twilight and created a blend of colors that took her breath away. Fiery red clouds were tinged with purple and orange. Vicki wished she had a camera.

When they heard movement on the road, everyone retreated into Wanda's hideout and watched the coverage by the Global Community News Network. Weather authorities tried to explain the killer heat wave, but every theory given by experts made Vicki laugh. Everyone in the world knew God had caused the heat.

Leon Fortunato spoke against Dr. Tsion Ben-Judah's claims that the Bible predicted the plague. "The enemies of world peace will twist these ancient words to fit their own agenda," he said. "His Excellency assures me that this change in weather is only temporary. And we reject reports that there is some god punishing innocent people for simply living their lives. That is not the kind of god I want to serve. I wish to serve the loving, generous god we have come to know, Nicolae Carpathia."

"Interesting that Leon is speaking to us from some underground cavern," Mark said, pointing out the background of the room.

Cameras picked up the effects of the devastation, since no one could photograph the actual burning during the middle of the day. Firefighters had to try and contain the damage to major cities at night and hope the next day things would get back to normal.

Judd was frustrated that he couldn't reach Vicki. The group in Ohio gathered shortly after Judd and Lionel returned from exploring and tapped into a secret feed from the Tribulation Force in San Diego.

Rayford Steele appeared on-screen. "We don't know how much time we're going to have, so we have to work quickly to take advantage of this opportunity. I've spoken personally with Dr. Ben-Judah, and he's given his blessing on our decision to go ahead with this operation.

"We'll need volunteers throughout the country to rearrange our storehouses of goods and products we trade through the International Commodity Co-op. We believe the Global Community and their followers will focus on survival, looking for relief from the sun. From what we can tell, thousands or maybe hundreds of thousands died today. In the coming days, we'd like to hear from believers and find out what help you need. Our goal is to move resources, but if we need to, we'll move people out of harm's way.

"This will not be easy, and it will be dangerous. We have no idea how long the heat wave will last. But we must take advantage of it as quickly as possible."

Judd wrote the Tribulation Force immediately and volunteered. *I'm hoping to be in Wisconsin by the time you need me, but let me know how I can join the effort.*

Judd and Lionel met with the leaders of the Ohio group and talked about how to proceed. Later in the evening Lionel handed Judd the phone and smiled. "The bride-to-be is on the line."

Judd grabbed the phone, and Vicki explained the situation with Cheryl and where they were. "We're going back to the campground in the morning, assuming the plague continues. What about you?"

"The leaders here have given the okay for us to head your way. They're concerned that with all the fires and debris on the roads, we might not make it in a day, so we're stopping at a midway point for the night.

"I can't believe we're actually going to see each other!"

"I just hope the plague doesn't end in the morning and we run into a bunch of GC officers."

Judd found it difficult to sleep that night. The group posted guards at the main entrance to the hideout and kept a couple of members up all night watching the property. Judd thought it was a miracle that even with the extreme heat, the group's outside cameras hadn't been affected.

There were tearful good-byes the next morning as the sun rose.

"Red sky at morning, GC take warning," Lionel said.

The doctor at the hideout who had helped with Lionel's arm examined it one more time and pronounced him healthy. Judd and Lionel thanked everyone for their help, and two men loaded enough supplies in the Humvee for a week. Another man made sure they had enough fuel, and the two sped off.

The fire's damage shocked Judd as he crossed the old border of Ohio and drove into Indiana. Trees and crops that had been green the last time they were there lay black and scorched. Judd had seen forest fire damage, but this seemed even worse.

Judd swerved to avoid several vehicles that had

burned the day before. Even worse than the dead trees, grass, and plant life were the charred bodies that littered the roadway, and Judd saw Lionel cringe several times while they drove.

"What do you miss most about the way things used to be?" Lionel said as they neared a city.

"I miss my parents and my little brother and sister," Judd said. "I think a lot about what they'd be doing if they were here. Marc and Marci would be in high school. But I also miss little things like going to Wrigley Field for a Cubs game or grabbing a burger at a local restaurant. I had dreamed of owning my own car and being my own boss. Going to movies—"

"Yeah, movies," Lionel said as they passed a destroyed theater complex. "The last time I went to a theater was with my sister."

"I know it sounds corny," Judd said, "but I miss just going to a church service too. I didn't like them when I was young, but now I'd give anything to be able to sing together and listen to teaching without being afraid."

"That's why I envy Sam for being in Petra. It must be one big church service every day." Lionel stretched his arm, put his seat back, and smiled. "So, how are you going to court Vicki?"

"Court?" Judd smirked.

"Yeah, what are you two going to do, take a walk in the fire?"

"I'll admit I'm a little worried about it."

"Why?"

"We've been apart so long, and we've both changed.

Plus, the last time we were together, we fought like cats and dogs."

Lionel chuckled. "Vicki sure got ticked at you a few times."

"Right. And how do we know we won't keep fighting?"

"Because God's been working on you."

"What do you mean?"

"I've told you this before. I was around you when we first started the Young Trib Force. You were . . . how do I say this . . . bossy. You knew you had the right plan, and anybody who got in your way was wrong."

Judd smiled. "Me?"

"Over the last few months, years even, I've seen God knock some rough edges off. He's humbled you."

"You talk like I was Frankenstein's monster."

"No, more like Frankenstein's selfish son." Lionel laughed. "I'm not saying you're perfect, and I expect you and Vicki are going to knock even more rough edges off each other, but you've come a long way. And I'm proud to be your friend."

"Thanks."

———————————————

Vicki's heart nearly broke when she watched Cheryl say good-bye to Ryan. Tom let her hold the boy before they left, and Cheryl sang a song she had made up for him. Through her tears she choked out the words and kissed him on the cheek. "I'm really sorry," she said as she handed Ryan to Tom. "Will you tell Mrs. Fogarty that—"

"You should tell her yourself," Tom said. "Write her or call her."

"I will. And I want you to know I'm going to get better. I've never been through anything like this before."

Tom opened the door and carried Ryan outside. Clemson put a hand on Cheryl's shoulder and smiled, showing his yellow teeth. "I don't excuse your behavior, but the truth is, I wouldn't have found God's peace if you all hadn't driven through our town. So I thank you for your part in that."

Cheryl nodded and hugged everyone. "I don't know what I would have done without you," she whispered in Vicki's ear.

"I look forward to having you back, but don't rush it. Talk this through with Wanda. Let God work."

The drive back to the campground went quickly in the daylight. Vicki wondered how many people had died in the houses that smoldered on hillsides. But she couldn't contain her excitement over Judd. She looked out the window and smiled for no reason. Marshall caught her and asked why she was so happy, but she turned and tickled Ryan in his car seat without answering.

Along with the good feelings, Vicki couldn't help being nervous. What if she and Judd didn't get along? Their friendship had grown, but what if things changed when they were face-to-face?

Before the disappearances, the way a guy looked had been so important to her. Whether a guy looked "hot" was the only test Vicki had used to decide whether to go out with him. Now she couldn't imagine being interested in anyone who didn't share her faith in God and want to reach out to others. She was sure there was nothing that would keep her from liking Judd.

Judd and Lionel made it safely to the midway point of their trip by early afternoon and thought about continuing but decided to play it safe. They found the group they had contacted packed into the basement of an old library and running out of food. Judd and Lionel took the food they needed from the Humvee for the rest of their trip and gave the rest to the group.

"We e-mailed the Trib Force about supplies, but they don't know when they'll be able to get here," the leader said.

"I'm hoping to help move supplies around," Judd said. "I'll put in a word about your situation."

If Judd had trouble sleeping the night before, this night was a disaster. One of the younger members argued with the leader, and another coughed most of the night. Judd and Lionel slept on the floor, which was a thin strip of carpet over a slab of concrete. Judd walked the floor above them through the early morning hours, looking out at the charred remains of cars, trucks, and trees.

Before they left the next morning, Judd warned the leader about GC movement in the area. "I didn't see squad cars, but people were definitely out last night. When they see this library still standing, they may try to take possession of it, so be careful."

The leader thanked them for the food and wished

them well on the remainder of their trip. Lionel pulled out the tattered map they had started with in South Carolina so long ago and traced his finger along the route they had carefully chosen for this final leg of the trip. It ran a hundred miles south of Chicago so they wouldn't have to deal with the new GC buildup outside the nuked city.

Judd had to keep from driving too fast on the sweltering roadway. He set the cruise control and let the Humvee keep speed until he came to a burning wreck or a melted bridge. Twice they were forced to drive through a small stream or find another route.

Finally, they reached the road to the campground Vicki had described.

Lionel folded the map and put it in his pocket. "How do you feel?"

Judd took a breath. "Remember when those GC guys were looking for us in Israel? It's like my heart's beating out of my chest."

"Settle down, big boy. It's just another stop on our way to the Glorious Appearing, right?"

"Maybe it is for you," Judd said. He let off on the gas pedal and slowed. "I want to remember this last part of the drive."

LIONEL felt a strange mix of emotions as he got out of the Humvee and walked toward the campground. A white van and another car were parked nearby, and he spotted a child's toy in the grass and picked it up.

Lionel had dreamed of this moment from the first time he suggested he and Judd return home. Through trips to New Babylon, France, Petra, and their ordeal in South Carolina, Lionel never let go of the dream of being back with his friends.

But how will they react to my missing arm? The thought sent a shiver through him and Lionel turned. Judd was still in the car, his hands on the steering wheel, peering into the afternoon sunlight. Lionel shook off the emotion and walked toward the first cabin.

The door opened and Conrad flew out, racing to his friend and embracing him. Lionel hugged him tightly and wept. Darrion followed, then Shelly and Mark. The rest was a blur as familiar faces and people he'd never seen surrounded him.

"You wouldn't believe how we've prayed for you," an older woman said. "You look just like I thought you would."

Lionel smiled and tried to speak.

"I'm Maggie," the woman said. "Vicki and the others helped me get out of Des Plaines."

A woman holding a child stepped forward, and Lionel handed her the toy. "Where is Vicki?"

Zeke stepped forward and grabbed Lionel's hand. "Vicki and Janie have been down at Cheryl's cabin fixing the place up. Down at the end."

Lionel glanced back at the Humvee. Judd was still inside.

———

The emotion of seeing Lionel connect with his friends was too wonderful for Judd. Years ago, when Judd was a kid, he'd had relatives visit his family. At the end of the visit there were hugs and tears as Judd's parents said good-bye. At that age, Judd couldn't understand why older people cried so much.

Now, as he saw the friendships formed during the earth's last days, he shook with emotion. These people had prayed for him, had faced death together, and had lost many friends. The gathering seemed like a breathtaking dream.

———

Vicki and Janie had worked on Cheryl's old cabin since Vicki had returned from her trip. Food wrappers littered the floor. Clothes were thrown about, and Cheryl's cot hadn't been made for weeks. Though Marshall had assigned cabins and put at least two people in each (he said the partner system was best), Cheryl had stayed alone, which was fine with everyone else. But Cheryl's solitary life had come with a price. Vicki wondered what might have happened if the girl had roomed with some-one who could have helped her think through the situation with Ryan and the Fogartys.

Janie had finished moving a bed into place when Vicki heard a commotion outside. Janie went to the window and noticed several people walking toward the cabin.

"Are they here?" Vicki said.

"Only one way to find out," Janie said, then rushed out, the screen door banging behind her.

Vicki tried to move but couldn't. "God," she prayed, "you know how long we've prayed for Judd and Lionel to come back. You know all that's happened, so before I even see them, I want to thank you for loving us and sending them back. Whatever happens between Judd and me, even if we just become friends, I pray you'd get the glory for it. Amen."

The screen door opened, and Lionel walked inside. He looked older, his eyes somehow wiser. Vicki had first met Lionel when he was only thirteen. Now he was almost nineteen, and he had grown taller than Vicki by a few inches. She rushed to him and hugged him, forgetting about his arm injury.

"I'm not hurting you, am I?" Vicki said when she could speak.

Lionel smiled. "Nothing there to hurt."

"Oh, Lionel, we've missed you so much. I thought you'd be gone a couple of weeks, maybe a month tops."

"So did I. Guess things don't always turn out the way you think they're going to."

Vicki glanced at the door, and Lionel stepped aside. "Were you looking for somebody else?"

Vicki smiled. "He's with you, isn't he?"

Lionel took her hand and pulled her toward the door. "Come on."

The first one to reach Judd after he stepped out of the car was Mark. There were no words, just hugs and slaps on the back. Judd and Mark had disagreed about a lot of things through the years, beginning with Mark's involvement with the militia movement, but now all that seemed forgotten. They had both seen enough death and had been chased by the Global Community enough to know that any squabbles in the past were easily put aside.

"You don't know how good it is to be back," Judd said.

Zeke gave Judd a hug that nearly squeezed all the air from his lungs. "Looks like you got a few scratches during your travels."

"You haven't changed much, Zeke. Still have the tattoos."

"I'm thinkin' about gettin' a new one here," Zeke said, pointing to his right hand. "It'll be a GC symbol with the words *Carpathia stinks.*"

"Judd!" Shelly screamed. Zeke and Mark made way for her as she embraced Judd.

"It's a big family reunion," Zeke said.

Judd studied the faces outside the cabins while he walked this gauntlet. He recognized Tom and Josey Fogarty and hugged them tightly.

"Vicki told me you'd finally believed," Judd said to Tom.

"It took me a while to come around, but I finally realized the truth."

Darrion pecked Judd on the shoulder. "Remember me?"

Judd couldn't believe how much Darrion had changed. When he had first met her, she was just a kid. Now she was a young woman with long hair and a beautiful smile.

"Everybody's changed so much—it's hard to believe."

"I think there's somebody down there who wants to see you," Darrion whispered. "She's been really nervous."

Judd watched as Lionel came out of a cabin pulling someone behind him.

Vicki stepped outside the cabin and saw the glow on the faces of those before her. Somehow Vicki felt she had seen this moment before or had dreamed it. At the top of the hill, a few yards from the main cabin, a young man moved slowly toward her.

Judd had never felt so focused. He knew everyone was watching, wondering what he would do, but he concentrated on the girl at the end of the path.

Vicki had changed since Judd had been gone, like the

others, like he had. Her red hair was shorter, and Judd liked how it accented her face. She looked older, more mature.

On the drive to the airport, shortly after Judd and Vicki had first met in that cataclysmic moment after their families had disappeared, Judd hadn't even considered Vicki as anything but a fellow traveler, a lost and lonely survivor. When everyone he loved was gone, his first instinct was to shut down and keep people at a distance so he wouldn't be hurt even more.

The loss of Bruce Barnes had been another huge blow to Judd. But over the past two years, Judd had opened up to others in a way he had never done before. As he walked past this band of brothers and sisters, he wasn't just returning to his friends—he was truly coming home.

The thought overwhelmed Judd the closer he got to Vicki. Could God have loved him so much to take him safely through the past years and bring him back to the person he loved most? Had his adventures, his fighting the Global Community all been part of a plan to draw him closer to the God who loved him?

Somewhere deep inside, the pride, self-reliance, lack of trust in others, the guarding of his heart, and even the focus on his own sins was breaking down. For so long Judd had tried to figure things out. He knew the Bible, how things would wind up when Christ came back, and how everyone should act and fit in with his views. But the more Judd had tried to control things and people, the worse he felt.

He was a few feet from Vicki when the emotion he

was trying to control crashed. He had stayed in the car to compose himself, to keep himself guarded again, but the sight of that old dog Ryan Daley had brought home sent Judd over the edge. Phoenix bounded past Vicki and ran toward Judd, his tail wagging, barking with delight. Judd fell to his knees and put his hands on the ground, tears streaming.

At first Vicki thought Judd had fallen, then realized he was overcome. When Phoenix jumped up and licked his face, Vicki couldn't tell if Judd was laughing or crying.

She knelt and put an arm around Judd's shoulder and the other around Phoenix. Everything else in the world faded—the people around her, the hot sun, all the death and destruction, the Global Community.

Judd whispered something through his tears—she could tell they were tears now. "What did you say?" she said.

"I'm so sorry, Vicki. I'm so sorry."

"It's okay, Judd. You're back. What do you have to be sorry about?"

"For Phoenix. For Ryan. For the way I've been."

Vicki smiled and started to make Judd feel better, but then she realized that God was doing something. Here. Now. God was burrowing into Judd's soul, working in a way she had seen only when a person came to faith in God. To others it probably seemed like Judd was happy to see Vicki, but she sensed something more.

Vicki placed both arms around Judd's neck and whispered a prayer. "Oh, Father, you're so good to us. You've brought my friend back. Thank you."

Judd looked at Vicki, and she handed him a tissue. His face was shadowed by a couple days' growth of beard. He had aged beyond his twenty-one years. Vicki looked at the others gathered around. Josey Fogarty smiled and cradled Ryan tightly in her arms. Zeke had his hand over his mouth, studying the scene. Darrion and Janie and Shelly hugged each other and cried. They had been such good friends for Vicki.

"I'm through with just surviving," Judd choked. "I want to live. Do you think I can change?"

"I think you already have."

39

JUDD had never experienced a celebration like the one that evening in Wisconsin. He had been to birthday parties, anniversaries, and victory celebrations, but they didn't compare with the joy in the main cabin.

Zeke pulled out a boxful of different juices that no one knew he had. "I was waiting for the right time and place, and this is it!"

Josey Fogarty had baked several cakes, which she said was therapy for her. "I hated waiting for word about Ryan, so while I prayed I baked."

"You could have saved the oven and just stuck the cake outside," Zeke laughed.

Ryan couldn't take his eyes off Lionel. He was fascinated with Lionel's skin color and the fact that one of his sleeves was empty. Lionel seemed to take the attention in stride and let Ryan see the way his arm had healed.

Vicki left Judd to talk with Josey. Judd assumed it was

to explain what had happened with Cheryl the day before.

After everyone had eaten, Judd asked Vicki if she would like to take a walk before the sun went down.

Zeke stepped in front of Judd, blocking the door. "As Vicki's substitute dad, I'm going to have to ask your intentions."

People snickered.

Judd planted his feet and took a breath. "Sir, I'm here to renew an old friendship, if that's okay with you."

Zeke looked at Vicki. "Are you open to this young man renewing your acquaintance?"

"I am."

"Then go on, but have her back by dark." Zeke leaned forward. "I'm serious about that last part. We've been doing a lot of moving around. I don't want any surprise visits from the GC in the middle of the night."

Vicki led the way, showing Judd each of the cabins and telling him who lived where. She came to Zeke's workshop, which no one visited anymore. "Z's really excited about what he's been working on for Lionel. After the people stopped coming for fake IDs and cosmetic work, he started developing it."

When they had seen all the cabins, Vicki led Judd through the woods a short distance to a knoll overlooking the camp and the surrounding countryside. It seemed like years since Judd had been outside in daylight and he loved it, even if the devastating fires still raged. Smoke hovered over the valley, and in the distance Judd saw houses and farms ablaze.

The fire hadn't touched the woods surrounding the camp, and Judd was amazed. Like the other plagues, this could only be explained by the awesome power of God.

Judd and Vicki sat on a tree stump, side by side, and looked at the scene.

"This world is on its last legs," Vicki said.

"I can't wait to see what the new one's going to look like." Judd shifted nervously. "That wasn't the kind of entrance I'd hoped to make earlier. I had planned a private kind of thing, sneaking up on you and seeing if you'd recognize me."

"You had a lot of time to plan it out," Vicki said.

"I didn't think there would be so many people."

"It was a wonderful way to return."

"Zeke said I really lost it, and I guess I did."

"It's funny how people react to emotion. A lot of people are really uncomfortable, but I don't think you should ever be sorry about that. It was so genuine. I could tell God was doing something special in your heart."

"I used to sit in church and watch people go forward at the end of the service and try to figure out how they got the guts to do it. It seemed so humiliating to get up there in front of all those people, sometimes crying, other times just standing there. But when I saw you and Phoenix, I finally realized what a jerk I've been. I've seen it before, but it was like God showing me wave after wave of truth. I don't feel like a very worthy candidate to be your friend, let alone be . . ."

"What?" Vicki said.

"You know . . . more than that."

Vicki took Judd's hand and squeezed it. "I know we only have a little more than a year left before the Glorious Appearing, but I'd like to take this slow. Get to know each other better. There are things I need to tell you and things I need to hear from you."

Judd nodded. "Where do we start?"

"Tell me about Nada," Vicki said.

Judd did. He spilled the whole story about Nada, from their first meeting to Nada's eventual death in an Israeli jail cell. Vicki listened with interest, asking questions and falling silent when Judd told her about the plague of horsemen and the jailer who had killed Nada.

"Did you love her?"

Judd hesitated. "I'm not sure. I'd be lying to say I wasn't interested in her. She was an incredible person." He pulled a tattered piece of paper from his wallet and handed it to Vicki. "She wrote this, and her mother gave it to me after she died."

Vicki opened the paper and spread it out on her leg.

> *Dear Judd,*
>
> *My mother suggested I write this down so I won't forget. Maybe the GC is going to execute us, and if that happens, you can take comfort in the fact that I'm in a better place. Being with Christ is what our lives are all about. If they've killed me, I'm there, so don't be sad for me. I love you very much. From the moment you came to our family, I felt close to you. You were like a brother to me. Then, as my feelings grew deeper, you were more than that.*

But I have to tell you something. I feel it's only fair that I express this. As close as we became, in our talks and the time we spent together, I always felt there was something missing. I couldn't put my finger on it until we came back to Israel and you backed away. I feel what I'm about to say is something that God wants me to say.

I have prayed many nights about this. I've asked God to show me why I'm feeling this way. Honestly, I think something is holding you back. At first, I thought it was God. You're so sold out on him, and you want to live for him. But the more I thought and prayed, it became clear that God wasn't coming between us. I really believe there is someone else. You've never talked much about your friends in the States, but I sense there is someone there you care about deeply.

Maybe I'm making this up. If so, I apologize. But if I'm right and you find this letter, go back to her. You're a wonderful person with so much to offer. I have loved being your friend. I'm sorry for the trouble I caused you in New Babylon. I'm sorry for being difficult at times. (You had your moments too.) I'll look forward to seeing you again, whether it's in this life or the next. May God bless you.

Love,
Nada

Vicki's hands shook as she gingerly folded the page. "I can't believe that. She knew you well."

They talked more about Nada and her sacrifice as they returned to the main cabin. The sun had gone down, and

Judd wanted to be sure to honor Zeke's request that they return before dark.

"Let me ask you something," Judd said. "Remember when I called and you were out with that guy in Iowa?"

Vicki nodded. "His name was Chad Harris. He actually showed up here a little while after you made it to Ohio." Vicki told Judd what Chad had done and how the GC had caught and executed him.

Judd couldn't believe it. "You obviously didn't want to hurt his feelings, but you didn't feel the same way about him as he felt about you?"

"Right. I felt really bad about it for weeks."

When they reached the main cabin, everyone had gathered around the computer for the latest from the Global Community News Network. The reporters showed more death and devastation throughout the world. Famous sites around the world that had survived the wrath of the Lamb earthquake were burning. The GC had tried to adapt, but it was clear this plague had paralyzed the enemies of God.

"In the United North American States, one man has risen to the challenge of the killer fires," the reporter said.

A face flashed on the screen, and Vicki groaned. "Fulcire," she said under her breath.

"Commander Kruno Fulcire says he won't let this latest natural disaster keep him from his duty," the reporter said.

"I've pledged my life to the ideals of the Global Community," Fulcire said from some darkened GC bunker. "My main mission over these past few months and years has been to ferret out rebels and punish them.

I'm sticking with that mission, and we're offering even more money to any citizen brave and resourceful enough to bring in rebels during this time."

"How can people do that with all the fires?" the reporter said.

"Hunt them at night. We're watching radar and surveillance cameras for any movement and tracking down that movement when the heat allows. We may find more rebels now than at any other time."

"So there's truth to the rumors that the rebels, at least some of them, are immune to this wave of heat?"

Fulcire shifted in his chair. "I'm not saying that we know exactly who or what is out there during the day. I don't want to give the rebels any more credit than they deserve, but if they're foolish enough to go out in the fire and survive, we'll find a way to catch them."

Marshall Jameson smiled. "Sounds like they're trying to bluff us into staying put."

"Which is another good reason to go on the offensive," Judd said.

They watched the coverage a few more minutes. Then Colin Dial called for everyone's attention. "Before we sample some of Josey's desserts, I'd like to propose a toast." He held up a glass of juice, and the others grabbed full glasses from the table. "To Judd and Lionel, for surviving the long journey home."

Lionel held up his glass. "If I could add to that?"

Colin nodded.

"For the prayers of our friends. God answered in ways we couldn't have imagined, and we thank you."

"I might as well give mine and not let you two hog the spotlight," Zeke said. The others laughed. "To all the people we've known who believed and are no longer with us. And to my dad." He looked at the ceiling and gave a short salute. "I hope I can live long enough to make you proud."

Judd looked around to see if anyone else would add a toast. Charlie stepped forward. "I have one. To Judd and Vicki."

"To Judd and Vicki," everyone said.

Judd couldn't remember the last time he had eaten homemade cake. He devoured his first piece and went for seconds. The warmth of the group, the laughter and happy faces, were the perfect end to the evening. Though they had all experienced loss and the world was winding down like a huge clock, it felt good to have fun again.

Before the group went to their cabins, Marshall gave final instructions. "We're awaiting word from the Tribulation Force about the movement of supplies and people. Everybody be ready to help or welcome additions if we need to."

After an emotional time in prayer, everyone moved to their cabins. Judd lingered, talking to Conrad and Mark about the possibility of joining the Tribulation Force to move supplies.

Vicki talked with Becky Dial and others about Judd's return. As everyone filed out, Vicki touched Judd on the shoulder to say good night, but he excused himself and walked her to her cabin. The air was cool compared to the daytime temperature, and Vicki rubbed her arms.

"Great night, wasn't it?" Judd said.

"The best I can remember."

"I have something to apologize for."

"What?"

"Your birthday."

Vicki chuckled. "The whole world is burning, and you're worried about my birthday?"

"I had it written down to send you a message on your birthday, but we switched computers and it slipped my mind. When I finally remembered, it seemed kind of lame to just apologize, and I couldn't send this."

Judd pulled out a small package and Vicki gasped.

"I ran short on wrapping paper," Judd said.

Vicki unwrapped the newspaper and opened the box slowly. Shelly peeked out the cabin door, then closed it. Vicki heard snickers from inside, and Judd blushed.

"When we moved from Indiana to Ohio, we met a doctor who treated Lionel's arm. His wife had disappeared in the Rapture, and he'd kept this ever since he found it on her pillow."

Inside the box was a beautiful gold chain with a heart-shaped pendant. A diamond sparkled in the middle. Judd turned the heart around and pointed at elegant writing on the back that said *Ich Liebe Dich*.

"What's that mean?"

"The doctor said it's German for 'I love you.' He had studied in Germany and brought that back as an engagement gift for his wife. When I told him our story, he wanted me to give it to you." Judd took the necklace from the box and fastened it around Vicki's neck.

"I love it. And I'm glad you waited to give it to me." She gave Judd a hug.

He smiled and squeezed her hand. "See you at breakfast?"

"Wouldn't miss it."

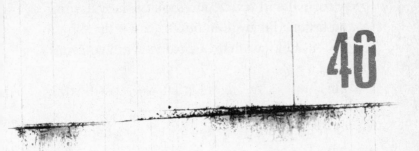

40

THE FIRST night was the hardest for Lionel. He told Marshall he would take the first watch for any GC activity, and when Marshall protested, Lionel put his hand on the man's arm. "It would do me good to stay up. I'm not doing too well with all the changes."

Zeke volunteered to stay at the computer with Lionel, and they had a good talk. "Must be kind of hard for you with all the excitement over Judd and Vicki."

"I expected it," Lionel said. "I don't know which was harder, running from the GC these last few years or keeping up with Judd's love life."

Zeke smiled. "You've seen a lot more of the inner workings of the GC than any of us here."

"And I've seen a lot of death." Lionel told Zeke about Conrad's brother, Taylor Graham, and how he had died. Zeke asked about Pavel, their young friend who had invited them to New Babylon, who had also died. When

Lionel got to the stories of Nada and her brother, Kasim,
he shook his head. "I think we need to change the subject."

"Good idea. Tell me what God's done with you since
you left."

Lionel held up the stump of his left arm. "He did this."

"Are you upset about it?"

"No. I just don't understand why it had to happen."

"Accidents happen."

Lionel nodded. "I guess that's one thing that changed
while I was away. Before the Rapture, I thought about
God in terms of him being way out there and us down
here trying to do stuff for him. When I became a true
believer, I realized he wanted to be with us, helping us.
But I still thought living for God meant doing stuff for
him, trying to convince people he's there and he loves
them. All the pressure was on me to perform, you know?
If somebody didn't become a believer, I felt responsible,
like it was my fault."

"And that's changed?"

"Big time. I know I need to reach out as much as I
can, but the past few years have taught me this is God's
battle. He's the one drawing people to himself and fighting the enemy. If I talk with someone and they don't
become a believer, I feel sad, but I don't feel guilty. God
really is in control."

Zeke nodded. "That's a hard lesson to learn. We want
to keep control of things and make it all about us when
this is all about God." He paused. "But how does that
affect your arm? If God's in control, he let it happen."

Lionel stared at the computer screen. "Sometimes at

night I'll reach out for a drink of water or rub my eyes, and I'll realize I'm still reaching with my left hand. And then I'll have nightmares about the rest of my arm under that rock."

"Ever have any pain in the arm that's gone?"

"You bet. It shoots up and down the tendons and into my fingers . . . fingers that aren't even there."

"They call that phantom pain, but it's supposed to be just as real as if your arm were still there."

"I thought it would go away, but it hasn't."

"Give it time," Zeke said. "I watched you tonight during the celebration. You've adjusted well to the physical part, eating with one hand and everything else. But there's a mental side to this, an emotional thing you have to adjust to. I can't say I can help much, but if you need somebody to talk to . . ."

"Thanks," Lionel said.

"And there's something I've been workin' on since I heard about the accident." Zeke walked to a storage closet and pulled out a box. He laid it at Lionel's feet.

Lionel gasped when he opened the lid. Inside was a plastic replica of the lower portion of his arm. "How did you—"

"As soon as I heard what happened, I went looking on the Internet and through our sources at the Co-op for what they call prosthetic devices. Then I realized I had most of the materials right here, so I went to work. The hard part was making a mold for the plastic. I must have tried a dozen times before it came out right. Go ahead— try it out."

Lionel lifted the gadget into place. It fit perfectly against the end of his arm.

Zeke helped him fasten it. "You ain't gonna be lifting with it or using two pistols to fight the GC, but it does move with pressure." He showed Lionel how to turn his hand and move the lower arm by shifting his weight.

"It's perfect," Lionel said, holding out his new left hand. "Put her there."

Zeke shook Lionel's left hand and smiled. "I don't know why God allowed that to happen either, but I wouldn't doubt it if he was preparing you for something."

"He's going to have to hurry if he wants to use me," Lionel said. "There's only a year left before Jesus comes back."

Vicki liked the fact that Judd hadn't kissed her good night. The slower they took this, the better, as far as she was concerned. As she lay in bed, she held the golden heart up to the moonlight streaming in the window and watched the reflection dance against the ceiling. Shelly and Janie had moved into the room with her and had gushed over the present.

"It's so romantic!" Janie had said.

"Is that an engagement necklace?" Shelly said.

Vicki grinned. "The reports of our wedding have been greatly exaggerated."

Now, as the others slept, Vicki wondered what would happen. She had been waiting for so long she didn't know how to act now that Judd was actually here. She closed her eyes and thought of a scene from a movie where two people had been married in a secret ceremony. She drifted off to sleep clutching the golden heart.

Over the next few days, Judd tried to help out with whatever jobs needed to be done at the campground. The latest news from the Co-op suggested they would need to make room for a group that had been hiding south of Chicago, where the GC were more active.

"It's easier to move people than supplies," Rayford Steele had said, "and this will get our people out of harm's way."

Judd kept in contact with Sam Goldberg for the latest in Petra. The boy continued his Petra Diaries, and each new writing was filled with facts and observations about Tsion's and Chaim's messages.

Judd also spoke with Chang Wong in New Babylon and encouraged him to use the heat wave to escape Nicolae Carpathia and the palace. Chang resisted, saying the Tribulation Force needed him there now more than ever.

"There's so much to move—equipment, aircraft, food, and other supplies," Chang said. "If I can hang on long enough, we'll all be in a lot better shape for the final year."

"What's it like there?" Judd said.

"Everyone is obsessed with finding shelter from the sun. The first couple of days were the worst. People went underground and set up their offices and living quarters. They work at night and try to sleep during the day, but some don't even want to go out at night because of all the bodies and burned-out vehicles."

"What about Carpathia? I hope he's mad about all this."

"He says the heat's not bothering him at all."

"You're kidding."

"No, the sun comes through the glass ceiling and roasts the whole floor. His secretary is underground, but Nicolae orders people around all day from his office."

"Can anyone work in the palace?"

"On the lower floors, they've painted the windows black to keep out the sun, and some can work there. The weirdest thing happened the other day after Nicolae told his secretary he was going into the courtyard to sunbathe."

Judd shook his head. "And I suppose he did it."

"I snuck to a corner window and scraped a hole in the black coating. Carpathia took off his shirt and lay on a concrete bench and soaked in the rays."

"How long did he stay there?"

"He was out there at least an hour. Flames were licking at the concrete and all around him. I listened to a recording of Leon Fortunato with their head security guy, Akbar. Leon said he couldn't stand within twenty feet of Nicolae after the sunbathing incident because it was too hot."

"We should start calling him Nicolae the blowtorch."

Chang laughed. "Leon said Nicolae's shoes smoked. There were sparks in his hair. Even the buttons of his suit had melted."

"It just shows he's not really human."

"You won't believe what happened after that," Chang continued. "I listened in to a conversation between Smoky Shoes and Technical Services. He wanted a tele-scope set up so he could look directly at the sun at noon."

"What could he possibly want that for?"

"He said he wanted to record whether the sun has grown and if bursts of flame from its surface would be visible."

"Don't tell me he actually did it."

"I watched him. He looked at the sun for several minutes. He left, and when he came back the telescope had melted. That night he told the technician he had seen the flares dancing on the sun's surface. The techie laughed, thinking it was a joke, and Carpathia turned mean."

"What did he say?"

"He said, 'The sun, moon, and stars bow to me.' "

Judd felt a chill. He knew Carpathia was the Antichrist, but he was more than that now. Since Nicolae had risen from the dead, Dr. Ben-Judah and others believed that the man was literally indwelt by Satan. God's enemy would be defeated, but not before he did everything he could to hurt God's people. Satan, as Jesus had said, was a liar and a murderer from the beginning. He would use all his weapons to try to block God's plan.

"Carpathia has to know his time is running out," Judd said.

"Don't think the guy will ever think logically. He's trying to convince everyone around him that he's still king of the world."

"Even though everybody's burning up? Chang, this is the perfect time for you to get away. Think of what they'll do to you if they find out who you really serve."

"There's still too much to do with the Tribulation Force. Besides, nobody suspects me."

"Just don't make any mistakes. The first could be your last."

───────────────

Vicki was pleased with the progress they were making with the cabins. Clemson Stoddard turned out to be a great carpenter. When he wasn't helping repair old cabins or construct new ones, he was reading Tsion Ben-Judah's Web site or sitting in on classes Vicki and the others offered newer believers.

Clemson had gone from looking like a hermit to being neatly dressed. He was always polite, and he had as many questions as anyone about the end of the world and what was going to happen next.

Vicki was answering one of his questions by drawing a time line of the Tribulation when she turned and noticed Judd had slipped into the back. She continued, trying to keep her focus on the class.

Marshall called everyone to dinner, and Judd walked with her to the main cabin.

"Don't do that again," Vicki said.

"Do what?"

"It makes me nervous when you're back there."

Judd stopped her and turned to face her. "You are one of the best teachers I've ever seen. I was only in there a few minutes, but the way you explained the time line was incredible."

Vicki blushed and rolled her eyes.

"I mean it. You don't know how proud I was when we were in Israel and you showed up on the video screen above the stadium."

"Bet you were surprised too."

"You bet and a little bit scared for you. But when 'Vicki B.' started talking about God and telling people how to become a believer, I was in awe."

"So you didn't think I could do that kind of thing?"

"I didn't take the time to think about anybody else back then. But it's clear now that God had something more planned for you, and if I hadn't gotten out of the way, it might never have happened."

Vicki smiled. "Care to escort the teacher to dinner?"

"I'd be honored."

As the sun went down, Judd and Vicki met with Marshall and Zeke. Judd was excited because he knew Marshall had had a phone meeting scheduled with Rayford Steele earlier in the day.

"The Trib Force heard from the group you stayed with in the library, but they haven't been able to get back in touch with them," Marshall said. "They're wondering if you could meet them and help lead them to those people."

"I'm there," Judd said.

"Before you agree, you have to understand that we

don't have any idea when this plague will lift. You could be in the air when it gets cool, and the GC could converge on you."

Judd bit his lip. "In that case, I have one request."

"What's that?" Marshall said.

"That Vicki goes with me."

41

AS SOON as the sun came up two days later, Judd drove Vicki south in the Humvee to meet a Tribulation Force plane. The small airport lay in ruins, skeletons of planes smoldering under the wrecked hangar. The runway was still in good shape though, and it wasn't long after they arrived that the plane touched down.

Judd had hoped Rayford Steele would be aboard or perhaps another of the higher ranking Trib Force members. Instead, the door opened and Westin Jakes appeared. Judd introduced Vicki, and Westin shook hands with her. "So you're the reason Judd was so eager to get back to the States."

Vicki smiled. "And you're one of the reasons he made it back in one piece."

"Have a seat. We'll get in the air, and I'll explain our mission."

"This is an awfully big plane for the three of us," Judd said.

"Hopefully on the way back we'll have the thing full of your friends from that library," Westin said. He asked Judd the specific location of the library, and Judd told him.

Westin went to the back of the plane as Judd buckled in behind the pilot's seat. He told Vicki more about what Westin had been through and the episode in Paris.

"If Judd and Lionel hadn't been there to help, my head would be in some bread basket in France right now," Westin said when he returned to the cockpit. "I heard about Lionel's arm. Tell him I've been praying for him."

"He'll appreciate that," Judd said. "Have you heard anything about Z-Van lately?"

Westin smiled. "You didn't hear about the concert a few days ago?" He held up a hand, taxied the runway, and got them airborne.

When it was safe, he put the plane on autopilot and turned. "Z-Van was doing his pro-Carpathia show, I guess trying to make people think there's really nothing wrong with the world, when it starts getting hot onstage."

"This was the day the heat wave started?" Vicki said. Westin nodded.

"And you were there?" Judd said.

"I was delivering supplies to a group of believers near the event. It was a night job, real secret kind of stuff. I had dropped the supplies off and was heading back to the plane when I found out about Z-Van's appearance. I couldn't help myself."

"Don't tell me you showed up at the concert!" Judd said.

"I kept a good distance. I was wearing my fake GC outfit, so nobody paid much attention. Normally Z-Van doesn't perform in the daytime, at least he didn't while I was with him. But the GC must have convinced him to do this late-morning gig."

"I don't guess they needed a warm-up band." Judd laughed.

"Good one," Westin said. "I noticed people in the crowd were getting restless way before show time. They were wiping their faces and shielding their eyes from the sun. Some held blankets or umbrellas over them. Well, the music started and Z-Van came out, but people were getting so hot that they couldn't pay attention."

"And you probably had no idea what was going on," Judd said.

"Right. I was a little warm, but these people were going crazy. Z-Van runs out expecting some kind of ovation, and there are nothing but screams. He reaches for the microphone and then drops it on the ground like he's picked up a poisonous snake. That's when I noticed something funny about the video screen onstage. Images of Nicolae and Leon Fortunato were flashing when all of a sudden the screen started rippling. Then a big brown spot appeared in the middle, and it burst into flames."

"I'll bet that got Z-Van's attention," Judd said.

"He was still trying to pick up the microphone, but the thing had melted. He pried it up with a drumstick, but it was fried."

"What did the crowd do?" Vicki said.

"Everybody panicked. It was as if the heat just

411

descended like a swarm of bees, and they ran for cover. Problem was, they ran over each other. Hundreds were killed from being trampled before the first person ever caught fire."

"How awful!" Vicki said.

"One of those miracle workers came onstage and tried to calm the crowd. He was wearing a long, black robe and had a lapel microphone on. The speakers started crackling and popping like something was wrong with the lines, but when I looked closer, it was the miracle guy with flames licking at his outfit. He ran screaming to the back with the rest of the band members."

"You think Z-Van survived?" Judd said.

"The GC hasn't said he's dead, but they also didn't report anything about the concert. There must have been thousands on the ground, their bodies just piles of ashes. The stage, lights, all their instruments—everything went up in smoke."

As they flew, Westin told them the other things he had experienced while flying for the Co-op. Judd was amazed at all God had accomplished through this man he and Lionel had reached out to.

When they neared their destination, Westin outlined the plan for the group at the library. He handed Judd a printout of a message the Tribulation Force had received two days earlier.

> Dear Captain Steele or anyone else in the Tribulation Force,
>
> A young man named Judd Thompson gave us this

address and told us if we felt in danger in any way we should contact you. The power has been spotty in our area, but there have been sightings of GC near us at night. If you could please get back to us with an escape plan, we would be grateful. I don't feel I should give you our location in case this gets intercepted by the GC. Below you'll see Judd's e-mail, and he can tell you where to find us.

The group signed the note, "Waiting in the stacks." Judd thought of the people he had met at the library. "How are we going to get from wherever you'll land to the library?"

"Good question. You'll have to ask God that one. We have people praying about the transportation question right now."

Westin used his phone to call San Diego and confirm the nearest landing strip that could handle their large airplane. "I was right. The nearest strip is about twenty miles from your friends." He glanced at his watch. "If everything goes as planned, we can get back to Wisconsin with a couple hours to spare and have your friends at the camp meet you with another vehicle."

"What if we don't get back before sundown?" Vicki said.

"That's why we have people praying," Westin said.

_____

As they flew close to the ground, Vicki looked out the window at plumes of smoke rising from buildings. There were no other planes in sight, which was an eerie feeling. The earth looked like a shell that had been used and thrown away. The most drastic change had come with the wrath of the Lamb earthquake, but even with that, the GC leaders had found a way to bounce back and restore services. With this plague of heat, the earth had come to a standstill during daylight hours. It was an advantage Vicki had never dreamed of for believers, but she couldn't help feeling sad for the poor people who had chosen Carpathia.

Westin told her and Judd that the Tribulation Force members were free to come and go as long as they were careful to plan their travel into time zones that kept them in daylight as long as possible. There was news that the polar ice caps were melting faster than at any time in history, and huge weather systems threatened the coasts on every continent. Many coastlines were already buried under massive floods.

"What are you doing after this assignment?" Vicki said.

"We're trying to coordinate our planes and store-houses. Chang Wong in New Babylon has it all graphed out. If this heat wave continues, we'll have enough food and supplies for believers for at least a year. That's what we hope."

The plane touched down on a runway so short Vicki thought they were going to run off the end. Westin led them off the plane and secured the door, though there was no reason to think anyone would get to it before they returned.

When they were on the ground, Vicki saw the devastation of a more populated city for the first time. What appeared to be million-dollar homes looked like the remains of old campfires. Fencing around the airport had melted from the intense heat.

Vicki noticed a creepy silence. In the woods she had sensed the lack of animals during the day, but here, where there should have been traffic and honking and buses, the only sound was the occasional collapse of a building or the crackling of fires.

"Follow me," Westin said. He led them to a concrete parking garage. "We haven't used this airfield as a base of operations, but I'm willing to bet there's a vehicle—" He paused, staring into the distance. "Would you look at that?"

Vicki glanced to her right at a small bus sitting in front of what was left of the main terminal building. It looked like the kind of bus used to transport disabled children. She was shocked that in the midst of the heat, the vehicle hadn't caught fire.

"Is this your answer to prayer?" Judd said as they ran to the bus.

"Works for me," Westin said.

They climbed in and Westin chuckled. "Even has a full tank of gas."

Though they had found transportation quickly, finding the library proved to be more difficult. It was nearly 3:30 local time when they finally pulled close to the structure. Judd said he had worried that the building wouldn't be there, but it still stood.

Vicki was glad to retrace some of Judd's steps. She had

heard about the library and pictured it in her mind, but seeing it in person made her feel more a part of his story.

Judd opened the front door and called for his friends. There was no answer. "They're probably downstairs. Come on."

Judd took the stairs two at a time and bounded through the lower floor of the darkened library. He flipped on the light switch, but nothing happened.

"They said they were having power problems," Westin said.

Vicki was immediately hit by the smell of old books. She hadn't spent that much time in the library as a kid, but the times when she had to do a research project or look up something on the Internet had been fun. Each time she walked through her library in Mount Prospect, she wondered why she didn't read more.

Westin snagged Judd's shirt and pulled him back toward the stairwell. "Something's not right."

"There can't be GC here," Judd said. "The building would have—"

Someone moaned from behind the stacks of books. Vicki was startled when she heard pounding on the window upstairs. The three moved back up the steps cautiously, and Vicki gasped when she saw a face at the window.

Judd hit the front door and rushed outside.

Judd grabbed the leader of the group's hands and shook furiously. He introduced Vicki and Westin while the man caught his breath.

"Two nights ago . . . the GC came . . . we only had a few seconds to get out the back," the man gasped.

"Where is everyone?" Judd said.

"Scattered. Some of us have hidden in a burned-out building a few blocks away. We prayed you'd come."

"And there are Peacekeepers hiding downstairs in the library?"

"Some are just citizens, but others are officers. I think they have guns."

"I don't get it," Vicki said. "If everybody in there is loyal to Carpathia, why hasn't the building burned?"

Westin pursed his lips. "Let's get the rest of your group and get out of here."

The man led them to three separate sites and gathered more than twenty people into the bus. All were overjoyed to see Judd, glad they wouldn't have to spend another night hiding. One of the last to be picked up was a woman in her forties who scanned the bus and turned to Westin. "We can't leave yet. Howard's not here."

"Who's Howard?" Judd said.

"My son. You probably met him when you were here."

"I remember a young guy who argued—"

The woman nodded. "That's him. I don't know if he made it out of the library. I haven't seen him since that night."

"Where else could he be?" Judd said.

"Wait a minute," Vicki said. "If the library is still standing, maybe Howard's hiding there."

Westin looked at his watch. "Listen, people, we're running out of time. If we don't get in the air soon—"

"We have to try," Vicki said, glancing at Judd. "If the GC find him tonight—"

"Who's to say they haven't already found him and chopped off his head?" a man behind them said.

Howard's mother put a hand to her mouth and started crying.

"Don't worry," Vicki said. She looked at Judd. "We are going to try, right?"

Judd motioned for Westin to move outside, and the man followed. "I can't pull rank on you because I don't have any, but I'd like to go back and see if this kid is inside the library. Vicki's got a hunch, and usually she's right."

"Don't let your judgment get clouded," Westin said. "If we get caught out after dark, we could jeopardize the whole Tribulation Force. If we're in the air, the GC could launch a missile or track us with radar."

Judd looked at his watch. "Let us go to the library, and you head to the plane. If we're not there in an hour, leave."

"I can't do that. And you know if Captain Steel or anybody else hears about this, you won't go on another mission."

Judd looked at Vicki, who had her arm draped around Howard's mother. He jumped back inside the bus and called for quiet. "Does anyone know of a vehicle near here?"

An older man raised a hand. "I have an old Beetle in a garage a couple of blocks that way. It was still there yesterday when I checked."

"Where are the keys?" Judd said.

The man fished in his pocket and threw them at Judd. "Go left at that stop sign, and then two blocks. It's the only garage still standing."

"You can't do this," Westin said as Judd raced down the stairs.

Judd turned. "One hour. We'll meet you at the airstrip." He looked at the distraught woman. "And don't worry, ma'am. If your son's there, we'll find him."

"Bless you," she said.

The air brakes sounded behind them while Judd and Vicki hurried toward the garage.

"You think we can make it in an hour?" Vicki said.

"If we don't, it's going to be a long night."

42

THE CAR sputtered and coughed when Judd turned the key. The Volkswagen wasn't just old—it was ancient, with rust spots on the body, balding tires, and an inch of dust. Vicki coughed as she jumped in the passenger seat. Judd tried to start the engine again, but it wheezed and shook.

"Maybe we should walk to the library," Vicki said.

"We'll never make it back to the airport in time," Judd said, pumping the gas pedal. He turned the ignition again, and blue smoke poured from the exhaust pipe. He revved the engine, put the car in reverse, and backed out.

The car chugged and clunked its way through the smoky streets, leaving a trail of smoke of its own. Judd glanced at Vicki and smiled. "You think the GC will stop us for polluting the air?"

Vicki gritted her teeth. "You're doing this for me, aren't you?"

"In a way, but I'm doing it for Howard and his mother too."

"I saw Westin's face. If we don't get back to that plane in time we're in big trouble, right?"

Judd made a sharp turn, and the tires squealed. "This is the right thing to do, and not just because it was your idea. We're going to find Howard and get to the plane. Besides, Westin owes me."

Judd parked on what had been the lawn of the library. All the grass had burned, along with the flowers and shrubbery that surrounded the building.

"How do you want to do this?" Vicki said.

"We don't have time for strategy," Judd said.

"If there are GC here and they have guns, they'll use them."

Judd scratched his chin. "Maybe we can make them think there are more than two of us."

"It doesn't matter how many they think we are—if they start shooting, we're in trouble."

———————————

Vicki already noticed a change in the way Judd handled things. In the old days, he would have simply rushed inside without talking with anyone. He might have dismissed the idea of coming back altogether. But something had changed, and it made Vicki want to follow him inside.

Judd stopped, picked up a huge rock, and pointed to the tinted glass below them. "That's the stairwell. Grab a rock and see if you can break that glass."

Judd's first throw glanced off and landed below. Vicki moved for a better angle and heaved a chunk of concrete. The glass crashed and fell inside the stairwell.

"Good job," Judd said, picking up another stone. A minute later the stairwell was filled with glass, and the sun reached the fire doors below.

Judd climbed down the small hill and carefully crawled through one of the broken windows. He reached back to help Vicki through, then propped open the fire doors with two rocks. Immediately Vicki heard voices whispering inside. A woman was crying, and someone tried to shush her.

Vicki moved into the basement and thought about the GC's perspective. They were trying to stay out of the fire, and here were people walking through it as though it was nothing. "They must be terrified," she whispered.

Judd pointed to the opposite end of the building. "I saw two windows down on that end. There must be an office or something. The more light we can get in here, the better."

Vicki nodded, grabbed two rocks, and hurried in the shadows to the other end of the room. Judd was right. A sign on a door at the end said *Library Director*. Vicki tried the doorknob, and to her surprise the door opened. She hurled stones at the window behind the desk, and the glass shattered, letting in some of the deadly heat.

Another crash on the other side of the library and a shaft of light lit the room. Judd walked into the light.

"What do you want with us?" a man yelled, his voice full of fear.

"Why are you trying to kill us?" a woman sobbed.

Vicki froze and strained to see the people. "It's getting really hot," someone said.

"We don't want to hurt you," Judd said. Vicki had never heard this voice of Judd's. It was full of authority, though he wasn't yelling. "Throw out your weapons, and we'll get what we need and leave."

"Don't do it," someone whispered. "It's a trick."

"That blacked-out window behind you will come down if you don't slide your weapons out now."

Vicki held her breath.

Several guns clattered on the floor. Judd gathered them up cautiously and returned to the shadows. "All right, step forward and come to the front of the stacks."

"He's going to shoot us!" a woman said.

"You won't be harmed. Step forward."

"The sun's too hot," a man said.

Judd kicked the rocks from the stair doors and let them close. The room darkened, and several people stepped forward. "Sit," Judd said.

Vicki counted twelve people, four of them wearing Global Community uniforms. They sat in front of the bookshelves, sweating and breathing heavily, eyes darting from Judd to Vicki.

"Is this all of you?" Judd said.

"It's everybody," an officer said.

Judd placed the guns on the floor and squatted. "How did you find this place?"

The officer laughed. "What do you mean? It's the only building standing for blocks. We ran in here to escape the heat. More come every night."

"Did you see anyone in here when you came?"

"Nobody," the officer said.

"I thought I saw some Judah-ites run out," a younger woman said. "They ran into the sunlight just like . . ."

"Just like what?"

She hesitated. "Just like you."

As Judd spoke with the group, Vicki wandered down the corridor, looking for a hiding place. She noticed movement in one of the locked study rooms along the north wall. A series of doors opened on small, five-by-five-foot rooms. Vicki got on all fours and crept toward the door at the end. She stood and looked through the window. A young man with the mark of the believer on his forehead moved behind a desk. He was startled when Vicki knocked on the door.

"Howard?" Vicki said.

The young man's mouth opened in shock. "How did you know my name?"

"Get out of there. We don't have much time."

Howard was thin and no taller than Vicki, with a slight beard. His clothes were tight, and his hair stuck up in the back.

"I've been waiting two days for someone to come get me," Howard said as he snatched his backpack and followed Vicki. "Do you know where my mom and—"

Vicki put a finger to her lips. "Keep quiet until we get

out of here." She led Howard to the stairwell door and cleared her throat. "I have him."

Judd grabbed the guns from the floor and stood.

"I thought you said we could have our guns back," the officer said.

"You don't need guns to survive this plague by God."

"You *are* Judah-ites," a woman said.

A gun clicked from the back of the library, and Vicki ducked as the wood above her head splintered. Automatic weapon fire filled the room, and Judd hit the stairwell doors hard, spreading light onto the people sitting in front of the stacks. All of them screamed and ran for the darkness as Judd, Vicki, and Howard bolted upstairs.

"Get in the car!" Judd yelled as they jumped over the broken glass on the stairway. More gunfire erupted, but the shooter quickly ran out of ammunition.

While Judd plopped the weapons in the backseat, Howard jumped inside. "Where are you taking me?"

"Hang on," Judd said, firing up the Beetle. "We're headed for the airport."

The car's tires spun on the lawn when Judd pulled away. Vicki looked back to make sure no one was following them and noticed more smoke. Judd slowed long enough to see the roof of the library begin to curl. Windows on the upper floor of the building shattered, and smoke billowed. Vicki put her window down a little, then rolled it up when she heard people inside screaming.

Judd had clicked his stopwatch as soon as Westin and the others in the bus pulled away. He looked at it now and shook his head. They had less than twenty minutes to make it to the airport before the hour was up.

He flew through the streets, made a wrong turn, back-tracked, then headed in the right direction.

"How'd you guys know I was there?" Howard said.

"Your mom noticed you were missing," Vicki said. "What happened?"

"Our leader told us to stay together, but I got fed up with all the rules. I went into one of those study rooms, and when I woke up the GC had moved in. I tried to slip out last night, but I got scared."

"You should have listened to your leader," Judd said.

Howard rolled his eyes. "Thanks."

Judd dialed Westin, but the call didn't go through.

"A lot of the big towers are down," Howard said. "I heard that before the power went out."

By the time they made it to the airport, Judd's watch showed the trip had taken an hour and a half. He jammed the keys in his pocket, slammed the door of the Beetle, and joined Vicki outside. The sun was fading, and they had only an hour of daylight left.

"Don't be too hard on Howard," Vicki whispered. "Westin will be back for us tomorrow, right?"

Judd sighed. "I hope so, but you know if he talks to anyone in the Trib Force they'll blacklist us."

Vicki shrugged. "Well, that'll just give us more time together."

Howard got out of the car and approached them with his hands in his pockets. "I'm sorry. I didn't mean to cause you trouble. Guess I've really messed things up."

Judd put a hand on Howard's shoulder. "Everybody makes mistakes. I just hope you live long enough to learn from them."

"We need to find a place to hide, right?" Howard said. "I think I might know the spot."

Howard pointed to the parking garage, and Judd parked the car behind some burned-out vehicles. They wound their way through the stairwell, made it to the roof, and found a spot by the door.

"I'm hungry," Vicki said.

Howard opened his backpack and pulled out a couple of sandwiches and some candy bars. "I had these stashed away in my little corner so I wouldn't have to go out and eat with the others." He gave the food to Vicki, and she divided it equally among them. Judd rushed into the terminal and came back a few minutes later with several bottles of water he had found in an employee kitchen.

"What do we do if the GC come tonight?" Howard said.

"The only people who knew about you are part of the ashes of that library," Judd said.

"What if somebody heard the plane?"

Judd shrugged, and Vicki huddled close to him as the sun finally went down. Judd tried calling Westin, but the connection didn't ring. He thought about calling the group in Wisconsin but decided against it. They were on their own for the night.

Vicki suggested they pray, and the three bowed their heads. Judd and Vicki prayed freely and paused to let Howard join.

After a few seconds he took a breath and struggled through a brief prayer. "God, I want to thank you for these people who helped me. If the GC had caught me back there, I don't know what would have happened. I ask you to forgive me for being so . . . hardheaded and help Judd and Vicki make it back to their friends."

43

JUDD was surprised at how fast the temperature dropped after the sun went down. Vicki snuggled close, and the two tried to stay warm. Though fires burned throughout the city, they feared building one on the roof would draw attention.

In the daytime, the only sounds Judd had heard, other than their car and plane, were the crackling fires and the whistling of the wind. At night, however, the city seemed to come alive. Dogs barked, motorcycles whined, and people shouted in the distance. But the worst sound was the cries of people who had lost family and friends. The high-pitched wails of men and women in pain echoed through the smoldering ruins.

"I feel so bad for them," Vicki whispered. "If they'd chosen God instead of Carpathia, they wouldn't be hurting."

Judd looked at Howard, who was looking out at the city over the concrete wall. "How long have you lived here?"

431

"All my life. I never thought I'd see anything like this."

"Tell us your story," Vicki said.

"You don't want to know about me."

"Come on," Judd said.

Howard sighed, turned, and slid to a sitting position. "My dad left when I was four or five. My mom did her best, but by the time I was a teenager, I didn't want anybody running my life. She worked two jobs, so she was out till all hours of the night.

"I hung out with a bunch of friends, and a lot of times I didn't even show up for school. We'd party all night, which meant we'd buy some beer—we didn't have much money for drugs. I guess you could say I was wasted. I was just kind of out there."

"You didn't know any Christians?" Vicki said.

Howard laughed. "I saw them on TV, you know, the evangelists and all. Preachers who wanted me to send money. I knew kids whose parents dragged them to church, but they pretty much did the same stuff I did.

"But there was this one kid, Kirk. He was just as wild as we were, only not in the same way."

"What do you mean?" Vicki said.

"He could do stuff on a skateboard you wouldn't believe. No helmet. No fear. He was skinny, like me, with a pointy nose. He kind of looked like a bird, come to think of it. His hair was always sticking up in the back, and his body was always moving. You know, even if he was standing still he was moving, cracking his knuckles, crossing his legs, snapping his neck. You just couldn't stop the guy."

"What happened to him?" Vicki said.

"We were hanging out one night when Kirk came by. He was riding a new scooter he'd saved up for. His dad didn't like him riding at night, but he had to show it off. You should have seen his face when he pulled up. You would have thought he had a Mercedes. He'd been talking about the thing for a whole year." Howard looked at the floor and pursed his lips.

"What?" Judd said. "Did you do something to him?"

"We made fun of it. We asked him why he threw away his money on a toy. Said it would probably only go ten miles an hour. I knew we hurt him. He just wanted to show it to us."

"When you get with a group, it's hard not to put others down," Vicki said.

"Yeah, well I never got the chance to tell him I was sorry."

"What happened?"

"He gunned the thing and drove down an alley, trying to show off. I told the other guys he was going to wipe out if he wasn't careful. He must have been going fifty when he came out the other side. We heard a squeal and a crash. And when we got there, a guy was standing by the scooter saying, 'He drove right out in front of me.' The impact had thrown Kirk about thirty feet into some garbage cans. He was still breathing when we got to him. The driver called an ambulance. Kirk wasn't wearing a helmet, and I'm not sure he had much of a chance, anyway."

"That must have been awful for you," Vicki said.

"Yeah. I went to the hospital, but I couldn't face his family. The next day I heard he'd died and that all of us were invited to the funeral."

"Did you go?" Judd said.

Howard nodded. "It was the first time I heard any kind of religion that made sense."

"What do you mean?" Vicki said.

"Kirk wasn't real religious, you know. He didn't push it on any of us. When we'd get beer or the occasional joint, he'd find some excuse to leave. He did smoke cigarettes, but I could tell he felt bad about it and tried like everything to quit. He actually invited me and my mom to church a couple of times, but I always made some excuse.

"Anyway, the funeral was at his church, and you wouldn't believe all the people. There were church kids sitting next to stoners and freaks. Just about every group in school had known Kirk. We were there to say good-bye and try to deal with the loss, but the family had asked a guy to speak."

"Someone from the church?" Judd said.

"Yeah, a youth leader. He had kind of a high-pitched voice and was short, but what he said made all of us want to listen. He talked about Kirk and nailed him. I mean, the guy knew him inside and out. Even talked about Kirk's struggle to kick tobacco.

"Then he told us that we'd all known Kirk for a reason. He was quiet for a moment, and I could hear people sniffling. He said God had called us to a divine appointment that day to hear Kirk's biggest hope for each one of us.

"He pulled out a wrinkled piece of paper and put on his glasses. It was so quiet you could have heard a mouse burp. I looked at Kirk's mom and dad, and I don't think they even knew what the guy was going to say."

Howard stopped his story and turned his head. "You guys hear that?"

Judd stood up. He had been so engrossed in Howard's story that he had forgotten they were keeping an eye out for the Global Community.

"Maybe this wasn't the best place to hide," Vicki said.

Judd peeked over the railing and scanned the area. A black dog pawed at debris below them, and Judd sighed. "Keep going. I want to hear what happened."

"So the guy pulls out this paper and starts reading. I guess Kirk had asked a bunch of questions, and the youth guy had told him to write down his thoughts and dreams."

"What was on the paper?" Vicki said.

"Kirk started with something like, 'I don't understand why God could forgive me for the stuff I've done and not forgive the others.' You know, he just kind of went off on God and asked why all his friends seemed so unhappy and how Kirk felt guilty for not reaching out to them and helping them. That was the main thing the youth guy said, that Kirk came to him feeling guilty that he didn't have the courage to tell all of us about Jesus.

"That's when he read the prayer. I'll never forget it. 'God, I'm asking you to give me the courage to help all my friends hear about you. I don't know how you're going to do it, but I ask you to work through me to tell them the truth.' That was it. The guy folded the paper and put it back in his pocket. He told us that God had worked it out to have all of us in one place so we could hear about Kirk's faith."

"What did he say then?" Judd said.

Howard bit his lip. "I remember him talking about Jesus and dying on the cross and wanting to forgive us, but I was so upset about being the reason Kirk was dead that I couldn't concentrate. I remember him saying that one day Jesus was going to come back for his followers and take them away. When the service was over, the youth guy asked people to come forward and give their lives to God. I slipped out the back door and went home."

"Did you ever talk with the youth leader?" Judd said.

"I was going to a couple of times but chickened out. I was also going to go see Kirk's parents and tell them how sorry I was, but I never got the chance."

"Why not?" Vicki said.

"They all disappeared about two weeks later. A lot of my friends I hung out with were gone. Some of the goths. A bunch of the drama kids. There wasn't a group that had been at that funeral that didn't lose somebody. There were all kinds of theories about what had happened—from space aliens to some kind of chemical reaction—but I knew as soon as I went back to school and saw all those people gone that it was supernatural. God had come back for his own, and I was left behind."

"What did you do?" Vicki said.

"I went back to the church. The youth guy had a bunch of Bibles and some stuff to read. I took a Bible and some of the papers and showed them to my mom. She was the first to pray, and then I did." Howard looked around the rooftop and pinched the bridge of his nose. "I know I haven't been a very good believer like you guys, but I really want to be."

"It's not about being good," Judd said. "If we all had to live perfectly after God forgave us, we'd be in deep trouble."

"But I've done just about everything I could to make my mom and the others who helped us miserable."

"God wants to change you from the inside out," Vicki said, "but you have to let him."

"I want that. . . ."

"Then tell him," Vicki said. "Pray right now and tell God you're giving him the rest of your life to use however he wants. Thank him for saving you and making you a believer, and ask him to help you grow. He'll do it. He really will."

Howard bowed his head, and Judd saw his lips moving.

A siren wailed and all three jumped. They crouched beneath the concrete wall and listened as a GC squad car pulled into the airport. The swirling lights cast eerie shadows through the hovering smoke. When Judd heard voices, he crawled to the edge and peeked over. A uniformed GC officer spoke with a man at the airport entrance. Their voices carried across the parking lot.

"He came inside looking for something to eat, I guess, but all he found was a few bottles of water," the man said.

"And he walked back outside?"

"I think so. I wasn't about to follow into the sunshine, but it didn't seem to bother him."

"How long after the plane took off?" the officer said.

"About a half hour. I heard a rattle and bang, like he was driving an old Volkswagen. You can't miss those engines, the way they whistle and ping—"

"Did you hear him drive off?" the officer interrupted.

"Come to think of it, I didn't. You suppose those were Judah-ites? I heard they weren't affected by the sun like we are."

"Don't believe everything you hear, old-timer. I'm going to take a look around. If you help, I'll make sure you get some food."

"Thank you. I've got some stashed away in the freezer. It's not that cold in there since the power's been off. But I wouldn't mind helping you look."

Judd slid back down. "Keep quiet. No movement. Now would be a good time to think of a better hiding place."

"What time does the sun come up here?" Vicki whispered.

"A little after seven, I think," Howard said.

It was 2:15 A.M. when the older man discovered the Beetle hidden below them. Judd moved to the wall and listened as the GC officer searched it. He kicked himself for leaving the guns in the backseat.

"Why would they leave a car out here where it would burn in the morning?" the man said.

"Maybe they're coming back before sunup. You stay with the car. I'll search the garage."

Judd hurried back to Vicki and Howard. "Officer's headed our way."

Howard pointed to a steel ladder that hung over the side of the concrete wall. It was on the opposite side from the Beetle. "When the guy comes up, we can just hop over and stay until he leaves."

"We'd have to time it so we don't go over until he's reached the top floor," Vicki said.

Judd nodded. "Good. You two stay by the ladder, and I'll crack the door and watch. When I wave, go over and I'll join you."

Vicki and Howard tiptoed to the other side of the roof. Judd propped the door open with a broken piece of concrete and strained to hear any footsteps. His heart beat faster, and he tried to take a deep breath. There was no room for panic now.

Judd couldn't believe the man had seen him in the airport, and he was frustrated they had stayed in the garage. There were a hundred other places in the blocks surrounding the airport that would have made much better hiding places.

Judd glanced at his watch—2:47. Stars shone clear in the sky, and he remembered Ryan Fogarty's favorite bedtime song: *"Twinkle, twinkle, little star, how I wonder what you are. . . ."*

Footsteps on the stairs. Judd moved slightly for a better view and heard a door below open and close. If he was right, the officer was on the third floor, one floor below them. It would take the man five minutes to go through the debris and head for the roof.

At 3:04 a door clattered below him and Judd stood. A flashlight beam darted back and forth on the wall below as the officer trudged up the last flight of stairs. Judd waved wildly at Vicki and Howard and flew across the garage roof to join them. They were over the edge and hanging onto the ladder when Judd scampered over the side. He was just below the top of the wall when the door banged open. Judd sighed and felt something tap his foot.

"Should we go to the third floor?" Howard whispered.

Judd shook his head and mouthed, "Stay here."

Judd listened to the officer and watched for the flashlight beam to come closer.

Suddenly, the man shouted, "He's been up here. I found the empty water bottles and some food wrappers."

"Just one of them or are there more?" the man at the Beetle yelled.

"Can't tell. But the door was propped open. They might still be around somewhere. I'm coming down."

The door hinges creaked as the officer swung it open. Judd smiled. Only four more hours and the sun would be up. A squeal pierced the night, and Judd's heart sank.

His cell phone!

JUDD turned off his cell phone and motioned for Vicki and Howard to climb down. The officer rushed toward them above while Judd quickly slid down the ladder and hopped onto the third-floor wall. Vicki and Howard were already running for the stairwell door on the other side of the building.

"They're on the third floor!" the officer yelled, out of breath. "Don't let them get the car!"

Judd raced to catch up as Vicki and Howard ran down the stairs. When Judd hit the door, the officer was still lumbering overhead.

Howard put both hands on the rails and slid down. Vicki took two steps at a time, and Judd caught up to her easily. They were steps away from the second-floor door when the officer burst into the stairwell shouting for them to stop.

"Where now?" Howard called from below.

"Keep going," Judd said. "I don't think the guy outside is armed. And stay close to the wall in case—"

A shot pinged in the stairwell. Vicki screamed, and Judd grabbed her hand as they sprinted down the last flight of stairs. They joined Howard outside and were confronted by the older man holding a metal pole.

"Stop right there!" the man yelled.

Judd pulled Howard to the door. "Jam your foot here and don't let the officer out." Vicki joined him and put her foot against the metal door.

"I'm warning you!" the man said. "Don't come any closer."

Judd had played enough football to know how to make himself look menacing to quarterbacks on the other side of the line. He gritted his teeth and lowered his shoulder. The older man dropped the pole, turned, and ran toward the terminal entrance, just as Judd heard a loud thump at the door behind him.

"What if he shoots?" Vicki said.

"The bullet can't go through—"

Bang!

A one-inch hole appeared in the door and missed Howard by less than a foot.

"Don't make me kill you. Get away from the door!"

Judd picked up the pole and raced forward.

"I'm going to give you one more chance," the officer yelled. "Now stand aside!"

Judd rammed the pole through the door handle and all the way to the other side. He pulled Vicki and Howard away as the officer threw his weight against the door again. It opened a few inches, but no farther.

"Head for the car," Judd hollered, pulling the keys out.

Judd jumped in the driver's side, and the car started with a rumble and clatter. Vicki yelled a warning from the backseat. The officer was aiming at them through metal bars inside the garage. Judd swerved and avoided the first shot. He yelled at Vicki and Howard to get down right before the next shot shattered the back window.

Judd floored the accelerator and pulled away. Unless the officer was a great shot, he'd never hit them, and he didn't. But as they raced out of the airport road, Judd noticed swirling lights.

"We've got a head start, but not much of one," Judd said. "Howard, any ideas on where we should go?"

The VW chugged along as Howard directed Judd through a maze of roads near burned-out buildings. Judd kept his lights off, driving by moonlight and the glow of fires.

"Take a left here," Howard said, and Judd turned into a skate park.

"This is too out in the open," Judd said. "We need to—"

"Go over the curb and down that little hill," Howard said.

"Hang on," Judd said.

They bounced over the curb and raced down an incline, stopping near a drainage pipe twice the size of the car. He pulled in and turned off the motor.

"We used to come down here when one of us was in trouble," Howard said. "You can't see it, but the opening goes all the way to the other side of the road."

"This is perfect," Vicki said.

"Yeah, unless somebody heard us and reports us to the GC," Judd said.

When a vehicle passed overhead, Judd pulled out his phone and turned it on. A call had come from Westin, so Judd dialed him back and explained what had happened. Westin said he had felt guilty for taking off without him. "Where are you now?" Judd said.

"We made it to Kansas before we lost the sun," Westin said. "Couldn't risk the Wisconsin trip because we were so late. I have some friends here who live close to an old airport. They took us all in. What about Howard?"

Judd gave Westin the good news, and Howard got on the phone and spoke briefly with his mother. He seemed moved by his mom's voice.

"I hope nothing bad happens to these two because of me," Howard said. "All they were trying to do was save me."

Westin told Judd he would fly to the airport with Howard's mother at noon the next day.

"What about the people we were going to take to Wisconsin?" Judd said.

"Change of plans. There's a flight coming from Wyoming in a few hours. These people will go there, while you take Howard and his mom to Wisconsin."

"I have to know, is this going to affect the way the Trib Force looks at me?"

Westin paused. "I told the Trib Force this was my idea."

"But that's not true—"

"Right. So kick me out of the choir. Steele chewed me out, said I was playing hot dog with people's lives, and I apologized."

"But this wasn't your fault. I was the one—"

"Judd, I took the blame. Maybe I shouldn't have, but I did. You're square with them, okay? See you at noon."

Vicki never felt so grateful to see the sun rise the next morning. Instead of being chased like animals, they were free to roam the neighborhoods and head back to the airport.

In a gesture of goodwill, Howard left food in front of the freezer for the old man. "We must have scared him to death last night. Least we can do is give him something to eat."

The flight to Wisconsin went as planned. Howard's mother couldn't stop thanking Judd and Vicki for their help and said she would make it up to them somehow.

The group in Wisconsin welcomed the two newcomers with open arms. Howard seemed most pleased to meet Zeke, who looked nothing like what he expected in an "assistant pastor."

The Tribulation Force continued moving people and supplies around the country and the world, though the Global Community had tried to adapt. News from Oregon disturbed Vicki and the others when they found out about a new GC plan that affected believers.

"The GC moved into the lava tubes in Oregon," Mark said a few days after Judd and Vicki returned.

"Lava tubes?" Charlie said.

"They're natural rock formations made by volcanoes," Mark said. "Miles of tunnels believers have been using since we were forced to go underground. Once the plague of heat hit, GC survivors decided to move into them at night because the temperature is so cool during the day. They surprised some believers, and a bunch of them were executed."

"Why couldn't someone have helped?" Vicki said.

"These believers were pretty cut off from anyone outside. They were living on their own."

Other members of the Tribulation Force passed along stories of believers eluding the GC in China, the Philippines, Australia, and other locations. The 144,000 evangelists continued their preaching, and many undecided became believers. This encouraged the Wisconsin group, knowing that there were still some without Carpathia's mark, but everyone knew the numbers were dwindling.

Though Vicki didn't like to be separated from Judd, they each took separate trips as requested by the Tribulation Force to help believers with supplies, food, and new places to live. In some cases, Vicki was asked to go because she had been the main contact for younger believers who had seen her at one of the stadium events. At other locations, the Trib Force needed help loading and unloading materials, and Judd volunteered. Most of these were daylong flights or drives, so they were back with each other the next day.

As time went on, Vicki wondered what Judd was thinking about their relationship. They had become more serious, and everyone in the Wisconsin group wondered if Judd would propose. "I'm content however things work out," Vicki told her friends, "but I'll admit I wouldn't mind being Mrs. Judd Thompson."

Judd agonized over the marriage question. He knew Vicki was the one for him, if he did decide to get married, but things seemed to be going so well that he didn't want to mess up their friendship. Judd pored over the Scriptures and asked people's advice.

Zeke was a big help, saying that if God planted a desire for marriage, there wasn't anything to hold him back. "You have to ask yourself—are you ready to love another human being the way God loves you?"

On a trip to Tennessee to help out a group that had befriended him, Judd opened the Bible to the passage in 1 Corinthians, chapter 13. Known as the love chapter, Judd read the verses, then wrote a segment of the passage in his own words.

Love is so patient and kind that others can see it, taste it, and smell it. Love isn't jealous when someone else succeeds, isn't rude, doesn't boast, and certainly isn't prideful. Love doesn't want things a certain way and doesn't get irritated over little things. Love doesn't keep a scorecard. When a wrong is committed, a person who loves doesn't hold that over the other person's head. A person who loves isn't glad about people who are treated unfairly, but is glad when the truth is seen and welcomed. Love simply does not give up, it never loses faith or hope, and in every circumstance, no matter what that circumstance is, love keeps on going.

Judd studied the list and shook his head. *Love is pretty tough to accomplish,* he thought. As he looked over his words and the other parts of the passage, he was struck by how many of these verses Vicki lived. She was never jealous of anyone who succeeded, was never proud or boastful about her accomplishments, and seemed to always put others ahead of herself. Even when Judd was asked to go on trips for the Trib Force, she seemed genuinely excited for his opportunities.

Though it scared him, it was on that flight that Judd finally made up his mind to ask Vicki the most important question of his life. *"Perfect love expels all fear,"* Judd thought. Zeke loved quoting that verse. Maybe he was right.

Vicki was excited when Judd asked her to help him deliver supplies to a Wisconsin group she had never heard of. Judd said they would be gone a few hours and that she might want to bring some food along, so she packed a lunch and they set out after ten that morning.

They chatted about the way things were going with the group, how much help Charlie had been, and how glad they were that he had become part of the group.

Vicki had received an e-mail from Wanda that morning reporting good progress by Cheryl.

"You think she'll ever come back?" Judd said.

"Wanda doesn't think it's a good idea yet, but if Cheryl keeps working on getting healthy—" Vicki pointed to her head—"I wouldn't be surprised to see her again."

"Ryan Victor sure is full of spunk," Judd said.

Vicki laughed and repeated a story about the boy Josey had told her the day before. Ryan had truly been the bright spot in their lives the past two years.

Vicki noticed a cloud of dust in one of the mirrors and turned. "Do you see that?"

Judd glanced back. "Looks like smoke from a building."

"No, it came from beside the road, like someone just pulled out." Vicki peered through the back windshield and yelped. "Judd, there's a car coming this way."

"Well, we don't have anything to worry about, right? It has to be a believer or the car would be burning up by now."

"I suppose you're right, but what if the plague's lifted? Or maybe the GC has figured out a way to overcome the effects—"

"I see lights on top of that car," Judd interrupted.

"Step on it. We can lose whoever it is in this Humvee."

Judd sped up, but the car gained on them. Vicki's heart beat faster and faster.

The car was right behind them and Judd slowed.

"What are you doing? Keep going."

"Let's see who it is."

"What are you talking about? That guy's GC. I know it!"

Judd pulled to the side of the road and stopped. Vicki stared in disbelief as a man in a Global Community uniform stepped from the car pointing a gun at the Humvee.

Judd rolled down his window and studied the rearview mirror. "Let's play this straight. Just do what he says and we'll be okay."

"Both of you step out of the car," the officer said.

Judd put a hand on Vicki's shoulder. "We'll be okay. Just get out."

Vicki opened the door and climbed out. She looked for a place to run, but the officer motioned her to the rear of the Humvee. The air felt warm, so the plague was still in effect.

"You, redhead, walk slowly toward me with your hands up," the officer said.

Vicki did as she was told.

"What do you want with us?" Judd said.

"Shut up and come with me, punk."

"No!" Vicki said.

"Hands on the back of the car!" the officer warned.

Vicki turned. She couldn't believe they had been caught. They had gone through so much, too much to have it end like this.

"You," the officer said to Judd, "on your knees."

Judd knelt behind the car, and Vicki glanced at the officer, who slowly walked toward them. The man stopped near Judd, holstered his gun, and pulled something out of his pocket. "I believe this is yours, young man. And I think you know what to do with it."

Vicki turned, her brow furrowed. The officer had given Judd a tiny box, and Judd smiled. The officer took off his sunglasses and pushed his hat up, showing the mark of the true believer.

"Zeke?" Vicki said.

"Pay attention to what's happening, redhead," Zeke said.

Vicki glanced at Judd, who was still on one knee. "Vicki, I have known you almost six years, and though we've had some difficult days, the last few weeks have been the happiest of my life."

Vicki covered her mouth with a hand as Judd opened the box, revealing a sparkling ring.

"I've come to love you, Vicki, and I want to share the rest of my days with you, before our Lord returns." He pulled the ring from the box and held it out. His voice broke when he said, "Will you marry me?"

Tears stung Vicki's eyes as she slipped the ring on her finger. Vicki fell into Judd's arms and they kissed. Her voice trembled as she whispered, "Yes."

45

WHEN Vicki returned to the camp in Avery, the others had put together an engagement party for her and Judd. Zeke had told everyone what was going on, and Josey had made a cake.

Lionel could hardly contain himself. He kept slapping Judd on the back, smiling, laughing, and shaking his head. "You finally did it!"

After Vicki recovered from the shock of the creative way Judd had asked her to marry him, she socked him in the shoulder for scaring her with the GC trick. "You just about gave me a heart attack! I thought we were both dead."

Judd smiled. "I thought it would be memorable. Who wants to tell everybody a boring engagement story?"

They both met with Marshall to talk about their next step. To her surprise, Vicki discovered there were a few at the camp who thought it wasn't a good idea for them to get married.

"I've had conversations with some who think these

kinds of things shouldn't be happening," Marshall said. "But this is a personal decision, and you two have shown good judgment through this dating process."

"What do you mean?" Judd said.

"Let's just say people have been watching you two to see if you'd become clingy with each other. You know, to see if you'd be so 'in love' that you wouldn't be able to concentrate on anything else. But we've been pleased with how you've handled this."

"Vicki and I were talking about dates for the wedding," Judd said. "Is there a set waiting period?"

"That's up to you, though I would suggest you go through a marriage counseling course."

"What will that do?" Vicki said.

"It helps prepare you for the big changes ahead. We could set up the sessions and have them done as fast as possible."

Judd bit his lip. "I know this is a long shot, but would there be any way to link with Dr. Ben-Judah and have him perform the ceremony?"

"We were talking," Vicki continued, "and outside of Bruce Barnes, the person who has mentored us most is Dr. Ben-Judah, even though it's been mostly through his writing."

Marshall scratched his chin. "Why don't you e-mail him and see?"

Judd wrote the e-mail and let Vicki read it. "Perfect," she said. He sent it directly to Dr. Ben-Judah and copied Sam

Goldberg and Mr. Stein. Vicki wrote Chloe Steele and a few others she thought would be interested in their news. Within an hour, a flood of messages came back.

I'm so happy for you, Vicki and Judd, Chloe wrote. *I think you'll find marriage one of the most challenging and rewarding things you'll ever do. I can't imagine not having married Buck, in spite of how little time we have left.*

Rayford Steele also wrote. Judd was a little anxious, but he was relieved when he read Rayford's message. *I've been married twice, and only once as a believer. Having someone share the good and bad times is one of the greatest comforts I've experienced. You two will be a great team!*

Westin wrote from his plane somewhere over the Atlantic Ocean. *I couldn't be happier for you. Actually, I might be able to give you a pretty good present. Let me know when you two are planning the ceremony.*

"What could he be talking about?" Vicki said.

Judd shrugged. "Knowing Westin, it could be anything."

The next day Dr. Ben-Judah wrote and congratulated Judd and Vicki. *I would be proud to unite the two of you if we can work out the technical details. In the meantime, you should both seek the Lord in prayer as to where you should live. It may be that he wants you to stay in Wisconsin with your friends. We could also use a young married couple here in Petra. Consider this and let me know when you would like to arrange the ceremony.*

Vicki's mouth opened wide. "I've heard so much about Petra, but I can't imagine actually living there."

"It would be a great place to start a new life," Judd said. "But what about our friends?"

"It'd be hard to leave, but if we're together, I could call anywhere home."

Two weeks later, just after a counseling session with Marshall, Mark held up the phone in the main cabin. "It's Westin. I think you'll want to take this."

Judd heard plane noise as he answered the phone. "New plan," Westin said. "And you should know I've cleared this with the Trib Force."

"What are you talking about?"

"Remember my surprise to you and Vicki? Well, I heard about Dr. Ben-Judah's offer to have you come to Petra. I have an important run next week to some believers near New Babylon, and I'd like you to come with me."

"Just me?" Judd said.

"Last trip as a bachelor," Westin said. "You help me with the New Babylon drop, and then we go to Petra so you can build your honeymoon cottage."

"I've seen the homes there, and there's not much to them."

"Still, you could get things ready for Vicki. Then she'd come on my next trip back."

Judd looked at Vicki and smiled. "What about my best man? He's here in Wisconsin."

"I can bring him with Vicki and anybody else who might want to relocate to the safest place on earth."

Vicki hugged Judd tightly and looked into his eyes. "The next time I see you, I'll be walking down the aisle—or the rocks or whatever they call it in Petra."

"I don't think I can find a tux," Judd said, "I hope you won't be too disappointed."

"Something about this plan scares me," Vicki said.

"We've waited this long. Another week's not a big deal."

"Just be careful."

Judd met Westin in Hudson, Wisconsin, and was amazed at the amount of supplies packed onto the plane. Westin said the believers near New Babylon were a little mysterious, not having much contact with the outside world, but they were prepared to ride out their remaining days right under the noses of the Global Community. The contact they had made with Westin wasn't through the Tribulation Force but from a man named Otto, who had moved to New Babylon from Germany.

"That's about all I know," Westin said, "other than they've been fighting the GC every chance they get."

"You mean fighting, as in guns?" Judd said.

"Hey, the last battle is coming, and you need to get ready. Armageddon. I'm not going to miss it."

"I thought Armageddon was where God smashed the armies of the Antichrist."

"It is, but God's used his followers up to now, so why wouldn't he use us in battle? You should hear Dr. Ben-Judah preach about it. He's really stirred me up to think I can be part of it."

Judd settled in for the long flight and sent Vicki an e-mail. *When the disappearances happened, it was scary and really sad. But part of it was exciting because we were on our own, without parents telling us what to do. But like Marshall told us in one of our sessions, everything we do from now on will be done together!*

The plane touched down near Petra, and Judd spent a day meeting old friends and scouting a place to build a small shelter. Sam Goldberg showed him several sites, and Mr. Stein said there would be plenty of help and materials.

"We don't have all the modern conveniences," Mr. Stein said, "but we have fresh food provided by God every day and wonderful teaching, not to mention fresh water."

After visiting the communications center and greeting Naomi Tiberius, Judd rested for the trip the next day to New Babylon.

Vicki watched the news coverage about changes in the past two days and felt concerned about Judd. The blood had turned back to water in streams, signaling the end of the third Bowl Judgment. An urgent message from Chang Wong came not long after.

In my monitoring of Carpathia over the last few days, I believe we have reached a turning point. He is still occupied with the "Jewish problem," as he calls it. Just when Carpathia and Akbar thought they had devised a plan to kill Jewish believers in Jerusalem, the sun plague hit and the GC were sent underground. In fact, the number of Global Community forces who have died is staggering. But they still have a lot of firepower available.

Of particular interest to me was a phone call I recorded between the potentate and his security chief, Suhail Akbar. I send this transcript not to scare but to warn you of the seriousness of the threat.

Carpathia: Suhail, these plagues have always had their seasons. This one has to end sometime. And when it does, that may be the time for us to pull out the half of our munitions and equipment that we have in reserve. Would you estimate that the confidentiality level on that stockpile remains secure?

Akbar: To the best of my knowledge, Excellency.

Carpathia: When the sun curse lifts, Director, when you can stand being out in the light of day again, let us be ready to mount the most massive offensive in the history of mankind. I have not yet conceded even Petra, but I want the Jews wherever they are. I want them from Israel, particularly Jerusalem. And I will not be distracted or dissuaded by our whining friends in northern Africa. Suhail, if you have ever wanted to please me, ever wanted to impress me, ever wanted to make yourself indispensable to me, give yourself to this task. The planning, the strategy, the use of resources should make every other war strategist in history hang his head in shame. I want you to knock me out, Suhail, and I am telling you that resources—monetary and military—are limit-less.

Akbar: Thank you, sir. I won't let you down.
Carpathia: Did you get that, Suhail? Lim-it-less.

After Judd's plane touched down in a remote area outside of New Babylon, he met with one of the leaders of the mysterious group, Rainer Kurtzmann, a former stage actor from Germany who had become a believer not long after the disappearances.

After Judd and the others loaded supplies into several of the group's vehicles and headed for Carpathia's city, Rainer took another route to give Judd and Westin a tour. The effects of the sun plague had left the city in ruins. Lavish parks with fountains and flowers were reduced to ashes. Judd noticed Rainer was wearing a gun, and Judd asked him why.

"We came from Germany, where fighting the GC was getting boring. One of the leaders of a nearby group, Otto Weser, convinced us from Scripture that there would be believers in New Babylon during this time. So we came, and we have survived."

"I can't imagine living here without the mark of Carpathia, right under his nose," Judd said.

"I couldn't either. Some said we would be killed before we ever found a place to stay, but here we are, moving supplies into our underground hideout."

"Have you lost any members?"

Rainer gave Judd a pained look. "Yes, but I'd rather not talk about that now."

Judd nodded.

Back at the safe house, Judd and the others enjoyed a meal together. Everyone wanted to hear about Judd's experience in New Babylon, and he described his adventures, though he kept the information about Chang Wong private.

The conversation was so interesting that Judd and Westin stayed past their deadline to get back to Petra before dark, so the group made room for them. As the sun went down, Judd watched the group go through their complex routine of securing the hideout. A few days after the sun plague began, the group had burned the top of their house to make it look like the others surrounding it.

Judd found it difficult to sleep in the enclosed hideaway. It was so different than the camp in Wisconsin, where they felt safe at all hours. A team kept watch over video screens throughout the night, looking for any irregular GC movement.

When morning came, Judd headed outside to watch the sunrise but was stopped by a female member of the group. "We aren't allowed out until the sun is fully up. I'm sorry."

Judd went to the breakfast area, where he wouldn't disturb anyone, and dialed Chang Wong.

Chang was out of breath when he answered the private line. "Judd, I hope you're calling from Petra."

"Actually, I'm not. Why?"

"Show's over."

"What?"

"Though I've been immune to the sun plague, I've still felt the difference in temperature and humidity. A few

461

minutes ago I woke up, and the air feels different." Judd heard Chang clicking at his computer. "Yeah, I'm right. The temperature here is normal."

Judd's heart sank. "Maybe when the sun gets higher—"

"No, usually at this time of the morning things have begun to burn."

Judd tried to hold back his emotion. He had tried so hard to get back to Vicki, and now he was a million miles from her in the most hostile location on the planet.

"Where are you?" Chang said.

"You're not going to believe it," Judd said.

ABOUT THE AUTHORS

Jerry B. Jenkins (www.jerryjenkins.com) is the writer of the Left Behind series. He owns the Jerry B. Jenkins Christian Writers Guild, (www.ChristianWritersGuild.com), an organization dedicated to mentoring aspiring authors, as well as Jenkins Entertainment, a filmmaking company (www.Jenkins-Entertainment.com). Former vice president of publishing for the Moody Bible Institute of Chicago, he also served many years as editor of *Moody* magazine and is now Moody's writer-at-large.

His writing has appeared in publications as varied as *Time* magazine, *Reader's Digest, Parade, Guideposts*, in-flight magazines, and dozens of other periodicals. Jenkins's biographies include books with Billy Graham, Hank Aaron, Bill Gaither, Luis Palau, Walter Payton, Orel Hershiser, and Nolan Ryan, among many others. His books appear regularly on the *New York Times, USA Today, Wall Street Journal*, and *Publishers Weekly* best-seller lists.

He holds two honorary doctorates, one from Bethel College (Indiana) and one from Trinity International University. Jerry and his wife, Dianna, live in Colorado and have three grown sons and three grandchildren.

Dr. Tim LaHaye (www.timlahaye.com), who conceived the idea of fictionalizing an account of the Rapture and the Tribulation, is a noted author, minister, and nationally recognized speaker on Bible prophecy. He is the founder of both Tim LaHaye Ministries and The PreTrib Research Center.

He also recently cofounded the Tim LaHaye School

of Prophecy at Liberty University. Dr. LaHaye speaks at many of the major Bible prophecy conferences in the U.S. and Canada, where his prophecy books are very popular.

Dr. LaHaye earned a doctor of ministry degree from Western Theological Seminary and an honorary doctor of literature degree from Liberty University. For twenty-five years he pastored one of the nation's outstanding churches in San Diego, which grew to three locations. During that time he founded two accredited Christian high schools, a Christian school system of ten schools, and Christian Heritage College.

There are almost 13 million copies of Dr. LaHaye's fifty nonfiction books that have been published in over thirty-seven foreign languages. He has written books on a wide variety of subjects, such as family life, temperaments, and Bible prophecy. His current fiction works, the Left Behind series, written with Jerry B. Jenkins, continue to appear on the best-seller lists of the Christian Booksellers Association, *Publishers Weekly, Wall Street Journal, USA Today,* and the *New York Times.* LaHaye's second fiction series of prophetic novels consists of *Babylon Rising* and *The Secret on Ararat,* both of which hit the *New York Times* best-seller list and will soon be followed by *Europa Challenge.* This series of four action thrillers, unlike *Left Behind,* does not start with the Rapture but could take place today and goes up to the Rapture.

He is the father of four grown children and grandfather of nine. Snow skiing, waterskiing, motorcycling, golfing, vacationing with family, and jogging are among his leisure activities.